THE ANONYMOUS SOURCE

BY

A.C. FULLER

A.C. FULLER BOOKS
HANSVILLE, WASHINGTON, 2017

This is a work of fiction. Names, characters, businesses, places, events and incidents are either the products of the author's imagination or used in a fictitious manner. Any resemblance to actual persons, living or dead, or actual events is purely coincidental.

ISBN-13: 978-1540584564
ISBN-10: 1540584569

Cover design by Greg Simanson

Edited by Julie Molinari

A.C. Fuller Books
Hansville, Washington
www.acfuller.com

Dedications

To my dad: for modeling the curiosity, persistence,
and joy it takes to write a novel.

And to my wife, Amanda: my first editor,
my greatest supporter, and the love of my life.

Prologue

World Trade Center, South Tower, 99th Floor
September 11, 2001, 8:46 a.m.

Macintosh Hollinger heard a faint rumble. As he set his comb on the edge of the sink, he noticed a small vase of pink carnations wobbling on the marble vanity. When had New York City last been hit by an earthquake? He tried to recall as he checked his short gray hair in the mirror and adjusted the lapel of the blue suit his wife had given him that morning for his eighty-fourth birthday. It wasn't worth the four grand Sonia had probably spent on it, but he *did* look sharp. When he glanced again, the vase was still. It was probably nothing.

Winking at himself, he walked out of his executive bathroom into his sprawling office. On the east wall were photos of Hollinger with Elvis Presley, Muhammad Ali, and Presidents Reagan and Clinton. A large gold frame held a photo of Lou Gehrig smiling in front of the dugout at Yankee Stadium.

Hollinger, who was short, but spry for his age, walked briskly across Persian carpets toward the floor-to-ceiling windows that faced west across the Hudson. The morning was bright and clear and he squinted at the horizon, trying to glimpse the conical spire of his New Jersey estate. He hoped Sonia would get soup for the party—but of course she had, she knew how much he loved soup. Lobster bisque, or maybe crab.

A stream of black smoke drifted toward the window. Hollinger lurched back, spun around, and scanned the three flat-screen TVs on the wall. On WNYW, a wobbly shot showed the top of the north tower, partially obscured by leaves.

He grabbed a remote and unmuted the TV. A male reporter's voice filled the room. "Just a few moments ago, something believed to be a plane crashed into the north tower of the World Trade Center. I just saw flames inside. You can see the smoke coming out of the tower. We have no idea what it was."

He switched to CNN—a live shot of the smoking tower—and read the headline at the bottom of the screen: "World Trade Center Disaster." His body tensed. His feet felt strange, leaden. Sheets of smoke clouded the windows. A pang of terror shot through his head.

He was going to die. This struck him as a bodily certainty and his first thought was that he had to tell someone about the money. He walked to the phone and picked up the receiver, but paused before dialing. Smoke billowed past his windows. He heard Sonia's voice in his head, warm and grating at the same time. *Vamos!*

His eyes darted around the office and landed on the photo of Lou Gehrig. He dropped the phone and scrambled across the room. Up on his tiptoes, Hollinger yanked the photo off the wall and tucked it under his left arm, then jogged into the lobby of his firm.

"Susaaa—" He tried to yell, but the sound caught in his throat. His secretary wasn't there. The two other offices in his suite were empty.

He passed a marble placard that read "Hollinger Quantitative Investing" and followed the hallway to stairwell B. He peered down and counted the stairs between him and the landing. Nineteen stairs per floor. Ninety-nine floors. 1,881 stairs. He wouldn't make it. Sonia. If she were there, she'd tell him what to do. He stepped back toward the hallway, but, again, Sonia's voice cut through the fog of his indecision. *Vamos!* He blinked twice and stepped down.

Ten minutes later, he stood on the landing of the eightieth floor, sweating and shaking. He leaned the photo against the wall and cupped his palms over his knees. People rushed past as images flooded his mind—smoke pressing on windows; a sea of blue seats at Yankee Stadium; Sonia's blonde hair, dark at the roots. He heard an explosion above him and froze in terror as the building shook. Within seconds, he smelled what he thought was kerosene. Smoke drifted down the stairwell toward him.

A woman bumped into him on her way past. "We got hit, too," she shrieked into a cell phone.

He heard crackling a flight up, then screaming. He looked at the photo leaning against the wall and smiled back at Lou Gehrig, then continued down the stairs without it. His knees buckled with each step and he gagged on the sour smoke that followed him down. He saw his wife's athletic legs walking on hot sand—her smooth skin the color of milky coffee. *Vamos!*

At the fortieth floor, people packed the stairwell. Most were quiet but some yelled into cell phones pressed to their ears. A young man asked, "What happened?" to no one in particular. Hollinger heard sirens and men shouting from below. He fought to keep up with the crowd, but his lungs burned and his legs had gone numb.

At 9:25 a.m., he stumbled into the crisp morning air. A small piece of steel struck his shoulder as firefighters rushed past him into the towers. "Get the hell out of here," one yelled. "Run!"

At the corner of World Trade Center Plaza, Hollinger stood in line for a pay phone, watching the charcoal smoke fill the sky. Glass and steel smashed down on cars parked around the towers. He doubled over and coughed violently, then looked up again. A woman in a blue dress fell to the street from a hundred stories above.

"Please, God, no," he said. He spat blood that tasted like charred iron, then closed his eyes as hard as he could, trying to drive the image from his mind.

After a few minutes it was his turn to use the phone. He pulled some coins from his pocket and dialed, then waited until the answering machine picked up. He hung up. "Damn it, Martin."

He fished out more change and dialed another number. "It's Mac. Come get me." His voice was raspy, dry.

"Where are you? Are you all right?" Denver Bice spoke in a calm, thin voice.

"I made it out. Come get me."

"Can't you get any help down there?"

"Everyone's running *into* the buildings."

"Why didn't you call Sonia?"

"I can't call *her*." He coughed into the phone and wiped his mouth on his sleeve. "She's at the Farm."

"It'll be ten minutes, at least. I'm at the Standard Building."

"I'll be walking up Church Street."

***

Sonia Hollinger was on her final set of crunches in the gym of the New Jersey estate she and her husband referred to as "The Farm." As she brought her elbows toward her knees, Juan Carlos wiped the sweat from her forehead.

"Thanks, baby," she said as she exhaled.

"Three more," he replied.

Sonia breathed hard. "*Vamos*," she said, dropping her head onto the mat. Before she could come up for a crunch, the phone rang.

"You want I should get it?" Juan asked.

"No, honey," Sonia said. "Who calls this early anyway?" She finished the set and lay on the mat, stretching her long, tan legs onto his lap. "All this sweat has me feeling a bit *excitada*. Is it nine yet?"

Juan lay beside her. "Five to nine, and you are done for the day, Mrs. Hollinger. We have time." He put his hand on her taut thigh.

The phone rang again and Sonia shot a look across the gym. "Who would be *rude* enough to call twice before nine?"

Juan slid his hand up to her waist.

She moaned lightly and put her hand behind his head. "I have Mac's party to prepare for, honey. We should probably wait until after lunch."

"The caterers will not be here for an hour, and I can do a lot in that time."

"I know you can." She sat up and pulled her blonde ponytail tighter. As she stood up, she rubbed her hand over her belly. "I feel *gorda*."

"Mrs. Hollinger, you are the sexiest fifty-five year old woman in the world. Why you think I do what I do for you?"

She smiled. "Because my husband pays you seventy-five thousand a year."

"He pay me to cook and work you out. The other things I do for fun."

The phone rang again.

"Well!" Sonia barked, walking across the gym past a single-lane swimming pool and a row of cardio machines. The pink cordless phone on the wall was studded with rhinestones. "Hello?" she said, irritated. "What? Slow down … what happened?" She grabbed a remote and clicked on a wall-mounted TV. Smoke billowed from the north tower. "*Meu Deus*," she said. She dropped the phone, knelt, and made the sign of the cross. "I need to call Mac."

Juan ran across the gym and took her hand. "*Que*?"

"A plane hit the trade center." She picked up the phone and dialed her husband's office. "Pick up. Pick up. Pick up." She slammed the phone back down and looked at Juan. "What should I do?"

"Try again."

She dialed again, but this time the call wouldn't connect. "Phone lines must be overloaded," she said. "We've got to go there, find him."

Juan put his hand on her shoulder. "Mrs. Hollinger, no. It will be too much chaos. They'll close the tunnels."

She tried five different numbers. Three of the calls didn't go through and when the others did, she left frantic messages. For the next hour she stared at the TV and called her husband's office every few minutes. At 9:58 a.m., she and Juan watched live TV coverage as the south tower collapsed. "*Meu Deus*," she said again, this time under her breath.

***

Macintosh Hollinger stood at the corner of Church and Duane, studying each car that passed. Where the hell was Bice? As the south tower began to collapse, he heard the slow, rhythmic crash of each floor crumpling into the next. Smoke filled the sky and Hollinger gagged on a smell that reminded him of the Polo Grounds—cigarettes and sauerkraut.

A black Lincoln pulled up next to him. Hollinger fell into the front seat and looked into the pale gray eyes of Denver Bice.

"Den, what hap—" Hollinger's voice stuck.

Bice wore a black suit and his dyed black hair was stiff with gel. "No one knows yet. What happened to you?"

"Smoke. Something hit my shoulder."

Bice made a U-turn, drove north a few blocks, and turned left on Canal. "Did you call Sonia after we spoke? Does she know you made it out?"

Hollinger closed his eyes and slumped in the soft leather seat. He pressed his shoulder with the tips of his fingers. "No," he said. "Take the West Side Highway up to Roosevelt Hospital. They know me there. Then call Sonia for me."

At the highway entrance, Bice glanced at Hollinger and gripped the wheel tighter with his long, tan fingers. He turned south. Hollinger opened his eyes when he felt the direction of the turn. "Where are you going? North. Go north." He coughed and wiped blood on his sleeve.

Bice stared straight ahead. "You need immediate attention," he said, his voice steady and slow.

"What are you doing?" Hollinger asked weakly.

Bice took the Albany Street exit and made a soft left into an alley at Albany and Greenwich. Dust shrouded the car as he shut the engine off. Tiny bits of debris pinged on the windshield. He glanced at his golf bag in the back seat, then stared at Hollinger, who was coming in and out of consciousness. Slowly, Bice reached back and pulled a black velvet club guard off of his seven iron.

"What's happening?" Hollinger asked, opening his eyes. "Are we at the hospital?"

Bice leaned toward him and looked into his bright blue eyes. "Who else knows about the money?" he demanded.

"What money?"

Bice leaned in closer and raised his voice. "The stock. I got a call from Sadie Green."

"What?"

"I'll take you to the hospital," Bice said, his tone softer now. "Just tell me, have you started the process?"

Hollinger stared back at Bice, then closed his eyes. "No."

Bice passed the club guard from his right hand to his left. With a sudden thrust, he crammed it into Hollinger's mouth and halfway down his throat. Hollinger's eyes flashed wide. Bice pressed hard as Hollinger kicked at the underside of the glove compartment.

After ten seconds, Hollinger went still.

Bice pulled the wet club guard from Hollinger's mouth, dropped it onto the seat, and stared at the lifeless body next to him. He slammed his fist into Hollinger's chest. "Damn it!" he shouted. "Why did you make me do that?" He slammed his fist down on his own thigh. "I wasn't supposed to do that." He leaned toward Hollinger, so close that his nose nearly brushed the dead man's bloody lips. Bice's cheeks and jaw tightened, then shook. He spat into Hollinger's face. "Why did you make me do that?" he asked quietly as the yellow phlegm dripped from Hollinger's chin.

Ambulances wailed from all directions as Bice started the car. He propped Hollinger up, eased the Lincoln out of the alley, and drove through a cloud of dust. A few minutes later, he stopped at the half-collapsed entrance of the Marriott. Seeing no one around, he leaned over the body, opened the passenger door, and pushed it out. Hollinger's head struck the sidewalk with a deep thud. Bice pulled the door shut and made a slow U-turn.

At Washington Street, he let an ambulance pass and followed it to the West Side Highway. He heard a slow rumbling followed by a giant crash. In his rearview mirror he saw the north tower collapse.

***

Sonia sat on a weight bench, drinking bottled water and staring at the TV. Juan stood behind her, rubbing her neck. The towers collapsed over and over. Each time she felt tears rise up, she gripped the bottle tighter and told herself to be strong.

"In Cuba," Juan said, "this would never happen."

"That's because no one cares enough about Cuba to bother," Sonia said. "Everyone wants to be us. That's why they attack us. You're too young to know it, but you're lucky to be in this country."

"What about Brazil?" Juan asked. "Doesn't this make you wish you had stayed? Maybe no one cares enough to attack you, but also you don't get attacked."

She grimaced at the replay of bodies falling from the towers. "I'm American now," she said. "Brazilian-American. And proud. You should learn to be proud as well."

The phone rang. She lunged at it and almost fell over. "Mac?" she yelled.

"No, it's Denver Bice."

"Mr. Bice, have you heard from Mac? He should have been in his office when it happened."

"Sonia, I'm so sorry. I haven't heard from him."

Her shoulders dropped. "And you, Mr. Bice? Are you okay?" Juan pressed his hand into her lower back, adjusting her posture.

"Denver, please call me Denver. And yes, I'm fine. Don't worry. The police will find him. It could take a few hours, but I know you'll hear from him soon."

"Thank you, Mr. Bice. You will call me if you hear anything?"

"Of course, and you as well."

"Of course," she said, sitting up as straight as she could, struggling to hold back the tears.

***

Denver Bice closed his cell phone and scanned the parking garage of the Standard Media building through the windshield of his Lincoln. He scooped up the club guard and put it in his pocket as he got out of the car. He opened the door to the back seat and pulled the guards off the rest of his clubs. He buried them in the dumpster in the corner of the garage, then took the elevator to the thirty-third floor.

The corporate offices of *The New York Standard* were bustling. Employees hurried back and forth, called loved ones, and gathered around televisions. Bice set up a meeting with his VPs for later in the afternoon and sent his assistant home for the day. "Go be with your family," he said gravely. "Our people downstairs will get the story. I want to make some calls and see what I can do to help."

As he closed the door to his office, Bice heard the thud of Hollinger's head. His breath tightened. He saw the body in the shadow of the Marriott and all his muscles contracted at once. *It's not my fault. He didn't give me a choice.* He locked the door, then sat at his desk and focused on an orange spot on the vast art deco carpet. "You can choose to be in control," he whispered. He took ten deep breaths. His muscles relaxed.

He unlocked the bottom drawer of his desk and pulled out a thirty-eight-caliber Iver Johnson pistol. He stashed the club guard in the drawer, next to a flattened, navy blue NYU hat. He closed the drawer and heard the thud again. *It wasn't my fault.*

He ran his index finger up the thin, silver barrel of the pistol. *Mac wasn't my fault. Dad wasn't my fault.* When he closed his eyes he was twelve years old. He saw his father stumbling up the steps of their Connecticut farmhouse, belt in hand, reeking of Scotch. He felt the welts on his back. His chest contracted. *It's not my fault.* He took five more deep breaths and his chest relaxed. He saw his father again, lying face down in freezing gray mud on the riverbank behind the house. He felt himself running toward his father's body, the pistol laying next to it, as blood pooled in the man's frozen shoe prints. A note stuck out of a muddied pocket. He heard the roar of the river and felt the cold steel on his belly as he stashed the gun under his shirt, hoping to somehow undo his father's act by hiding the weapon. He heard the crinkle of paper as he read his father's note. *When you hurt someone, you deserve to be punished.*

Bice opened his eyes and looked at the gun on his desk. "It wasn't my fault," he said.

He picked up the phone, dialed, and left a message. "Chairman Gathert, it's Denver. Everyone here is safe. I went down to get a first-hand look, but there was nothing I could do.

I want you to know that this isn't going to derail the deal. Let's meet later this week, once things have settled down."

He hung up and opened his laptop, clicking on an MP3 recording that he had downloaded from his cell phone. "Hello?" he heard himself say on the recording. As he listened he stared at the gun.

"Bice, you asshole. You evil prick. We finally have a fair fight." Now it was a young woman's voice, drunk and happy. "Mac Hollinger is pulling his money from *The Standard.* He has *seeeeeen* the error of his ways. It took a year, but I did it. *I* did it!" He heard laughter and a steady drumbeat in the background. "You bastard."

"Who is this?" Bice's voice demanded.

"You're in trouble. Not you, personally. I would never threaten a man as pathetic as you. But I know about the merger." For a moment the woman's voice was silent, the music thumping louder. Then she spoke again. "You and your company are screwed."

There were a few more seconds of heavy breathing, then the recording ended.

Bice looked down at the gun and back at the laptop. "You made me do it you stupid dyke. It's *your* fault."

He listened to the call twice, closed his laptop, and took five more controlled breaths. His face tightened, then shook, and he smashed his fist on the desk three times. "Stupid! Fucking! Dyke!" Heat coursed through his body.

On the TV, people ran from a wave of dust, screaming.

"None of this is my fault." He opened the desk drawer and slid the pistol past the club guard and under the NYU hat. "I will never be like him," he said quietly. "I will never kill myself."

Part One

Chapter One

Thursday, September 5, 2002

Alex Vane rolled out of an unfamiliar bed, naked and confused, his head pulsing in a steady rhythm interrupted only by one thought: *Where the hell am I?* He rubbed at a pain in his shoulder, turning his head to look. Bite marks. He glanced around the room and saw a rolled-up yoga mat leaning against the wall. An empty sake bottle sat on top of it.

"Oh, right," he said under his breath.

He stared at the long, slender body in the bed. The woman lay on her stomach, her straight black hair glistening on her pale back. He felt vaguely guilty but told himself it was nothing as he crept out of her bedroom.

He rummaged through her kitchen looking for coffee, but found only tea. None of it was caffeinated. "What kind of girl was I *with* last night?" he mumbled.

He found an envelope on the kitchen table and scrawled a note:

> Greta-
> Had a great time. Had to get to work. Call me sometime.
> -Alex

He didn't leave his number.

He returned to the bedroom, pulled on his jeans and polo shirt, then grabbed his laptop bag and walked out into the cold, sunny morning. He stopped on the steps of the brownstone, his head pounding as the light hit his eyes. He was on Tenth Street in the West Village, and as the night came back to him in flashes, he wondered why he felt guilty. He walked in place and stretched his legs. She seemed to have had a good time, he told himself. He'd done nothing wrong. So why did he feel like he had?

He dropped and did thirty push-ups on the porch of the brownstone. The cold, gritty stone felt good under his large hands. From the push-ups, he moved into downward dog, held it for ten seconds, then sprang up. He shook out his arms and legs and did a few circles with his head.

He felt a bit better and knew that a hit of caffeine would bring him all the way back to himself. At the cart on the corner, he bought a cup of coffee and a copy of *The New York Standard.* He leaned against a ginkgo tree and scanned the front page.

"Damn," he said to himself. They had trimmed his story by half, but at least it was above the fold.

> Trial of Student Killer Begins Today
> By Alex Vane
>
> Opening remarks are expected today at the New York County Criminal Court in the murder trial of Eric Santiago, the NYU student accused of murdering Professor John Martin in Washington Square Park on New Year's Eve, 2001.
>
> Santiago, a 19-year-old biology major, has pled not guilty.
>
> Prosecutors are expected to argue that Santiago encountered Martin at approximately 1 a.m. on January 1, 2002 and administered a lethal dose of fentanyl, a synthetic narcotic.
>
> It remains unclear what motive prosecutors will claim, but sources describe Santiago as "sick" and "cold-blooded." One officer familiar with the case said, "Motive? What motive? Sickos like Santiago don't need a motive."
>
> Martin's murder, and the revelation that police were investigating a student, gripped New York City

earlier this year, but the trial has been delayed with jury selection and motions for over six months.

Alex finished the coffee and stepped back over to the cart to buy an egg sandwich. He threw the roll in the trash and then leaned back against the tree, chewing the egg as he read another story.

Nation Corp. Acquisition of Standard Media Clears Hurdle
September 5, 2002

The proposed merger between Nation Corp. and Standard Media cleared one of its final hurdles Wednesday when federal antitrust regulators concluded their three-month review and gave the deal the green light.

The merger would combine Nation Corp., the top Internet service and cable provider, with Standard Media, the world's largest media conglomerate. The combined company—Standard Media/Nation Corp.—will hold dominant positions in many industries, including music, publishing, news, entertainment, cable TV, and high-speed Internet.

"Together, they represent an unprecedented powerhouse in media," said Bill Dickens, an analyst with Morris Investments. "The best content will now have the best distribution. This deal is a game changer."

But media critics oppose the deal. According to Sadie Green, executive director of the Media Protection Organization, "If allowed, this deal will create the most powerful company in the world. A company that will put hundreds of small papers out of business and will, eventually, use its power to strangle open access to the Internet. It will make an already gutless media way, way worse."

According to industry sources, Standard Media CEO Denver Bice is expected to lead the new company

> after the merger. Formal approval of the deal from the FCC is expected next month.

Alex dropped the paper on a bench and tilted his head back to stare at the yellow leaves above him.

"Hello," he said to himself. "I'm Alex Vane. Court reporter with Standard Media slash Nation Corp." He looked down at the paper. "Damn."

He flipped open his cell phone to check the time, then hailed a taxi heading south on Seventh Avenue.

Chapter Two

The taxi stopped behind a CNN van in front of the downtown courthouse, a twenty-story, marble-faced tower. It looked to Alex like a bland office building, nothing like the stately southern courthouses he had come to expect from reading John Grisham as a teen. When he'd decided to become a reporter, Alex had chosen the courts with an expectation of exciting cases and dramatic courtroom scenes, a fantasy—he realized quickly—that had little to do with the day-to-day grind of the law. He had been covering the court for a year and rarely got a story beyond the metro section. But now TV trucks, out-of-state reporters, and curious citizens surrounded the building. The Santiago trial would land him on the front page for weeks.

He scanned the faces of the reporters but avoided eye contact as he made his way through the throng and up the steps. The courthouse furnishings were outdated and its halls smelled of cleaning supplies and wet cement. As he stopped at the security desk, Alex said, "Hey, Bearon," and flashed an ID.

Bearon Decoteau, wearing a dark blue uniform and courthouse badge, smiled as he held out a clipboard and said, "Name and address."

"You think I don't know the routine by now?" Alex shook his head as he took the clipboard.

"Bosses make me say it." Bearon pulled back his long, black ponytail and studied Alex. "You look terrible, man. I mean, for a pretty boy like you. You look like one of the Backstreet Boys the morning his agent checks him into rehab. How'd it work out with Greta?"

Alex scribbled on the visitor sheet. "We had a good time. How'd it go for you last night?"

"Let's just say I could use a little of that Alex Vane charm. City girls don't seem to appreciate gorgeous Native men from the Pacific Northwest."

Alex laughed. "Not like back home, huh?" He rubbed his eyes and patted down his dark brown hair. "Any good gossip for me today?"

Bearon leaned in. "Looks like Sharp is gonna take the lead on the Santiago prosecution, along with Davis and Morganthal."

Alex handed the clipboard back. "Then Santiago's even more screwed than we thought. Sharp is good. I heard he might challenge Bloomberg for mayor in a couple years."

"Everybody knows that. His people are already leaking his slogan: 'At Last, a Democrat Who's *Sharp* On Crime.' You heard from WNYW?"

"Not yet."

"You're a shoo-in, though, right?" Bearon switched to an exaggerated news anchor voice. "This just in: young, handsome, arrogant newsman Alex Vane to become New York's next big TV reporter."

Alex smiled and turned down the long marble corridor. "I hope so," he said under his breath.

Across the hall from Courtroom Four, Alex sat on a wooden bench and leaned his head against the wall. Court wouldn't start for ten minutes and he was half asleep when he heard his ringtone—a tinny, Muzak version of Nirvana's *In Bloom*. When he pulled the phone out of his bag, he saw that the caller ID read *000-0000*. He sighed, tired of telemarketers, but answered anyway. "Hello. I'd like to purchase ten of whatever you're selling."

He heard quiet, steady breathing on the line.

"Alex Vane?" The voice was distorted, deep and metallic.

Alex realized it was being run through a voice scrambler. He looked around instinctively and ran a hand through his hair. "This is Alex. Who's this?"

"The one who knows."

Alex got calls from sources almost every day, some reliable and some crazy. He decided this was one of the crazy ones. "Knows what?" he asked.

The voice spoke slowly. "Knows who killed Professor John Martin. You are covering the trial for *The Standard*, right?"

"I am. Again, may I ask who this is?"

"The one who knows."

Alex paced the hallway. "Oh right, you told me already."

"Eric Santiago did not kill Professor Martin. I could get in a lot of trouble for telling you this."

"Then why are you telling me?" Alex asked.

Silence.

"Hello?"

"Are you familiar with John 12:25?"

Alex smiled. "Let's assume I'm not."

"'He who hateth his life in this world shall keep it unto life eternal.'"

Alex chuckled nervously. "That's why you're calling me?" He waited. "Hello?"

The line was dead.

Chapter Three

Giant granite columns supported the rounded ceilings of Courtroom Four and rows of wooden benches held more than two hundred spectators. Alex found a seat in the back and scanned the crowd as Santiago was led to his seat. His eyes landed on a woman in the front row. In her mid-thirties, she had curly brown hair so voluminous that it blocked his view of Santiago. When she turned toward Alex, he tried to catch her dark brown—almost black—eyes, which stood out against her light tan skin. She looked separate from the proceedings, out of place. And she seemed to look right through him.

At 9:05 a.m., the judge gaveled the session to order as spectators packed the courtroom to its corners.

Alex looked up at Assistant District Attorney Daniel Sharp, who was leaning on a wooden railing, talking with the other prosecutors. Sharp was forty years old but could pass for thirty, even with his bald head beaming under the fluorescent lights. Several times over the last year, Alex had watched him shatter a witness in one moment, then turn to address a jury with grace and kindness in the next. If he planned to run for mayor in a couple of years, Alex thought, this trial was sure to get him some attention.

Sharp approached the jury. "Ladies and gentlemen, this is one of the simplest cases I've had the honor of prosecuting. At one o'clock in the morning on New Year's Eve, 2001, Eric Santiago entered Washington Square Park from West Fourth Street. He walked the diagonal toward the fountain and stopped at the towering bronze statue of Giuseppe Garibaldi."

Sharp paused and looked at the floor gravely, then continued. "Santiago—"

Alex tuned him out and studied the waves of the mystery woman's hair. He knew most of the people in the courtroom that day—Santiago's mother, Professor Martin's daughter, a few NYU professors—but he couldn't place the woman.

Sharp raised his voice. "Fentanyl is designed as a slow-release drug. After receiving a concentrated dose orally, the professor would have felt nothing for three or four minutes. As his stomach heated the liquid fentanyl to 98 degrees, he probably experienced a few moments of relaxation, even well-being. Then, suddenly, his heart rate slowed, his blood pressure dropped, and his skin became clammy. Soon after, he fell to the ground, overcome by drowsiness. Seconds later, he was in a coma. In another minute, he was dead."

Sharp paused and looked at the defendant with contempt. Santiago was slight and pale, his face scarred from untreated acne. His eyes didn't move from the table in front of him.

"After killing the professor," Sharp continued, "Mr. Santiago strolled to Sixth Avenue where—theater workers will testify—he bought a ticket to the one-thirty a.m. showing of *Erotic Advances*. An hour later, he was back in his dorm room, where police found the spray bottle of fentanyl two days later."

Sharp paced in front of the jury box. "You will hear from the defense that Mr. Santiago had no motive. But we will show that Mr. Santiago did not only have *a* motive, he had *the* motive. Did he kill because he wanted better grades? No, he did not have any classes with the professor. Was it about a girl? No, they had no mutual acquaintances. Perhaps it was payback for some old slight? Again, no. Santiago's actions sprang from the motive of a *true* killer—a simple love of death. He's an icy, detached man who, as a child, burned insects in his backyard for pleasure. He is *remorseless*. He did not even bother to destroy the murder weapon! To the man before you, killing is its own reward."

Sharp stopped pacing and looked at the jury. "We may not be able to understand this man's evil, but we know it when we see it. And, ladies and gentlemen, we are confident that you will make sure he *never* has the opportunity to kill again."

Sharp let his words sink in, then took his seat. Alex jotted a few notes, yawned, and moved his gaze back to the woman's hair, hoping she would turn around again. His head throbbed and he wished he'd eaten a few more eggs.

Defense attorney Cynthia Baker wore a cream-colored suit and her long dreadlocks were tied in a neat bun. She was young and Alex thought she must be inexperienced because he had never seen her before. "Mr. Sharp is right about one thing," she began, "Mr. Santiago *was* in Washington Square Park from one to one-fifteen in the morning. But he was not there to kill Professor Martin. The defense will show that Mr. Santiago—lonely, confused, and away from home for the first time—made an error in judgment. He went to the park that night to purchase marijuana. But he did not purchase marijuana, just as he did not kill Mr. Martin.

"The defense will show," she continued, "that Mr. Santiago entered the park at one, wandered around for fifteen minutes, then attended part of a film. He was back in his dorm by two-thirty. And we will show that the so-called murder weapon, the spray bottle of fentanyl, was in Mr. Santiago's dorm room on the night in question. Further, we will provide proof that Mr. Santiago had a prescription for the drug.

"Finally, we will demonstrate that—despite Mr. Sharp's best efforts to obscure this fact—there is not a man or woman alive who saw Mr. Santiago commit this crime. Not one."

Alex listened with one ear. His thoughts danced between Greta's pale, naked body, and what he would have for lunch—then landed once again on the woman in the front row.

Chapter Four

When the trial broke for lunch, Alex followed the woman outside and down the courthouse steps. The afternoon was cool and cloudless. He took a deep breath and felt refreshed, despite the fumes from the garbage trucks backed up along the street.

The woman turned down Broadway and paused at a red light. She took something out of her purse and passed it from hand to hand. When she began walking again, Alex flipped open his phone and called his editor.

"Colonel, it's Alex. Laptop's dead … I know … Yeah, *I know*. I've got the first hit from this morning. You ready?"

He dodged a car as he crossed an intersection and dictated the story using his "evening news" voice. "In a surprising twist in the Eric Santiago trial, the defense admitted that the defendant was in Washington Square Park the night Professor John Martin was murdered." He paused. "Got it? *The Post* might lead with the new prosecutor, but this is the story … Yeah, okay, I'll drop the voice."

The woman turned left onto Canal and started walking faster. When he lost her in the crowd, he jogged until he saw her again.

"Colonel, you still there?" he asked in his normal voice. "Good. Both defense and prosecution acknowledge that the case hinges on a fifteen-minute period, from one to one-fifteen a.m. on January first, 2002. Prosecutors argued that Santiago sprayed Martin with a lethal dose of fentanyl during that period, but the defense claimed that Santiago had nothing to do with

Martin's death—Got it? New graf … No, I'm not reading from notes. This is how I roll, Colonel."

The woman stopped in a crowd at a red light on West Broadway. Alex waited a hundred feet behind her.

"In another development, the District Attorney's Office surprisingly appointed Assistant DA Daniel Sharp as lead prosecutor, showing its determination to win a conviction in the high-profile murder trial—Wait, cut 'surprisingly' okay? Got it? Good. Sharp, who has served as assistant DA since 1995, is known for prosecuting narcotics cases and is rumored to be laying the groundwork for a mayoral campaign—can we get away with saying 'is rumored?' I mean, everyone knows it, but I can call around later and get someone to say it on the record if you want."

When the light changed, the woman crossed West Broadway.

Alex pulled out his notebook. "Sharp portrayed Santiago as a cold-blooded killer." He glanced down at his notes as he walked. "Quote: 'We may not be able to understand this man's evil, but we know it when we see it,' end-quote, Sharp said during opening arguments. The prosecution is expected to call its first witness on Monday … Yeah, that's all the new stuff, but I'll add B-Matter when I get back … Yeah, I'll be in later."

The woman entered the subway at Varick and Canal. Alex closed his phone and considered what he was doing. When he was interested in a woman, he generally wasn't shy about it, especially if she was connected to a story. If she wasn't interested in him, he could pretend that he had approached her for professional reasons. And if they hit it off, he could always find another source. But there was something about her that made him hang back. Even in the subway she appeared out of place, aloof, and this made Alex nervous.

The station was in its midday lull. A man sat on a bench reading a book and another stood on the edge of the platform, leaning out every few seconds to look down the tunnel. Alex's head pounded as he breathed the stale air. He saw her sitting on a bench at the north end of the station and leaned on a wall fifty feet away, pretending to read his notebook while watching her out of one eye. She stared straight ahead and passed something between the fingers of her left hand. Alex thought it was a coin.

He heard the slow screech of a train approaching from the south. She stood and threw the coin in the air. The screech became a high-pitched, metallic scraping as she caught the coin and looked down at it. She crinkled her nose at the coin, then walked into the first car once the train stopped in front of her.

Alex took a step toward the train, then paused. He wanted to follow but he was frozen.

The train pulled out and Alex turned toward the exit. He had to get back to court anyway.

Chapter Five

Inside the train, Camila Gray sat next to a large woman and scanned the ads along the top of the subway car. Her mind was blank and she read slowly. "Live a Life Without Fear," a workshop with someone she'd never heard of; "¡Hablemos Español!" a law firm specializing in deportation issues; "Sex in the City," a singles club.

The woman beside her touched Camila's leg. "You okay, honey?" she asked.

Camila turned toward her and let her eyes go soft so she saw only a brownish blur. The woman smelled of cinnamon and bleach. "Why do you ask?" Camila said quietly.

"You look sad. Is it 'cause of the 9/11 anniversary comin' up?"

"I'm sorry," Camila replied. "No, it's not that. I don't mean to make you sad as well." She smiled. "My ex-boyfriend was murdered. My father is dying. This is just how I am right now."

The woman patted Camila on the knee and turned away. The smell of bleach reminded Camila of the first time she had done her own laundry.

She'd been eight at the time and had poured in half a bottle of bleach, then hid under her bed as the scent spread throughout the house. It was the first time her father had slapped her. "You'll learn not to be so precocious," was all he'd said. Afterward, her face aching, she had sat in a small white oak tree below her bedroom window, flipping a silver and gold Argentinian peso coin. When giving her the coin, Camila's grandmother had said, "When you feel lost, choose two possibilities, one for heads and one for tails. Then flip. But you do not have to do what the coin says. Instead, when you see the outcome, put your hand to your heart and feel. Is there disappointment? Or is there relief? This way you can get out of that head of yours and find out what you truly want."

In the tree, Camila had been trying to decide whether or not to run away from home. With each flip, she'd felt her heart with her hand, just like her grandmother had told her. And though the stream of angry thoughts had softened, no answer had come. As she'd scratched the ashy bark with the edge of the coin, Camila had stared up at the light blue sky and slow-moving clouds, which had looked to her like mountains from a fairy tale. She hadn't been able to tell whether they were truly moving. She'd been deeply sad, but had then forgotten to be sad. And the more she'd stared at the clouds, the more she'd disappeared to herself. Finally, she had forgotten to be anything at all and had vanished into the sky.

Only when she had heard her father's harsh voice through the window, "Cam, what are you *doing*?"—the last word biting and cruel—had she come into herself and wondered what had happened. As she'd placed the coin in her pocket and gone inside, she'd wondered, *Where did I go?* Alone in her bed that night, and for some weeks to come, she would think about how she'd felt in the tree. *How can it be that I am not the sad one I think I am, but something else entirely? Something I don't yet understand.*

At 96th Street, Camila took the escalator up from the station, squinting in the bright sun. Her phone rang and she stared at the caller ID. *Mom.* With the phone in her left hand, she pulled her grandmother's coin out of her pocket with her right. She flipped and read the result. Tails.

Putting the phone back in her purse, she walked north.

Chapter Six

As the elevator opened onto the thirtieth floor, Alex smiled. His head had stopped hurting during the afternoon court session, and the brisk walk fifty blocks north had left him feeling energetic. He did not always like reporting, but he loved the bustle of *The New York Standard* newsroom, a sprawling landscape of fluorescent lights and cubicles, with a few corner offices. People hurried back and forth, keyboards clicked, phones rang. The place gave him a feeling of organized frenzy, of urgency. Alex didn't finish anything unless he had a deadline. Here there was always a deadline.

He walked up behind Lance Brickman—a pudgy black man wearing a brown suede jacket and fingering a fat cigar—and leaned on his desk, which was empty except for an old computer and a single sheet of laminated paper that listed over two hundred contacts with the Jets, Giants, Knicks, and Yankees.

"How was Triple X today?" Alex asked.

Lance turned. "Same shit, different day." He had a silky, deep voice that made Alex think of Lando Calrissian. "Our business is in decline, son. Back when we could smoke while we worked, I used to churn out two thousand words a day. I would sit here and write three damn stories in a row, surrounded by fresh ink and smoke."

"Did you crank the printing press by hand back then, or was it coal powered?"

Lance smiled. "Screw you."

Alex ran his hand across the top of Lance's computer screen. "Lance, I'd like to introduce you to someone. This is HAL."

Lance stared at Alex blankly and nibbled the tip of his cigar.

"Never mind," Alex said, shaking his head. "Dive Bar tonight? I'll buy you a cognac and we can drown our sorrows about a newspaper culture on its way to hell."

Lance nodded. "I'll be there."

"By the way, you ever had a source call you and use a voice scrambler?"

"No, but I had one who claimed to be the reincarnation of Len Bias. I asked the guy how old he was and he said he was forty. When I told him Len Bias had died when he was twenty-something, he hung up."

Alex leaned toward the computer. "Uh, Lance, why have you typed 'fuck' seven times in a row?"

"It's nothing."

"Did the Colonel drop another story on you?"

Lance tapped the cigar on his desk. "Let me put it this way: I'm seven words into a thousand-word column about whether the local teams are paying proper tribute to 9/11."

"You already wrote a column this week."

"Colonel said it wasn't up to '*New York Standard* standards.' Like we *have* standards at this point. I think it might be time to change the name of this piece of shit paper."

"How long did he give you?"

"An hour."

"That's such bull," Alex blurted, turning abruptly and locking his eyes on a door in the corner.

Lance grabbed Alex's arm. "It's not the Colonel's fault," he said. "It's the folks upstairs. Why pay me when they can pay someone like you half as much?"

When Lance let go of his arm, Alex pulled a chair from a nearby desk and sat down. "Because you're a legend. Because you have actual contacts with every team in the city. Because—"

"Don't get all worked up, son."

"How many months until you're vested?" Alex asked.

Lance twirled his cigar and sighed. "I get my options in three months."

"We're keeping you here until then."

Lance laughed. "And they say your generation is lazy and disaffected. It's not worth it. Really. This is just what happens. Young bucks move in and old fatties like me are put out to pasture in the journalism department at Queens Community College."

"How much time do we have?"

Lance looked at this watch. "Forty-one minutes."

Alex rolled Lance's chair out of the way and scooted himself in front of the computer. He held down the delete button, then started typing. "While I write, call three sources you can reach in the next fifteen minutes. One from the Jets or Giants, one from the Yankees, and someone from a high school—to give it some local flavor. I'll leave room for quotes."

"But you don't know what they're gonna say."

Alex stopped typing and looked at Lance. "Yes, I do. You're gonna get them to say that they're doing everything they can to honor the victims through memorials, moments of silence, and so on, and that sports can be a way to heal after tragedy. That's what they've already said in twenty stories this week. That's all their PR departments are gonna let them say. That's all they know how to say."

"What about the facts?"

Alex started typing. "It's a sports column. We don't need any facts."

Lance stood and grabbed the laminated sheet and the cordless phone.

As Alex typed, Lance cracked a few jokes into the phone before asking, "So, how do you feel about how you guys are handling the 9/11 tributes?" Then he clicked over to speakerphone so Alex could transcribe the answer.

Lance called two more sources, repeating the routine of small talk, question, and speakerphone.

After thirty minutes, Alex looked up. "Done," he said, standing up so Lance could sit down.

Lance read the story slowly, changing a few words as he went. He read the last few sentences aloud. "Despite their best efforts, our New York sports franchises can't heal the wounds from the tragedy that occurred almost one year ago. They can play their part, and they will, but only New York sports fans themselves can show the indomitable spirit of this city. The fans who stream into our stadiums from project apartments in Queens, from high rises in Manhattan, or stone row houses in Williamsburg. Only New Yorkers themselves, and their love of sports—which is in fact a love of life—can honor the dead, inspire the living, and heal New York City."

Lance looked at Alex, who looked at the carpet.

"You can change it if you want," Alex said.

"Nah, I'd say we got it. You know, that piece has a whiff of sincerity. Kind of a surprise coming from you."

"I couldn't help it."

With a few clicks, Lance submitted the story, then turned back to Alex. "Doesn't take much to wake you from your slumber, does it?"

"Just don't want to see you get screwed."

"This might have bought me a few days," Lance said, "but I'm still gonna get screwed."

Alex shrugged and started walking away.

"Hey, Alex," Lance called after him, "where you going?"

"Gotta talk to the Colonel."

"'Bout what?"

Alex glanced back and winked. "An interesting woman."

Chapter Seven

When Alex pushed the door open, his boss looked up from his desk, which he'd been polishing with a rag, and asked, "Anything new since you called?"

"You've got a speck of dust there, Colonel, about thirty degrees south-southwest of the stapler."

Samuel Baxton was not really a colonel, but had been an Air Force lieutenant in the Vietnam War. He wasn't much of a writer, but he had discipline and organization—qualities Alex admired, knowing he lacked them himself.

Baxton looked at his desk, which was gleaming, then smiled at Alex. "Like I said, anything new?"

"Usual motions for this and that. Evidence stuff mostly. Seems like he probably did it, but it's surprising they don't have anything more solid on the kid."

Baxton ran his hands through his thin, brown hair. "Everyone knows he did it. But can the lawyers get him off? That's the story now."

"I don't think they can. Sharp is a pretty good prosecutor."

"A lot of people love that kid. Want to make him a martyr for idiots everywhere. The ACLU even said New Yorkers are using him to take their minds off 9/11. Assholes. *Dallas Morning News* ran a thing saying it's New York's elitism on trial. Can you believe that? I'm from Abilene! They must be talking about people like you."

Alex laughed. "Not me, Colonel Baxton, sir. I grew up in the mossy forests of western Washington."

"Yeah, but you were *born* here."

"Six months, sir. I only lived here for six months before we moved."

"That's all you need, Vane. Upper West Side, I'll bet. Parents probably hung out with Yoko and all the other beatniks snorting hash."

Alex looked at the carpet.

"Sorry," Baxton said. "I didn't mean to bring your parents into it."

Alex returned his gaze to eye level. "It's all right."

"But anyway, I never thought I'd be the boss of an aspiring TV model." He paused, raising his eyebrows. "Yeah, I heard about *that*. Why do you want to get into TV when you can write a news story in the time it takes most people to wipe their ass? You know how many people would kill to have what you have?"

Alex's face reddened. He fingered a piece of lint in the pocket of his jeans, struck by a familiar sense of pride tinged with guilt. He was talented. He knew and he appreciated this fact, but he also knew he'd been born on third base. He felt uncomfortable when people treated him like he'd hit a triple.

"You get the job?" Baxton asked.

"Don't know yet."

Baxton smiled. "Guess that's why you scarf down all those salads and sashimi platters. Staying pretty for the cameras."

Relieved that Baxton seemed to have moved on, Alex smiled broadly. "I'll have you know, Colonel, last week I ate food out of a carton. A *carton*! It hurt me to do it, too. I mean, what would my Aunt Winifred up at the Vineyard say? There I was, sitting on a sofa—not a chair at a table, but a *couch*—watching men in helmets run around with a ball made of pigskin, eating with—and this is the worst of it—sticks. I was eating with sticks!" He acted out the motion of shoveling food into his mouth.

Baxton laughed hard, smacking his thigh.

As Alex turned to leave, he added, "I don't even think the chopsticks were monogrammed." Before he left Baxton's office, he stopped in the doorway and glanced back. "By the way, I saw a woman in court today I didn't recognize."

"Who is she?"

"Dunno, but she must be connected to the case," Alex said. "I'll track her down."

"The professor's ex-girlfriend no one's been able to find?"

"Maybe. Just an FYI, I'll be in and out the next couple days." Before Baxton could respond, Alex was out the door.

***

Back at his desk, Alex dialed the courthouse. "Bearon, I need the name and address of a woman who was there today. Brown hair. Mid-thirties. She looked South American. Beautiful but not fancy."

"You mean the one who looked like Evita with a better butt and cheaper clothes?"

"And darker hair. Yeah, that's her." Alex paused. "She was stunning somehow." He heard papers shuffling.

"Last name Gray, first name Camila, with one *l*," Bearon whispered. "Two-hundred West 98th. 4A."

"She's practically my neighbor. Thanks, Bearon."

When he hung up, Alex opened his browser and searched "Camila Gray, NYC." After a few clicks, he found her bio on the NYU Journalism faculty page. He scanned her last few years of classes, including Media Law, Digital Communications, and Communications Theory. He saw that she had presented at various NYU events, such as the Women in the Digital Age Forum and the Millennium Writers Symposium.

He read her official bio:

> Camila Gray is a tenured Professor of Communications at NYU and has been on the faculty since 1999. Her articles have appeared in magazines such as *Wired*, *Digital Woman*, and *The Columbia Journalism Review*, as well as Web sites such as Salon and Media Review.
>
> She was a featured speaker at the Future of Media Conference in 2001, where she presented a paper entitled "Stories in the Digital Age." (link)

> A native of Des Moines, Iowa, Professor Gray had a brief career at *The Des Moines Register* before beginning her graduate work. She holds a BA from Iowa State (1988) and a PhD in media studies from Case Western (1993).

Alex clicked the link to the paper and scanned it, then opened a video at the bottom of the page. In the video, Camila sat on a small stage as the president of Barnard College introduced her. Alex fast-forwarded to the middle and saw Camila standing at an oak podium, looking nothing like the distracted woman he had seen in court. Her hair was pulled back in a tight bun and she addressed the crowd with confidence and a quiet passion.

"Humans love information. We love connection. But most of all, we love stories. From oral traditions to stone tablets, from papyrus to the printing press, from radio to TV, and now the Internet, the medium that delivers our stories is always changing. But our need to connect by sharing stories has been the same for millennia.

"By sharing information, we have built societies and mastered the physical world. By sharing stories, we have slowly taught ourselves what it is to be human.

"We are living at the edge of the greatest storm the media world has ever seen. Before the printing press, all our stories came from the small group of people in our town or village. That's how we learned what it meant to be a person. Soon, every story humans have ever told will be available digitally. As individuals, we are often so mesmerized by the onslaught of new content that we don't see that what matters is the new structure—and what the new structure is doing to us. The printing press was important because it created the possibility of widespread literacy. Television mattered because it ushered in a global culture, for better or worse.

"With each new medium, we have more access to stories, a wider network of connections, a larger village teaching us what it is to be human. So, as we enter an era in which we can easily connect with everyone on earth, we must ask: what will be the impact of The Digital Age on human consciousness?"

A man in the front row of the auditorium turned his head to cough. Alex paused the video and stared into the stiff, wrinkled face of Professor John Martin.

Chapter Eight

Camila lived in a small, fourth-story walkup in one of the cheapest buildings on the Upper West Side. As she walked into her barren kitchen, she imagined a thick chopping block in the center, copper pans and dried herbs hanging from hooks, and the rich scents of roasted fish, garlic, and cilantro. She was not much of a cook, but thought she could be some day.

She took a small carton of coconut water from the mostly-empty fridge and went to sit on her maroon couch. She closed her eyes, lifted her head, and relaxed her shoulders. Her memory of the tree and the sky were still present and the feeling of that day moved through her body. She thought of her father, his hair black that day but thin and white now. After a minute, her father faded and her mind buzzed with random thoughts and images, mostly food related. She watched her mind take on a life of its own, desperately moving from subject to subject as though trying to maintain its existence. After a few minutes, she noticed herself composing a shopping list in her head. She thought about slow cooking a leg of lamb with prunes and apricots and saffron. Maybe Persian food would be the next big thing.

She opened her eyes and stared at a seventeenth century Japanese woodblock print on her wall—a woman in a flowered orange and black kimono, struggling against a diagonal rain under a paper umbrella. A single, angry-looking cloud hovered over her. Camila scanned the print, wondering why she had hung it in her dorm room when she was eighteen and then carried it from apartment to apartment for the last sixteen years. Her eyes landed on the woman—sad, determined, graceful. Camila felt a bond with this woman, and as she stared she began to feel like she was staring at herself. After a minute, she saw the print not as a print but as an idea of herself that lived inside her: the one who struggles. As soon as she saw it, the identification dissolved and she found herself staring only at a piece of paper with patches of color.

She closed her eyes again and slowed her breath. Her butt sank into the couch. Her mind went black. After a few minutes, thoughts started coming more slowly. What would she teach the next day? Possibly dissolution of identity in the digital age. But she was hungry and her thoughts quickly switched back to food. Sweet potato *guiso* with cumin and raisins. Suddenly, thoughts of her father took over. *Papa.* She wondered why he was so cruel. Just as fast, the *guiso* popped back into focus—she'd need copper pans. And pork shoulder—very tender. And onions.

Her belly rumbled and she laughed out loud at herself. She knew she'd never actually cook *guiso.* She just wasn't the kind of person who would spend four hours braising a pork shoulder. Who would she cook for, anyway?

Her thoughts stopped and her mind was black again. Images moved slowly through the black. Steaming enamel pots and smashed cloves of garlic. Her father and uncle, throwing a mini Kansas City Chiefs football on a small rectangle of grass. The images passed through the black, then disappeared. For a moment, her attention shifted to the black space itself and she was gone. *Where am I?* She wiggled her toes and felt her butt on the couch. *I am here, but where is my mind?* A stream of thoughts came, this time about her lack of thoughts.

Her father appeared again—scowling and floating slowly through the black—then disappeared. Her conscious mind drifted in and out until she was aware of only an endless, luxurious blackness.

After a few minutes, she smelled bleach and smoky meat. "Cam, what are you *doing*?" Her father's growl from the kitchen window. She opened her eyes and a shudder ran through her body. Her chest tightened. She was salivating. Her mind returned.

She looked over at her phone, which was ringing. *Mom.* She watched the screen until it read "1 missed call." An overwhelming sadness spread through her body.

Then she began to cry.

Chapter Nine

Alex stopped by his studio apartment at 105th and Broadway to shower, shave, and change into a black button-down shirt and dark jeans. A king-size bed took up most of the floor space and from it he could reach his mini-kitchen with one large step across the center of the room. He thought that the owners of his building must have divided the apartments many times—adding kitchens in closets, converting living rooms to bedrooms—until they ended up with his one-window cell.

After changing, he walked to the door, then turned back and opened his laptop. He had a new e-mail.

> From: magdalena@wnyw.com
> To: alex_vane@hotmail.com
> Subject: Re: Application for Junior Reporter Position
> Date: September 5, 2002 5:32:15 PM EST
>
> Dear Mr. Vane,
>
> Thank you for your recent application to join our team at WNYW New York News. Regretfully, we are unable to offer you a position. We feel that you need a few more years of experience and perhaps some on-air practice before making the transition to television.
>
> We encourage you to try us again in the future.
>
> Sincerely,
> Maria Magdalena
> Co-Producer, WNYW News at 5

Alex read the e-mail twice, then flopped down on his bed. He stared at a black speck on the ceiling and tried to picture his parents in their vegetable garden back on Bainbridge Island. All he saw was their blue Camry swerving off the road, crashing into a cedar tree. For the first few years after their deaths, seeing his name in print had given him a feeling of existing when nothing else did, but he no longer got that rush. His job had become routine, easy. In his boredom, unpleasant images were arising. He hadn't actually been there when his parents died, but he was seeing the crash almost every day now.

He had heard that live TV is like a newspaper on speed. Fast paced and dangerous. A lot of attractive people working hard. He wanted to feel that, to be busy and productive. Most of all, he wanted to fill the blank space in his mind that images of the crash were occupying.

He stood up and read the e-mail again. "Damn," he said to himself, slamming his laptop and heading out the door.

***

The Dive Bar on 92nd street was full of New York sports memorabilia and poorly lit by dusty, colored lights. Alex saw Lance stooped over a glass of something brown. He thought of the e-mail again, then collected himself and flashed a smile. "How does it feel to live in a town where even the names of bars are ironic and self-referential?" He sat on an empty barstool next to Lance.

"Go to hell with all that," Lance said. "One glass of booze is as good as another."

Alex ordered a vodka and soda with lime.

Lance smiled. "Wouldn't want to accidentally ingest a carbohydrate, would you?"

"Wouldn't exactly hurt you to cut the carbs a bit," Alex replied, reaching over to pat Lance's belly. Lance swatted Alex's hand away.

"How'd that story go over?" Alex asked.

"Fine. Looks like I'm safe for one more day."

When the bartender brought his drink, Alex squeezed the lime into it.

Lance shook his head. "This whole food obsession is getting out of control. Half the country is killing themselves with food and the rest treat food the way we treated the Holy Spirit at Trinity Baptist on Sundays."

"Huh?"

"With *reverence*. Man, what the hell happened to just eating?"

Alex sipped his drink. "Why didn't you go into radio? You preach like a radio guy."

"Didn't have the looks for it."

They both laughed as the bartender refilled Lance's cognac.

"Speakin' of different careers ..." Lance said, taking a long sip.

"I didn't get it."

"No?"

"She said I need on-air practice. I don't wanna talk about it. You got anything good on opening week in football?"

"Got a thing about some guy in the Giants locker room being Muslim. Couple teammates went on record saying they don't trust him. It's a bullshit story, but they said it so we're gonna print it. What have you got?"

"Santiago. The Washington Square Park murder."

"That's a career-maker, if you play it right. Depending on how the trial plays out, you could be doing segments on CNN before you know it. But pray for something dramatic at the trial—sexual abuse, some dirt about the professor. Maybe it'll turn out the kid's innocent. If the trial goes national you could ride it ... hell, who knows where?" He turned to the bartender. "Ma'am, another for me and get this young man one, too. He needs to learn how to drink the good stuff."

Lance emptied his glass and turned to Alex. "Why do you want to leave for local TV anyway? This merger goes through and we might *be* a TV station."

"I've heard they're gonna keep the paper if the deal goes final," Alex said.

The bartender set down a curved glass and poured the liquor.

"When the guys from Nation Corp. move in, *The Standard* will be a one-page flyer," Lance said. "And you'll be doing two-minute segments on Court TV."

Alex ran his finger around the rim of the cognac glass. He turned to Lance. "You think Santiago did it?"

"Doesn't matter if he did it, matters how big the story gets. Not that it could get much bigger."

"But do you *think* he did it?"

"You're askin' the wrong question."

Alex picked up the glass and smelled. "I don't drink brown liquor."

Lance shook his head. "You got a lot to learn, son."

"So school me."

"First of all, journalists don't drink vodka."

"Why not?"

"Who knows, but I heard Edward R. Murrow say it when he gave a talk at Syracuse in 1963, so it must be true." Lance was slurring his words now. "Second, you're screwed unless you go for it when you get your chance, which is now. I started at *The Standard* ten years before ESPN was born, when the sports section was all people had. I knew athletes were gonna run the world soon. That job was my shot and by the time I was thirty we had the best sports section in the city. I did coke with half the pro-athletes in New York in the eighties. We were kings back then. Now? For a kid like you there's nowhere to go in this business but down. Or, if you're lucky, sideways."

"So what are you saying?"

"Don't screw up this story. Do what the Colonel says, get your pretty face on CNN, and use *that* to get a TV job, if that's what you want."

Alex emptied the glass and grimaced. Lance shook his head. "You just shot a twenty dollar glass of champagne cognac."

"Was I not supposed to?"

Lance smacked him on the back of his head. At the same time, someone touched Alex's shoulder. He turned.

Greta Mori stood before him at about five foot six, with long, black braids hanging in front of her shoulders. Alex was surprised but stood up and gave her a brief hug. "Sorry I'm late," she said. "I'm always late."

"Greta," he said. "Oh, uh, late? Um, this is Lance. We work together. Lance, this is Greta. She's a … yoga teacher."

Lance smiled into his drink.

"I'm a body worker," she said, holding one hand out to Lance while smacking Alex on the shoulder with the other. "Wait, you don't even remember that you invited me to meet you here tonight." She smoothed her white linen dress under her as she sat on a barstool next to Alex.

Alex flushed. "What had happened was … I had been *planning* to meet you here … and then Lance called and I … and *then* what happened was … Never mind. I'm an asshole. But enough about me. What do *you* think of me?"

Greta turned to Lance. "Asshole pretty much sums it up."

Lance laughed. "But at least he knows he's an asshole. That's a start."

Alex leaned forward between them. "You guys know I'm still sitting here, right?"

***

An hour later, Alex and Greta walked out of the bar, arm in arm. "My apartment is ten blocks north," Alex said.

"Then let's hurry."

The streets were mostly deserted and they walked in silence. At 88th street, Alex glanced back and saw a tall, rail-thin man walking about half a block behind them. Alex stopped and the man stopped.

"What?" Greta asked.

The man stepped into the shadow of a streetlight as a panic rose in Alex's chest.

Chapter Ten

Camila sat up on the couch, catching a glimpse of herself in a mirror that hung from the bedroom door. She looked like hell. Her cheeks were red and her hair was a wild, tangled mess. She gathered it in her hands and pressed it down over her eyes. Sirens and car horns blared from the street below.

Her cell phone rang. *Mom.* She walked to the kitchen, found a stale cookie in the cupboard, nibbled the edge, and threw it in the trash. When her phone beeped, she walked back to the living room, flipped open her phone, and called her voice mail.

"Cam, it's Mama. I thought you having a cell phone meant that we could *reach* you. Papa's not doing very well, dear. Your cousins are coming down from Kansas City this week, and *su tío* is coming from Rosario. Please come. Your papa might not make it until Christmas break and we haven't seen you in so long. I just was telling Georgette—"

Camila closed her phone and looked at herself in the mirror. *I need to eat.* She pressed her hair into shape, untangled some curls, and walked to the door.

***

The Gaslight Diner on 89th Street was empty. Camila slid into her regular red leather booth in the corner, catching the eye of the old woman behind the counter. "Hi Mirna. The usual," she called over.

Mirna was thin, her face wrinkled but bright, and her silver-gray hair was pinned up in a beehive style. She turned and shouted back to the kitchen. "Bacon and Brie burger, rare.

Sweet potato fries. Roasted garlic aioli." She turned to Camila. "You're here late tonight. Been crying again?" she asked in a harsh but motherly voice.

"Guess," Camila croaked across the diner.

"About Martin or your dad, or something else?"

"At this point I'm not even sure anymore."

"Drink?"

"At least one."

Mirna grabbed a shaker from the bar behind the counter, added a shot of gin, a dash of simple syrup, a splash of lemon juice, and a scoop of ice. She shook it hard. "You know, the boys in the kitchen talk about you," she said. "Couple days ago, Fernando said, 'How can someone so beautiful and so smart be so sad?'" She poured the mixture into a champagne flute and topped it off with champagne before garnishing it with a lemon rind.

Smiling, she approached Camila then set down the drink. "I told him I had no idea."

Camila took a long sip and looked up at Mirna, but said nothing.

"I've worked here forty years," Mirna said, "and you're the only person who's ever ordered a French 75."

"You want to know why I started drinking them?"

"Okay, but talk loud, I gotta wipe down bottles." Mirna turned and started pulling ketchup and mustard bottles off empty tables, running them through a wet rag and replacing them.

"We're all about the glamour, huh?" Camilla smiled. "Two girls living the dream in New York City."

"You know it."

After dropping the lemon rind into the drink, Camila took a long sip, then turned toward Mirna. "When I was in my twenties, before grad school, I lived in Paris for a year. I thought I was going to be a philosopher."

Mirna smiled. "When I was in my twenties, I thought I was going to be Marilyn Monroe. You know, I slept with Joe DiMaggio before she did."

Camila laughed. "I'll bet you did."

"If I looked like you, you know what a good time I'd be having?"

"I'm not going to become a Derek Jeter groupie, if that's what you're suggesting."

"Wouldn't hurt you to have a little fun." Mirna set down a saltshaker and looked back. "Have you been with anyone since John died?"

Camila shook her head and sipped. "Do you want to hear why I drink this silly thing or not?"

"Shoot."

"I lived in Paris for a year and I'd stay up all night in cafés, reading the French philosophers and psychoanalysts—Derrida, Lacan. I wanted to be hip, French, something different. And I was a little self-involved."

Mirna smirked. "You don't say."

Camila tossed a napkin at her. "Hey, leave me alone. I'm fragile right now. Anyway, I wanted a drink that sounded cool and no one else drank, so I started drinking French 75s."

"And now that you've stopped trying to be cool, why are you still drinking them?"

Camila finished the drink in one long sip. "It's like drinking a glass of joy, bitterness, and fire."

A man shouted from the kitchen. "Burger's up!"

Camila raised her glass. "And I'll take another one of these, please."

Mirna retrieved the burger from the window and set it in front of Camila. "You're gonna eat that whole thing, huh?"

"Damn right," Camila said. "I need to refuel so I can go home and cry some more."

Chapter Eleven

Alex took Greta's hand and walked on. At 90th, they stopped at the window of a small grocery store.

"Lots of energy in fruit," Greta said.

Alex looked back and saw the man standing next to a pay phone a half block behind them.

"What's wrong?" Greta asked.

"Nothing," he said, nudging her and continuing up the street. "I think I need a coffee for the walk home."

They stopped at the Starbucks on the corner and stood in line. Alex looked out the window. After a moment, the man appeared under a streetlight. He wore a puffy black jacket and his curly black hair peeked out from under its hood. Alex thought he recognized him. The man glanced inside, then looked away and lit a cigarette.

Greta didn't want anything, so when they reached the register Alex just ordered a small coffee for himself. While they waited, he turned back to the window.

The man's face was pressed against the glass. He had a yellow and red bird tattooed on the left side of his neck and his wild green eyes were fixed on Alex. Frozen, Alex held his gaze. He thought of the call from earlier in the day. This was real.

"Two dollars and nine cents, please."

Alex turned around and the barista handed him his coffee.

"Why not two dollars even?" he asked, trying to sound confident. He handed her three dollars. "Right now, there are probably ten thousand Starbucks employees counting out ninety-one cents and handing it to guys like me."

“Most people just drop it in the tip jar,” she replied, unimpressed.

“But that’s a 45 percent tip,” Alex said, smiling.

Greta gave his arm a gentle tug toward the door. He dropped the money in the jar and looked back toward the window. The man was gone.

Alex looked both ways as they stepped out onto the sidewalk. No man. He took Greta’s hand and they walked north. Every few minutes, Alex glanced back into the shadows, trying to remember John 12:25.

Chapter Twelve

Friday, September 6, 2002

Alex read his story on the Santiago trial standing in front of the NYU journalism building, a fifteen-story stone tower a few doors up from Washington Square Park. The sun was still behind the buildings and a thin fog hung in the air. He thought of all the people across the city reading his story. Ten million people in the five boroughs, three-hundred thousand of whom bought *The Standard* each day, including home delivery. Probably only half of them looked at the front page, and maybe half of those actually read it. Seventy-five thousand readers. In an eighteen-hour day, about four thousand readers per hour, about seventy every minute. And that wasn't even counting the web edition.

When Camila stepped out of the taxi, her eyes looked puffy and her hair was even more disheveled than it had been the day before. As she walked past Alex into the journalism building, he slung his laptop bag over his shoulder and followed her in, careful to stay a few yards back.

Nearing the front of the elevator line, Alex saw a sleepy-looking security guard checking IDs as the students filed past him. When he was a student at NYU, they hadn't had security. "Checking IDs?" he asked when he reached the front, smiling and looking straight at the security guard.

"They got us doin' it ever since 9/11. Gotta be safe, I guess. Students and employees only."

Alex noticed that the students were just flashing their IDs at the man as he waved them through. "I'm neither," he said.

"Here as a guest speaker in Professor Gray's class. I should be on the list. Fourth floor, right?"

"Sixth floor. All journalism classes are on six."

Alex waved his *New York Standard* ID under the man's nose. "That's right, *sixth*. She has me here to talk about the case of the murdered professor from last year. You know the one?"

"Sure, I know the case. It's *huuuuuge* around here. Everybody's talking about that Santiago kid. I used to do security for his baseball games. He was a shortstop, right?"

Alex was inching toward the elevator. "That's right."

The guard waved him through. "Head on up."

Alex rode the elevator to the sixth floor and walked down the hallway. He saw her through the window of a theater-style lecture hall filled with about three hundred seats. He filed in with the students and took a seat in a crowded section near the back.

Camila stood on a large stage at the front of the room fiddling with a laptop and projector. When she plugged in the laptop, an image appeared on the screen behind her: a generic-looking man in the center, surrounded by the logos of Microsoft, Yahoo, Hotmail, CNN, and *The New York Times*. Above the logos, in large text, Alex read: "Communications 235: Media and Identity in the Digital Age."

Camila looked out from behind the lectern as students pulled out notebooks and laptops. She looked tired, but her face lit up as she began to speak.

"How many of you are journalism majors?" she asked. Most of the hands in the room went up. "And how many of you plan to work in the media in some capacity?" Most of the raised hands stayed up. "Why is that? I mean, why do you want to work in the media? You." She pointed at a tall boy in the front row.

"Uh, I don't know. What's that quote? 'Sunlight is the best disinfectant,' or something like that? Journalism can be like a light shining onto the parts of the world we miss. Exposing things we don't see."

"Good. That's good. Journalism is a noble endeavor. But I should tell you now that most of the media has nothing to do with journalism, and most journalism has little to do with reality. At its best, journalism is a skewed reflection of a tiny piece of reality." Camila paced the stage. "And there's nothing wrong with that. But when we start confusing the media with reality, we run into some serious problems. 'The cradle rocks above an abyss.' Anyone know where that's from?" She scanned the room. Alex caught himself pulling a thin reporter's notebook out of his back pocket. He had sat in classrooms like this almost every day during his four years at NYU. The habit had come right back. "It's Nabokov. It ends, 'And common sense tells us that our existence is but a brief crack of light between two eternities of darkness.' If that's true, then we live in the center of that crack of light."

The class had settled down. Alex was mesmerized.

"We live in the center of a national tornado called the media, and those of us in this room, in Manhattan, live in the eye of the storm. We can't see it, but it's whirling around us all the time, shaping our thoughts and experiences. It's an exciting time to be here, even if there *is* darkness on both sides. All the information we want is right here in this hunk of metal and silicon." She patted her laptop. "We are beginning to exist in the digital world. And even though we are the ones creating that world, we don't yet know what it is. We don't know what we're creating.

"When I was a little girl, I lived on a small street in Iowa. Neighbors. A palpable context. A *world* in which to live. A world that shaped and defined me. Now there is no world, no context, even for those still living on small streets. We are all trying to create worlds out of the endless stream of information—the images, words and sounds that go by on screens." She paused. "Is it working?

"There is a loneliness when we stare at the screen, right? And the loneliness becomes heartache when we realize that the screen has nothing to tell us. But it's not the screen's fault we feel so disconnected. It's not *its* fault that it's not human. It's *our* fault that *we're* not human. At least not as human as we're meant to be."

Just then a young man walked in with a huge stack of papers. "Ms. Gray, the syllabi."

Alex watched dozens of shoulders relax in front of him.

"Ok, class, enough of that," Camila said. "This is Greg, the TA. He will be handing out the syllabi. Welcome to Media and Identity in the Digital Age."

***

An hour later, Camila dismissed the class. Alex stayed in his seat and watched her chat with a few stragglers. Her formal demeanor was gone and she looked young enough to be a grad student. He wanted to approach her but felt stuck. What the hell? Why didn't he just talk to her?

He stood as the last of the students left, but something caught his eye through the window in the top half of the door. A bright bird on an ashy black neck. Then it was gone. Alex stared at the window a moment longer, then looked toward the door, both hoping and fearing that he would see the man again.

"Can I help you?" Camila stood in front of him.

"Um ... I ..." Alex's eyes darted back and forth between the doorway and her face, which appeared to be acutely focused on him, while at the same time relaxed, even soft.

"Do you have any questions about the syllabus?"

"No, I just ..." He glanced at the window; the man was back.

"I gotta go," he muttered, jogging past Camila and into the crowded hallway.

The man ducked his head and disappeared down the staircase next to the elevators. Alex fought through a swarm of oncoming students and bounded down the stairs two at a time. "Wait!" he called, still about a flight behind the tall, lanky frame moving awkwardly down the stairs.

Alex caught up to him on the second floor. When the man moved to the inside of the staircase to evade a group of students, Alex grabbed at his shoulder. The man lost his footing, then stumbled down the final few steps.

Alex took him by the arm and pulled him down the last flight of stairs and out into the street. The fog had burned off now and the sun was peeking over the buildings with a sharp, raw light. Alex squinted and looked at the ground, waiting for his eyes to adjust.

As he brought his eyes up he saw the gun.

Chapter Thirteen

After class, Camila returned to her office, a small room with brick walls and books stacked to the low ceilings. She locked the door, sat at her old metal desk, and stared at the wall. The bricks were painted white and the more she watched them the more they seemed to move. The grout lines between the bricks waved and pulsed as her mind softened. The wall took on a glow, then began to shimmer as her eyes relaxed. Every few moments, the strangeness of this overcame her and she shifted her head and focused her gaze, which reestablished her mind.

After a few minutes of this, she closed her eyes and saw John Martin. He was standing in her apartment—shoulders slumped, tears in his eyes—three weeks before he died. She did not like this memory of him. She stood and opened a small window that looked onto Fourth Street. The day was warm and hazy. It was going to rain. Students came and went and delivery trucks double-parked. Taxis honked behind them.

Leaning out the window, she closed her eyes and saw him again.

"We can't have a baby," she had said to him. The heater had been stuck on high for days and they'd propped the window open, so an occasional snowflake had drifted into their conversation and then melted in midair.

"Why not?" Martin asked.

"I love you, but we're too old."

"You mean *I'm* too old."

She sat on the couch, not looking at him. "Look at us," she said. "How are the two of *us* going to raise a baby? We're both solitary intellectuals."

"Camila, this is my last chance. I didn't think I'd find anyone I'd want to have another child with, but I did." He sat down next to her and his chin dropped to his chest as he pulled at a loose thread on the white longshoreman's cap in his lap. "And I thought you said you liked older men."

She stared at him with pity, then sadness. She was able to imagine his parents from the stiff wrinkles on his forehead—their neglect, their depression, their anger. They had filled him with fear. He looked like a little boy, shocked by an external force until the life in him just stopped. He had walled off enough of his mind to be brilliant on occasion, but his strength and vibrancy were gone.

"You said I make you feel safe," he continued. "I know how your father was. I would never hit a child."

Camila knew he would be a good father. She had met his daughter a couple of times, and she had turned out okay. He would try his best and he would never be violent. But he was weak. Too weak and too broken.

The snow started coming down hard and she walked to the window and watched it mound on the cars below.

"I'm fifty years old, Cam. I have enough money. Even if you don't want to stay with me, I want to have a baby with you."

He had smiled as she'd looked at him. Turning away, she'd leaned out the window and caught some snow in her hand. "I never said I liked older men," she had said, watching the snow melt in the white-gray light. "I said I tend to choose safe men. Some of them have been older. I love you, but I don't want to do that anymore. I can't do *this* anymore. I want to feel okay enough to be in a relationship that isn't just safe."

Her cell phone rang and she opened her eyes. She moved to her desk, glanced at the caller ID, and paced her office, trying to relax. She had to answer this time. On the fifth ring, she did.

"Mama? Yeah, I'm fine ... I should have called you back ... I know ... And there's *nothing* else they can do? How long did the doctor say he might ... Okay ... I can't just leave in the first week of the semester … Okay … Right … I'll see if I can come … Bye, Mama … Yeah, love you, too."

She put the phone down and looked back at the wall, staring until her vision blurred and the bricks morphed into a colorful fog.

Chapter Fourteen

"Demarcus Downton," the man said. He had a Brooklyn accent mixed with something else Alex couldn't quite place. They had crossed the street and were sitting in a small coffee shop where Alex felt safe.

"How'd you get upstairs?" Alex asked.

"Known the security guard for a long while."

"Why the gun? I saw it in your belt."

"It's not for you. Plus, *you* the one threw *me* down the stairs."

"Sorry about that," Alex said. "How's your head?"

"Had worse."

Alex believed him. His face was more than thin—concave almost, and scarred. His dark green eyes looked tired. In addition to the bright bird on his neck, Downton had a fading Tweety Bird tattooed on his left forearm. On his right wrist, the number *76845* in blocky lettering. But despite Downton's ragged appearance, the more Alex studied his face, the safer he felt.

The waitress came and they both ordered coffee.

Downton looked up at Alex. "You writin' the case of the boy they say killed the professor?"

"Santiago. Yeah."

"What you know about him?"

"Why do you want to know about Santiago?"

"'Cause the kid didn't do it, at least not like the police have been sayin'. Wonderin' why he's takin' the fall."

Alex was skeptical but pulled his notebook from his bag. "The fall for what? What the hell are you talking about?" He remembered the strange voice from the call the day before. "Did you call me yesterday?"

"I ain't even got a phone."

Alex couldn't think of a reason not to tell Downton about Santiago. Everything he knew was in the paper anyway, and it would give him a chance to study Downton's reactions, and possibly draw him out.

"Santiago's from a military town near the bases in San Diego. His father was killed in Iraq in 1990, leaving his mother with seven-year-old Eric and sixty hours a week in a department store. Don't know much else about her or the rest of his family."

The waitress brought the coffee. Alex sipped his black as Downton added teaspoon after teaspoon of sugar.

"As a teenager, he won chess tournaments and baseball games. He was small, but a good shortstop. Made the all-star team in little league and the all-county team in high school. In old photos, he looks like a pretty normal kid."

Downton stirred the sugar into his coffee. "He was on the baseball team here?"

"Yeah, why?"

"Used to play a bit myself."

"With your height, I would have thought you played basketball."

Downton smiled. "Played a bit of that, too."

"In high school, Santiago had a terrible problem with acne. Not just normal outbreak stuff but boils all over his face. Left deep scars. Can't figure out why he came across the country, because he got offers from a bunch of California schools that actually care about baseball.

"People who know him from school aren't talking, and in court he just stares into space. Must be smart enough if he got into NYU, but he just gives you this weird feeling, like he's not all there. He's never spoken to a reporter, and nobody knows why he killed Professor Martin."

Downton rubbed the numbers on his wrist. "Maybe that's because he didn't."

Alex sighed. "Yeah, the boy didn't do it. So you said. But why follow me? Why not just e-mail me like everyone else with a story to sell?"

Downton laughed. "E-mail? Gotta get to know you a bit 'for I can truss you."

"How do you know he didn't do it?"

Downton leaned in and spoke in a whisper. "Saw it go down." He looked over each shoulder before adding, "I'm the guy who made the anonymous call to the cops that night."

He had Alex's attention now.

Over the next fifteen minutes, Downton explained that he was a small-time pot dealer who sold mostly to NYU students in Washington Square Park. Alex had spent quite a few afternoons there as an undergrad, and realized now why he had recognized Downton.

"Was workin' the night the prof died," Downton said. "Hangin' 'round the west end of the park, a ways from the statue, when the prof come through. He wasn't staggerin' too bad, but you could tell he'd had a few. Looked like just another drunk in the park."

"Did you know Professor Martin before you saw him that night?"

"No. Didn't know neither of 'em. But I *see* everybody. That's my business. You get to know who's who—where they goin', who dey hang wit'. You got to, so you can tell if somethin' ain't right."

"You sure you didn't know Santiago?" Alex asked. "Defense said he was in the park to buy pot that night."

"I told you, I never sold to him."

"Okay. So what happened when Professor Martin came through?"

"He stopped at the statue and stood there a few minutes."

"What was he wearing?"

"Dark clothes, white hat—one of those kinda golf caps or captain's hats. I don't know what you call 'em but only white people wear 'em."

Alex perked up. If Downton was lying, at least he'd taken the time to learn a few details. "Then what?"

"The kid come from the east end of the park and walked straight by the prof. I was workin' a deal, watchin' the prof out the corner of my eye, and a few minutes later he was on the ground."

"How do you know the kid didn't attack him while you weren't looking?"

"Look, I don't know exactly *what* happened, but the kid never went near enough to do what they say. You all ain't been writin' the truth."

"I write facts," Alex said. "The truth is different."

"The truth is the truth." Downton leaned back and looked around the coffee shop.

Alex usually knew if a source was lying within a few minutes, but he was still unsure about Downton. He looked down at the man's tattooed wrist.

"Prison number," Downton said. "Did three years at Eastern, upstate."

"For what?"

"Didn't do it."

"What were you convicted of?"

"Assault."

Alex leaned back in his chair. "Look, I appreciate you coming forward, but I need another source on this, someone who will go on record and isn't a ... well, someone who will go on record."

Downton looked at the table.

"What's wrong?" Alex asked.

Downton closed his eyes, then opened them. "You ever dunk a basketball?"

"What?"

"You know that feelin' you get when your daddy is proud of you? First time I dunked a ball I was thirteen years old. It was my birthday and I got a real leather ball from my daddy. Was the only kid on the block who had one and he took me to the park and I dunked it. He looked at me like I was somethin' and my chest got all warm and I felt like I could do anything."

Alex nodded. "Yeah, I know that feeling."

"I knew then that he would sit courtside and watch me play at The Garden someday. Then he died and, well …" Downton went quiet and ran his fingers along the grain of the wooden table.

"My father died, too," Alex said. "And my mother."

"How?" Downton asked.

Alex sipped his coffee. "You have any kids?"

Downton smiled. "Had a wife. Left me when I did the bit upstate. She never minded the dealin'. Never did more than sell twenty-sacks to rich teenagers. But she couldn't stick with it when I went upstate. Gotta daughter who's grown now. Lives up in Queens near my mama."

"You seem like you have something else to say."

Downton looked into Alex's eyes, then stared down into his coffee cup. "There's a video," he said quietly.

"Of what?"

"The night. The kid. You know, the night in the park."

Alex shot up in his seat. "What?"

"You need another source, right? I don't have another source for you, but I've got a video."

"What? What's on it? Why didn't you tell me this before?"

Downton scanned the coffee shop. "Well, didn't want to give it up. Could be bad for me. I told them I don't have it."

Alex finished his coffee in one long sip. "Told who? What are you talking about?"

"I'll tell you everything, but you gotta do something for me."

"What?"

"Get me into a Knicks practice. Want to see how it looks from down on the floor."

Alex reached into his bag and took out his mini tape recorder. He set it on the table. "Okay, but let's start from the beginning."

Chapter Fifteen

"Need everything on Demarcus Downton!" Alex called, approaching a desk in a dark corner of the thirtieth floor.

James Stacy sat, headphones on, staring at two giant computer screens, his desk littered with papers, chip bags, and soda bottles. His wide back spilled over both sides of the chair. He was a college dropout who had been at *The Standard* about a year, and looked like he was still a teenager to Alex, but he could always find things online that Alex couldn't.

"Hey Jaaa-aaames." Alex stood behind him, pulling the headphone away from his left ear. "Hellooooooo?"

As James turned, the chair squeaked and buckled under his weight. His skin was pasty white, his blond hair tied into a long, messy ponytail. He pulled the headphones off and waved Alex away.

"What's that case thing?" Alex asked, pointing to a white device on James's desk.

"An iPod. They're the f-f-future. They're—"

"That's great," Alex cut in. "But *right now* I need everything we have on Demarcus Downton."

"Who is he to us?" James asked. His eyes shifted back and forth from Alex to the screens on his desk as he spoke.

"Possible source. He deals pot in Washington Square Park, was arrested at some point, did time at Eastern. Inmate number 76845. May have played sports locally, too."

James took a long sip of root beer. "He involved in the S-S-Santiago case?"

"Might be," Alex said. "Hey, do you know any way to trace one of those zero-zero-zero numbers that comes up on a caller ID?"

"Not without a court order and special equipment. C-Companies are using them to get around new t-telemarketing laws."

Alex walked to the other side of the desk and looked over the screens into James's eyes. "How do they work?"

James looked up. "You just run a regular phone l-line through a box that hides the c-c-caller ID. Costs a few hundred bucks."

"How long on the other thing?"

"Half hour."

"Fifteen minutes," Alex said over his shoulder, walking across the newsroom. "I need everything you can get in fifteen minutes."

***

Alex knocked as he pushed the door open. "I've got something, Colonel."

"Ever considered waiting until I actually tell you to come in? What if I'd had someone from upstairs in here?"

Alex smiled. "I knew you didn't. I can tell when you have a boss in here because everyone in the office gets this look like they're working hard. They don't have that look today."

Baxton adjusted a stack of papers so they made a ninety-degree angle with the corner of his desk. "What do you have?"

Alex looked at the papers. "They look straight to me, Colonel." Baxton didn't look up, so Alex continued. "I've got a guy on the Santiago thing who says he was there that night. Says Santiago didn't do it."

Baxton shot up in his seat. "You serious? Is he credible?"

"Not sure yet."

"Why didn't he go to the police? Why isn't he a witness?"

"Let's just say he lives slightly outside the law. He doesn't want to have anything to do with the police."

"A criminal?" Baxton asked.

"You could say that."

"What does he say happened?"

Alex put his hands in his pockets and paced the office. "Says he saw Santiago in the park that night. Saw the professor, but Santiago never touched him. He identified the professor's hat, too."

"He could have gotten that from police reports, or even the paper. We published that. Hell, everyone published that."

"There's more. He says—"

"This sounds pretty thin, Vane. I'm not saying don't work it, but you're gonna have to do a lot better."

Alex was startled. He usually got a fatherly pat on the back from Baxton when he had a good lead. "Don't work it? It may not be true, but if it is, it could be huge for us."

Baxton stood up. "And get you on TV? You don't *have* anything yet. We can't be the paper that blows up the Santiago case. You know how important it's been for the city. We love hating this kid." Baxton smiled. "Are you sure you don't *want* there to be something to what he says?"

"What? This isn't about me."

"Vane, c'mon. We all know you—"

"Colonel! Listen! He says he has a video."

"Of what?"

"The night."

Baxton reached down and straightened his papers for a moment, then slowly looked up. Alex had never seen Baxton look afraid, but his sharp eyes appeared to have receded further into his head.

"What's on it?" Baxton asked. "How'd he get it?"

Alex felt a knot in his stomach. He had never lied to Baxton before, but he had never had a reason to feel suspicious of him before either. "I don't know yet. Gonna get it tomorrow."

Baxton peered over Alex's shoulder and moved pencils from one cup to another. Alex knew the conversation was over.

When he was halfway out the door, Baxton asked, "Alex, by the way, what happened with the woman from the courthouse? You get anything on her?"

"Nah. She was just a court fan. No connection to the case."

Chapter Sixteen

Alex sat alone at Dive Bar and sifted through the research James had given him. Downton's name had come up in dozens of articles, most from local papers in the mid-seventies. It took Alex an hour to piece together his story.

Downton grew up in the Bed-Stuy neighborhood of Brooklyn, raised by his African-American father and Sri Lankan mother. In the seventh grade, and already standing six-foot-five, Downton led his basketball team to the state finals. The next year, coaches from St. John's and City College started attending his games and the old folks in the neighborhood began calling him "Baby Wilt." His coaches and peers called him "Downtown D."

By his junior year, now six-foot-nine, Downton was a local celebrity. He dominated the competition in high school—averaging twenty points, ten rebounds, and five assists—and was known as a great kid around the neighborhood. Article after article mentioned his volunteer work and good grades. Alex laughed out loud when he found a photo of Downton helping a lady up some steps with her groceries. Who was this guy?

In 1977, Downton accepted a full scholarship to play at St. John's. He never attended, but Alex couldn't figure out why. The next year, his name appeared in an article about a deadly fire at a meat packing plant. One of the victims was Tyree Downton, Demarcus's father. In 1985, Downton served six months for dealing marijuana. In 1988 he did another year for the same crime, and in 1992 he was sentenced to three years for beating up a man in Washington Square Park. He hadn't appeared in the papers since.

Alex was on his second drink when Lance walked in. "I was hoping you'd show up," Alex said.

Lance took the stool next to him, ordered a beer, then glanced Alex's way. "Vodka and soda again? Be careful. That lime wedge might have a third of a net carb in it."

Alex half-smiled and looked up from his drink. "Have you ever known the Colonel to sidestep a story?"

"What? No, 'How was your day, honey?' I'm *deeply* hurt."

"Seriously," Alex said. "You've been here forever. Has the Colonel always been straight with you?"

The bartender delivered the beer and Lance took a long sip, smacking his lips. "If I'm gonna be your therapist tonight, you're buying."

Alex turned to face him. "I mean, I know stories sometimes get stuffed for political or financial reasons, but today he didn't want me looking into something. Something big. I just got the feeling that—"

"That you're not the golden boy anymore?" Lance laughed then took another long swig of beer.

Alex mashed the lime wedge into the bottom of his glass with a little red straw.

"Boy, you're really hot for something, huh? Got that youthful exuberance and everything. The Colonel? Yeah, he'll stonewall you every now and then."

"What should I do?"

Lance took a moment to finish his beer then waved at the bartender. "Nothing you can do. You know that invisible wall between the news people and the ad people we talk about?"

"Yeah."

"It's getting thinner. Time was, we never even thought about the ad guys. They did their work and we did ours. But it changed in the nineties. Started getting the sense that, when assignments were handed out, we could never afford the personnel to do certain kinds of reporting."

Alex glanced at a group of women at the end of the bar, then back at Lance. "But I'm talking about when you've got something real, already in hand."

Lance took a cigar out of the inside pocket of his jacket and ran it under his nose. "You know they're gonna ban smoking in bars any minute now. Next, they'll probably ban carbs. Then we'll all look like you."

"Lance, please. You ever had a big story just stuffed?"

Lance put the cigar on the bar and rolled it back and forth with his thumb. "Remember a few years back when they changed the name of the football stadium from the Meadowlands to SunLife Tech Stadium? I had a column ready on how the Giants' owner had been on a board with the CEO of SunLife way back when. Everyone knew they were buddies, but I found something solid enough to print. So I wrote that maybe the Giants could get more money for the naming rights if they opened up the bidding instead of just making this back room deal. I'm no crusader, and the piece didn't come off like that. It was from a fan's perspective, you know? I was saying, 'If you're gonna sell out and name the stadium after some damn company, at least make the bidding competitive so you can drop the price of hotdogs by twenty-five cents.'"

"So, what happened?" Alex asked.

"Never found out. Colonel pulled it and ran a feature on some kid who overcame something or other and ran some race for charity. We'd had that piece on the kid sitting around for a week—wasn't even timely when we ran it." He shook his head. "Never felt right. And I noticed we started running quite a few ads for SunLife broadband soon after."

Alex sighed. "You think the Colonel gets it from upstairs, or is it his call?"

"What the hell are you asking for, boy? Sometimes stories get stuffed. Even yours. It's just the business being the business. Doesn't happen much, and when it does, we usually don't know why."

Alex leaned in. "Can we go off the record here?"

"Oh, for Christ's sake, Woodward. Don't be so dramatic." Lance waved down the bartender. "Ma'am, two cognacs. And leave the bottle. It's on my young friend here."

Alex waited as the bartender poured the drinks and set down the bottle. "Do you know Demarcus Downton?"

"Downtown D? Hell yes, I know him. He came up right after the King, Bernard King. Was a better prospect, too."

"Why'd he start dealing?" Alex asked.

"Usual story. Got his girlfriend pregnant and went to work instead of college. Then his dad died and he never made it back. In the neighborhood, we looked at him like a god. He was as close to a sure thing as there was in New York at the time." Lance picked up his cigar and dragged it between his lips.

"You think he'd lie to me about a story?" Alex asked. "I mean, a *big* story."

"Tough to say. Don't know him well, but everyone in the neighborhood knew Demarcus was on the straight path. His mom was real strict. She used to throw rice on us to get us off her stoop." Lance picked up the cognac bottle, shook it a bit, and put it down. "How big a story are you talking about?"

"If he's telling the truth? The biggest of my life. By far."

"Then, what can I do to help?"

Alex smiled. "Can you get Demarcus and me into a Knicks practice?"

Chapter Seventeen

Alex sat on the edge of his bed and took out his mini tape recorder. Downton had said he needed to get the video from his mother's house in Queens and they had arranged to meet at Jack's Bar in Brooklyn at noon the next day.

Alex pressed play and walked to his closet as Downton's voice filled the room.

"A couple months after 9/11—November, I think—two cops picked me up. White guy and a black guy. Fresh faced. You know, all 'us against the world.'"

Alex leaned into the closet and slipped a four-foot-long wooden pole out of a thin bag made of blue velvet. After draping the pole over his shoulders, he paced the room, rotating from his waist every few seconds as he listened.

"They said they had me on dealin' in the park and I could get ten years 'cause I was on parole. They'd looked me up, you know? Said if I helped 'em, they could get me out of it. NYU was their beat. Said they'd let me operate as long as I stayed small."

Alex heard the occasional thud of a coffee cup on a tab-letop in the background.

"Said they'd seen a kid buyin' from me who might be connected to 9/11. Wanted me to wear a camera for a few weeks, see if I could catch him buyin'. Man, how any of my customers could be connected to 9/11, I don't know. Plus, how are they gonna press a terrorist if all they have him on is buying a twenty sack? But it sounded like a get-out-of-jail-free card, so I said, 'what the hell.'"

Alex stopped pacing when he heard himself speaking on the recording. "It's possible the guy they were after was related to a suspected terrorist. Maybe they wanted to leverage your guy to get to the family member overseas." Hearing his own voice made him feel like he was being watched.

Downton continued. "Maybe, but it wasn't *my* business. I was lookin' at ten years, so I did it. It was a tiny black box I clipped to the inside of my jacket. Front looked like a button. They told me to click it on when I started workin' and click it off at the end of the night. Wore that thing for a couple months."

"Did you get the cops' names? They're supposed to show you a badge and ID."

Downton laughed. "It's not TV. When two guys in a cop car pick you up, they don't read you your rights or anything. You just get in the car."

"Did they take you to the station?"

"Nah, man. Just drove around. Black one drove and the white one told me the deal. Dropped me off at the park 'bout a half hour later like nothin' happened. Next day, they outfitted me with the camera in the bathrooms on the south side of the park. Every Monday after that, they'd come get the camera, then bring it back 'bout an hour later."

"How did they know if they got their guy?" Alex asked.

"Oh yeah, forgot about that. They asked me to keep an eye out for Arabs. 'Sandniggers' is what the white guy called 'em. He would do the bit like Joe Pesci from *Casino*. You know that movie? The part where Pesci's selling the diamonds? The white cop was Irish or something—all freckled—and he's trying to do an Italian accent like Joe Pesci. He was a racist asshole, but it *was* right after 9/11. Anyway, I'd tell 'em if I thought I'd had any Arab customers and when I'd seen 'em."

Alex did squats, using the pole to keep his shoulders level. "So how'd it end?" he asked on the tape. "Why didn't they come for the recorder once Professor Martin died?"

"They just stopped showin' up. Didn't make no sense. I figure it's an expensive camera, why wouldn't they want it?"

"When did they disappear?"

"Musta been about mid-December, end of the semester, because I remember my crowd was thinnin' out."

"Why'd you keep recording?"

"Only did another couple weeks. Didn't know if they'd show up again. After that prof got killed, I put the camera away and that was it."

Alex reached a hundred squats and began pacing again, using his abs to rotate side to side.

"So why now?" Alex's tone in the coffee shop had turned harsher. "You could have gotten Santiago off earlier if the video shows what you say it does."

The tape played chatter in the background. Neither spoke for a full minute.

"Thought about that hard," Downton said. "I mean, what was I supposed to do? Figured I probably broke laws about privacy or somethin', plus there's the dealing. In my line of work, you never look for attention."

Alex slid the pole back into the bag and placed it in the closet. He sat on the bed as he listened to himself asking Downton a question. "Then why not mail the video to the police anonymously?"

"Truth is, I'm not sure what's on it. Don't know how to use the thing, but I know it didn't go down like the police have been sayin'. Plus, you think just mailing in a video would get the kid off? Once the police have their guy, they run with it no matter what evidence shows up. And once they seen the video, they'd come lookin' for me."

"Then why not send it to the defense attorney?"

"Lawyers?" Downton laughed. "Either way it leads back to me."

"So, like I said before, why now?"

"The two cops showed back up. Got the sense they *really* wanted their camera back. Figured if I brought it to a reporter, people could see it for what it is."

"But if I put out the video," Alex said, "it will still lead back to the park that night. To you."

The voices in the background grew louder and Downton's grew softer. "Maybe, but it's just time. Never knew the city would make such a big deal outta this Santiago kid. I seen how the papers made him out to be a monster, talkin' about him torturing bugs, watching porn all the time. But I thought somehow he'd get off since I knew they had the wrong guy. But when those two cops came back? Well, I'm not sure I'll be around long enough to get in trouble anyway. That's why you gotta get me into a Knicks practice as soon as possible."

Alex clicked off the recorder and lay down on his bed. He stared at the black speck on the ceiling. In the coffee shop he had been angry, but he realized now that Downton was right—the video might not lead to Santiago's release. He knew he couldn't use Downton as the only source in a story, but no one else could verify his account. If Santiago was innocent, he needed another source. And he needed to see that video.

He thought of the strange call from the day before, opened his laptop, and searched for "John 12:25." After clicking a few dead links, he found a site that listed bible verses with interpretations from different pastors. The complete passage read, "He who loveth his life shall lose it; and he who hateth his life in this world shall keep it unto life eternal." Most thought the verse meant that if we love our worldly life—the life of sin—we'll lose our eternal life in heaven. Instead, we should recognize the limits of temporal life and turn our attention to Jesus. But one new age pastor Alex read had an opposite interpretation. He wrote that the passage was about suicide and reincarnation. If we live this life correctly, it will be our last, and we will end the cycle of reincarnation. But if we hate our lives in the world—if we don't value the gift of life—we might kill ourselves and be damned to continue the life we hate again and again, back on earth.

Alex had no idea how any of this could be relevant to Santiago, or to anything else, and fell asleep reading an article about how 9/11 had ended the popularity of boy bands.

Chapter Eighteen

Demarcus Downton leaned back in an old brown recliner and turned on SportsCenter. His apartment was a one bedroom on the first floor of a four-story brownstone in Brooklyn Heights. He had only one small window that faced the street and was covered with bars.

Sirens wailed and Downton turned up his TV. "The Knicks are going to suck again this year," he muttered. "Jordan's out of the league and they still can't win the east."

He heard a knock at the door and muted the TV. "Neese, is that you?" He picked up his gun from the table beside the recliner and slid it into his belt as he walked toward the door. "I *know* the TV is loud. Deal with it. I'm already depressed about the Knicks and the season hasn't even started." The sirens grew louder as he peered through the peephole, his left hand on the gun at his waist. Seeing nothing but the empty street, he slid the deadbolt.

An ambulance sped past his building as he opened the door. Downton turned away from the deafening shriek of the siren just as he felt his knee shatter. He wobbled forward as a scream caught in his throat, then fell onto his back into the apartment. His gun hit the floor and slid across the room.

Looking up, Downton saw what he thought was a child standing over him dressed in black jeans, a white t-shirt, and sunglasses. He heard the door slam shut as the pain in his knee coursed through his whole body. He was confused. He blinked slowly and when he opened his eyes he was staring into the barrel of a long, thin gun.

"Why are you, eh, talking to a reporter?" The figure above him spoke with a high voice and a strange accent Downton could barely understand. The voice—along with the thin, rectangular mustache and shoulder length, black hair—convinced Downton that this was not a child. Just a very short man.

"What?" Downton said.

The man spoke more slowly. "Why are you talking to this reporter? Is it possible you have something you are not supposed to have?"

Downton spoke weakly through stabbing pain. "Man, I don't know what you're talkin' about."

The man stepped away from Downton and picked up a framed photo from the windowsill. "Is this you?" the man asked.

"Me and my dad." Downton remembered every detail of the photo. Christmas Day, 1974. Knicks, Warriors. Third-level seats at Madison Square Garden.

"Look down at your knee, black man. Do I not look like someone who is good at what he does? Would I come here and break your knee if I did not know who you have been talking to?"

Downton looked at his knee and saw a bloody knob of bone sticking out just above it. His head dropped back to the floor.

"Here is what is going to happen. You will tell me about this reporter, about this video, or you will die right now, tonight, in this room."

"I don't know who you are man, but I really don't know—"

"Stop."

"Man, I'm tellin' you. I don't know nothin' about no reporter."

The man set the photo down and turned to Downton. "You fucking Americans. You never say the truth. Tell me about this reporter."

"He ain't done nothing to you."

"A minute ago you did not know what I was talking about? Now you know he has done nothing to me?" He stepped toward Downton. "Tall man, this is it."

Downton tilted his head to the left to look at the man, who squatted and stared into Downton's eyes.

Downton turned his head away and closed his eyes. He saw his dad, smiling at him from his red plastic seat at the Garden, rafters in the background. "I don't know who the hell you are, but I don't know nothin'."

The man stood quickly from his squat, and in the same motion, fired two quiet bullets into Downton's head.

"I am Dimitri Rak."

Rak pulled black leather gloves from his jacket pocket, put them on quickly, then rummaged through the TV stand and ran his hands across the fabric of Downton's recliner. He walked to the bedroom and went through the small dresser, inspecting every piece of clothing. He flipped over Downton's mattress and patted up and down the stained fabric. Finally, he searched the bathroom and kitchen.

Finding nothing, he bolted the front door from the inside and walked into the kitchen. From there, he opened the sliding door and stepped onto a tiny brick patio enclosed by a rusty fence. A dog barked in the distance.

Rak looked around, climbed over the fence, and walked down the street.

***

Alex slept in short bursts interrupted by vivid dreams.

In one, he stood in the doorway to his father's writing room in their Bainbridge Island house. It was the Christmas break before his college graduation, six months before his parents died. His father clicked away on a beige computer while Alex stood silently, his throat scratchy, and watched him write. Finally, he said, "Dad, why don't you and mom visit me in New York?" His father turned slowly, his eyes glassy and ineffectual, and spoke in the tinny, distorted voice Alex had heard over the phone two days prior. "We don't like it there." Alex's mother appeared behind his father, placing her hand on his shoulder. "We don't like it there," she repeated. Alex surveyed her with sadness, then dread. The dread intensified until he shot up in bed.

He checked his phone. It was 4:35 a.m. He must have slept a little.

He lay back and stared at the ceiling, thinking about his brief interaction with Camila. He tried to form a clear picture of her standing in front of him, but couldn't. The images of her morphed into scenes of his parents and his childhood home. He felt shaky. Why did he keep thinking about her?

He sat up in bed and leaned against the wall. Despite the crime and corruption he covered on a daily basis, Alex always felt safe, like he lived on an invisible solidity while the world around him shook. But trying to picture Camila made him feel uncomfortable. She was amorphous, complicated, and clearly strange. She was an academic. Not his type at all.

She might be the source he needed, but when he thought of calling her, the dread from the dream crept into his chest. "It's fine," he said to himself. "I'll call her at eight."

He lay back down and sprawled out on the bed. "I'm fine."

Chapter Nineteen

Saturday, September 7, 2002

Dishes clanged in Sweet Marie's diner as Alex breathed in the smell of bacon and fresh muffins. From his seat at the counter, he saw Camila come in. She wore jeans and a silky red shirt, her bushy hair tied back in a messy ponytail. She scanned the restaurant, found him, and navigated aisles crowded with strollers. He waved at an empty stool beside him.

"You were in my class the other day," she said, sitting down. "You didn't tell me you were a stalker."

He held out his hand. "I'm an alum. Alex Vane, *New York Standard.* I looked you up after I saw you in court." Alex tried to gauge her response. He couldn't read her. "Like I said on the phone, I'm covering the Santiago trial. Can I ask you some questions about Professor Martin?"

"Sure, but I don't know anything about John's death, and I won't be in the paper. I know how it works, and I'm only willing to be interviewed on deep background. Also, you're buying breakfast."

"Deal. How well did you know him?"

"I knew him a bit."

"That's it?"

"What do you want to hear?"

"Well, guys like me have been trying to find his reclusive ex-girlfriend for a long time. Are you her?"

A waiter appeared from the kitchen and asked for their orders. Camila ordered a vanilla latte, a croissant with butter, and a side of bacon. Alex ordered a six-egg-white omelet with spinach and two shots of espresso over ice.

Camila studied him as he ordered. "Keepin' it tight for TV?" she asked, smiling. "I get students in my classes every year who plan on putting in a few years at a paper before breaking into TV. Some have connections at a station, others land a couple big stories in print and make the transition. You've got that 'I need to be seen' look about you."

Alex was stunned and a little hurt.

She continued, "You know, pretend to be a journalist when what you really want to be is an entertainer. Maybe one of those guys who pontificates about trials on a multi-box talking-heads show?" She paused. "Do I have it right?"

"Maybe there's something to that," Alex said. "I've been looking into TV jobs, but I *do* have a job to do now. A *reporting* job. So, can I ask you about Martin?"

The waiter put down the croissant and coffees. Camila reached for the croissant and took a bite as Alex sipped his iced espresso and turned to speak.

Before he could, she said, "So why switch to TV?"

"I don't know. I mean, I don't think there's anything wrong with wanting to move into the form of journalism people *actually* consume."

Camila laughed and spat out croissant flakes. "You just called TV a 'form of journalism.'" She took a long sip of her latte. "C'mon, you wanna be famous. It's okay, so do half the people in this city."

Alex raised his voice. "You seem to know a lot about me for someone who's known me for five minutes. So let me ask you this: why hide away in academia? I saw on your bio that you were only a real journalist for about a week."

"Touché," she said. She took another big bite and spoke through a sprinkling of crumbs. "So why do you want to interview me anyway?"

"Way to change the subject. I'm doing a feature on the murder for next week's Sunday edition. Just trying to get a better sense of Martin's life. I saw you at the trial. How'd you know him?"

"We had sex for a while. Maybe a year."

The waiter put down the omelet.

Picking up his fork, Alex said, "I think they call that a relationship."

"Yes, it was actually fairly sweet."

"What was he like?"

"What do you have on him?"

Alex took a bite of his omelet and pulled his thin notebook from his bag. He pretended to read from notes. "Taught creative writing. Finished his PhD at forty after working at it for ten years. Published, but not widely—mostly short stories and a few poems in obscure literary magazines. Originally from Alabama. Attended Tulane, where he met his wife and had a daughter, who is now in her mid-twenties and lives upstate. Wife divorced him while he was in graduate school. Worked at a few lesser schools before landing the NYU job."

"I met his daughter once," Camila said. "Why aren't you talking to her?"

"I tried. She's only talking to *The Times*."

"Smart girl."

Alex smiled. "That hurts. Tell me more about him. What kind of man was he?"

"Hard working, but not especially gifted. John had a difficult time just getting through the day. His parents were both depressed when he was growing up. He was bright and sensitive in a household with oblivious parents. I liked his writing, and I think he was a good teacher—you'd have to talk to his students about that—but he was fragile."

"I've heard he was a little OCD," Alex said.

"Those diagnoses are BS—just a title they put on a bunch of symptoms no one understands. But he did keep *everything*. In file cabinets, cupboards, drawers. He kept every record of every class he ever taught—teaching notes, old student papers. He was proud of being a professor. He had to struggle to get anywhere in life."

Alex rattled the ice cubes around in his glass. "So if he wasn't OCD, how would you describe him?"

"John was wound tight, but held together tenuously. Like he was afraid of getting hit. Not physically hit. Just like the world would strike out at him at any moment, from any angle. Like his nervous system was on high alert. You know when you feel into someone and get a sense of what it's like inside them?"

Alex stared at his half-empty plate. "Uh, no. Not really."

"Think of it as an internal frequency. Yours is relaxed, easy, confident. It's what comes from having an easy life, a supported life. From being tall and handsome and white and heterosexual in America. John had a rough childhood. His energy was, well, constricted." She extended her right arm over the counter and clenched her fist so tightly that her whole right side shook. She made a sharp buzzing sound between her teeth. "He felt like that."

The waiter returned and Camila ordered another croissant.

"So why were you with him?" Alex asked.

"Honestly, I loved him. He had a sweetness he was trying to protect."

"Then why did you break up? If you don't mind me asking."

"I think I do mind. I like you, but I'd rather not talk about that."

The waiter slid the croissant down the counter. Alex stared as Camila covered it in butter and then mopped the plate with it to pick up flakes.

"Did you know the Santiago kid when he was a student?" Alex asked.

"No, and if you're asking whether I know of any hidden motive, I don't. The police already asked. Many times."

"Are you sure that Martin and Santiago didn't know each other?"

"If they knew each other, he never mentioned it to me."

"And you can't think of anyone else who might have had an interest in hurting Martin?"

"No."

Alex sucked on an ice cube. He could tell that, despite her bluntness when she arrived, she was comfortable with him. "Just humor me," he said. "Let's say you magically found out that Santiago was innocent. God came down and told you or something. If you had to name another reason Martin was killed, what would you say?"

Camila stared at him for a long moment, then looked away and began to spread jam over the butter on her croissant. Before she took a bite, she said, "I think you know something."

Alex leaned back in his stool. "No. I'm just asking as a thought experiment."

"You're lying."

Alex wasn't used to being seen through. "I'm just … gathering information."

She leaned toward him. "What do you know?"

He looked down and flipped pages in his notebook. "At least tell me why you two broke up. When was it, again?"

"I never told you when we broke up."

Alex smiled. "You'd be surprised how often that works."

Camila's phone rang in her purse. She wiped the splotches of jam on her plate with a corner she'd torn off the croissant and then popped it into her mouth. She took her phone out and looked at the caller ID. "It's my mother," she said. She put the phone back in her purse and closed her eyes. "My father is dying."

Alex stared at her but said nothing.

She looked up. "I'll keep talking, but let's get out of here."

Chapter Twenty

"So how did you and Martin meet?" Alex asked as he and Camila walked along the outside of the gravel path around the Central Park reservoir. A steady stream of joggers in colorful attire passed them on the inside. The air was cool but clear and the leaves were yellowing on the Norway Maples.

"We met at a faculty luncheon sponsored by the NYU humanities council. The idea was to promote interdisciplinary studies. You know, if the creative writing professors know the business professors, the students will have a better chance of success. That kind of thing."

"Sounds romantic," Alex said.

"I thought it was a waste of time—most faculty events are—but there's always free food."

"You seem to like food quite a bit," Alex said.

"Don't you?"

"I only eat vegetables and protein—you know, meat, eggs, fish. Don't really care about food."

Camila laughed. "Is this a medical or guilt-based diet?"

Alex took a few long strides and Camila jogged to catch up with him. "Did you hear me?" she asked.

"I used to be fat," he said, not looking at her. "A while back, I binged for a couple years. Food, sometimes alcohol. Then I regained control."

"And now you feel like you have to hold onto control as tightly as possible, right? It's what's making you an asshole."

"Thanks," he said. "That's sweet of you to say."

"I've been told I use criticism as a way of flirting. Not that that's what I was doing."

Alex glanced at her, but couldn't tell if she *was* flirting, or just making fun of him. They walked in silence and watched a pack of skateboarders pass on the walkway to the south of them.

"So, what was the relationship like?" Alex asked.

"It was good, overall. He didn't ask too much of me. We met a couple times a week, had a good time, and then led our separate lives."

"Until what? I mean, why'd you break up?"

"It just didn't work out."

"You're lying," Alex said.

"That's true, I'm lying." She walked to the inside of the path, leaned against the fence, and looked out across the reservoir. The sun was bright and the crisp air reminded Alex of the morning of 9/11. He walked over and leaned on the fence next to her.

"Where were you when it happened?" he asked. "9/11, I mean."

"When the planes hit I was asleep in John's bed. Every Monday night I used to sleep at his place because neither of us had early classes on Tuesdays. His phone rang and woke us up around 9:30."

"Who was it?"

"They didn't leave a message. Hung up when the machine came on, before John could answer. We'd been up half the night reading Wallace Stevens and we always slept in on Tuesdays. Anyway, John learned about the attacks when he turned on the stupid morning show he watched while he drank his coffee. Woke me up a few minutes later and we watched CNN all day like everyone else."

They left the fence and continued their stroll around the reservoir. "Why did you ask about 9/11 just then?" Camila asked.

"The weather is the same today. Do you want to know where I was?"

"Not especially," Camila said. "But I can see that you want to tell me."

He hadn't told anyone where he'd been that day. And she was right. He did want to tell her. "Never mind. I just—"

"Let's get back to the thought experiment you mentioned in the restaurant."

"You *do* like to change the topic abruptly, don't you?"

"Do you want me to do the thought experiment or not?"

They sat on a bench that overlooked the park at the south end of the reservoir. Alex stretched his long legs out in front of him and Camila sat facing him with her legs crossed over each other. "Sometime last December, we were at a funeral for one of John's old professors. Something Hollinger, I think it was. Billionaire who died in 9/11."

"Yeah, I remember him," Alex said. "Macintosh Hollinger. We ran an obit on him when they found his body. Richest guy to die in 9/11."

"Anyway, he taught at Tulane when John was there in the seventies. He and John stayed friends over the years. We were at Hollinger's funeral a few weeks before John died and he had a weird interaction with Denver Bice. You know him?"

Alex laughed. "Know him? He signs my checks. Not literally, but he's the boss's boss's boss. I know *of* him."

"John made some crack about it being lucky that Hollinger died when he did and Bice got weird about it. I don't know Bice—I only spent those few minutes with him. Seemed like he was trying to keep his cool."

Alex smirked. "How could you tell? Did you *feel his internal frequency*?"

She flashed her eyes at him. "Don't be so skeptical. When you're a kid growing up in an unsafe environment, you either go numb to it or you learn to sense the mood of everyone in the house, for self-protection. Most people lose that sensitivity as they become adults."

"And?"

"I didn't."

Alex's mind dismissed what she was saying. But he had to admit that she *had* read *him* pretty accurately. "How did Martin know Bice?" he managed.

"They were in a class taught by Hollinger. I guess they both kept in touch with him."

"So, what else about the interaction at the funeral?" Alex asked.

"John and I were breaking up at the time, so everything was a bit messed up. But that night, after the funeral, John was upset. More than usual. Like his internal frequency had gone all the way to this." She held her arm out and clenched her fist so hard that her whole body shook and her face turned red. "Something was wrong."

"What?" Alex asked.

"I asked him about it, but he wouldn't say. He was mad at me for other stuff, but something about the funeral had set him off, or something about the interaction with Bice."

Alex stood up and leaned on the bench. "My editor is fond of saying, 'Alex, we can't print your feelings.'"

"It was *your* thought experiment, and I'm not telling you to print anything. I'm just saying I got a funny feeling that night. We broke up that week, and a few weeks later he was dead. I told the cops about it, but it was nothing more than a feeling. And by then they were already convinced it was Santiago." She stood up and met his eyes. "But it sounds like you know Santiago didn't do it."

Alex flipped open his phone and checked the time. "Well, I'll find out for sure in an hour or so. I'm meeting a source who says he has a video that could break this story wide open."

Chapter Twenty-One

Jack's was a small bar in Brooklyn Heights, dark and unclean. Alex sat in a sticky booth in the back for twenty minutes before approaching the bartender.

"Are you Jack?" he asked an old man who shuffled back and forth behind the bar.

"Ain't no Jack," the man said. "Never was. Owner just thought it sounded homey."

"Do you know Demarcus Downton?"

"Sure I know him. Used to be a regular here before he went upstate."

Alex held out his hand. "Alex Vane, *New York Standard*. I'm writing a piece that might include something on Downton."

The bartender looked skeptical. "You a sports reporter? What you writin', a retrospective or somethin'?"

"No, nothing like that. I'm wondering if you know where I can find him. I was supposed to meet him here for an interview."

The man frowned. "You writin' a thing about people who did time for somethin' they didn't do?"

"No, not that, but what do you mean?"

"Demarcus, you know, the bit he did upstate. Everybody knows he deals. Hell, half my customers buy from him. But he ain't do what he got sent upstate for."

"The assault?"

"Yeah, he ain't do that. He was here that night, but the police didn't want to hear it. I tell ya, only upside to 9/11 is that the police have a different group to arrest without cause now.

Leave us black folks alone." He laughed and wiped the bar with a rag.

"Can you tell me where he might be? Like I said, I was supposed to meet him."

The man stopped cleaning and studied Alex. "Yeah, he live nearby."

Alex wrote down the address and walked out into the hot sun.

***

He saw the flashing lights from a few blocks away and broke into a jog up 61st Street. The worry he'd started to feel in the bar sank into his stomach and became a dense ball of dread as he approached Downton's building. Stopping near the police tape that blocked the entrance, he scanned the faces of the police and paramedics, but didn't see any he recognized. He didn't see any reporters he knew either.

Off to the side, a frail-looking woman of about fifty smoked a cigarette. She was dressed in a pink polyester robe and worn slippers. Alex noticed four cigarette butts around her feet. She was shaking and blinking her eyes rapidly in the bright sun.

He walked over and stuck out his hand. "Alex Vane, *New York Standard*." She blew smoke in his direction then turned her head away.

"Crystal Neese," she said hoarsely. She crushed her half-smoked cigarette under her slipper, then reached into the pocket of her robe and pulled a new one from a near-empty pack.

"Can I ask you a few questions, ma'am?"

"Demarcus. Police say he got shot. Killed."

"What happened?"

"Leave me alone," she said, shaking her head. "Don't like reporters."

Alex tried to catch her eye. "Ma'am, I—"

"Get outta here," she said. "I said I don't like reporters."

Alex stepped toward the police tape, recalling the anecdote about a group of reporters standing outside a burning building, taking notes as others saved people from the fire. His reporter instinct had kicked in so quickly that he forgot it was Demarcus who was dead inside the building.

He turned back to Crystal Neese. "I don't like reporters either," he said.

At the police tape, he tried to wave down an officer and a team of paramedics as they entered the building. They ignored him. He spoke with a few neighbors gathered in front of the building, but all he could learn for sure was that Demarcus was dead.

After passing out business cards to anyone who would take one, Alex jogged to the subway on Fourth Avenue.

Chapter Twenty-Two

Alex wedged his head under the faucet and took a long drink of cool water. He did forty push-ups on the floor of his kitchen, drank again, then lay on the bed. He was sweating.

For the first time, he realized he might be in danger. He had never been in danger before—at least he didn't think so. The closest he had come was when Bainbridge Island had been hit by a string of burglaries when he was ten. The paper had run sketches of two suspects and for weeks he'd worried about the two men climbing through his window at night. That was the closest he'd come to danger, and it had been imaginary.

His head buzzed. Maybe he should just drop the story and get out of town. But he couldn't be in any *real* danger—he never even saw the video. He pictured Downton sitting in the coffee shop and his eyes filled with tears. They felt cold rolling down his hot face. He wiped them away with his sleeve. He knew he didn't have time for this.

His instinct was to write everything he knew—Downton's claims about the night Martin was killed, his story about the two cops, and his murder. He would need to find out more about Downton's murder, but he was certain that it was connected to Martin and Santiago. Putting everything out in the open felt like it would shield him from any danger. But the video—he'd need the video. Downton had mentioned that it was at his mother's house in Queens. She couldn't be too hard to find.

He stood and called Baxton. "Colonel, it's Alex," he said, pacing the small apartment as he spoke.

"On a Saturday afternoon? Have I finally instilled a work ethic in you?"

"This is serious, Colonel. You know that source I talked to you about who had something on Santiago?"

"Yeah, the criminal. I remember."

"He got killed last night. Shot in his apartment."

"Well, you said he was a criminal, right? What happened?"

"I'm not sure. No one at the scene would talk."

"You were there?"

Alex stopped pacing and stared out at the traffic on Broadway. The late afternoon sun cast a golden light on the tops of the buildings and the street below was marked by long, irregular shadows. "Yeah. I was meeting him to get the video."

"You showed up and he was dead?"

"Yes. Look, Colonel, you've gotta do something for me."

"Where's this video supposed to be?"

"I don't know, maybe Queens. Look, I need you to call someone to find out what happened. You still have people in the department, right? Find out what sort of gun was used, who they are looking at, and whether there's any connection to Santiago, or to drugs."

"Your source was into drugs? What was he, a dealer or a user?"

Alex hesitated. "A dealer."

"I'll make some calls, but no one is going to go on record for this, you know."

"I know. Tell them it's for informational purposes only."

"If I do this for you, and it turns out to be just another drug-related homicide in Brooklyn, will you drop this guy?" Baxton asked. "Trial starts again Monday morning and I need a thousand words a day on it."

"Just call me back when you get something."

Alex put his phone on the desk and lay on the bed. His gaze followed the tiny cracks in the ceiling paint from one corner of the room to another as he imagined Downton, bloodied and lifeless, lying on the floor. He wondered whether he liked Downton, something he had never considered about a victim. Journalists were supposed to remain neutral and many had to set part of themselves aside to achieve this. For Alex, neutrality came easy. Sometimes he thought he had no feelings, no opinions, nothing solid that needed to be set aside. He was an excellent reporter, but it had never occurred to him to care about what he was reporting on—the sources or the victims he covered. But Downton had been attempting to do something good, had taken a risk, and it had gotten him killed.

He was relieved that Baxton was going to help him, and when his phone rang he sprang across the room.

Then he looked at the caller ID: *000-0000.*

Taking a deep breath, he answered, "Hello?"

"He was not the only one who knows what happened." The voice again. Deep and distorted. Metallic.

"Who is this?" he managed.

"We have been over that. I can't tell you. But I can say that Downton was not the only one who knows what happened."

Alex swallowed hard and looked at the clock on his desk. Downton's body had been discovered only a few hours ago.

"He's gone now," the voice continued. "I couldn't stop it. But you need to keep looking."

Alex wiped sweat from his forehead and sat on the bed. "How did you know he … I mean, can you give me anything else to go on?"

"No. But you're smart, Mr. Vane. Put your education to good use."

Medilogue One

East 128th Street, New York, New York
The Morning After 9/11

Sadie Green leaned over her laptop and clicked refresh. She scanned the list of the deceased, but didn't see his name. It was 8:30 a.m. Still too early to call.

She walked in circles around her couch—reading the headlines of the five newspapers spread across it again and again—then stopped in front of a long mirror on the wall. She looked tired. She had slept only three hours and still wore baggy Batman pajamas over her slight frame. Using her fingers like a comb, she smoothed her short brown hair.

Each of the three TVs on the floor played a different station. On CNN, two talking heads debated when President Bush should visit Ground Zero. She switched to CNBC, where Denver Bice was being interviewed by a perky blonde woman. He wore a black suit with a USA pin attached to the lapel and his hard jaw popped under the studio lights.

"Mr. Bice, in the weeks before the attacks there were rumors in the business community about a possible merger between your company, Standard Media, and—"

Bice held up his hand. "Deborah, I'm sorry. We know that American business will continue in the face of these horrific attacks. We know there will be a time for that. Right now, America needs to focus on—"

Sadie muted the TV. *Asshole.*

She threw the remote on the couch and stared at two small picture frames on the wall. The first was black and held a piece of white linen paper on which she had typed two quotes in a neat, cursive font:

> *Any dictator would admire the uniformity and obedience of the US Media. -Noam Chomsky*
>
> *Whoever controls the media controls the mind. -Jim Morrison*

She took down the second frame and sat on the couch. It was a letter printed on the official stationery of Hollinger Quantitative Investing. She cradled it in her small hands.

> December 16, 1999
> Sadie,
> This morning I sat at my desk and read about stocks, baseball, and fashion. May the people of the Sudan one day have the same luxury, with your help.
> Mac Hollinger

Sadie had begun corresponding with Hollinger while working as the executive director of Free Sudan, a not-for-profit whose mission was to set up the first independent TV station in the region. During her two years in Africa she had taught English, trained would-be journalists, and tried to convince wealthy donors to pay for equipment. After six months of letters to Hollinger, Free Sudan had received a $300,000 donation, which she had used to train a crew to produce a local newscast with digital cameras.

When she returned to New York to manage the Media Protection Organization, her first call was to Hollinger. He declined to meet with her for a few months, but she called him every week.

In the summer of 2000, her persistence paid off. By October they were meeting for lunch every few weeks and, over the next ten months, Hollinger donated about $500,000—a quarter of MPO's annual budget. Sadie found him to be naïve about the modern media, but genuine, thoughtful, and kind in a way that unnerved her. She often wondered why a billionaire investor allowed her to lecture him about the media. But each time his secretary scheduled an appointment, Sadie arrived with soup from his favorite deli and tried to chisel away at his view of the world.

She turned the frame over in her hands and looked at the clock: 9 a.m. Finally. She walked to her desk where she carefully set down the frame. Then she sat down, picked up the phone, and dialed Hollinger's home number. As it rang, she tugged at a tuft of her hair. The pain made her feel more awake.

A woman answered. "Hello?"

"Uh, hello," Sadie said. "Is this Sonia? Sonia Hollinger?"

"Yes."

"I'm calling for Mr. Hollinger, I mean to see if he's okay. If he, you know, made it out."

Sonia spoke quietly. "He's missing."

"I really need to speak with him. He promised a massive donation that will—"

Sonia gasped. "*Meu Deus*! I said he's missing."

"I'm sorry. So you don't know if he—"

"We don't know anything. No one has heard from him. Good-bye."

The line went dead.

Sadie hung up and read his note again, remembering the day five weeks earlier when she had realized that sports would be the way into his wallet. He had been in a bad mood when she'd walked into his office in the south tower that day. He'd eaten his soup in silence as she'd paced the room, trying to explain the importance of net neutrality.

Growing uncomfortable, she pointed at the framed photo of Lou Gehrig. "Big Yankees fan?" she asked. "Be nice if they could get one of those sluggers. Sosa or McGwire. Think the Yanks will ever have a hitter like that? I mean, seventy home runs in a season?"

Hollinger frowned and dipped bread in the paper cup of soup.

"I thought that was one record that would always be held by a Yankee," Sadie continued. "It just feels like it's ours, you know?"

He looked up, scowling. "If you ask me, The Babe still holds the record. Neither of those guys could hit fifty playing at Yankee stadium, and Maris did it with eight extra games. These new guys … well, the ball must have changed or something. A record doesn't stand for forty years then get broken by two guys in one season. I know numbers, and the odds just aren't there." Then he looked at his soup with disgust. "What is this, *lentil*? Whatever happened to beans? It's always lentils these days."

Sadie studied his face and smiled. "Different drugs. If The Babe had the drugs these guys have, he would have hit eighty."

"What?" Hollinger asked, looking up again.

"I mean, look at the size of these guys."

"What do you mean?"

"Steroids," she replied.

Hollinger shook his head. "No, they test for that. We're not the East Germans."

Sadie suppressed a laugh. "Sir, if a story is too good to be true—like two guys breaking the record in one season—that's usually because it's false. The East Germans, Ben Johnson, now these guys."

He waved a hand at her. "No, if baseball players were on drugs we would hear about it."

She chuckled. Before leaving for the Sudan, she had interned at the Chicago Tribune, often tagging along with the Cubs beat reporter. During the summer of 1998, she had asked him whether Sosa, McGwire and other recently-muscled players were on steroids. It was an innocent question, but he had laughed derisively and said, "Of course they are." When she'd asked why he didn't write about it, he'd replied, "First, even though a lot of us know it, we don't have proof. Second, my editor doesn't want proof. Seventy home runs is a story that's gonna save baseball and keep us all employed for a few more years."

Sadie took a step toward Hollinger's desk. "Mr. Hollinger, sir, you know how I've told you that sometimes the media colludes with the government, or certain people or businesses, to keep things out of the news?"

He grimaced as he ate a spoonful of soup. "Yes."

"Well, if you think sports reporting is any different, you might be in for a bit of a shock. I don't just mean leaving personal business out of the news, which is fine. I mean deliberately ignoring drug use, cheating, gambling, domestic violence, and more."

"Why would they do that?"

"To protect the players, to protect the team, to protect the journalist's *access*. Sometimes to protect advertisers or the brand of the sport. You have to understand—the media companies and the sports companies aren't in it for journalism or athletics. They are partners in *business*."

"Maybe, but they wouldn't ignore cheating in baseball."

"Mr. Hollinger, you're a businessman. The world of sports reporting is a big, big business pulling off one of the greatest misdirections in history. People get all worked up over one little detail that slips out here and there. Ever heard of Hemingway's Iceberg theory?"

"Yes."

"The idea that for every sentence he wrote there was a glacier of information left unwritten?"

"I said I'd heard of it," Hollinger replied, frowning.

"Reporters know all sorts of things they never write. Things you can't even imagine. All your heroes, they created them. After a while, they'll tear them down. That's what they do. When a character is no longer useful, they J. Jonah Jameson him."

"Who the hell is that?"

"*The Daily Bugle*? Spider-Man? Never mind."

Hollinger walked to the window and stared out at the Hudson, shushing Sadie any time she tried to speak. Finally, he turned and smiled broadly. "I knew it," he said. "That means The Babe is still the single season home run leader."

For the next few months, Sadie tried to convince Hollinger that similar omissions were happening everywhere. She railed about the deregulation of the media in the eighties, the weakness and corruption of the FCC in the nineties, and how the Founders had supported not only a free press, but also a government-subsidized press. By the end of the summer, Sadie felt certain that a donation was coming. Hollinger was fanatical about investing and the Yankees, *that* she'd known, but she'd had no idea that his fanaticism would turn so quickly in her favor.

In mid-August, Hollinger called Sadie over to his office and told her that he was selling five hundred million dollars in stock, much of it invested in the Standard Media Group. He was donating it to the Media Protection Organization.

Sadie tried to remain calm, managing only to hug him and say, "Thanks, Mr. Hollinger, you're doing the right thing."

"You're welcome," Hollinger said. He was quiet for a moment, then walked in small circles around his office, stopping occasionally to stare out at the Hudson. "I've always hated reporters but respected the press. I know as well as anyone that the press can be lied to and manipulated. I've done it myself quite a few times. Businesses and politicians are supposed to lie and journalists are supposed to hunt down the truly crooked ones and expose them. That's how it's always been. That's what keeps America from turning into a tyranny. But to think that the press would ignore cheating in baseball. Just ignore it? In *baseball*! I trust that, with my money, you'll do what you can to clean things up."

On the subway home that afternoon, Sadie had realized what the donation meant. She would become the executive director of the best-funded media organization in the world. For the first time, there would be an organization with the resources to fight the decline of the US media. And she would be running it. In particular, she planned to do everything she could to disrupt the merger that would create the largest media company in the world. That evening she had called a few friends and, between tequila shots at the White Elephant Bar, she'd left a drunken, rambling message for Denver Bice.

Sadie stood up, hung Hollinger's note back up on the wall, then came back to her desk and sat at her computer. She clicked refresh. His name had not been added to the list of the deceased. She rested her head on the desk and fell asleep.

***

The intercom buzzed and Denver Bice closed his laptop. "Mr. Bice, Chairman Gathert is here to see you." Bice stood and muted the TV, which showed members of Congress singing "God Bless America" on the steps of the Capitol.

"Send him in," he said, striding toward the door and extending his hand as it opened. "Chairman Gathert, how are you holding up?"

Gathert wore a blue suit and small round glasses. He took small steps toward the couch in the center of the office and ran a hand across his bald head as he sat. Bice sat in a leather chair across from him.

"Not well, Denver. I have three friends still missing. One confirmed dead. What about you?"

"Just one. Mac Hollinger. He's missing."

Gathert shook his head. "I heard. It's terrible."

"He was like a father to me at Tulane."

"I know," Gathert said. "I assume our editors are doing what they do, but I wanted to make sure that you're doing everything necessary to postpone the announcement."

"Well, I was thinking it might still go forward. By next week we might—"

"Denver!'

Bice stood up and looked down at Gathert. "I'm saying I think we can still do it. Here's the line: Despite the attack, American business will move forward. Two great American companies, Standard Media and Nation Corp., coming together in the face of terrorism."

Gathert stood up. "Are you crazy? There are people alive in the rubble fifty blocks south of here and you don't want to postpone the announcement of the merger?"

Bice clenched his fist. He heard the thud of Hollinger's head on the sidewalk. *When you hurt someone, you deserve to be punished.* "Chairman Gathert, I …" *You can choose to be in control.* "What I mean is, it's not just another merger. This is the deal that will—"

"Denver! The president will be in New York City in two days. I'm not saying the merger won't happen, but the announcement will be at least a couple months from now."

"Not happen? Do you know what I've done to keep this merger together?" Bice walked around the couch and softened his tone. "At least there may be a silver lining to the attacks. With all the coverage they're going to get, no one will notice when we announce the merger."

"Denver, what the hell are you saying?"

"War is the best time to conduct otherwise controversial business. The liberals will be too busy protesting our response to the attack and the conservatives will be too busy selling it."

Gathert stared at him for a moment, mouth open, then said, "Denver, I need to go. Just get with the people at Nation Corp. and let them know we need to put off the announcement for at least a month." He paused and shook his head. "I'm sure they'll agree."

When Gathert left, Bice sat at his desk and stared at the bottom drawer. Once again, he was standing on the riverbank, twelve years old, staring at his father's lifeless body. He felt the pain of the latest beating, his love for his father, and a rage that froze on top of it all. *When you hurt someone, you deserve to be punished.* He took the key out of his pocket and placed it on the desk. He took five deep breaths and looked at the drawer again. He put the key back in his pocket.

A minute later he pressed the button on his intercom. "Get me the CEO of Nation Corp. We have to postpone the announcement."

Part Two

Chapter Twenty-Three

Monday, September 9, 2002

At 9 a.m., the judge invited the prosecution to call its first witness. Daniel Sharp stood slowly and called to the stand the city's chief medical examiner, Bruce Irving, who wore thin-rimmed glasses and a neat beard. As Irving was sworn in, Alex ran a hand through his hair and heard the voice again: *Downton was not the only one who knows what happened … I couldn't stop it.*

He hadn't heard back from Baxton, and had spent the last day trying to decide what to do next, his fear battling his desire to get the story. When he'd woken up, he'd decided that court would be as safe a place as any. If the video was the reason Downton had been killed, the killer must know that Alex didn't have it. But he needed to get it, and he needed to find the caller. He figured that his source must be inside the police department or close to the case. How else could someone know about Downton's murder and connect it to Santiago so quickly?

Alex glanced around the courtroom, looking for Camila, as Sharp asked a series of routine questions to establish Irving's expertise. He didn't see her.

When he heard Sharp say, "I'd like to ask you a few questions about a drug called fentanyl," Alex turned to the front of the courtroom. The series of questions took Irving two hours to answer and traced the history of the drug and its physiological effects. Alex knew it was a synthetic pain reliever created in 1960 and now available as a patch, a lozenge, and a lollipop, and he was bored by the time Sharp asked Irving about Martin.

"And how much fentanyl does it take to kill a man of Professor Martin's size?"

"It varies based on the person's tolerance for opiates, but 125 micrograms is considered a lethal dose, though regular recreational users can withstand much more."

"One hundred and twenty-five micrograms? That doesn't sound like much," Sharp said.

"It's the equivalent of five or six grains of salt."

"Mr. Irving, what are some of the ways you have seen fentanyl abused?"

"Lots of ways. The patches are designed to provide the body with a steady stream of the drug for forty-eight to seventy-two hours, but recreational users try to speed up the delivery—applying multiple patches, scraping the gel off the patches, even eating patches whole. We've seen cases where the gel was dissolved in liquid and used as a nasal or topical spray. In some cases, we have even seen it dried and used to cut heroin."

"So, in your expert opinion, just how deadly is fentanyl?"

"Mr. Sharp, when taken incorrectly, fentanyl creates euphoria, followed by a steep drop in blood pressure and heart rate. Sweating, shaking, and panic then overtake you, but your consciousness is so dulled you do nothing about it. Instead, you fall into a murky, painless sleep, then die."

As Sharp took Irving through a series of questions about the tests he'd administered on Martin's body, Alex wondered why someone close to the case would make the phone calls he was receiving. Who would benefit from Santiago being proven innocent? Why that bible quote? And he kept hearing that voice. *I couldn't stop it.*

Sharp's voice boomed through the courtroom. "And can you say with certainty that Professor Martin died from an overdose of fentanyl?"

"Yes."

On cross examination, just before lunch, Defense Attorney Baker had only one question. "With all your tests and years of experience, is there any way to tell who administered the lethal dose of fentanyl? That is, is it possible for you to tell us whether the dose was administered by the defendant, by someone else, or perhaps by Martin himself?"

"No," Irving said. "Of course not."

***

At the lunch break, Alex stood on the steps of the courthouse and called into *The Standard*. He had himself transferred to James Stacy's voice mail.

"Hey, it's Alex. I need you to put together a list of everyone who would have access to Santiago's police or case file. Cops, lawyers, judges. Someone is feeding me information and I need to know who it is. I need phone numbers if you can get them. Pay special attention to anyone with a strong Christian background."

Just as he closed his phone, he felt a hand on his shoulder. "If your head wasn't so full of thoughts, you might be good looking." Startled, he turned to find that Camila Gray had come up behind him.

"Didn't see you in there. Did you come in late?" he asked.

"Yeah, I was in the way back. You want to get lunch?"

"Don't you ever work?"

"Evening classes on Mondays."

"Office hours?"

"It's the second week of school. No one's going to want to talk to me until something is due."

"Okay," Alex said. "We can go to Suzy's."

He started down the courthouse steps, but Camila just stood, staring at him. "What's wrong?" she asked. "Your energy is a bit frozen."

"Don't tell me you're feeling *my* internal frequency now. You hippie."

"Seriously, you seem afraid."

I couldn't stop it. Alex couldn't shake that voice. "I'll tell you at lunch."

Chapter Twenty-Four

Suzy's was a lawyer hangout on Broome Street that delivered lunch to offices throughout the court district. They took a booth in the back and ordered, then Alex told Camila everything he knew about Demarcus Downton, including his promise of the video and his murder. He also told her about the two calls from the anonymous source. "Just waiting to hear back from my editor now," he concluded.

The food arrived and Camila chewed on the pickle that had come with her Reuben sandwich as Alex picked at a seared salmon salad with extra spinach and no croutons.

He looked down at her sandwich. "How do you eat like that and look like you look?" he asked.

Camila shrugged. "Demarcus didn't say anything about what was on the video?"

"Just that it showed that Santiago didn't do it."

"But not who did?"

"Didn't say anything about that," he said, "but I assume he would've mentioned if it did."

"And the source who called—who do you think it is?" She took a big bite of her Reuben as Thousand Island dressing dripped onto the plate.

"Don't know. Obviously someone close to the case—cop, a lawyer maybe—and someone who knew that Demarcus knew something. But if someone in the police department knows Santiago is innocent, and knows that Demarcus knew, why would they call *me* about it? Why not tell the lawyers, the judge? Someone who can actually do something."

"Probably because you're a few more steps removed," Camila said. "Look, if there are even a handful of people who know Santiago is innocent, anyone who steps forward and goes against the police department and Sharp is taking a big risk. Talking to a journalist is a safer bet than a lawyer or a judge."

"I guess."

"So why aren't you going after the video right now?" she asked.

"I will. But I'm waiting to hear from my editor. I still can't be certain Demarcus's death is connected."

"You can't? Are you kidding me?" She leaned in. "You think it's a coincidence that this guy would turn up dead the day he was supposed to give you a video that would blow up the Santiago case, humiliate the police department, and piss off the entire city? Not to mention make a lot of you guys in the press look *really* bad. *You can't be certain*?"

Alex sat back in the booth, feeling berated. "My editor said to just sit tight. And it *could* just be a weird coincidence. Stranger things have happened," he said weakly.

"No, they haven't. And what did you just tell me the source said? Something like, 'He's gone now, I couldn't stop it.'"

"Something like that."

"Why would he say that if they weren't connected? It means the source knew Demarcus was gonna get killed *before* he got killed. You need to get that video."

"I know you're right, but that's another problem. I can't just barge into his mother's house and say, 'I'm here for the video your recently murdered son promised me.'"

Alex's phone rang. Baxton. He excused himself and walked out onto Broome Street. Horns blared and Alex could barely hear his boss over occasional shouts of "move it" or "fuck you" from backed-up cars.

"Colonel, speak up. I'm out on the street."

"I checked out your murder."

"And?"

"Looks drug related. No forced entry so they probably knew him. Happened around one a.m. I was told there was a struggle. Most likely angle is that he was meeting with a supplier and the deal went wrong. Took him out and took the drugs."

Alex pressed the phone to his ear and cupped a hand over it. "Did they find anything in the house?"

"Like what?"

"I don't know. Any actual evidence that it was a drug deal gone wrong? This isn't adding up."

"No, but the people I talked to knew he was a dealer. He was low level, but he had a sheet. But you probably know all this. I know how meticulous you are in your research."

Ten feet away, a garbage truck blew a long, low horn.

"Shut up!" Alex yelled. His anger surprised him and he took a deep breath, trying to calm himself. The smell of garbage filled his lungs. "I'm sorry, Colonel. I'm just a bit on edge right now. Just never had a source turn up dead at the hour I was supposed to meet him."

"No worries," Baxton said. "It's a weird coincidence."

"What about the video?" Alex asked. "He might have had the video on him."

"If they found any video, they weren't telling me. Are you sure it even exists?"

"I guess not. Suspects?"

"Nothing, but my guy in the department says a neighbor heard a crash, looked out her front window, and saw a burly black guy running from the scene."

***

Camila was picking the crispy salmon skin off Alex's plate as he sat down. She crunched a bite. "I don't know what it is about raw spinach," she said. "I mean, I understand the concept of salad. I just don't think spinach is one of the things God intended us to eat without cooking. Something in the texture, maybe."

"I see you have no trouble with salmon skin, though," Alex said, pulling the plate back to his side of the table as she tugged at the last bit.

She smiled. "You used to be fat, right? What did your editor say?"

"Cops are telling him it was a fight over drugs, totally unrelated to me and the Santiago case."

"You're not buying *that*, are you?"

"I know he sidesteps things from time to time, but the Colonel wouldn't lie to me."

He took a small bite of salmon and shoved a few spinach leaves into his mouth, then pushed his plate toward Camila.

"You sure about that?" she asked.

"Maybe the cops are lying to him, but he and I have a good relationship."

She reached for the little cup of dressing he had neglected and poured it over the spinach salad. She took a few bites, then picked up her Reuben and wiped the corner of it around the inside edge of the dressing cup.

"What's going on with your father?" Alex asked.

"Like I said the other day, he's dying."

"I'm sorry. I really am."

She took a bite of her sandwich. "Esophageal cancer," she said through a mouthful of food.

"When are you gonna go see him?"

Camila swallowed and took another bite.

Alex watched her. "*Are* you gonna go see him?"

She put down her sandwich. "I gotta head back and prep for a class."

"Camila—"

"Right now I'm a bit distracted by the trial, and I just started a new semester, and …"

Alex tried to take her hand but she pulled it away. "Camila, it's your dad. Why aren't you going to go see him? I mean, it's your *dad.* Whatever your deal is with him, now is the time to come down from the ivory tower."

"Alex, please. You don't know anything about him. Or about me."

"Camila, I'm sorry. But I know what it is to lose a parent."

She stood and stared down at him. Her eyes seemed to burn through him, then soften. "You do? Do you also know what it is to be trained to be quiet, obedient, subservient? Do you know what it feels like when your father treats you like your existence is an imposition? Or when he explodes in a rage and hits you because you fail to live up to his standard of female docility?"

Alex looked down at the table. "No. I don't."

"Then you don't have any idea what I'm going through."

"I'm sorry," Alex said, looking up, but she was already walking across the restaurant.

Chapter Twenty-Five

Back in his apartment that evening, Alex wrote his story on the Santiago trial, e-mailed it to Baxton, then searched public records for an address for Demarcus's mother, Malina Downton. After a few minutes, he gave up and scanned the homepage of *The New York Post*. When he saw the picture of Demarcus, he rocked back in his chair and held his breath. He read the article the first time through without taking a breath, then read it again more slowly.

> Post Exclusive
> Pint-Sized Perpetrator Slays Supersized Star
> Brooklyn Heights
>
> Early this morning, a shooting in an apartment in Brooklyn Heights took the life of former high school basketball star Demarcus Downton. According to an eyewitness, the killer was less than 5 feet tall.
>
> At around 1 a.m., Downton's upstairs neighbor, Crystal Neese, heard a knock on Downton's door, followed by a loud sound, "like someone hitting the ground." A few minutes later, she watched out her back window as a "very short man" exited the victim's back door dressed in dark jeans and a white T-shirt. She did not hear a gunshot.
>
> Neese said she called in the disturbance immediately, but police did not arrive until 9 a.m. She described the man she saw as a white male, aged forty-to-fifty, with a thin mustache. But his defining trait was his size.

> "He was real small," she said. "I'm only 5 foot 3 and he looked smaller than me."
>
> Police would not comment on whether the man is a suspect and the department has made no official statement about the shooting.

Alex stared at the picture of the suspect that accompanied the article, a digital sketch like the police make from witness descriptions. He knew the software *The Post* had used to create it. The man was thin, as well as short. His mustache was a small, perfect rectangle and his eyes held a digital, lifeless gaze.

Alex chewed at his cuticles, thinking about what Baxton had said earlier, that the police had seen a "burly black guy" running from the scene. Had the Colonel lied to him? Or had the police lied to the Colonel? Alex hoped it was the latter.

He dialed Lance Brickman. Lance did not have Internet access in his Brooklyn apartment, so Alex read him the story over the phone. Then he told him Baxton's version.

"No way," Lance said. "The Colonel isn't bullshitting you this time. Maybe he would nudge you off a story but he's not gonna lie about who's out there killing people."

"Then he was lied to—or maybe *The Post's* source is lying, but I doubt it."

"They paid the woman to talk," Lance said. "Those bastards at *The Post.* How does *The Standard* expect us to compete when *The Post* can pay for stories and we can't?"

"I know. I had that woman, too. I was talking to her forty-eight hours ago. And just because they paid their source doesn't mean it's not true."

"That's what I'm saying," Lance said. "It probably is true."

"How do I find out?"

"If I was you, I wouldn't want to. Who *knows* what you're into here?"

"It gets worse," Alex said. "I know why he was killed. There's a video."

"What?"

Alex contemplated for a moment, then told Lance Downton's story. When he finished, Lance was silent.

"So?" Alex asked.

Lance sighed. "You want my advice? Drop the whole thing. Pretend it never happened."

"I don't know if I can do that," Alex said.

"Who the hell knows what's on that video? And if finding out could get you killed, it's just not worth it. Don't get all riled up."

"I can't just drop it. I need to see what's on that video."

They were both quiet until Alex said, "Can you get me Downton's mother's address in Queens? I think her name is Malina but she's not listed anywhere."

"Don't you have anyone in the courts or the DMV who can look her up for you?"

"Yeah, but I don't want to involve anyone else in this right now."

Lance snorted. "So you're involving me?"

"C'mon, I figured you might know her address off the top of your head. You know everyone out there. You're the man in Queens, right?"

"I'm not the Colonel, Alex. Flattery doesn't work on me."

"But you'll do it?"

"I'll call you back."

Alex hung up and stared at the eerie face on his screen. He wasn't sure why, but he needed to see Camila. He put his laptop in his bag along with the recording of Downton he had made at the café.

The face hung in his mind as he walked out the door.

Chapter Twenty-Six

Dimitri Rak walked into Vasyl's Pierogi Shop on Second Street in Williamsburg and looked around. The restaurant was empty except for an old man with thin gray hair, who came out from behind the counter.

"We are closing now," Rak said. The man nodded.

Rak turned and locked the door, then walked over to the counter and sat down on a stool. He picked up an old beige phone that sat next to a dirty cash register. The air was hot and smelled of rancid grease.

"Six pork and potato," he said to the man, who then disappeared into the kitchen.

Taking a piece of paper from the inside pocket of his denim jacket, Rak dialed Denver Bice. He spoke with a smooth Ukrainian accent. "Mr. Bice, have you seen it?"

"Calm down," Bice said, irritated.

"Am very calm. But you are not the one with your picture on the newspaper."

"Things have not gone as planned."

"No," Rak said. "When we meet early in January, after the job on the professor, what did you tell me?"

"I don't remember everything we said but—"

"You tell me that police are finding a suspect and they have good evidence. You tell me that your people in the police say he will be found guilty. Do you remember telling me this?"

"I do," Bice said. "But we have bigger issues than—"

Rak interrupted, "And then, when you learned that a man might have a video—the black man—do you remember what you tell me then?"

"Yes, I told you that he must be taken care of and that this would end the matter."

Rak pounded the counter with his right fist. "Well, it was not the end. Was it? Now we have a reporter and a woman, and who knows who else? And now we have my picture on the newspaper."

"Don't worry about the picture," Bice said. "Only one paper ran it and the police haven't found anything on you."

"That's good. Very good." Rak smiled and turned toward the kitchen. The old man emerged and set down a paper plate of greasy pierogies and a bowl of yogurt sauce. The grease bled through the paper onto the cracked linoleum counter.

Rak dipped a pierogi in yogurt and moved it to his mouth. "Have you ever had pierogies?" he asked as he took a bite.

"No," Bice said.

"Very good. You try mine sometime." He spoke through his food, crumbs of pork and flecks of grease sticking to his mustache.

"I don't know. Maybe."

Rak put the pierogi down. "We both have make mistakes here," he said. "If you are right this time, we have two more to deal with. You pay the regular price?"

"I'll pay the regular price, but I don't want Alex Vane killed. The girl, I don't care."

"Why not kill them both?"

"Make sure they do not have a copy of that video, hurt him if you need to," Bice said.

"Mr. Bice, do you know how sensitive the flesh under a fingernail is?"

"What?"

"If the black man gave them the video, they will give it to me." He picked the pierogi back up, dipped it in the yogurt, and stuffed it into his mouth.

"That's fine," Bice said. "Just make sure he lives."

"What for?" Rak asked, but the line was dead.

Chapter Twenty-Seven

Camila was on stage when Alex slipped in a side door and sat in the back row. She paced for a minute, then stopped to point at a graph of major media conglomerates on a projector screen. "If any of you end up working in the media," she said, "you will probably work for one of these six companies. In 1982, it was fifty companies. In 1962, hundreds of companies. We have gone from *hundreds* to *six* in the last forty years. Now, there *are* some smaller, independent ones, but these six produce 90 percent of the news, TV, music, movies, and so on."

She surveyed the class and pointed at a lanky boy in the front row. "Where are you from?"

"Me? Uh, Green Bay."

"Good, Green Bay. Up until 1980, a company based in Green Bay owned the major paper there, *The Press-Gazette.* For a hundred years it had been locally owned and controlled. Maybe it wasn't the best paper in the world, but it responded to the needs of the community. In 1980, Gannett purchased the paper. Gannett is the country's largest newspaper publisher and also owns a dozen or so TV stations. Now, what effect do you think that purchase had on *The Press-Gazette's* news coverage?"

The boy raised his hand. "Aren't Gannett's TV stations NBC affiliates? That would mean the paper's more liberal now because NBC is a liberal station. Right?"

Camila smiled at him. "Okay, that's a thought. Anyone else?"

A girl in the back with pink hair raised her hand. "Made it more conservative because Gannett is a big corporation and they're, like, republican?"

Camila smiled again. "And that's how it happens," she said, looking down at her notes.

"From page 171 in the McChesney text: 'Policy debates focus on marginal and tangential issues because core structures and policies are off-limits to criticism … ' Now, what does that mean? It means that we tend to think in terms of liberal and conservative, left and right. NBC is for the democrats and Fox is for the republicans, right? By splitting the debate this way, we give ourselves something to believe in, something to argue about, something to stand in opposition to. The fewer media options we have—the fewer voices we hear—the more we are structured by these small dichotomies.

"But there's a fundamental misunderstanding here, which is that the media is a reflection of reality. It's not. Imagine if six publicly traded companies owned 90 percent of restaurants. Would their main goal be our nourishment and health? Would they offer an accurate reflection of world cuisine?" She paused. "Or would they produce cheap food that appealed to a wide base of diners while trying to maximize profit at every moment?"

Alex smiled. He felt berated again, but in a way he was beginning to like.

"If you ate at those six restaurants long enough," Camila continued, "you'd start to believe that they represented food. You'd begin to find significance in the tiny differences between them, forgetting that there is a vast world of flavors and textures beyond them."

The lanky boy put up his hand. "What does that have to do with Green Bay and *The Press-Gazette*?"

"What happened in Green Bay—what is happening to the media and what it does to us—is much more complex than liberal or conservative."

The pink-haired girl raised her hand again. "But what about the Internet? Isn't that bringing the diversity back?"

"Quite possibly," Camila said. "And we will get into all of that. But, I'm afraid, class is over."

As the crowd thinned Alex made his way up the aisle and caught her eye.

"Sneaking in again?" she asked.

"We have problems."

"We? What problems do I have? Other than all the ones I haven't told *you* about."

"Okay, I guess *I* have problems, and I'd like your help."

Camila watched the last of the students file out. "Talk," she said.

Alex told her about the story in *The Post* and his conversation with Lance as she packed up her papers.

"So your editor lied to you. Does he do that often?" she asked.

"Not that I know of. Honestly, I usually feel like I'm in charge."

Camila smiled. "I bet you're used to that."

Alex sighed and ran a hand through his hair. "This is serious."

"Maybe he was lied to or maybe a witness lied to the cops. It happens."

"Yeah, but I already felt like he was pushing me off the story."

Camila sat on the edge of the stage, leaned back on the palms of her hands, and stared at him.

Alex turned away. "You're not feeling into me again, are you?"

"Just seeing what's going on," she said.

"And what's going on?"

"You're scared. You're scared and excited."

He was beginning to accept the fact that she saw right through him. "I don't like all this uncertainty," he said.

"You still didn't tell me how I'm involved in this."

"It just feels like you are."

They sat in silence until his phone rang. "Hello? Yeah … 301 168th, apartment 3-A? Got it. Thanks, Lance."

"Who was that?" Camila asked.

Alex smiled. "Want to take a trip to Queens?"

"I guess it's that or Des Moines."

Chapter Twenty-Eight

Outside the journalism building, they hailed a taxi in a light, warm rain.

"Queens, 301 168th," Alex said to the driver. He turned to Camila. "This is going to be an expensive ride."

"My guess is that you have extra money somewhere. Trust-funder?"

Alex eyed a wet cigarette butt on the floor and ran his finger along a gash in the glossy plastic seat. "Not really," he said.

"What do you mean? You seem upset."

"My parents were beatniks. They had a little money but they didn't give me much. I mean, they paid for college and everything."

"What do you mean 'were'—is that what you were talking about at lunch?"

"They died six years ago."

"At the same time? How?"

Alex picked bits of foam from the seat cushion.

"I guess you don't want to talk about it?"

He looked up at her. "What makes you think I have money?"

"Just the way you carry yourself. You look like someone who was raised in affluence."

"We weren't poor, but we weren't rich either."

"Where are you from?"

"Bainbridge Island. Near Seattle. I was born in the West Village and we moved when I was a baby. Maybe it's all the fresh air I grew up with that makes me look rich. Plus, they did leave me a bit of money when they died. You weren't wrong about that."

His leg was almost touching hers and Alex felt an electricity surge through his knee, up his thigh, into his hip. He tried to pick up on her cues, but she didn't seem to give any.

"I know Bainbridge Island," she said. "A lot of writers out there."

"My parents were two of them."

"Writers? Both?"

"Yup, or trying to be. I think they might have liked the lifestyle more than the writing part, though. They lived in the Village in the early seventies. Dad was in the fancy paper business and Mom taught poetry at Barnard. After I was born, they fled the city. Traded in their two-bedroom apartment on MacDougal for a four-bedroom waterfront house."

The taxi stopped abruptly and they both rocked forward, then sat back. Horns honked all around them.

"Lemmee guess," Camila said, "wine and candles and poetry readings. A vegetable garden that ended up costing your mom three dollars per carrot, and a tweed jacket in a wood-paneled room?"

Alex laughed. "You're pretty close. I lived there 'til 1992, when I came back to go to NYU as an undergrad."

"How long have you been a reporter?"

"When I graduated, I worked as an intern before I realized I wasn't going anywhere. Went to Columbia Journalism School and was hired to do obits and other small assignments for *The Standard* when I graduated. Woulda been summer of '99."

"So why do you want to be on TV?"

Alex pretended not to hear her. He leaned forward and spoke to the driver, "Can you take Queens Boulevard? It's quicker this time of night."

The driver mumbled something and Alex leaned back. "Are you ready to tell me why you and Martin broke up?" he asked.

She looked out the window. "He wanted to have a baby and I didn't." Alex didn't say anything. "I miss him," she added.

"Do you wish you hadn't broken up with him?"

She turned to Alex. "No, I don't wish I hadn't ended it. I needed to do something different, to *become* something different. I don't know. I just miss him."

"Why are you helping me?" he asked.

"I don't know. I did love Martin and I don't want Santiago to be convicted if he didn't do it. But I don't know why I do half of what I do. I used to think I knew what I was doing, that things were under control. Now it's like I'm standing on water but not quite sinking."

Alex tried to think of a way to change the subject. He hadn't wanted the conversation to get so personal. "Maybe you need therapy," he said.

"You asshole!" She turned abruptly and looked out the window. "I don't need therapy. Most *therapists* need therapy more than I do. I don't need to rearrange my ideas about myself. I'm talking about things coming apart—the fabric of identity, of people, of matter …" She sighed and rested her head on her knees, then sat back up. "A few years ago, I wouldn't have come with you, I would have known what I was doing. But now, John is dead, I'm alone for the first time in years, and I have no idea what I am or what I'm doing. You don't know what I'm talking about, do you?"

"I wish I did." He dug into the hole in the seat, picking at the foam. "Why do you flip that coin?" he asked, then immediately regretted it.

Camila glared at him. "You followed me?"

Alex said nothing.

"Can you turn this up?" Camila asked the driver, tapping on the divider. He was listening to a local radio debate about what sort of tribute the Yankees should have at their September 11th game. "I just *love* sports talk radio."

Alex nudged her playfully. "Look, I followed you just the one time. I was curious. It's what I do for a living. I'm a reporter. I'm supposed to be an asshole."

She looked at him with a look he didn't understand. Staring at her, he felt like he was being pulled into a blank space where he could no longer see himself, where he disappeared. He leaned away but still felt like he was being pulled in.

"But you're not an asshole," she said.

"Yes, I am."

"You're not. You're a decent guy pretending to be an asshole."

Alex wanted to reach for her but he looked out the window instead. They both went quiet as the rain pattered the metal roof.

"We're almost there," he said, rolling down the window. The rain was coming in fat drops and the smells of the city wafted through the car.

Camila rubbed her hands together in her lap and Alex saw a tear roll down her cheek. She rolled down her window and reached out. "I love how all the smells happen at once when it first starts to rain. Somehow the streets hold decades of smells."

The taxi stopped in front of a tall, brick building.

"It makes me miss him," she said.

"What, the rain?"

"Yeah, and the smells."

"Why?"

"I don't know."

"You really think I'm not an asshole?"

"Yeah. I mean no, you're not."

Chapter Twenty-Nine

The door to the apartment building was closing slowly, but Alex reached out to grab it before it latched. It was quiet in the stairwell as they climbed to the third floor.

"It feels like no one lives here," Camila said. "There are no smells."

"Probably a gentrification building. They're trying to clear them out so the owners can renovate and attract people like us to live here. You know, 'young professionals.'"

"In my building," Camila said, "each floor is a unique olfactory experience. You might get the smell of chicken on one floor, Indian spices on another, and, when you get to my neighbor Charlie's floor, it's always cakes and cookies. Sometimes all the smells waft together and I feel like I've discovered some new dish from a fantasy land—like curried chicken cookies."

Alex chuckled as they came to the landing and knocked on a red door marked "3-A."

"Let me ask the questions," Alex said. "And tap your feet if you think she's lying."

"A signal? Are you serious?"

The door cracked and they saw a woman's bright green eyes peering out over a silver chain. "Who are you?" the woman asked.

It sounded more like an accusation than a question. "Alex Vane from *The New York Standard.* This is my assistant, Camila Gray."

The door slammed. "Wait," Alex said, "I'm not here to do a story about your son."

"He's moved on," the woman said from behind the door.

"We know. That's why we're here," Alex said, directing his voice toward the crack between the door and its frame.

Even through the old, solid wood, the woman's voice was stern. "I do not wish to speak to a reporter."

Camila tapped on the door. "Alex was with your son the day before he died," she said.

The door reopened a crack.

"Your son told me about your husband," Alex said. "About the basketball he gave Demarcus for his birthday. He may have left something here he wanted us to have."

The door closed and they heard the chain slide against it. As it opened, the woman blocked the doorway and Alex thought he could see a bit of Demarcus in her. Her skin was lighter than her son's and her black hair reached all the way down her back, but she was tall and lean and had the same long, narrow nose. She was draped in a long white sari. "Malina Downton," she said.

"We're sorry to show up so late and to interrupt your mourning," Camila said.

"And we are so sorry about Demarcus," Alex added.

Malina stared at Alex and, after a moment, led them into a large living room with clean, worn-out carpeting and bright walls. "Thank you, but we do not mourn," she said. "He will be cremated tomorrow and will be back again soon enough."

As they sat on the couch, Camila nodded at a silver statue on a small table against the wall. "Are you Tamil?" she asked. The statue was about twelve inches high—a man with thick shoulders sitting cross-legged, holding a trident.

Malina sat in a chair across from them. "Yes, we are. You are not Hindu are you?"

"No, but it's beautiful," Camila replied. "It's Shiva," she said to Alex.

They heard a clicking sound and saw a child playing behind a stack of wooden blocks near the kitchen.

"That is my great-grandson, little Tyree," Malina said. "Demarcus's grandson."

"Demarcus never mentioned a grandson," Alex said.

"Well, that is just like him. Demarcus never valued family."

"The way he spoke about you," Alex said. "I could tell he loved you and his father."

"But he never learned responsibility. This one will be different." She smiled at the boy, then turned to Alex and Camila and folded her hands in her lap. "So, why are you here?"

"Are you familiar with Eric Santiago?" Alex asked.

Malina nodded.

Alex told her about his meeting with Demarcus and how he had planned to meet him the day after he was killed. "He said he had a video," he concluded. "A video of the night John Martin was murdered."

"I do not know anything about a video."

"Did he come by in the last week or two?" Alex asked.

Malina turned to watch Tyree in the corner. "No."

Camila tapped her foot and looked at Alex. Then she leaned over and tried to catch the woman's eyes. "Malina," she said, "I knew the man who died in the park. I did not know your son but I know that he was trying to help a boy who might spend the rest of his life in jail for something he didn't do."

Malina looked up. "I know what Demarcus was doing in the park that night, and I do not want any part of it. He has not been around here."

Tyree came from the corner and curled up on Malina's lap.

"How old is he?" Camila asked, smiling.

"I'm two and three-quarters," he said.

"And precocious," Malina added.

Camila smiled at him as Malina stroked Tyree's hair. He looked up at her. "*Muppāṭṭi*, you said not to lie. Grandpa *was* here."

"I said never to lie to a friend, to an honest man. This is a reporter."

Alex laughed loudly, but when Malina shot an icy look at him, he realized she hadn't been joking.

"But the lady is nice," Tyree said.

Malina smiled at the boy and spoke to Camila. "Demarcus came by last Thursday."

"That's the day I first noticed him following me," Alex said.

"He stayed for about an hour. He walked from room to room talking about basketball. The times he had played with his dad in the park. He even asked if I remembered particular games from high school. Honestly, all those games are the same to me, but he was talking about them like they had just happened."

"Did he take anything with him?" Camila asked. "A bag? A package?"

"Not that I saw."

"Mrs. Downton, that video *has* to be here," Alex said.

"What he means to say, Malina, is that Demarcus intended for us to have this video. Do you know where he might have put it?"

"No, but you are welcome to look through his memory box. It's on the top shelf in my *peyaran's* room now."

Malina led them into a small bedroom furnished with only a twin bed and a few plastic buckets filled with toys and stuffed animals. She opened the sliding door of a wide closet and pointed at the top shelf. "Up there."

Alex took down a box and placed it on the bed.

"Please be brief," Malina said from the doorway.

Alex rummaged through the materials until Camila pushed him out of the way. "Have some respect," she said.

Alex sat on the bed and folded his arms. Camila took items out one by one, scanning them and placing them in a neat pile. "Mostly old photos and news clippings," she said. "Yearbook. Old report cards. Some finger paintings and old assignments from school. No video."

"He said it was a little black thing. A tiny box or something." Alex thumbed through the papers and photos, hoping to find the video stuck between the pages.

"Come here," Camila said. She was inside the closet, pointing at its ceiling.

Alex got a chair and climbed up, running his fingers along a crease in the ceiling. "It's a storage space," he said.

He pried it open from the corners, revealing a small compartment. Reaching in, he felt plastic and pulled out a thick garbage bag. When he looked down to hand it to Camila, she was no longer there. He stepped down and saw that she'd left the room. He opened the bag and pulled out another bag from inside it, then another. By the time he got to the fourth bag, Alex smelled the sweet, rich aroma of high-end marijuana. He sifted through dozens of small baggies before pulling out a small piece of rag.

Wrapped in the rag was a black box, about one by two inches, with what looked like a black jacket button attached to the front and a tiny silver wire on the back.

Alex smelled food. He put the baggies back in the plastic bags and returned them to the storage space. He walked down the hall but paused in the doorway when he saw Camila playing with Tyree on the floor of the kitchen. She stacked blocks up to the level of his head, then sat back as Tyree slapped them down, a huge smile spreading across his face.

As the blocks scattered across the kitchen, Camila laughed. "Hey, I was building that," she said in a deep, booming voice. Tyree laughed and gathered the blocks.

Camila started building again as Alex stepped into the kitchen. "Found it," he said.

From the floor, Camila said, "Is that turmeric, Malina?"

"Yes," Malina replied, "I try to feed this one a little more traditionally. Sometimes I think Demarcus went bad because of all the food in this country. The only connection he had with Sri Lanka was that silly tattoo. Do you cook?"

"Not much, but I do eat," Camila said.

"What tattoo?" Alex asked.

"That tattoo on his neck was a jungle fowl. National bird of Sri Lanka. Instead of living the values of his culture, he got a tattoo to represent them. That was when I knew he had become an American." She looked into the simmering pot, then at Camila. "Would you like to stay for dinner?"

The tower was a foot above Tyree's head when he knocked it down with both arms, cackling as blocks flew across the kitchen.

"Hey. I. Was. Building. That." Camila's laughter cut through her mock angry voice.

"Looks like you're part of the family already," Alex said.

Camila hugged Tyree, stood up, and walked to the stove. "You asked if we wanted to stay for dinner?"

"We really ought to be going," Alex said.

Malina turned toward Alex but did not look at him. "You found what you came for?"

"I did. I found—"

She held up her hand. "I do not wish to know anything about it."

"Thank you so much for the dinner offer," Camila said.

"Yeah," Alex added as Malina led them into the hallway, "and thanks for your help. Really."

"You're welcome," Malina said, "I hope you two find whatever you're looking for. Good-bye."

When she had closed the door behind them, Alex handed Camila the recorder. "How do we watch it?" Camila asked, burying it in her purse.

Alex smiled. "Ever been inside a real newsroom, or do you just critique them for a living?"

Camila punched his shoulder. Alex faked a wince. They both smiled.

Chapter Thirty

Alex and Camila scanned the dark, quiet newsroom. A fluorescent light flickered above them. "The layout and design people are finalizing the paper," Alex said. "Most everyone else has gone home. I hope our researcher slash tech-guy is still here."

They found James Stacy at his desk in the corner, staring at spreadsheets on both of his giant screens. "I figured you'd still be here," Alex said. He pointed at the screens. "What's that?"

"Web traffic l-l-logs. They're having me keep track of site visits, ads served, that kind of thing."

James turned toward them, then lurched back in his chair. He stared at Camila with his mouth open, then turned quickly back to the screens.

"Don't worry," Alex said. "It's just a woman. She's not here to eat your soul or anything."

James took a long swig of soda as he handed Alex a manila folder. "Your l-l-l-list," he said. "It's l-l-long. Seventy-five p-people. It's a b-b-big case."

Alex opened the folder and looked over the three printed pages, stapled in the corner. James had organized the list alphabetically, by last name, with a separate column explaining each person's connection to the case. "Nothing about their religions?" Alex asked.

"Didn't think you were s-serious about that."

Camila pointed at the soda can on James's desk. "You drink Jolt?" she asked. "I used to love Jolt. I thought they'd stopped making it."

James looked at her timidly. "You can still get the original cans on-on-on." He cleared his throat with a giant cough. "Get them online."

"That's awesome," Camila said. "All the sugar, twice the caffeine."

James smiled and turned back to the screen. "What do you need, Alex? I thought you turned into a p-pumpkin if you stayed past four-thirty."

Camila retrieved the recorder from her purse and dangled it in front of James's face.

"Do you know how to watch whatever is on there?" Alex asked.

James studied it. "Why? What's on it? Anything to do with the Santiago c-case? Things were weird around here today. The Colonel was in his office all day and a couple suits came down."

"Nothing's going on," Alex said.

"Then why do you have a thousand dollar surveillance camera and why are you bringing it to me at ten on a Monday n-night?"

"Can you help me or not?" Alex asked.

James opened a desk drawer and pulled out a box of wires and connectors. He tossed cable after cable onto his desk before finding a thin white wire. He connected it to the silver wire on the recorder, then connected the other end of the white wire to his computer. He opened a program called "Video Codec 5" on the large screen on the left side of his desk. He stood up. "I suppose you want me to l-leave?"

"I promise I'll explain at some point," Alex said.

"I n-need to get another s-s-soda anyway," James said, walking away.

Camila sat in James's chair. Alex leaned over her and pressed play. The video was dark and grainy and showed the fountain in the center of Washington Square Park.

"Damn, no audio," Alex said. "But there's a time stamp. Scroll forward."

Camila scrolled until the time stamp read 1 a.m. The video now showed trees and a garbage can, but was panning slowly across the park.

"It's weird to think that that's Downton moving the camera," Alex said. "Looking for customers."

"There," Camila said. The shot had steadied, though the camera still wobbled.

It was a wide-angle shot about fifty feet from the bronze statue of Garibaldi. On the left side of the frame there was darkness and a few trees. On the right, just the towering statue lit by a streetlight. The fountain sat between them. Alex leaned over Camila's shoulder and squinted. Just under the statue, at the bottom-right of the frame, a man moved. He was medium-height and wore a white longshoreman's cap. He rocked back and forth from leg to leg.

Alex touched the screen with a finger. "That's Martin."

"Yeah."

"What's he doing?"

"I don't know."

Alex pointed at the darkness on the left side of the picture. "That's the path that leads in and out of the park."

After a few minutes, a figure appeared and walked past the statue and toward the camera. Alex recognized Santiago right away. He was short, and as he got closer to the camera, Alex could make out his brown hair and expressionless face.

When Santiago was about twenty-five feet from the camera, in between the statue and the fountain, he stopped and turned around. He appeared to be staring straight at Martin.

Under the statue, Martin rocked back and forth, his white hat now lower in the frame.

"What's Martin doing?" Alex asked.

Camila tapped on the screen. "Looks like he's sick or something. Was he drunk?"

"I don't think so. People I've talked to say that witnesses from the bar are going to say he'd only had one glass of wine."

They watched in silence. Santiago stood motionless and Martin rocked back and forth in a doubled-over curl. The camera shook slightly, then Martin fell over.

His hat hit the ground and landed about a foot from his head. Santiago took two quick steps toward him, then stopped. He stood for a few seconds, turned, and walked away from Martin, toward the center of the park. As Santiago neared the edge of the frame, the camera caught his face.

Alex thought he saw a smile spread between the young man's pockmarked cheeks. He turned to Camila. "What the hell?"

Chapter Thirty-One

Tuesday, September 10, 2002

"He just stood there, watching," Alex said, looking down at his plate.

By just after midnight, they were sitting in the Apollo Diner a couple of blocks from the newsroom. The restaurant was empty except for a table of drunk twenty-somethings and a few people reading in booths. They had watched the video four times and scanned the thirty minutes on either side of it, but found nothing else of interest.

Camila looked at Alex's plate. "I watched a show about bodybuilders once and they eat just like you—five-egg omelet with triple spinach and coffee." She stirred cheese into a bowl of onion soup. "What are you thinking?" she asked.

"I'm trying to figure out what to do. I could write a story or call the cops, but part of me wants to just disappear."

"First of all, you're not giving the video to the cops, at least not yet." She swallowed a spoonful of soup. "Those guys can lose a video like this even faster than a newspaper can."

"And if my boss lied to me about who killed Downton, I don't even want to tell him I have the video. But I have to, I can't just ..." He trailed off and took a sip of his coffee. "Look, I know what you're thinking, and there's no conspiracy. Just a bunch of reporters and editors and owners, doing their best to handle pressure exerted from every direction while making a living. It only looks like a conspiracy from the outside because the final product is so often shitty. There is no 'media.'

There are just thousands of people making millions of independent decisions, many out of fear, or just stupidity."

"Yeah but—"

"All you academics who write books about 'liberal bias this' or 'Fox news that,' have no idea what actually goes on."

Camila put her spoon down and raised her voice. "But doesn't the stuff that gets left out bother you? I'm not especially political, but I think it's better to have more voices, more stories, more perspectives."

"People are lying to us and using us all day, every day, from every angle. Most of us are just doing our best to make a living and, if we're lucky, get some truth out."

"That's not exactly inspiring. You know, the fourth estate safeguarding democracy and all that."

She smiled but Alex went quiet and pushed eggs around on his plate. After a moment, he said, "It's a chicken and egg thing. Do people get stupid by listening to us or do they listen to us because they're stupid? A well-informed public has never existed. We just give the people what they want." He paused. "Too many people are making a living bashing journalists."

"I don't bash journalists. It's not *your* fault." She sighed. "None of this matters now. This is a real thing. Can you live with the way Santiago got executed in the press? The way your boss is sidestepping this story?"

Alex sipped his coffee. "I don't know ... no. I can't live with that."

"So what do you want to do?"

Alex took a bite of omelet, chewed slowly, swallowed, and looked up at her. "I'm confused as hell, but I know that video directly contradicts the version we've been hearing from police and prosecutors for a year."

"And?"

"Despite what you said in the taxi—which I appreciated, by the way—I *am* an asshole." He paused. "I have to do *something*."

"But if your boss lied to you about Downton..."

Alex finished his coffee and waved to the waitress, who came over and refilled his cup. "What's your name?" Alex asked her with a broad smile.

Short and stocky, she wore a brown Apollo Diner uniform and black rectangular glasses. "Mary," she replied.

"And, Mary, can I ask you a question?"

"Sure."

"Do you consider yourself well informed?"

"Pretty well informed, I guess."

"Do you believe what you read in the paper?"

"Uh, well, I guess so," she said.

"And do you trust reporters?"

"Hell no. Buncha lyin' bastards, if you ask me."

Alex smirked at Camila, then looked back at Mary. "So reporters are lying bastards, but you trust what you read in the paper?"

"Hmmm. Guess I never really thought about it," she said, turning and walking away.

"Touché," Camila said. "So what are you gonna do?"

"I'll do what I do. I'll write it."

"What about your boss?"

"I have to believe he's not in on it. And once he knows the video is real, he'll have to run it."

Chapter Thirty-Two

The newsroom was dark and quiet. The first staff wouldn't arrive until 5 a.m. and James had fallen asleep with his head on his desk. Camila watched over Alex's shoulder as he stared at the blinking cursor on the blank screen.

He knew he could approach the story from one of two angles. The first was to present only the content of the video, leaving out how it was obtained. The second was to connect the video to Downton, his story about the two young cops, and his murder. But this would mean trying to track down the two cops—days of work that might prove fruitless.

He got out of his chair and paced. "I'm gonna leave Downton out of it," he said, looking at Camila but speaking to himself. He sat down. "For now, the video is the story. I can track down the rest of it later."

"What about the weird calls you've been getting?"

"Can't run anything on those. Too vague at this point. If I can convince the caller to go on the record, or find out how he knows what he knows, that would change things."

"Do you know it's a him?"

"No, but that reminds me." Alex reached for the manila folder James had given him and scanned the list. He recognized only a few of the names. He could cold-call them but doubted it would yield any results, especially at 1 a.m. He set the list aside, turned back to the computer, and started typing. Camila lay on her back on the floor and stared at the ceiling.

After twenty minutes, Alex got up and did fifty pushups.

Camila rolled over on her elbows to watch him. "Why do you do that?" she asked, laughing.

"Clears my mind. You know, you might try moving your body at some point. It's that thing just below your head." He smiled at her. "Hey, can you go back to James's desk, watch the video again, and find out exactly how long Santiago stood and stared at Martin?"

"The details, huh?"

"Yup."

***

Alex finished writing at 2 a.m. He printed two copies of the story, folded one and put it in his pocket, and put the other in a folder with a sticky note.

> Colonel-
> I'll call around for police and attorney denials after 8. Do we have any partnerships with TV stations we can leak the video to? —AV

He put the folder on Baxton's desk, then led Camila to a ragged couch in the corner of the newsroom. "You can have it," he said. She lay down on the worn upholstery and Alex lay on the carpet.

"You write well, and quickly," she said, yawning.

His whole body was tired and he felt it melt into the floor as he stretched his legs. "That's the first nice thing you've said to me."

Camila yawned again and rolled over, burying her head in the cushions. "Unless we count when I said you're not an asshole."

"Yeah, unless we count that. Good night."

After a minute, Alex said, "Camila, what do you think my boss will do with my story? Camila?"

She was already asleep.

Chapter Thirty-Three

Alex woke with a start to find Baxton hovering over him.

"I didn't know you existed before 0800," Baxton said.

"Colonel? What time is it?"

"Five."

Alex rubbed his eyes as he stood up. "Check your desk."

"Who's that?" Baxton pointed at Camila, asleep on the couch.

"Camila Gray, ex-girlfriend of Professor Martin. She helped me track down the video."

"The video? You have it?"

"Check your desk."

"Okay, my office in ten."

***

Alex watched Baxton through the large window that looked into his office from the newsroom. As Baxton read his story, Alex pulled the copy from his pocket and read it again.

> A video recording exists that casts doubt on the series of events that led to the death of NYU Professor John Martin on New Year's Eve, 2001.
>
> According to police statements and opening arguments in the trial, Eric Santiago—the NYU student accused of murdering Martin—administered a lethal dose of the opiate fentanyl in Washington Square Park at around 1 a.m. on January 1, 2002.
>
> But the video, which was obtained by *The Standard* from a confidential source, shows a different version of

the events of that night. In the video, Santiago enters the park from the east as Martin stands under the statue of Giuseppe Garibaldi, where police found his body at 2 a.m. For one minute and 21 seconds, Santiago can be seen staring at Martin, but it is clear that the two never came into contact.

The video does not show any other figures and does not give any indication as to the cause of Martin's death. It does, however, call into question police and prosecutor statements regarding Martin's death.

[B-Matter]

[Police denial or no comment]

[Attorney's denial or no comment]

Santiago is currently being tried in the Manhattan Criminal Court and has maintained his innocence since his arrest last January.

Alex took a few steps toward Baxton's office, but stopped when he saw Baxton pick up the phone. A knot formed in his stomach as he watched him speak, then listen. Baxton hung up and straightened papers on his desk, then waved Alex into his office.

"Helluva piece of work." He held up Alex's story. "But we can't run it."

"Why not?" Alex asked. The knot in his stomach tightened.

"You know how the Santiago case has gripped the city. Biggest story since 9/11. If we're gonna blow it up now, we need something more than a video, which we don't even know is authentic."

"It's authentic, Colonel. Watch it yourself."

"It's not enough."

"What if I write about the source? I can write about how Downton got the video. I can find the two cops who gave him the recorder. I can talk to Santiago."

"That could take weeks, and it still might not be enough. You've got daily reports due on the trial and I can't have you running around the city on this. Alex, your desire to get yourself on TV is clouding your judgment."

Alex looked at the phone on Baxton's desk. "You know, Colonel, I'm starting to feel like Josef K. here. Can't you tell me what's *really* going on?"

"Who's that?"

Alex pointed at the phone. "Who did you call earlier?"

Baxton stood up. "Alex, I know we're informal around here, but spying on me during calls crosses a line. What I need from you is a story a day on the Santiago trial. Can you handle that?"

"Colonel, if we don't run this, someone else is going to get the story."

"Not without the video. It's property of *The Standard* and we need it to stay here."

"We?"

"*I* need it to stay here," Baxton said.

Alex raised his voice. "Please tell me you're at least going to give a copy to the police. At the very least, it complicates the trial." He was surprised by his own anger. "Santiago may be *innocent*."

"I'll watch the video and look into the matter," Baxton said loudly. "Where is it?"

"But I received it—"

"On company time. Your notebooks and stories—everything is the property of *The Standard*. Have you made any copies of it?" Baxton looked over Alex's shoulder. Alex turned and saw that a handful of staff members were listening to their argument.

"Shut the door," Baxton said.

Alex shut the door and turned to Baxton, who was sitting down. "Colonel," he said, "If Santiago is innocent, that *has* to mean more than anything else."

"Look, Alex. This will blow over. You'll see." His tone was final.

Alex felt his chest fold in on itself. "Just tell me one thing. When you said that a witness had seen a large black man fleeing the scene after Demarcus was killed, were you lying or had the police lied to you?"

Baxton adjusted pencils in a coffee mug. "Did you make any copies of the video?"

Alex dropped his head and turned to leave. "No. No copies," he said weakly. "I'll keep working the daily Santiago developments. James has the video. He hasn't seen it." He walked out without saying good-bye. He saw Camila from across the room and waved her toward the elevator.

***

Alex gave the driver his address, then stared out the window as the taxi drove north along Broadway.

Camila watched him. "What did your boss say?" she asked. "Alex, talk to me."

"I'm such a coward."

"What? Why?"

"The video. I barely even put up a fight."

She put a hand on his knee. "You had no choice. It's *The Standard's* property if you got it while reporting for them."

"That doesn't help. The only piece of evidence that could get Santiago off and I barely put up a fight."

The taxi turned onto Eighth Avenue. Alex stared at passing shops and restaurants, cursing himself in his mind. His cell phone broke the silence as they rounded Columbus Circle. He looked down at the caller ID and froze.

"It's the guy again." Alex flipped open his phone and tapped the speakerphone button. "Hello?" He braced himself in anticipation of the voice.

"Martin is the end, not the beginning. Go back in time."

The voice echoed in the taxi and Alex slid the plastic divider so the driver couldn't hear. He looked at Camila and raised an eyebrow. She shrugged.

"Okay," Alex said, "I know you're going out on a limb here, but can you be more specific? Two people are dead and an innocent man is about to go to prison for the rest of his life. Is there any way we can meet?"

"We might meet at some point, but not yet."

"Are you an officer?" Alex asked.

"I won't answer that."

"A lawyer? A witness?"

"I won't answer that."

Alex looked at Camila, who just stared at the phone. The voice said, "You must find out why Professor Martin was killed. You must go back in time."

"How do I do that?" Alex asked.

"You said two people are dead, right?"

"Yes."

"There are three."

Chapter Thirty-Four

Alex stood at the door to his apartment and turned the key. "Something's not right," he said. "I usually have to jiggle the key after a quarter turn, but this time it moved easily." He swung the door open. "What the hell?"

Clothes, books, and papers littered the bed and floor. His dresser drawers and closet door were open.

"Didn't take you for a slob," Camila said as they walked in. "Not with the way you take care of your body."

"This isn't me," Alex said, scanning the room. "Someone's been here. The lock. Someone picked it."

Alex threw his bag on the bed and crossed the room with two large steps. He shuffled through papers scattered over his desk. "They took some of my notebooks. At least I had my laptop and the Downton tapes in my bag."

"They? Who?"

Alex grabbed the wooden pole from the closet, letting the blue cloth drop to the floor. "How the hell would I know? Can we go to your place?"

"Why the pole?" Camila asked.

"Let's go."

***

They each held their breath as Camila opened the door and peered into her apartment. "Everything seems to be in order," she said.

Alex followed her in and leaned the pole against the couch as he sat. "What do I do now?" he asked. "At this point, I don't know who to be more afraid of—the guy who killed Downton or my newspaper."

"Your boss might be more pathetic than sinister," Camila said. "He may just be getting word that the story shouldn't be pursued. Doesn't mean he knows what's really going on."

"But I was wrong about him."

Camila walked into the kitchen and opened the fridge.

"I don't like being confused," Alex called after her.

Camila returned and sat next to him. She handed him a coconut water. "Yes, I can see that about you." Alex studied the bottle's label. "Just drink it," Camila said.

Alex took a small sip. "I could go to the police and tell them everything. Tell them to get the video from the paper. They'd probably put me in some sort of witness protection program."

"You're not going to the police. First of all, the paper wouldn't have to give them the video. The police could subpoena it as part of the trial, but the paper would withhold it since it's confidential source material. The cops would get it eventually, but it could take weeks or even months."

Alex looked at the woodblock print of the woman struggling against the rain. It made him uncomfortable so he got up and walked to the window. "What do I do?" he asked.

"I'm not sure, but do you want to know one of the things I do when I don't know what to do?"

"Flip a coin?"

"Other than that. You want to know?"

"Not really, but you're going to tell me anyway."

"I don't do anything. I literally sit still and don't do anything."

She got up, took his hand, and led him back to the couch. He sat and she pushed his shoulders down gently and straightened them. "Sit up straight. Feet on the floor. Uncross your legs. Take a few deep breaths. Good. Now close your eyes and just sit still for a few minutes."

Alex complied for a few seconds, then asked, "But what should I *do*?"

"Be still. That's all."

He opened his eyes. "Look, I'm freaking out here."

"Just try it."

Alex closed his eyes again and sighed.

"Just be confused for a while," he heard her say. "Feel your feet on the floor."

Alex felt his feet on the floor. After a minute, he became aware of a stream of images passing through him. Downton leaning over his coffee. The jungle fowl tattoo on his neck. Baxton, holding the phone. Greta in the bar the night Downton started following him—her long black hair and toned arms. Then he heard the voice, metallic and strange. *There are three.* Martin's hat hitting the ground. An imagined memory of Downton playing basketball with his father. He felt a pang of sadness but quickly dismissed it. *There are three.* The look on Santiago's face as he walked away from Martin. Why the smile? Was he in on it? What a sick bastard. Then Camila, walking in the park. Her image blurred with one of his mother, standing in the park the day before his graduation. Then the smell coming through his apartment window after 9/11, sour and dusty. What was in that smell? Then back in the park with Camila. Baxton again. The voice: *There are three.*

A name appeared in his mind. Denver Bice. Baxton works for Denver Bice.

"Alex?"

He opened his eyes. His forehead hurt and he had forgotten about Camila.

"Alex, what's going on in your head?"

"How long was I sitting there?"

"Three minutes."

"What?"

"I know. The mind can do a lot in three minutes, huh?"

"I've had enough of this." He stood and walked back to the window. "Remember when you said that Martin kept everything? Where did his stuff end up?"

Camila crossed her legs on the couch. "Most of his records are with his daughter upstate, but I have a few cartons of papers from the last year or so."

"Good. The source said to look into why Martin was killed, so maybe there will be something there."

"Maybe, but—"

"And remember when you mentioned Martin's interaction with Denver Bice at the funeral?"

"Yeah."

"Well, you had that hunch, and now I have my boss, who works for Bice, stonewalling me, and—"

There was a quiet tap on the door. Alex swung around on his heels.

"Don't worry," Camila said. "That's Charlie from across the hall. I heard his door shut."

Camila opened the door and a tall, brawny man of about fifty walked in.

"Hello! It's just me, your friendly 'gaybor.'" He was neatly dressed in black and wore thick black glasses and a tidy beard. He leaned forward and hugged Camila. "Can I borrow some sugar, sugar? I'm having the girls over for drinks and need to make some simple syrup." He looked at Alex on the couch. "Mmm … Who is *this* young man?"

Camila led Charlie to the couch. "This is Alex Vane," she said. "He works at *The Standard*."

"Are you going full-on cougar?" Charlie asked.

Alex looked at the floor.

"No, it's not that kind of thing," Camila said, walking to the kitchen. "We're working on something together. He's covering the Santiago trial. You know, John's case."

"Oh yeah. Well, I'm glad to see him here. I was a little worried when I saw the guy coming out of your place earlier. I thought 'Ooohhh, she's slumin.'"

Camila walked into the living room. She stared at Charlie blankly. "What guy?"

"Your uncle," Charlie said. "The guy who stayed with you last night."

Alex walked over and took Camila's hand.

Camila said, "Seriously, Charlie, what guy?"

"The little guy. Said he was your uncle visiting from Europe. Left early this morning. He said he was staying with you."

Alex shot glances around the room. Camila's mouth dropped open. "How little was he?" she managed.

"Tiny. Weird accent, too. You mean that's not your uncle?"

Chapter Thirty-Five

"I left my pole," Alex said. They had bounded down the stairs of Camila's building and hailed a taxi headed west on 98th.

"What's the deal with that pole?" Camila asked.

"My dad took it from the gym near our house when it shut down. He brought it from home and gave it to me the day I graduated NYU. The next day, they died."

"How?"

Alex looked out the window and closed his eyes. Camila put a hand on his knee.

They rode in silence, north on the West Side Highway. "We have to go to the cops," Alex said at last. "I know some are corrupt, and some are inept. But most aren't. And we don't have any other options."

"Right now, I feel safer in the back of a moving taxi than I would in a police station," Camila said, staring out the window.

Alex took her shoulders in his hands and turned her toward him. "We *have* to go to the cops."

"What do we do then?" Camila asked.

"Well, we—"

She put her hand over his mouth. "We tell them that, A, there's a video that *may or may not* prove Santiago innocent and that, B, the guy who made the video is *dead*, and that, C, my neighbor saw a guy come out of my apartment who looks a lot like a guy who *may or may not* have killed the guy who made the video that *may or may not* clear a kid who everyone believes is a *twisted killer*? Is that what you want to tell them?"

Alex pushed her hand away. "But they don't know Demarcus was killed right after contacting me about the video. They could use that to tie his murder to Martin. There could be a million little threads to the Martin investigation that never got reported."

"And you think if you tell them they'll drop all charges against Santiago and put the full weight of the department behind figuring out what really happened? That would humiliate the department, embarrass the press that ran with the story, and piss off millions of New Yorkers. If you think that's what the cops would do, then you're even naïver than I thought."

"Naïver?" Alex asked.

"It's a word. Plus, do you know the department's record of protecting witnesses? Even if they did the right thing, *we'd* still be screwed. That guy was in my home!"

"I do know their record. It's pretty good."

"Good enough to bet your life on?"

Alex stared across the Hudson River at New Jersey as the taxi passed 125th Street. At the George Washington Bridge, the driver leaned back. "Where we headed?" he asked.

"Still don't know, just head north," Camila said.

"Bridge toll coming up in a few minutes," the driver said. Alex handed him a ten-dollar bill and they rode in silence across the Henry Hudson Bridge. The driver looked at them in the rearview mirror. "You want to take the Sawmill or the Cross County Parkway?" Alex dropped his head and sighed.

"I have an idea," Camila said. "On the couch you asked about Bice, right? The interaction between him and Martin is our only lead."

Alex looked up. "We can't talk to Bice because he runs the paper that killed my story. And Hollinger isn't around to help us."

"His wife is," Camila said. "John told me she lives in Hawaii. Kona. He talked to her at the funeral."

"Okay, but what good will she do us?"

"I don't know," Camila said. "But where else can we turn?"

Alex shrugged.

"How much money do you have?" Camila asked.

"I have enough saved up to buy us a couple weeks, but what's the plan?"

Camila tapped on the glass divider and spoke to the driver. "Cross County to Ninety-Five East."

Chapter Thirty-Six

The captain's voice jolted Alex as it echoed metallic and scratchy through the cabin. "At the present time we are experiencing significant precipitation, which may delay our anticipated takeoff time by at least twenty minutes or more."

Alex slid his laptop bag under the seat in front of him. "Why not just say it's raining so the flight is delayed?"

Camila laughed.

"We will be heading to Kona, Hawaii today with a layover in San Francisco," the captain continued. "So if one of these two cities is not in your travel plans, please let a flight attendant know."

"Politics, lawyers, and television happened," she said, moving into the aisle to make way for a large man in a tight suit who was pointing at the window seat.

Alex swung his legs into her seat to let the man pass. "How did I get stuck in the middle anyway?" he asked Camila as the man lifted up the armrest and wedged himself into the window seat.

"Sorry," the man said.

"Heading all the way to Kona?" Alex asked, trying to sound like a flight attendant. "Or is SFO your final destination?"

"Kona."

Alex tried to pull the armrest down but it stuck on the man's shoulder.

"Sorry," the man said again, putting on headphones and leaning against the window.

Camila sat and Alex scrunched as close to her as he could. "I'm still pissed at myself," he said.

"Why?"

"I can't believe I left that video with Baxton. He's not going to get it out there. The trial will go on like nothing has changed. And I can't believe I'm about to fly across the country. The Santiago story is the biggest of my career and I'm bailing on it." He leaned back. "I think I need to sleep."

"We both do. But you're not bailing on the story, you're following it. The real story isn't what's happening in court." She paused. "Out of curiosity, what would you do with the video if you had it?"

"I don't know. I'd just have it. I'd feel a little less crazy. Maybe there's something on it we didn't see. Maybe I'd leak it to a TV station at least." He looked at Camila and was surprised to see that she was smiling. "We're in a pretty messed up place for you to be smiling right now. I mean, three hours ago you found out a killer was in your apartment."

"And what offer would you be willing to make to a beautiful woman who had the video? Would you—I don't know—give her your share of peanuts, or steal her a bag of the animal crackers they only give to kids?"

"Stop messing around."

Camila reached into her purse and pulled out a silver USB drive. "I don't know what this is, exactly, but your friend James said he loaded the video onto it."

Alex sat up straight and took it from her.

"When I put my hair up," she continued, "his eyes rolled back in his head. I asked him to make me a copy while you were writing."

Alex smiled as the plane started moving. "You trollop! You used your devastating beauty to take advantage of him." He passed the USB drive between his hands.

"He's a sweet guy."

The captain's voice came through the cabin again. "Ladies and gentlemen, the precipitation has halted and we anticipate departure in three to five minutes. We're currently fourth in line, so please bring all tray tables and seat backs to their full, upright, and locked positions in preparation for our impending departure."

"For God's sake," Alex said in a whisper, "why can't he just say it stopped raining so we're leaving?"

"You ever read Orwell?" Camila asked.

Chapter Thirty-Seven

At SFO they bought carry-on bags, toiletries, and a few clothing items, then took a booth at a seafood restaurant so Camila could eat clam chowder from a sourdough bowl. Alex ordered two grilled swordfish steaks and a side of steamed vegetables.

She laughed at him when the waitress left. "What is that, like a hundred grams of protein and four-hundred calories?"

"What are we doing?" he asked.

"What do you mean?"

"I mean, we need to do something besides trying to track down Sonia Hollinger. She's a long shot at best."

"What about your source?"

Alex pulled out the folder James had given him, scanned the names, then threw it on the table. "I'll try some things after we eat."

While they waited for the food, Alex checked his voice mail. He had four new messages.

The first message was Baxton, and Alex immediately recognized his irritated tone. "Alex," he said, "it's Tuesday at three. Why haven't you gotten me Santiago copy? I've talked to the folks upstairs and they are considering sending the video to the police, but they want to meet with you, so get your TV-model ass in here."

The second message was from James Stacy. "Something's going on h-here. The Colonel has been on the phone all d-day. Some suit came and asked me about helping you with whatever that file was. I played dumb. I mean, I am dumb in this case." James was breathing heavily and whispering. "I didn't tell them

I gave your friend a copy of the v-video. They didn't ask but I didn't volunteer it. And Lance is looking for you, too." James told Alex to call him at home and left his number.

Alex looked at Camila. "They want to meet with me."

She laughed. "To find out how much you know? Or to kill you?"

"Thanks," Alex said.

The third message was from Greta Mori. "Hey Alex," she said in a perky voice. "Just wanted to say hi and see what you're up to this weekend. We had talked about getting together again, maybe meeting at Dive Bar on Friday. I think your friend Lance wanted to flirt with me some more. Anyway, bye."

Alex looked at Camila but turned away before meeting her eyes.

The fourth message, left just half an hour earlier, was Baxton again. "Alex, I don't know what in the hell you're up to, but this is entirely unacceptable. I'll assume you're half dead with the flu or something. But I will only assume this until tomorrow morning at nine." He hung up without saying good-bye.

The waitress brought the food and Alex looked down at the fish.

"Looks dry, doesn't it?" Camila said, ripping off a piece of sourdough and dunking it in the soup. Alex poked at the fish with his fork, then ate a few vegetables.

When she finished her soup, Camila called the secretary of the journalism department and canceled her classes for the rest of the week. "It's the flu," she said, sounding weak. "It's going around."

"You're a good liar," Alex said when she hung up. "A true sociopath. You can lie without remorse."

Camila smiled at him. "I think a sociopath doesn't know she's lying. I *am* without morals, but I only use my powers for good."

As the waitress cleared their plates, Camila ordered a chocolate milkshake and Alex called Bearon, his friend at the courthouse. He explained why he hadn't been in court that day, then told him about the strange calls and Downton's video. It took him a few minutes to convince his friend that he was serious. Finally, Bearon said, "I guess it's not a huge surprise that they got a brown kid for something he didn't do. We're used to that, but I didn't see *this* coming."

"No one did, but I need to ask you a question. Can you think of any police employee who might have inside information on the Santiago trial?"

"Lots," Bearon said, "but none who would make the kind of calls you're getting."

"What about a disgruntled prosecutor who wants to stick it to the police? Anyone who could benefit from exposing a shoddy investigation?"

"I can think of a lot of people who'd want to embarrass the department," Bearon said, "but nobody would go about it that way. Have you considered the possibility that your source is crazy?"

"I'm assuming he is, but he's also been right so far." He pulled out James's list and read the names one by one. Bearon didn't recognize all of them, but he was able to eliminate three officers who had transferred out of the borough and wouldn't have access to the Santiago file. Alex crossed off their names.

"Plus, the last two," Bearon said. "Waxman and Yardley. I know them well enough to know they wouldn't leak that type of information. Sorry I can't be more help. What are you gonna do?"

"Better if I don't say. And Bearon, thanks."

Alex hung up and stared at Camila's milkshake. "That just leaves about seventy more names," he said, dialing Lance Brickman.

"Lance, it's Alex."

"You stupid bastard," Lance said. "You bailed, huh?"

"How'd you know?"

"I know because the Colonel is running some bullshit I wrote on the front page of the Metro section instead of the piece you were supposed to write on Santiago. We're gonna have to use the AP report."

"Damn," Alex said. "That's embarrassing. But it's not like I'm not justified. And at least it worked out well for one of us.

You got the front page of Metro. That'll make it harder for them to fire you before you hit your thirty."

"No. It won't. Where the hell are you, anyway?"

"I better not say, but look, I need to tell you something, then ask you something." Alex told Lance about the last two calls he had received from the source. "It's weird, right? I mean, if you're gonna use a voice scrambler and hide yourself, why not just tell me what happened so I can write it?"

Alex heard the click of a lighter and a loud puff. "Look," Lance said, "I don't know what you're into, but I don't want any part of it."

"Can you just tell me why the hell a source might do that? I mean, I would just ignore him if he didn't keep being right."

"Didn't you read *All the President's Men* in J-School?"

"I saw the movie. But so what?"

"Sources can be paranoid bastards."

When he hung up, Alex started making calls from the top of the list while Camila ate her milkshake with a spoon.

First, he called Betty Ableton, a records clerk, and pretended to be a pollster taking a survey of New York City residents. He asked her a series of questions about the Santiago trial and finished with, "Do you believe that Eric Santiago is guilty?" He thought that if he'd found his source, there would at least be a pause, a catch in her voice. Something. She said "Yes" without hesitation.

Next, he tried Timothy Alston, a detective, and got the same answer. The next name was Byron Deerborn, an officer in the evidence unit. The call went to voice mail and Alex hung up. After a dozen calls, he leaned back in the booth and looked at Camila. "This is pointless. Even if I happen to reach the right person, what good will it do?"

"It'll be better when we get to Hawaii. Sonia Hollinger will know something."

Chapter Thirty-Eight

Alex rubbed his palms over his eyes, then stared out the window as the flight to Kona took off. The sun was beginning to set over the brown hills of San Francisco, bathing the dry grass in a soft, warm light. He turned to Camila. "We haven't slept yet."

"I was just thinking the same thing. We must be approaching zombiehood."

Alex looked at the man next to him, hoping he had shrunk during the layover. His headphones were on and he was looking out the window.

"You ever read the bible?" Alex asked.

"I was raised Catholic for a few years. Then I studied it on my own when I grew up."

"'He who hateth his life in this world shall keep it unto life eternal.' It's John 12:25. Any idea what it means?"

"You left off the first part."

"I know. It's 'He who loveth his life shall lose it; and he who hateth his life in this world shall keep it unto life eternal.' What's it mean?"

"Why?"

"Well, the source who keeps calling me quoted the second half of that passage the first time he called."

"You didn't tell me that," Camila said, sitting up in her seat.

"Didn't seem important."

"I'm no biblical scholar, but I think it means that, in Christianity, you are supposed to love Christ more than you love yourself, more than you love your own life. You're supposed to see beyond this life in order to gain eternal life in heaven."

Alex nodded. "Yeah, that's what I read online."

"'In the world but not of it.' Ever heard that phrase? It's Sufi."

"What's Sufi?" Alex asked.

"It's the mystical, contemplative branch of Islam. Kinda like Kabbalah is to Judaism. 'In the world but not of it' means kinda the same thing. Participating in this world, in this life, without being limited by it. It means seeing beyond the self-imposed mental limitations that we project onto the world. Recognizing that there is another world—a *realer* world—beyond the everyday life of this one."

"Self-imposed? I thought it was all the fault of 'The Media.'"

"Screw you, I never said that. But seriously, did you see *The Matrix*? 'There is no spoon.' It's like that."

"But what's wrong with everyday life?"

"It doesn't mean there's anything wrong with everyday life. It's about seeing through the false." She paused. "Anyway, I could be way off. It could also be about suicide. If you 'hateth life,' you might kill yourself and be doomed to live that life for eternity in hell. It could also mean that."

Alex shrugged. "Yeah, I read that, too. I had just asked him why he was telling me about Santiago being innocent when he said it. Or she said it. That help at all?"

"Seems to me this person wants to do the right thing because he or she has an eye on the eternal."

Alex shook his head and looked out the window. "So we're looking for someone who believes in heaven and doesn't think he's getting in."

"Or she's getting in."

***

When the plane leveled off at 33,000 feet, Alex closed his eyes. His legs and feet were folded into a Z-shape and wedged under his seat. His head rested uncomfortably on top of the cushion and sleep came in fifteen-minute fragments. He wasn't sure if he was dreaming or thinking. First he saw Downton walking from room to room in his mother's apartment, talking about basketball. Next he saw him lying on the floor of his Brooklyn apartment, the man from the sketch standing over him. The plane hit a patch of turbulence. Alex's head dropped forward and bounced off the seat in front of him. He opened his eyes and felt a tenderness in his chest. He closed them again and saw Downton with his grandson, Tyree. Then he saw a grainy image of Santiago standing in the park, the dark trees waving behind him. His pockmarked face, smiling into the night, became disconnected from his body and hung in Alex's head. In the minutes before he awoke, his mind jumped back and forth between Santiago and Tyree, accompanied by a vague feeling of shame. He needed to do something.

When he opened his eyes, he turned to find Camila staring at him as she popped peanuts into her mouth. "What were you dreaming about?" she asked.

"Santiago. Downton. Tyree." He was groggy. Her eyes were tender and he thought she had probably been watching him for a while. He sat up a little. "Why did Santiago just stand there, for two and a half minutes, watching him die? And then it looked like he smiled. Why would he do that?"

"I don't know."

He stared back at her and the image of Santiago left him. His head felt relaxed, soft, and the softness expanded down his neck and met the tenderness in his chest. He thought that he would relax away into nothing. He tensed his shoulders and sat up straight. "When did your parents move to the States?" he asked.

"I just realized, you don't know what it's like being a foreigner, do you?"

"I don't know. What's that supposed to mean?"

She crunched a peanut. "You feel safe all the time and you make people comfortable. You're so sure of yourself that people can make you into whatever they need you to be."

He frowned until he realized she wasn't mocking him. "Well, in college I traveled all over and felt at home everywhere I went."

"You're like America."

"I get that," he said. "That's funny."

"You didn't laugh. Where are your parents from, anyway?"

"Upstate New York. They met in high school. Dad lived in New York his whole life before the move. Mom went to college somewhere else, but they never really talked about it. I think they wanted me to believe in the whole high-school-sweethearts thing."

"Or maybe *they* wanted to believe in the whole high-school-sweethearts thing."

"Maybe."

"In Iowa, we were considered foreign even though we were whitish. We looked different enough for people to ask where we were from, and most people thought Argentina was part of Mexico."

Alex laughed and rubbed his eyes. "But you weren't really raised Catholic?"

"It's basically a Catholic country, but we weren't raised anything. My parents gave up religion soon after I was born."

"So why do you meditate?" Alex asked.

"It's a concentration practice."

"But why?"

"So I can pay closer attention to what's going on inside me."

"But there's a lot more going on outside you. Why not pay attention to that?"

"It depends on what kind of action you're looking for. There's a lot going on inside, too. We just don't pay much attention to it."

"Some people have good reasons not to."

"That's true, but it's funny to hear you say that because, of all people, you seem to have the least amount of pain to avoid."

Alex looked down at his lap. "You mean besides my parents dying?"

"Yes, besides that. Sorry."

The elbow of the man next to him was digging into Alex's side so he scooted toward Camila. He looked back up and she smiled, then fished around in the bag for the last of the peanuts. As he watched her chew, he felt drawn in, and he wondered whether he was falling in love with her. Then, in an instant, he felt the floor drop out from beneath him and thought he would fall forever. He remembered the call he received when his parents died, and how he'd felt when he'd received it. Blank. Out of control. Terrified.

He felt the man's head drop onto his shoulder and he pushed it away, still staring at Camila. "Can I tell you something—I mean, ask you something?"

She threw a peanut at him. "In case you haven't noticed, you don't need the preliminaries and throat clearing with me. Just ask."

"It's just … well … I mean …" He swallowed hard. "In the taxi yesterday you said you felt like you were standing on water but not sinking. I'm not sure how to ask this, but … what's going on with you?"

The flight attendant came by to collect trash and Camila asked for another bag of peanuts. When the flight attendant left, Camila said, "I've dated mostly older men. John wasn't the first. Men who are not only not *of* the world, but not really *in* it, either. I have the same tendency. My whole life, I've only barely been here. My mind is here, sure, but the rest of me? Not so much."

The flight attendant came back with two bags of peanuts. "Plain *and* honey roasted," she said. She handed them to Camila and turned abruptly.

"Was she mocking me?" Camila asked.

"Well, your peanut consumption may put the whole airline in the red this quarter. But seriously, I get the thing about older men, but what's going on with you *now*?"

Camila passed the bags of nuts between her hands. They crinkled rhythmically and the man next to Alex squirmed. Alex put his hand over hers to stop the noise.

She looked up at him. "Have you ever felt bad in a way that's beyond everyday guilt, beyond moral judgment, beyond the little voice in your head that tells you what to do? Like something is wrong that can never be fixed?"

He wished he had, so he could feel what she felt, but his guilt was simpler than that. "I haven't."

She traced the words on the peanut package with her pinky finger. "Well, it's like that," she said. "And all I can do is feel it."

"But why? I mean, what do you feel bad about?"

"It started after John died. I dumped him and three weeks later he was dead. And it's my dad, too. He's dying, and I think I'm heartbroken, but all I can think about are the times he hit me. When he hit me, I walled off parts of myself for safekeeping. Other parts of me went dormant. Since John died, it's like everything I buried is slowly resurfacing. At the core, I don't feel bad *about* anything. I think sometimes the 'abouts' are just stories we tell ourselves to avoid feelings that are fundamentally unbearable."

"Yeah."

"Sometimes I think I'm holding all the suffering of my parents, grandparents, and great-grandparents. Like the accumulated sadness of our whole family lineage—the hard times, the abuse, even the everyday disappointments—are appearing in me, and I have to process what they couldn't. To feel what they couldn't feel. "

"Why?"

"I'm not sure there's a why."

They sat in silence.

Alex ran his hands through his hair. Finally, he said, "You know how you say everything is easy for me? Well, you're kinda right about that. But sometimes, as a teenager, I would wish something terrible would happen. Like my plane would crash, or my parents would die. I didn't really want to die, or want them to die, but I wished for some tragedy, some huge event. Like I wanted to be shaken awake or something. Then my parents did die and that didn't do it. It did the opposite."

"Will you tell me how they died? It might help."

"Car crash. They visited New York for my NYU graduation and died on their way home from the airport. They hadn't been back to the city since I was six months old. They took one trip—to see *me*—and they died."

Camila nodded but said nothing.

"I was sad. I mean, I'm still sad. I feel bad that I even had that thought about them dying. And on 9/11, I remember thinking, 'Maybe this is it. Maybe this will be the thing.' It wasn't. 9/11 was a lot of things, but it didn't wake me from the fog either. I remember having drinks in the Village with some friends a couple weeks later. I was looking around the bar, thinking, 'Everything is the same.' There we were, a mile from Ground Zero, and everything was the *fucking* same. And not just with me, but with everyone. We were the same bunch of assholes we were before the attacks."

Camila opened the bag of honey-roasted peanuts and put one in his mouth. He chewed as she took his hand. "Maybe *this* is it," she said. "Maybe this will be the thing."

He squeezed her hand and, a few minutes later, fell into a deep sleep.

Chapter Thirty-Nine

Rak sat at the counter, staring at the phone next to the cash register. When it rang, he glanced at the old man. "Beef and peas. Four." The man disappeared into the kitchen.

Rak picked up the phone. "Mr. Bice?"

"When we spoke two days ago, you assured me that you would find them."

"They did not go home all night."

"We have the video now. It will never come out."

"How do you know that they do not make a copy?"

"We can't be sure until you find them. They are in Hawaii. Kona. Maybe I don't need to tell you, but you have a personal stake in this as well. We were fortunate that the police found the kid and the charges stuck, but now that this case has gotten so big, if that video comes out, the pressure to find the real killer will be huge."

Rak glanced toward the kitchen, where the old man was standing at the stove. "But you have not yet tell me what it is, exactly."

"I'm not going to talk about the video. The less you know, the better. It doesn't implicate you, but it could get the kid off. You need to track them down and make sure they do not have that recording."

"When I track them down, I will kill them both."

"No, you won't. Like I said before, do what you want with the girl. Leave Alex Vane alive. As long as he doesn't have a copy of that video, he can't hurt you. Without that video, Santiago will be convicted."

"Mr. Bice, I took the job on the professor as a courtesy to Smedveb. He says you are okay. Now, you will tell me how this happened, or I will hang up, kill them both, and disappear."

The old man slid a paper plate down the counter and set a small bowl of yogurt next to it. Rak dunked a whole pierogi in the yogurt and popped it into his mouth.

"If I tell you what happened," Bice said, "will you do what I've asked?"

Rak licked tiny drops of grease off his pasty lips. "You have no choice but to tell me and find out."

Bice spoke in a steady monotone as Rak chewed pierogies. "After 9/11, two cops approached Downton, the black man—the drug dealer—in Washington Square Park. They were young, dumb cops trying to make names for themselves by looking into local kids who might have Al Qaeda ties. They wired him with a video camera. A week or two before you took out the professor, they were put on leave for brutality."

"What did they do?"

"Roughed up an Arab, but the department covered it up. Never came out in the papers. After nine months, they came back to the police force with a demotion. Went looking for the recorder. They found Downton and he told them he got rid of it after they disappeared. They asked him about the night the professor was killed and he said he didn't see anything. But they thought he was lying. Thought he knew something about the murder."

"And when was this?" Rak asked.

"End of August. They were angry because it was an expensive camera. Real stupid guys."

"And how are *you* connecting to these 'real stupid guys?' How did you come to know all this?"

"Before they went on leave, the two cops used to help me out. Kept an eye on certain reporters for me. Did odd jobs."

Rak smiled and sucked the filling out of a pierogi. "'Odd jobs.' Yes."

"One of the cops came to me two weeks ago and told me the story. Said that one of my reporters, Alex Vane, had a meeting with this dealer. He brought it to me because he was worried that Downton might be telling the reporter about *them*, about their attempts to get information illegally. Like I said, these are real stupid guys. The cop that came to me, this Irish piece of shit, had roughed Downton up a bit when he couldn't produce the recorder. He thought maybe Downton had turned on him. Wondered if I could do anything to get the reporter off the story."

"You sure the black man didn't tell the police anything about what happened in the park that night? About the professor?"

"Yes."

"And the police—this 'Irish piece of shit'—thinks you make Downton disappear to help him?"

"Yes, and now he owes me."

"Okay, I will finish the job. But, Mr. Bice, there is no reason to keep anyone alive. If the girl and the reporter saw this video, they both have to go."

"No."

Rak nibbled the doughy edges of a pierogi. "Mr. Bice, this is not about you anymore. I do not understand your business. I do not know why you want what you want. But I am not in the business of keeping people alive."

"I'm paying you to do as I say. I am in control."

Rak laughed. "No, Mr. Bice, no one controls Rak. Keep the money. I'm going to finish this." Before Bice could answer, Rak hung up, wiped his sleeve across his mouth, and walked to the door.

Chapter Forty

Wednesday, September 11, 2002

At the Kona airport, Alex and Camila stepped out of the plane into sweltering, wet air. They took the rolling staircase down to the tarmac where a young woman with curly brown hair was draping orchid leis over the heads of some of the passengers.

"How come we don't get one?" Alex asked Camila.

"I think you have to be with a tour group."

"That orchid scent is like a shot of caffeine. I think I slept hard the last few hours." He flipped open his phone. "It's past midnight back home. One-year anniversary of 9/11. And we are definitely not in New York City anymore."

Ten minutes later, they were sitting on a slatted bench under a wooden canopy, waiting for a taxi. Alex got up to stretch and do jumping jacks as Camila munched chocolate covered macadamia nuts. When he saw that she was watching him with a wry smile, he closed his eyes.

She laughed. "You know I can still see you when you close your eyes, right?"

He opened his eyes and bent at the waist, touching his hands flat to the ground. "I'm not sure that's how it works." He slowly arched up and smiled at her. "I'm fairly certain that when I close my eyes, the world stops existing."

"Remember what I said about you being a decent guy pretending to be an asshole?"

"Yeah."

"I take back the 'pretending' part."

Alex's phone beeped. He had a message from a man named Damian Bale, who worked at the Old Rhino Bar in the Village. He called him back as Camila watched from the bench.

"Damian Bale? This is Alex Vane. What's this about?"

"Are you the Alex Vane who's covering the Santiago trial for *The Standard*?" Bale spoke quickly and sounded young.

"That's me."

"I was working the bar last New Year's Eve, the night the professor was killed in the park."

Alex could hear clinking and music in the background. "Did you know him?"

"No, but I saw him that night. He was a regular. Always came in, ate alone, seemed kind of sad and uptight. Wasn't a big drinker or a big tipper. Always had wine, usually two glasses, but that night he ordered a bottle and only drank a glass. Kinda sad to be drinking a hundred-dollar bottle alone on New Year's."

"What kind of wine did he order?"

"Hellooo? You must already know the answer to that. Is this a test?"

"Yes, it is," Alex said.

"Châteauneuf-du-Pape, 1992. He was a Rhône guy. Liked the big, bold reds. I'm studying to be a sommelier so I watch what kind of people order what kind of wine. He was a small, weak guy. Maybe the big hearty reds made him, you know, feel like something."

"So what are you calling to tell me?" Alex asked, wiping sweat from his forehead.

"You heard of Demarcus Downton? Some random guy who got killed in Brooklyn Heights a couple days ago?"

Alex coughed into the phone. "Yes."

"Well, *The Post* ran a sketch of the guy who killed him. Now, I *do not* read *The Post*, but meathead guys leave it on the bar all the time. I was thumbing through it today and I recognized the guy who killed this Downton guy. He was in the bar New Year's Eve."

"Wait," Alex said, "the guy from the sketch in *The Post* was in your bar? White guy, mustache, real small?"

"I'm sure of it. Real funny looking. Strange accent. I spent a summer in the south of France and one traveling through Eastern Europe for my thesis on dessert wines. Anyhoo, this guy sounded European, but the accent was all jumbled together."

"And you think he was in your bar New Year's Eve?"

"I don't think, okay? I know. Look, I want to own my own place someday, a wine bar down here in the Village. I'm gonna specialize in wines that go with chocolate. Gonna call it Chocolate Bar. Clever, right?"

"So what?"

"So what I'm saying is, I notice what goes on in a bar. Hellooo? It's my job. And this guy *did not* belong. Was here maybe an hour. Drank a glass of krupnik. I mean, who *orders* that? Made me think he was Polish or maybe Lithuanian. And, other than Professor Martin, he was the only guy here by himself that night."

"Why not call the police about this?" Alex asked.

"I did. Called them right when I saw the sketch in *The Post.* They took my statement and told me not to talk to any reporters. There's one other thing, too. Guy was eyeing the professor. At first I took him for gay with how much he was looking over at him. But I know gay. I *am* gay. I threw some gay at him and it didn't stick, if you know what I mean. When the professor went to the bathroom, the guy paid for the krupnik and walked out right past his table."

"Did you get his name?" Alex asked.

"No."

"And I'm guessing he didn't pay with a card?"

"No, he left cash. A twenty for an eight-dollar drink. Seemed in a hurry to leave. Didn't seem that weird at the time, but when I saw his picture in *The Post*, it all kinda came back to me."

"If the police said not to talk to reporters, why did you call me?" Alex asked.

"I don't know, I figure, you get me in the paper, I can start building my brand."

"Your brand?"

"You run this in *The Standard*, mention my name, maybe people will drop by and see me at the bar. I'm looking for investors."

"And you think this will help you find them?"

"Hellooooo? You're a journalist, you know there's no bad PR."

Alex thanked him and said good-bye, then sat down next to Camila and filled her in on the conversation.

When he had finished, she said, "Well, if Santiago didn't do it, I guess we know who did." She stood. "I'm hungry."

Alex laughed. "Makes sense. It's dinner time here and you've only eaten four or five meals today, plus two-thousand calories worth of peanuts. You wanna get a taxi into town?"

"Yes, and I could use a cocktail."

***

They watched the orange sky darken to a rusty brown as they passed miles of black lava rock on the long, flat stretch of highway into Kailua-Kona. Neither spoke during the ride. As they pulled into town, Camila said to the driver, "Just drop us anywhere. We don't know where we're going."

They walked down Alii Drive, poking their heads into gift shops full of t-shirts and postcards as the last light faded from the sky. A reggae band on the sidewalk a block away started playing steel drums.

"I thought reggae was supposed to be Jamaican," Alex said.

Camila waved her hand at a throng of tourists blocking a storefront. "Do you think most of these people know the difference?"

"Is it possible for you to stop being cynical for a minute? We're not in the city anymore—you don't get points for being an elitist smart ass here."

She smiled. "It's two a.m. in the city and I'm too tired not to be a smart ass."

They settled into dinner at a small café on a side street. Alex ate oysters on the half shell and a tuna steak with sesame slaw. Camila had macadamia-crusted tilapia with lobster mashed potatoes and lime beurre blanc. Camila sipped a French 75 as Alex drank glass after glass of sparkling water.

When they had finished eating, Camila ordered another drink. As the waiter left, she reached out and took Alex's hand. "I feel …"

"Feel what?" he asked.

"I feel better around you."

"That's nice to hear."

"You're better than you think you are."

"That's nice to hear, too."

She leaned across the table, her face lit by a low candle. "I feel, I don't know. Like I want to kiss you." She leaned in more and Alex leaned toward her. They both closed their eyes.

"You here for the triathlon?" The waiter was beside their table, delivering Camila's drink.

Alex flushed red and sipped his water.

"Yes, he came in second last year," Camila said, laughing. "He's been training hard and is definitely gonna take it this time."

Alex rubbed his cheeks with both hands and glanced down at the table, then looked back up and smiled.

After dinner, Camila reserved a room at the King Kamehameha Inn.

Within minutes of checking in, they were asleep in separate beds.

Medilogue Two

Chambers Street, New York, New York
Ten Weeks After 9/11

Sonia Hollinger was in the back of her limo when the office of the chief medical examiner called to tell her that a team sifting through the rubble of the Marriott had found her husband's desiccated body. After she hung up, she told her driver to head downtown to the morgue. She slumped down in the seat, but she didn't cry. She hadn't cried once since her husband had disappeared.

In the days after the attack, Sonia had plastered pictures of Mac all over the city. She had questioned hundreds of people and had even found a few who thought they might have recognized him. One firefighter thought he remembered seeing Mac leave the south tower. But he had seen hundreds of people coming and going and couldn't be sure.

Each morning since the attacks she had risen early, done her hair and makeup, and gone from hospital to hospital, shelter to shelter. "Maybe he forgot his name," she'd told herself, "or was injured and can't speak and is lying in a room somewhere." Some days she'd wanted to quit her search, collapse onto the bed, and cry for hours. But each time she'd felt like this she'd forced herself to be strong, sit up straighter, and fix her makeup.

Sonia held her face tight as she walked into the white tent serving as a makeshift coroner's office. She had never seen a body so withered, a face so deformed. She only recognized Mac by the gold band on his left ring finger, which gleamed on his decaying hand. She stared at the ring, fighting tears, and pressed her hands into her thighs as hard as she could.

"Why was he in the rubble of the Marriott?" she asked the assistant, a young man with bright red acne on his pale cheeks.

"Well, since he was on a high floor, he could have fallen out in that direction—or, I'm sorry to say this, he could have jumped. We'll probably never know."

"So you don't think he made it out alive?"

"It's possible, but if he did, he would have been exhausted, disoriented. His lungs were badly damaged before he died. That we know for sure. The only unusual thing we found was a bit of black fuzz lodged in his throat. Velvet, or some similar material."

Sonia looked up and the young man met her eyes.

"But, honestly," he continued, "and I don't know how to say this without being insensitive, so I'll just say it. We found detached limbs and bone fragments everywhere. We found steel beams through skulls, keyboards lodged in ribcages. I've looked at over a thousand bodies and parts of bodies in the last forty-five days. This attack was a horror on a scale I didn't think possible. Nothing surprises me anymore."

***

Sonia was home by noon and slept hard for three hours.

When she awoke, she felt only a dull sadness. She got out of bed and locked the door to her bedroom, then lay back down, covered herself in a thick comforter, and wept quietly for two hours. At 5 p.m., she walked into the bathroom and splashed cold water on her face. "That's enough of that," she said, critiquing herself in the mirror. She brushed her hair, put on makeup, and walked downstairs to her husband's home office off the kitchen.

On his desk lay a list of names handwritten in her neat script. She rubbed her eyes and looked down at the list, then called Mayor Giuliani and told his secretary that Mac's body had been found. She knew it would spread through the city quickly now. She called her husband's two children, both in California, and made them promise to call his ex-wife, grandchildren, and cousins. Then she called his former business partners and a few personal friends. She put a neat check mark next to each name.

At 8 p.m., she walked to the kitchen. Juan sat on a stool, his head resting on his arms on the vast, granite island. "I'm ready for dinner," she said.

Juan sat up. "*Es verdad?*"

She nodded. "How did you hear?"

"I thought something was going on when I arrived and you were sleeping."

She smacked the counter with an open hand. "I was sleeping, Juan. I have the right to do that!"

"I know. I mean … I looked around the computer. *The New York Times* had it up a few hours ago."

She stood up straighter, dreading the wave of phone calls she was about to receive. "What's for dinner?" she asked.

Juan stood, walked to her, and placed his hand on her chest above her breasts. "*Lo siento.* Sonia, are you okay? Is there anything I can do?"

"I need to eat."

Half an hour later she was back at the desk, full of oysters. She emptied the last drops of a bottle of Dom Pérignon into a paper-thin champagne flute. She studied the names on the list that remained unchecked—mostly friends, clients, and vague acquaintances. She did not want to make the calls, but knew that she would.

Just as she was about to pick it up, the phone on the desk rang. She sipped the champagne and answered with the sweetest voice she could muster. "Hello?"

"Sonia, it's Denver Bice. I've just heard about Mac and I'm calling to offer my deepest condolences. I am so sorry."

"Thank you," she managed.

"Just know," he continued, "we're gonna get these guys. We're only two weeks into the bombing and we've taken out half of Afghanistan. I'm in touch with people in the White House—people Mac knew as well—and they assure me that we're not going to stop until we get them all."

She ran her finger around the top of the champagne flute and tried to speak, but nothing came out.

"Sonia, listen," he continued, "we'll be executing Bin Laden at this year's Super Bowl Halftime Show. I promise."

She laughed softly. "Thank you, Mr. Bice. I hope you are right."

"Call me Denver, or Den. Mac used to call me Den."

"Thank you, Denver." She emptied the glass and slumped down in her chair, then caught herself and sat up straight.

"You know," Bice said, "your husband taught the last class I took at Tulane."

"Yes, I know."

"I owe him a lot."

"Yes, thank you."

"Well I, I just wanted to let you know how sorry I am."

"Yes, thank you."

She hung up, looked down at the list, and put a check mark next to "Denver Bice." She walked to her bedroom, took a sleeping pill, and read a romance novel for fifteen minutes before falling into a dreamless sleep.

***

Bice hung up and walked to the conference room on the thirty-third floor of the Standard Media building in midtown. The twelve men and two women of the board of directors sat around a giant oval table, bathed in gray, early-winter light.

After the secretary called the meeting to order, Bice stood up. "Before we get started," he said, "I'd like to acknowledge what some of you have already heard. Macintosh Hollinger's body was found today. It is as we thought." He lowered his head. "Besides being a mentor and friend, he was this company's largest investor, one of its earliest investors. We owe him a debt of gratitude."

After a few seconds of silence, he said, "On the topic of the merger, a few rumors have leaked out, but we will make the official announcement on Monday, after the Thanksgiving holiday."

A small woman in a blue two-piece skirt suit said, "And how long do we expect it to take for the merger to go final. A year?"

"If things go well, six to eight months," Bice said. "It depends on how much of a show the FTC, FCC, and the antitrust people want to put on. And that depends on how much pressure they get from the administration."

"How much pressure do you expect them to get?" she asked.

Bice smiled. "Not much. People I'm talking to say approval should be easy."

The woman nodded and took notes, then looked up. "Did you solve the issue of how to present the acquisition?"

Bice walked around the table. "Technically, Nation Corp. will be acquiring us because they have the larger market cap, but we are going to sell it to the public as an even merger creating a new entity: Standard Media/Nation Corp."

The woman nodded her approval. "What about Europe? Will there be regulatory issues over there?"

"They'll just follow the wind over here," Bice said. "It won't be a problem." He stopped pacing and looked around the room. "Well then, if there aren't any further—"

"Just a second." Laurence Stevens, a stocky black man in a brown suit raised his hand. "Are we sure that the Nation Corp. board will approve you as CEO of the joint entity?"

"We're confident, Laurence," Bice said, sitting down. "But I'll defer to Chairman Gathert on this."

At the far end of the table, Chairman Gathert put on his round glasses and stood up. "I met with Nation Corp. last week and presented our case for Denver. They know he has spearheaded our growth over the last eight years, and—"

Laurence held up his hand. "If I may, Chairman Gathert. I'm sorry, but is now really the time to announce? Since the attacks we've seen a seven percent drop in the Dow, then an eight percent rise. We're ten weeks removed from the most devastating attack ever on American soil. We're at war already and who knows where *that* will lead us? I want to go on record and say that I think we need to put more consideration into how this will appear."

Gathert and Bice exchanged glances. Bice looked down and jotted notes on a yellow legal pad as Gathert spoke slowly, with warmth. "Laurence, we've been over this. We're not going to derail this deal because of nineteen terrorists or a dip in the market. Our stock is already up one percent from September tenth. This deal is meant to happen. This new company is meant to happen. And we're going to make everyone in this room a lot of money."

Laurence looked across the table at Bice. "What about the dot coms? Those of us who deal with finances actually have to face the fact that they're pariahs right now. Forget 9/11, this deal could backfire for a lot of reasons."

Bice capped his pen, then held it in his fist and squeezed hard as he looked around the table. "It's a blip," he said. "The Internet is not going away. And Nation Corp. is more than just an Internet company. They're our access to every mode of distribution." Bice's hand was turning red. He loosened his grip on the pen. "This is the deal, people. It's going to be hard. There *will* be some bumps in the road. But in the end, we'll be in charge of the information and entertainment that half the people in the world consume, *and* we'll be in charge of how they consume it."

Laurence stood up and glared across the table at Bice. "And you'll be king of the media?"

Bice put the pen down and took a few breaths. "Someone has to do it," he said quietly.

Gathert put his hands out over the table. "Gentlemen, please. This is a stressful time. The city is on edge. A lot is at stake. Let's all calm down."

"Fine, fine," Laurence said, sitting down. "But one last thing. We all know this deal is precarious. If the market falters, or our stock drops and theirs doesn't, the whole deal shifts. Down in finance, we've heard grumblings that Mac Hollinger intended to divest before he died. Have you heard anything about that?"

Bice swept his hand through the air. "I've heard the rumors. They are absolutely untrue."

"We don't need to tell you what a blow that would be, do we?" Laurence asked. "One big loss like that and we'll be buying tickets to the Nation Corp. board meetings."

A young woman next to Stevens said, "I've heard the rumors too, Denver. I guess it's a moot point—no offense to Mr. Hollinger's memory. But now's not the time to have people thinking our single biggest investor was going to pull out. Just the rumor could hit our stock hard."

Bice walked around the table and stood behind the young woman. He placed a hand on her shoulder and another on Stevens's shoulder. "Laurence, Sarah. It's just one girl spreading a rumor because she's pissed about the deal—Sadie Green from the Media Protection Organization." He took his hands off their shoulders and began pacing. "She's some radical media nut. I spoke with Hollinger's widow just today. I know her personally. If he even considered selling his stock, she didn't know about it and she has no plans to do so now. His will does not call for any change in his holdings. Plus, the rumor is already out there and our stock is fine."

Bice stopped pacing just behind Stevens, who looked up at him and asked, "Can you guarantee that nothing is going to come of this?"

"Absolutely," Bice said, smiling.

Part Three

Chapter Forty-One

Alex awoke at 3 a.m. and looked around the hotel room. There were two double beds and a small desk. Above the desk, a window looked out on the stairway and courtyard. Brown curtains framed French doors that led onto a small balcony facing the ocean, now illuminated by silver moonlight. Along the wall, a long dresser held an old TV.

"Crap," Alex whispered. There was no coffee maker.

Camila was asleep on the bed in the corner. Alex found the safe in the closet and locked up the recordings of his conversation with Downton and the USB drive James had given Camila. Next, he quietly dressed and left the room, then took the stairs down to the courtyard. The hotel lobby was open and the concierge on duty gave him a cup of coffee and directions to the business center, a ten by ten beige room with a row of old PCs.

First, he sent an e-mail to Baxton, telling him that he needed to take a leave of absence for at least a week. He tried to sound professional, despite the fact that he filled with rage every time he thought about his boss. Then he did a web search for Macintosh Hollinger and spent two hours reading everything he could find.

By 6 a.m., Alex was on the beach wearing a pair of Hawaiian shorts the concierge had lent him from the lost and found. The first streaks of pink were appearing in the sky and the day was warming. He left his clothes and shoes in the sand and started at a slow jog past cabanas and palm trees, picking up speed as he passed the last hotel and entered a long stretch of empty beach.

He tried to think about Hollinger and Bice, but instead thought about Camila. What was it about her? And why did he feel like he was being erased? As the dread pooled in his stomach, he laughed out loud at the fact that the dread was not related to the man who had rummaged through his apartment twenty-four hours earlier, but to his feelings for Camila.

Every eight minutes or so he stopped to do pushups in the sand. After an hour, he had completed a seven-mile loop and 150 pushups.

***

Camila sat on a plastic chair on the shady balcony and looked out at the ocean. She watched a giant turtle crawl off a rock into the water, then rise and fall with the waves. She felt the cool, wet air move through her nostrils and fill her belly. She looked down at her phone, balanced on the arm of the chair. Her mother would call again soon.

She closed her eyes and pictured Alex—stretching at the airport, making fun of himself. She imagined the crunchy bits of macadamia nut from the night before, the tiny bubbles from the champagne, and saw Alex smiling as she'd leaned in to kiss him. Then her father appeared, sitting in his old recliner, watching football as her mother shuffled from room to room. She remembered the way he spoke to her mother. His cruel words. His cold, bitter tone.

She felt the wind on her face and the cold plastic chair through her pants. She saw her father and felt a sting on her face, then an aching. Her whole body stiffened, contracted. Her head was warm and relaxed, her mind clear, but in her body she felt a creeping sickness, an unspeakable sadness. Like something was fundamentally wrong with her, without cause.

She was no longer aware of the wind or the sea. She wanted to get up, but instead focused on the sensation. In it she felt all her father's bitterness and anger. She adjusted her legs, but the awareness stayed. "Cam, what are you *doing*?" Her father's voice echoed in her, stabbed at her chest. His tone seemed to carry with it generations of cruelty.

She heard the door of the hotel room open. Alex's voice came softly through the room. "Honey, I'm home."

Chapter Forty-Two

When Alex saw her sitting on the balcony, he walked through the room and out the sliding door. Her body was still, which made him feel uncomfortable. "Is everything okay?"

"Fine," she said, turning toward him. She burst out laughing when she saw him. He still wore the borrowed shorts and was covered in sand-speckled sweat.

"You look like a commercial for Hawaii," she said. "Where are your clothes?"

"Left them down in the changing room by the pool. Concierge lent me these."

"Have you eaten? Wait, lemmee guess. You swam out, caught a baby shark, built a fire out of driftwood, then grilled it on the beach for a tasty, low-carb option?"

Alex smiled and wiped the sweat from his chest with a towel he'd grabbed from the bathroom. "You're just making fun of me because you've probably never seen a shirtless younger man up close."

Camila glared at him.

"I'm sorry," he said after a moment. "I didn't mean it that way. Look, the breakfast buffet is open downstairs. Let's eat and I'll tell you about Hollinger."

"Ok, but please put some regular clothes on first."

***

They piled their plates high at a forty-foot buffet of standard American breakfast foods—sausage, bacon, eggs, pancakes—and local foods like mango, pineapple, and crab legs. Camila led them to a table in the corner, and they sat overlooking a courtyard dotted with cedar planters filled with flowers and miniature palm trees.

Alex had read several bios of Hollinger and many flattering profiles in finance and investment magazines. He told her Hollinger's story as they ate.

"Mr. Hollinger was born on a New Jersey dairy farm on September 11, 1917, died on his eighty-fourth birthday. His dad went to fight in Germany just before he was born and never came back, so he was raised by his mom and three older brothers until he left for Princeton in 1933. Went there early, it looks like. His mother and brothers are all deceased and he has two kids from a previous marriage, both of whom live in California."

"From a farm to Princeton?" Camila poured syrup over pineapple pancakes that were already drenched in butter.

"From what I could tell, they weren't exactly farmers. They owned a large dairy operation, over a thousand acres, that sold milk wholesale to cheese makers. Anyway, his mom ran the business after his dad died. So, he goes to Princeton, majors in math, graduates in '37, and finishes an MA there in 1940. Spent World War II breaking codes for the Navy. Gets out of the Navy in '47 and decides to teach the world about math, about why numbers matter."

"So how'd he get so rich?"

"Hold on a sec." Alex walked to the buffet and returned with a plate covered in crab legs.

"That much crab would cost two hundred dollars in the City."

"I know. I'm thinking about moving here."

"So how'd he get so rich?"

Alex cracked a giant crab leg and dipped the meat in salted lemon juice. "At some point, he started investing a little of his family's money. They didn't have a ton, but enough extra during the boom of the fifties that they needed to do something with it. So he's hopping around between crappy teaching jobs and he starts to invest little pieces of his family's money. He lands a tenure-track job at Tulane in 1956. Taught there for fifteen years and left in '71 to start his own investing firm. Weird thing was, he was already rich. He was investing the whole time at Tulane. The financial magazines describe him as a pioneer. In the sixties and seventies, he used advanced math in his investing before anyone else. Used computers to design trades before the first computer appeared in the New York Stock Exchange."

"So he was some sort of genius?" Camila asked.

"Basically, yeah. Just made trades based on numbers, which everyone does now. I don't really understand it, but it worked. By the time he set up his own firm in '71, he had some *very* rich clients. Plus, he already had a personal fortune of over fifty million."

Camila nibbled a slice of watermelon. "Anything that helps explain the interaction at the funeral? What could John have meant when he said it was lucky Hollinger died when he did?"

"Well, we already knew that Martin, Hollinger, and Bice were all at Tulane at the same time. But I did find out that a good chunk of Hollinger's fortune came from an early investment in Standard Media. Ended up owning ten percent of their stock, more than five hundred million's worth. So that's a connection with Bice. But who knows what it means?"

Camila wiped her watermelon in a pool of syrup. "Mac's wife might."

Chapter Forty-Three

Back in their room, they checked the phone book for Sonia Hollinger but found nothing. Alex flipped open his phone and called James Stacy at home. James picked up on the first ring as Camila flopped down on the bed.

"Waiting by the phone?" Alex asked.

"Actually, y-yes. Where the hell are you?"

"We've been in transit."

"We?"

"I mean, I."

"What's going on?"

"Calm down, James. I need some help."

"More h-help? I'm already freaking out that I helped you with that video."

Alex walked to the balcony and stared at the beach. "James, calm down. Can you do research from home? I mean, do you have access to all the same stuff you have at the office?"

"Most of it, bu—"

"I need you to look something up."

"I'm not d-doing another thing until you t-tell me what's going on."

Alex held his hand over the phone. "He wants to know what's going on," he whispered to Camila.

She sat up in bed and nodded. Alex told James about the video, Baxton squashing his story, and the man in their apartments. "We're in Kona," he concluded.

James coughed into the phone. "I'm not involving myself in this any-m-m-m-m—" He cleared his throat. "Anymore."

"You're already involved," Alex said. "Please, we just need an address or phone number for Sonia Hollinger in Kona."

"Aren't you a reporter? Can't you go d-down to the town hall or something?"

"We don't want anyone to know we're looking for her."

James sighed. "Give me a half hour."

"Fifteen minutes," Alex said. He hung up.

Camila lay on her back across the bed. "I feel like I'm in a sugar coma."

Alex lay on his belly beside her, his feet dangling off the bottom of the bed. "Let's think about this, Cam. What do we know?"

"Cam? So we're doing nicknames for each other now?"

Alex pressed the nail of his index finger into his thumb then flicked her leg. "*You're* the one who held my hand on the plane," he said. "*And* leaned toward me flirtatiously last night."

She rolled away from him onto her elbow. "That was a mistake. I'm really not ... I mean ... it's not a good idea."

Alex stood up and walked to the window. "I could use another call from that source," he said after staring at the beach for a minute.

"What about your list? Read me a few names."

Alex took the list from his bag. "Well, Bearon eliminated five names. I called a few. About seventy are left. Brian Adler, officer on the NYU beat. Simone Bryant, assistant DA for Manhattan County. You're not gonna know any of these people."

"You're probably right."

Alex scanned the list, then looked up. "Weird."

"What?"

"James put the names of the prosecutors on here."

"What do you mean?"

"Well, he put Davis, Morganthal, and Sharp on here. The three lead prosecutors in the Santiago trial."

"You asked him for everyone who would have access to the file, right?"

"Yeah, but I figured he would eliminate people who obviously aren't my source."

"Did you ask him to do that?"

"Well, no."

Camila walked over and took the list. "Wait, that could fit," she said. "If Santiago is innocent, they are likely to know it. Maybe one of them has a guilty conscience."

"That's pretty farfetched. They're putting all their energy into *prosecuting* the guy. Why would they leak information to sabotage their own case?"

"Think about it," Camila said. "You said Sharp wants to run for mayor, right? Maybe he wants the case to get even bigger. Even if he loses, if it's not his fault, it won't matter. The more press the trial gets, the bigger his profile gets. For better or worse, he'd become a national figure."

"Maybe. But if it's him, he'll never go on record. He'd be disbarred. Finished."

"That's why he'd go to great lengths—like a voice scrambler—to make sure he stays anonymous."

"Let's stick with what we know, okay? I need to get this straight before we meet with Sonia."

"*If* we meet with Sonia," Camila said, dropping the list on the bed and sitting down.

"We know the guy from the sketch killed Demarcus and rifled through my apartment, probably looking for the recording. But why didn't he rifle through your apartment?"

"Maybe he heard Charlie next door and looked through everything quietly. Or maybe he was just waiting for us there and left when we didn't come home."

Alex closed the curtains, then opened them again. He closed his left eye and focused on a pair of surfers far out on the waves. "And if the bartender is right, we know the killer was in the bar on New Year's Eve. So somehow that night he dosed Martin's drink with fentanyl, probably while he was in the restroom."

"That would explain the wobbling and shaking on the video."

"Right," Alex said. "So he gets to the park as the fentanyl hits. He leans on the statue. Santiago walks through the park, stops, and watches him die."

"Any chance Santiago was somehow in on it, and is taking the fall?"

"I don't know, but he seems like a pretty weird kid. Seems like the kinda kid who could've done it."

"That's not exactly how these things are supposed to be decided," Camila said.

"Well, he had the drug in his apartment."

"Yeah, but lots of students get fake prescriptions." Camila walked over to Alex and looked out at the surfers.

"So if Santiago had nothing to do with it," he said, "we're back to motive. My source said we need to figure out *why* Martin was killed, that there are three dead, not two. It's possible that refers to Hollinger, but it's quite possible it doesn't." Alex paused. "Plus, Hollinger died in 9/11. How could his death be linked to anything else?"

Camila went back, sat on the bed, and closed her eyes.

Alex watched her. "What?" he asked. "I can tell you're thinking something."

"I'm just thinking about that interaction John had with Bice at the funeral. Maybe John knew something Bice didn't want him to know. Something connected to Hollinger."

"That would tie them together, but we need to talk with Hollinger's wife." Alex paced the room.

"What are you thinking now?" Camila asked.

"Before we ran out of your apartment, you said that Martin kept everything. Do you have an assistant? Anyone who can send you Martin's papers?"

"I can get Charlie to do it. He's got a spare key."

"What about e-mails? Can we get his e-mails?"

"John rarely e-mailed, and when he did, it was just for work. He didn't even have a personal e-mail account."

Camila called Charlie and explained where she was. Next, she asked him to send all the files from the bottom drawer of her filing cabinet, plus the letters Martin had written her, which were in her desk drawer. "Everything should be here Saturday," she said when she hung up.

Alex's phone rang and he looked at the caller ID. "It's James," he said, flipping it open. "What happened to fifteen minutes?"

"Rich p-people are harder to find."

Chapter Forty-Four

"How'd you find the number?" Alex asked.

"Called the c-county c-clerk in Kona and pretended I was a cop following up on some 9/11 stuff about her h-husband. Couldn't get an address but the woman gave me a number."

Alex took down the number. "Thanks," he said. "I promise we'll be in touch soon."

He dialed Sonia and got no answer. "Now what?" he asked Camila.

Camila's phone rang. She looked at the caller ID and walked out through the sliding door to the balcony. Alex sat at the desk and listened.

"Mama? Yeah, hi. What's going on with Papa? Yeah ... Yes, I'll talk with him ... Hi Papa ... Yes, Mama told me, I'm so sorry ... I'm going to try to come ... Yes, okay, go rest, Papa ... Hi Mama. Let me try to figure some things out. I'll see if I can make arrangements ... Yeah, bye."

She walked back into the room and closed the sliding door behind her. "My father is going to die this week," she said.

Alex tried to catch her eye, but she was staring at the carpet. After a moment, she picked up her purse and walked out of the room.

***

Alex didn't see her the rest of the afternoon.

He called Sonia every half hour and finally left a message at around 3 p.m. In between calls, he worked at the business center. First he looked up Damian Bale, who was listed on the Web site of the Old Rhino Bar as a wine expert, and even had a one-page Web site of his own at nycchocolatebar.com. Alex knew there was no way to confirm what the bartender had said about New Year's Eve, but he had a feeling the guy was reliable.

At 4 p.m., he checked the homepage of *The New York Times* for news on the Santiago trial. That day, prosecutors had called two police officers and both had testified that they'd searched Martin's apartment within hours of the murder but hadn't found anything helpful. The next day, they'd retraced Martin's steps from his apartment, to the Old Rhino Bar, to his walk across the park. By the end of the first day of the investigation, their only clue had been a law student who'd said she had seen a strange-looking kid in the park that night. After police questioned her, the strange-looking kid had become their only lead.

Canvassing the neighborhood the next day, they'd traced Santiago to the adult theater. They were in his room by noon, where they'd found the spray bottle of fentanyl. At that point, they hadn't had a cause of death for the professor. But when Santiago produced what had looked like fake prescriptions for numerous drugs, he'd been held and questioned. Once they'd had Santiago in custody, the police had ordered a fentanyl test on Martin's body. And when the test had come back positive two days later, they'd known they had their man.

As Alex read the AP story *The Standard* was running where his own work should have appeared, his phone rang. He flipped it open. "Mrs. Hollinger?"

Silence.

"Sonia?"

"No, this is Juan Carlos." The man's accent was thick and Alex thought it sounded Cuban. "I am her assistant. Is this Alex Vane?"

"Yes."

"You have called many times."

"Yes I—"

"What do you want with Mrs. Hollinger?"

"I am a reporter with *The New York Standard* but I am not here on an assignment. I believe she may be able to help us solve the murder of a friend of her husband. His name was Professor John Martin."

"I thought the police already solved that murder. You say you are a reporter or a police?"

"Reporter. But it's a long story. Please. We will only need a few minutes of her time."

Alex heard Juan whispering to someone. Finally, Juan said, "You can come by tomorrow morning around eleven. We are on Alii Drive, 1616."

Chapter Forty-Five

Camila sat on the beach, listening to the waves and watching a pair of surfers far out in the water. She saw a giant turtle and wondered whether it was the same one she had seen that morning. She remembered the cold chair from earlier in the day, then relaxed as her butt sank into the sand. She thought she could feel the weight of the earth pushing her up from below. She wondered whether it was because there were no pipes, subways, or people below her.

She dug her toes into the sand. A warm wind blew her hair across her face. Her body felt light as she closed her eyes.

"Cam, what are you *doing*?" Her father's voice in her head. She felt the words as an inner recoil, a tensing that started in her legs and moved through the rest of her body. It was like the phrase contained all his anger, all his cruelty, as well as that of his parents and their parents. A stabbing sadness coursed through her chest. She doubled over and cried for a few seconds, then sat back up, wiping sandy tears from her face. She dug her toes deeper into the sand.

She felt him throughout her body, and felt his parents and grandparents, too. Generations of congealed suffering moved through her. She opened her eyes. The beach and the sea were still there. She heard laughing in the water and saw blurry surfers through her tears.

She breathed deeply and felt her father drift through her. Maybe he was dead already, and this was him trying to move into her. She shivered and closed her eyes. Her father's mother appeared to her in a black dress, scowling on a dock in Buenos Aires. The cruelty had been in her grandmother, too.

She lay in the sand and covered her eyes to block the bright sun. She felt her father and grandmother settle over her, her sense of self crowded out until she could no longer track what was happening. They were both full of a sadness that came from a time before she was born.

She was too hot. She writhed in the sand, feeling that the sadness would kill her—that years upon years of cruelty had finally arrived within her, to take her away. She'd let it take her. She spread out her arms and legs in the sand and sobbed as the sadness stabbed at her chest. After a few minutes, her sobbing quieted into a soft whimpering and she became still. The heavy earth pushed her up and a lightness came into her. Her mind was empty and her father and grandmother were gone.

She sat up, rubbed her eyes clear of tears, and looked out at the water. Light glimmered on the edges of waves. The turtle was gone. She imagined it swimming away under the surf.

She felt new to herself. Light and unburdened.

She stood, stared at the water for a few minutes, then reached into her pocket and retrieved the coin her grandmother had given her. She flipped it.

***

She walked for twenty minutes before returning to the room.

"I need to see my father," she said to Alex, who greeted her at the door.

"Have you been crying?"

"Yes, but it's okay. I do that sometimes."

"What's going on?"

"It's … hard to explain. But I'm okay now. Really. I'll tell you about it sometime. Did you reach Sonia?" She sat at the desk and stared out the window.

Alex stepped toward her and put his hand on her shoulder. "You have sand in your hair." He brushed it gently onto the floor. "Are you hungry?"

"I don't know. I'm fine. Just tell me what happened with Sonia."

Alex told her about the call with Juan, then, sensing that she wanted to be alone, he went to the balcony and did twenty minutes of yoga.

When he came back into the room, Camila was emerging from the bathroom, her hair wet from the shower. "I'll stay until after we meet Sonia," she said. "After that, I'm going to see my dad."

Chapter Forty-Six

Thursday, September 12, 2002

Sonia Hollinger's estate sat high on a bluff just outside the town of Kona. The taxi turned up a thin road cut into a rock wall. They were buzzed through an iron gate and took the long, steep driveway toward the house, passing trees heavy with pomegranate, mango, and avocado.

"Feels like we're going through a tropical jungle," Alex said.

Camila leaned her head out the window. "We kind of are."

At the top of the driveway, the taxi stopped in front of a sprawling, glass house. Alex took the driver's card as they got out and stared at the house's thick glass walls supported by stainless steel beams. The day was hot but not yet muggy.

They could see through the front of the house into the entryway, kitchen, and dining room, and out the back to a patio and garden. The house slanted sharply from front to back, giving the appearance that it didn't have a roof.

"Talk about modern," Camila said.

"I didn't know houses like this actually existed."

On the left, beyond a low fence covered in flowering vines, they saw a disappearing-edge pool tiled in light blue granite. They opened a small gate, walked between the pool and the house, and found a small glass door. Camila knocked.

When the door opened, Sonia Hollinger stood before them in layers of flowery silk robes that half-covered a yellow bikini. She wore full makeup and her blonde hair was held up with pins, exposing her long, tan neck.

"Good afternoon, darlings," she said, sipping a bright pink cocktail from a tall, narrow glass. "I'd invite you in but I prefer to be outside."

She led them around the side of the house to the pool, which was surrounded by tomato plants, banana trees, and patches of basil and cilantro. They sat at a glass table supported by a single piece of stone shaped like a giant octopus.

"You seem to have a lot of good things to eat here," Camila said. "What's the growing season like?"

"Aren't you sweet, honey," Sonia replied. "We grow all year here. Do you garden?"

"No. I live in a tiny box in Manhattan."

Sonia frowned and studied Camila. "You're Argentinian?"

"Yes, how'd you know?"

"I'm Brazilian-American. You have that look about you."

"I was born here," Camila said. "Never actually been there."

Sonia gasped into her hand with feigned shock then smiled. Just then, Juan emerged from the glass door on the side of the house wearing a red Speedo and no shirt.

"Juan, darling, yes," Sonia called, waving him over. "Drinks for our guests, please. They've come all the way from New York City to see me."

Juan walked over to the table and looked at Alex. "Hola," he said. "You want I should make you two of those?" He pointed at Sonia's drink, then placed his hand on her shoulder.

Camila and Alex looked at each other. Alex frowned. "I usually don't do juice," he said.

"Oh, don't be ridiculous, honey," Sonia said.

Camila smiled at Juan. "Two of whatever fruity cocktails you like to make."

Juan headed off to the kitchen and the three of them spoke for a few minutes about the weather, Manhattan, and the Santiago trial, which Sonia was following.

"The news you poor New Yorkers think is important is so … limited," she said, looking at Alex and sipping her drink. "We have thousands of men and women in Afghanistan and will soon be after Saddam. And you run front-page stories about a little imbecilic killer from NYU. I know you're just doing your job, but your bosses really ought to be ashamed of themselves."

Juan appeared with their drinks, set them on the table, then sat in a chair by the pool about ten feet away.

"Mrs. Hollinger," Alex said, "let me tell you a little bit about why we're here."

Her face tightened. "You're here because of Mac. You're not the first people to show up, you know. First there were the estate people and the lawyers. Then journalists, journalists, and more journalists. Then that little bitch Green. She called for weeks before I agreed to see her."

"Sadie Green?" Alex asked.

"Yes."

"Sonia," Camila said, "the man Santiago is accused of killing knew your husband."

"A lot of people knew my husband. So what?"

"Your husband taught John Martin at Tulane," Alex said.

Sonia pulled a cherry from her drink and sucked on it. "Yes," she said. "I met Mr. Martin briefly at Mac's funeral."

"It's the day of the funeral we want to ask you about," Alex said.

Sonia finished her drink and nodded at Juan, who stood and walked toward the kitchen.

"I was there as well," Camila said. "I went with John. We were together then."

"He was a little old for you, no?" Sonia looked at Alex and smiled, passing the cherry stem between her fingers. "This young man is ... much more suitable."

Juan returned and refilled their drinks from a tall pitcher.

"*Comida por favor*," Sonia said. She looked at Alex and Camila. "Are you hungry?"

Alex said no and Camila said yes, but Sonia wasn't listening and Juan was already gone.

"Sonia, please," Camila said. "At the funeral, we spoke with a man named Denver Bice."

"Yes, I know Mr. Bice. He was one of my husband's more successful students. No offense to Mr. Martin, of course."

"John and Mr. Bice were making polite conversation," Camila continued. "But then John said the strangest thing."

"Did he now?" Sonia said, sipping her drink. "You know, Juan is the most amazing cook. He came from Cuba as a boy, but I think a piece of his soul comes from each Latin country. He can cook anything. He worked all morning preparing lunch for you."

Juan walked out from the kitchen carrying a metal platter covered with thinly sliced steak, roasted vegetables, chunks of mango and mounds of grapes, salad, two loaves of bread, and three kinds of cheese.

"Please, help yourselves," Sonia said. "I barely eat."

"Sonia, if I can just tell you about what happened," Camila said.

Sonia nibbled a grape. "Please continue, honey."

"At the funeral, John said it was lucky for Mr. Bice that Mac, your husband, died when he did."

Sonia put the half-eaten grape on the table and sipped her drink. As Alex ate a slice of steak wrapped around a lettuce leaf, he watched Sonia closely. He thought he saw a slight flinch in her cheeks as she drank. When she put the glass down, she said, "Hmm, that could mean a lot of things."

Camila reached across the table and took her hand. "You know something."

"Yes, but …"

Juan appeared behind her and held her shoulders. "Sonia, maybe it's time for your rest." He held her arm as she stood, but she wobbled and tripped on her chair. He caught her before she could hit the ground and led her into the house.

Alex looked at Camila. "What the hell do we do now?"

Chapter Forty-Seven

Rak approached the door of the plane and squinted. The evening air was warm and he had never felt such humidity. He leaned back into the plane for one last breath of cold air, then took the stairs to the tarmac wearing dark blue jeans, a black blazer, and sunglasses. Within a minute, his skin was clammy. He knew right away that he did not like Hawaii.

After claiming his bags—a standard brown suitcase and matching laptop case—he took a taxi to the Marriott and checked in under the name Sven Goldberg, using an Israeli passport for ID.

A teenage bellboy took his bags and led him to the elevator. "Where ya from?" the bellboy asked.

"Am from New York, but I come from Israel originally."

The elevator was empty except for the two of them.

"New York City?" the boy asked. "Boy oh boy. Were you there on 9/11? We felt for you all, even out here on the islands. That musta been some kinda thing."

"Yes, I was there that day."

"What was it like?"

Rak stared up at the boy, who was tall and smiled down on him. "I tell you a joke," Rak said. "What is the favorite football team of the Al Qaeda men who flew into the towers?"

The boy looked away. "Uh, sir? I don't feel comfortable hearin' a joke about it, sir."

"The New York Jets," Rak said, laughing.

When the elevator stopped, Rak handed the boy a ten-dollar bill. "I can find the room from here."

***

In his room, Rak ate a club sandwich while watching a bright green gecko crawl across the sliding balcony door. It crawled back and forth, stopping occasionally to touch its nose to the glass.

When he finished eating, he inspected the thickness of the glass door and the space it retracted into. There was about a quarter inch of space between the door and the doorjamb. He looked out the sliding glass door onto a vast lawn below, where a few staff members in crisp shirts were setting up a buffet under a tent. A woman stuck wooden torches in the ground every ten feet or so.

Rak looked back at the gecko, sitting still in the center of the door. With a sudden jerk of his arm, he slid the door open. The gecko slid with the door, its tail and the lower half of its body wedging into the thin space between the door and the opening, then exploding as the force of the door carried its body further in.

He picked up a cloth napkin from his room service tray and stepped onto the balcony, then closed the door and wiped the gecko's guts off the glass. What was left of the carcass had fallen to the ground. Rak used the napkin to pick it up and toss it over the side of the balcony, then went back inside and put the napkin on top of his half-eaten sandwich.

After showering, he dressed in the same clothes he'd been wearing earlier, then took the elevator down to the lobby.

Chapter Forty-Eight

Alex and Camila were sipping drinks in the pool, wearing swimsuits Juan had found them. Thick clouds had settled over the house and the sky was darkening, but they could see far out into the Pacific over the fruit trees. They heard pots and pans clanging in the kitchen and smelled smoke and pork.

"I didn't know situations like this really existed," Alex said. "I feel like we're in a cheesy sitcom about a rich widow. Why do you think Juan asked us to stay?"

Camila swam to him and sat on the steps of the shallow end of the pool. "She knew something, right?"

"Yes, she did."

"Maybe Juan wants to help us."

"Maybe. I think she knows something about Sadie Green. Do you know of her?"

"I've heard the name," Camila said, dunking her head in the pool.

When she came up, Alex said, "She's the director of the Media Protection Organization. Right up your alley, actually. They lobby against media conglomeration and for things like net neutrality."

"I'm not politically active."

Alex smirked, "Yeah, no kidding. Why is that, anyway? From what you said in class, I would have thought you'd care about this stuff."

"I do, and I'm happy people like her are out there. But we're living in the path of an avalanche. Digital media will smother us in the next twenty years. There's no stopping that on a political level. Anyone who thinks they know how it's going to go—or how it *should* go—is naïve about how technologies develop. But, on a personal level, we can still protect ourselves from what's coming. We can safeguard our inner lives against turning into ones and zeroes."

Alex swam the length of the pool and back without coming up for air. Breathing a little harder, he said, "Sonia said Sadie Green was in touch with her after Hollinger died. Why would that be?" He swam another lap and came up breathing even harder this time.

"Didn't you already work out today?" Camila asked.

"Yeah, but I'm drinking all these sugary cocktails. It wouldn't hurt you to—you know—move your body in a manner that raises your heart rate. I'm not sure they have it in academia, but in the outside world we call it exercise. It's like eating but without the food."

Camila splashed him and swam to the deep end of the pool. Alex swam after her. They reached the wall at the same time and both hung on with one hand, facing each other.

"Can you stand up here?" Alex asked. Camila let herself sink to the bottom and extended her toes, leaving only her eyes above the water. "You're short," Alex said.

"Is that your way of flirting with me?"

"I guess so. I feel a bit like a first grader who throws sand on the girl he likes at recess."

She splashed him again. "Yeah, that's how you seem." She fished a few leaves out of the water and placed them on the edge of the pool, then she turned to him and studied his face. "Do you know why you feel so much anxiety about me?"

He turned to look out toward the ocean. "Kind of."

"You're afraid of what you might feel, afraid of getting hurt, and you know I won't take care of you."

"Why won't you?" he asked, sliding toward her along the wall but still not looking at her.

"I don't do that."

He turned to look into her eyes. "Why are you so … I don't know … stiff, hard, distant?" He leaned toward her but she tilted her head away slightly.

"You just said three words that mean the same thing. Writers aren't supposed to do that."

Alex pulled himself up and sat on the edge of the pool. "What about your dad?" he asked. "Yesterday, you said that you needed to go see him."

"I will," she said. "I figured out yesterday that I will."

"How? I mean, how did you figure it out?"

"Remember on the plane, what I said about the sadness without cause?"

"Yeah, I remember."

"It turns out it's not my fault. None of it is. None of it is me."

"Whose fault is it?"

"No one's. It's just what happens."

"When will you go?"

"I want to give this another day or two." She splashed him again. "Plus, you'd miss me too much if I left. You'd positively fall apart without me." She spoke with a high-pitched English accent, the back of her hand against her forehead. "You wouldn't know what to *do* without me, you'd—"

Alex looked up when he heard a door close. Juan was walking toward the pool.

***

Juan had led them to a spare bedroom. While Camila changed in the bathroom, Alex turned on the wall-mounted TV. He flipped to CNN.

A red, white, and blue graphic on the bottom of the screen read, "WMDs in Iraq?" Two men in their fifties sat at a desk, a moderator in a bowtie sat between them.

The man on the left said, "The International Institute for Strategic Studies is saying that Iraq does not have any nuclear weapons—a point our president has been trying to obscure for months. And our national media has printed dozens of anonymous quotes, all hinting at WMDs. But there's no actual evidence."

The man on the right said, "The IISS report is full of speculation and innuendo. Tomorrow the president will issue a new report detailing a decade of deception by Saddam Hussein and the Iraqi military. It will show them to be an imminent threat to the United States. And—"

The man on the left interrupted. "But will it show *any* proof of WMDs?" He looked at the moderator. "And will your network *demand* any proof? And—"

The moderator interrupted. "And I hope we can have you both back to debate that report in the coming weeks. I'm afraid that will have to do it for today. Up next—"

Alex switched to Court TV and saw Cynthia Baker, Santiago's lawyer, walking down the courthouse steps flanked by two assistants. Photographers and journalists snapped pictures and shouted questions at her.

Camila walked out of the bathroom, smiling. "Have you ever been in a bathroom with heated floors?" she asked. "They're incredible."

"Shhhh!" Alex held up a hand and turned the TV up as a reporter's voice came in over the images.

"The fifth day of the murder trial of NYU student Eric Santiago concluded earlier today with prosecutors calling their second witness, twenty-four-year-old Tamar Joseph, a law student, who testified to seeing Santiago in Washington Square Park on New Year's Eve 2001—the night that Professor John Martin was killed."

Camila sat next to Alex on the bed.

"Defense Attorney Baker, in cross-examination, tried to discredit the witness, questioning whether she could have seen Santiago clearly given that she admitted to drinking heavily at a party that night.

"In one stirring exchange, lead prosecutor Daniel Sharp objected to Ms. Baker's line of questioning, arguing that bringing up Ms. Joseph's drinking was an inappropriate attempt to smear her. In his objection, he cited Matthew 5:10—'Blessed are they which are persecuted for righteousness' sake.'"

Alex muted the TV and looked at Camila, who was smiling.

"What was it before?" she asked. "John 12:25?"

Chapter Forty-Nine

They joined Sonia around a small black table in an informal dining room off the kitchen. Photos of Hollinger's children hung on the wall next to a large, framed black and white photo of a boy standing in front of a dugout. Lou Gehrig's arm was draped around his shoulder.

"Is that Mac?" Camila asked, pointing at the picture.

"Yes, it's from 1927, when Mac was ten. He loved the Yankees, and Gehrig especially. Thought he embodied America. Excellent mind, excellent body, and a work ethic that wouldn't allow him to waste it."

Alex looked up at the photo, recalling Gehrig's streak of 2,130 games played. Fourteen years without missing a day of work. "I wanted to ask you, Sonia, if you hate the papers so much, why do you invest in them?"

Sonia looked toward Juan, who was carrying in a steaming platter of shredded pork with handmade corn tortillas, guacamole, pineapple relish, roasted corn and peppers, and a half dozen stone bowls filled with garnishes. When he put the platter down, Sonia turned to Alex. "As I said before, Juan is a brilliant chef, among his many talents. Now, how long have you two been together?"

"We're, um, not together," Alex said. "About the newspapers."

"Oh, I have nothing to do with the investments," Sonia said. "Mac handled all that. We had our arrangement and I had plenty to live on, but I never got involved in the finances."

Alex felt irritated and impatient. He didn't know if it was the sugar in the drinks, his conversation with Camila in the pool, or the thought of Sharp using him to sabotage his own case, but he had an urge to get to the point.

"But you *are* involved now, Mrs. Hollinger. Sorry to be blunt, but you are still the single biggest investor in Standard Media. You own ten percent of the biggest media company in the world, which is about to merge with the biggest cable and Internet provider in the world. Surely you must know that."

"Yes, I own a lot of things now."

Camila layered a tortilla with pork, guacamole, diced cucumbers, and charred chilies, then squeezed some lime juice on top and took a bite. She looked over at Juan, who stood in the corner. "I would marry you," she said to him with her mouth full. "*Te amo.*"

"I told you he was amazing," Sonia said.

Alex continued, "Earlier today you mentioned being pestered by Sadie Green. Would you be comfortable telling us what she wanted?" Alex tried to sound casual, but noticed that his hands were shaking as he reached for the hot sauce and shook it onto his pork.

Sonia poured herself a tall glass of red sangria. "I knew of her before Mac's death. She was one of many people my husband supported. She had some thing helping Africans. Personally, I never saw why we didn't just donate our money to the Church, or at least to veterans. But Mac liked to support all kinds of things. She started calling me right after 9/11. Can you believe that? While we were still searching for Mac?" She looked down at her glass, then emptied it and refilled it. "She said that my husband had planned to donate five hundred million to her little do-gooder media thing. Five hundred million! She claimed that my husband had agreed to it a few weeks before 9/11."

"What?" Alex said, almost standing up. He glanced at Camila, who was wiping tortillas in a pool of sauce on her plate. "Did she have any evidence of that?" he asked.

"No. I figured she was just trying to get me to feel sorry for her, trying to get me to give her some of Mac's money. A lot of folks did that, you know. Half of being rich is turning people down when they ask you for money. But the way she did it! A few days after America had been attacked? While I was still searching for my husband? She was off-putting, to put it kindly."

"Did you give her any money?" Alex asked.

"My husband's will had her little group in there for a quarter million out of his cash reserves. So I *had* to give her that when his will was settled. But I wasn't about to add anything to it."

Camila said, "Sonia, when she approached you about the money, did she seem desperate or demanding? Did it *feel* like a con?"

Sonia picked up a long metal fork and stabbed at a grape floating at the bottom of the sangria pitcher. "You know how in Argentina you have big cookouts?"

"Well, I was raised in Iowa, but I know the tradition," Camila said.

"What a pity, darling. In Brazil, we had *churrasco* the last Sunday of the month after church. The whole family came over and my father cooked. We talked some politics but mostly football—you know, soccer—and ate all day and drank beer and then whisky. Sometimes my father let my big brother tend the meat, which had to be done very carefully. Spray the fire, keep it just right, rotate the meat. It was the most important position in the family on *churrasco* day.

"My little brother always wanted to tend the meat, but my father never allowed it. My big brother would spray him with the water bottle if he even got close to the fire. He could drink sangria when he was twelve but could never get near the coals. He used to demand it, then beg, cry, and pout. He was not good at taking no for an answer." She nibbled on a cucumber slice. "Sadie Green was like that. Anyway, even if Mac had been considering what she said, he didn't actually do it. And I wasn't going to help her. Not with the way she treated me."

***

After the meal, they accepted Sonia's offer to have Juan drive them to their hotel. Minutes later, they were speeding toward town in the back of a silver Mercedes convertible. Latin dance music blasted through speakers in the seats and they rode without speaking. Alex's head spun.

When they got into town, Juan turned down the music. "You believe her story?" he asked.

Alex and Camila looked at each other. Alex said, "We, uh. I'm not sure what to think. What story?"

Juan made a sharp right turn into the hotel parking lot. "Green. The girl. You believe her story about the money?"

"We're really not sure," Alex said.

"Yes, I believe her story," Camila said. "I think John Martin was murdered because he knew about Mr. Hollinger's intention to sell stock and give the money to Sadie Green."

Alex glared at her. She shrugged.

"But who knows what really happened?" Alex said loudly.

Juan stopped the car in front of their hotel, then turned in his seat and smiled. "I have to get back to Sonia now," he said, "but there is something I need to tell you."

Chapter Fifty

Friday, September 13, 2002

Alex rose early and went to the business center. First, he researched Sadie Green and the Media Protection Organization. He found their tax records for the last ten years, along with dozens of press releases most of the newspapers had ignored. He learned that Sadie Green had been hired in early 2000 and that donations had risen by fifty percent in her first year. Donors were not listed by name, but Alex assumed the increase was due to her relationship with Hollinger. After reading for an hour, Alex thought he understood the mission of MPO and the particular slant that Sadie Green brought to this mission. Their four biggest priorities were slowing media conglomeration, reversing the deregulation that had occurred during the 1980s, increasing funding for public media, and protecting net neutrality. He printed out a typical MPO press release to take back to the room for Camila.

Next, Alex looked up Daniel Sharp, landing on his official bio on the New York City Web site. Sharp was born and raised in the Bronx and attended Princeton and Harvard Law before serving as a Law Clerk from 1988-1990. After seven years in private practice, Sharp became assistant DA in Manhattan. Alex couldn't find anything on his religious affiliation, but he did learn that Sharp had attended the top-ranked Catholic high school in the city. Alex still could not believe that Sharp would sabotage his own case, but he could see how, if played right, a mistrial in the Santiago case might raise his profile more than a conviction would.

***

When he returned to the room, Camila was sitting on her bed wearing a bright orange cloth wrapped like a sari.

"Visit the gift shop?" Alex asked.

"I was sick of wearing those clothes from the airport. I got you a present." She threw him a balled-up t-shirt, which splayed out as it flew through the air. Its pre-faded yellow fabric bore blue lettering that read: "It's hard work looking this good." The two sets of *o*'s looked like pairs of sunglasses.

"Uh, thanks," he said. "This will go great with those Hawaiian shorts you're so fond of." He was distracted by the gift and felt short of breath. He hadn't been prepared for her to do something nice. "I need to run. The sugar in those drinks is messing with me."

He changed into his shorts in the bathroom. "Come for a run with me," he said when he came out.

In response, Camila fell forward onto the bed.

"C'mon," Alex said, pulling her up and pushing her toward the bathroom. "I'll read you something as you change."

Camila sighed and Alex read loudly in his "evening news" voice as she changed in the bathroom, the door slightly ajar.

"Thousands Sign Petition Urging FCC and Congress to Act on Net Neutrality. June 20, 2000. For immediate release.

"The Media Protection Organization (MPO) submitted a petition to Congress and the FCC today that was signed by over 20,000 citizens. It urged Washington to protect Internet neutrality and block corporate mergers."

"Do others find that voice as annoying as I do?" Camila called from behind the door.

"Yes, they do," Alex said. He continued in his normal voice. "The petition is part of MPO's effort to slow the rapid conglomeration of media resources that has taken place since the unprecedented deregulation of the 1980s. In particular, it is aimed at stopping efforts by Standard Media and others to consolidate control of information by abandoning the decades-old custom of treating all data on the Internet equally."

He paced in front of the bathroom door and continued loudly. "According to MPO Executive Director Sadie Green, 'These companies want to be the gatekeepers of the Internet. It's just a matter of time before rich people can get their data through, or get their sites to load, and poor people can't. This would kill competition, kill freedom of information, and kill the Internet as we've come to know and love it. Though the companies argue that they funded the broadband networks, MPO and the petitioners recognize the fact that the basic infrastructure was publicly funded, with private companies providing only the 'last mile' of wiring. Essentially, these companies want to take a public resource—the pipes and wires that make the Internet work—and privatize them for profit.'"

Alex looked up as Camila emerged wearing a white swimsuit top and the new orange cloth tied into a skirt just below her navel. "You look amazing."

She looked at him and smiled. "You know how I said I'm not very political? If I was gonna be, it would be about net neutrality."

"Why?"

"She's right about the Internet. Most of it was designed and built with Pentagon money. Now a handful of companies want to privatize the profit. If I were teaching this week, I'd be laying out how the press plays a huge role in shaping our identities—how we see ourselves and know ourselves—and how the net is the first time in a long time that there's been a chance for a real diversification of voices. Not that information alone will save anyone, but it's a decent start. And the fact that Standard Media and others want to control the Internet can't be anything but bad for actual people."

***

They jogged down the beach toward town, the sun peeking over the hills to their right and casting long shadows on the beach. "MPO is one of the most savvy and well-organized media groups," Alex said. "They're not very big, but they're growing, probably because of the influx of cash from Hollinger. So, let's say it's true that he was going to take five hundred million out of Standard Media and give it to MPO. That would hammer the stock, right? But Standard Media is finalizing the deal to merge with Nation Corp. and—"

"Gotta … walk … for … a … minute," Camila stammered between breaths. "I … know about … the deal."

They slowed to a walk.

"It's not the time you want a world-famous financial guru divesting," Alex said. "And it's also not the time you want him giving five hundred million to a company that's going to do everything in its power to keep the deal from happening. Can you imagine the negative PR they could have thrown on the deal with that money?" Alex gave her a nudge and they started jogging again.

"I don't think they could have stopped it," Camila said, still trying to catch her breath. "Even with all that money."

"Maybe not. But if Sonia is right about Sadie's persistence, she could have caused a lot of headaches."

Camila looked at him and raised an eyebrow. "Oh, she's 'Sonia' now? What happened to 'Mrs. Hollinger'?"

"Jealous?"

She ran ahead of him a few steps. She was sweating and her skin had reddened.

"Try to land on your mid-foot, not your heel," Alex said. "So anyway, Hollinger tells Green and Martin that he's planning to make this move with his money. Let's say that's during the summer before 9/11."

"Okay."

"And then he dies on 9/11 before he could actually do any of it. At some point in October, maybe November, Sadie Green meets with Sonia and starts spreading rumors that Hollinger was going to make this move."

"Yeah."

"And then Martin says something to Bice at the funeral in December, showing that he knew Hollinger's plans."

"And then … Bice … has Martin killed." Camila was out of breath and slowed to a walk again.

Alex took her hand and they turned back toward the hotel. "If all that's true," he said, "then I have four questions. First, how and when did Hollinger tell Martin about his plans? Second, who else might Hollinger have mentioned his plans to? I can understand not telling Sonia, given their relationship, but maybe he mentioned it to one of his lawyers or financial advisors. Even if he didn't start making the move yet, he must have consulted someone. Third, if Hollinger told Martin, did Martin tell anyone else before he was killed?"

"He wouldn't have. He was constantly lost in his writing and barely thought about that kind of thing. If he didn't tell me, he wouldn't have told anyone else." She pulled her hand gently out of his. "What's your fourth question?"

"What kind of man is Denver Bice? What I mean is, if you learn about Hollinger's plans in October or November, then learn that Martin knew about them in December, why resort to murder? The law doesn't care if Hollinger *contemplated* changing his will. Bice must have known about the rumors for weeks before the interaction with Martin at the funeral. And Martin wasn't the only one who knew. Nothing was going to change, so why have Martin killed?"

"So you're saying he must have had another reason to want Martin dead? I don't know, maybe he was just being super-cautious. When I met him, he seemed like someone who was very practiced at concealing explosive rage. He came off as polite, even affable. But I could tell that he was the kind of guy who could get angry quickly if something didn't go as planned."

"I guess you don't get to where he is without being a bit megalomaniacal." They were approaching the hotel and Alex stopped and looked at her. "It comes down to what I said: what kind of man is Denver Bice?"

Alex's phone vibrated in his pocket. *Juan.* He flipped it open. "Are you ready to tell us what you wanted to tell us?"

"Yes, meet me at the pier by your hotel at three o'clock today."

Chapter Fifty-One

When they came back from their run, Camila toweled off and changed clothes, then went straight to the buffet. Alex took a quick shower, then called the courthouse.

Bearon picked up on the first ring. "You shouldn't be calling me here," he said.

"I need some help," Alex said, walking out to the balcony. "I'll be quick."

"You better."

First, Alex quizzed him on the Santiago trial, but Bearon knew nothing more than Alex had learned from the online reports and TV. "Sharp really seems to be enjoying himself," Bearon said. "Making sure to enter and exit with witnesses, leaking stuff to journalists. He's gonna be the most well-known Democrat in the city off this case."

"That's what I called to ask you about. I mean, if Santiago is innocent, couldn't that bring even *more* profile to the case?"

"What do you mean?" Bearon asked.

Alex closed one eye and focused the other on a wave moving toward the beach. "Sharp already has a good prosecution record. No one can call him soft on crime. To be mayor in a couple years, he needs money and exposure, right? And maybe some of the far-left voters?"

"He's already getting the exposure."

"But what if the case had some huge twist that wasn't his fault? Wouldn't that raise his profile even more?"

"I guess, but what are you getting at?" Bearon asked.

Alex paced the balcony. "Think about it. What if *he's* the guy who's been calling me? Maybe he *wants* the case to explode.

If Santiago is innocent, Sharp would get national exposure. Meanwhile, he appears magnanimous by dropping the case, blaming the police department. That would play well with some of the left-leaning voters."

"No way."

"I'm not saying I'm sure, but keep an eye out for me, will you? What are you hearing about the Demarcus Downton investigation?"

"Well, folks from *The Post* are telling everyone that the police used the sketch from their story to ID a Ukrainian assassin named Dimitri Rak."

"Sounds like *The Post*," Alex said. "Rak? Like R-A-K?"

"Yeah, Dimitri Rak. Once the police matched the sketch to the name, it leaked within five minutes. Apparently, he's already suspected in the killing of a member of the Polish legislature and a theater bombing in Belarus. Everyone is talking about it, but no one knows why a professional like him would kill a small-time pot dealer in Brooklyn. All sorts of theories flying around."

"Are there any rumors about a possible connection to the Santiago trial?" Alex asked.

"What? No. But there will be now. What's the connection?"

Alex watched a gecko crawl across the balcony. "Rak killed Professor Martin, too. I know how and I think I know why."

"What?"

"Bearon, I need you to listen. I can't say anything more but I wouldn't mind if that rumor somehow slipped out, especially to anyone involved in the Downton investigation or the Santiago trial."

"If you're in Hawaii working the story, why would you want that leaked? Don't you want the scoop?"

"I wouldn't mind the scoop," Alex said, "but I may not be able to break the story in any real way. Meanwhile, I've got to get Santiago off."

"Are you sure on this? If I spread this around, I could end up looking like a prophet or a fool."

"Have I ever been wrong? I mean on something like this?"

"There's never *been* anything like this," Bearon said.

"I guess that's true. And Bearon, one last thing. You cannot, must not, mention my name or where I am. Just say enough to get people to look into it. If you need to, mention a bartender named Damian Bale. He has information the police may be ignoring."

***

Camila returned to their room from the buffet and handed Alex a plate piled high with eggs and steamed vegetables.

"Thanks." He pointed to a napkin tied into a pouch in her other hand. "What's that?"

"For later," she said, unfolding the napkin and setting two blueberry muffins on the desk. She handed Alex a couple of pieces of folded paper. "Did a little research. That's everything I could find on the Internet about Hollinger divesting."

Alex scanned the articles. Both were short pieces printed in October 2001—one from *The Standard* and one from *The Post*. Both quoted only one unnamed source. He crumpled them up and threw them across the room into the garbage. "Just business gossip. Nothing substantial," he said. "Looks like Green didn't have much luck spreading her rumor around."

"I guess not. Did you reach Bearon?"

"Yeah, and I forgot to tell you, I researched Sharp a bit. Looks like you could be right about him sabotaging the Santiago case."

"So, what's your next move?"

"I don't think it will do any good, but, after we find out what Juan knows, I'm gonna call him."

Chapter Fifty-Two

They walked a mile down the beach and out onto a pier. The sun was right overhead and the day was unusually hot and dry. Alex turned toward the beach and saw Juan walking down the pier. "Let me ask the questions, okay?"

"Fine, I think he was into you anyway."

Alex looked at her, squinting into the sun. "I think he's into Sonia."

"The two aren't mutually exclusive."

As Juan strolled down the pier, he pulled off his shirt, revealing an evenly tanned physique. "*Qué bolá?*" he asked, leaning up against the railing and looking at Alex.

"So, what do you know?" Alex asked.

"Let's walk," Juan said, stepping between them and walking down the pier toward the beach. They walked in silence until they reached the sand.

Juan glanced at Alex. "What the Green girl says is true."

"How do you know?" Alex asked.

"A few weeks before the attacks, I overhear Mr. Hollinger have a call." They turned up the beach.

"With who?"

Juan laughed and patted Alex on the back. "I can only hear one side of the call, Mr. Alex."

"What happened on the call?"

"I hear Mr. Hollinger talking about selling stock. He was talking about selling it slow, kept saying he wanted to 'do it right.'"

"Did you listen to his calls often?" Camila asked.

"Sometimes. When you work for a family like I do, and they trust you, sometimes it's okay."

"Then why aren't you telling this to Mrs. Hollinger?" Alex asked.

"She has been so upset since Mac died. This would just upset her more."

"On the call, did he mention Sadie Green?" Alex asked. "Or what he planned to do with the money?"

"No, but he said five hundred million. So when that girl came around, I knew she was telling the truth."

They stopped when they came to a cabana on the beach that rented snorkel gear and boogie boards. Alex picked up a red snorkel mask and turned it over and over in his hands. "Why do you think he would want to give away all his money?"

"Five hundred million is not *all* his money. He have lots of money. But I don't know why."

"Juan, this is important." Alex set down the mask and put his hand on Juan's shoulder. "Can you remember the day that call took place? The date and time?"

"No."

Alex let go of Juan's shoulder and picked up the snorkel mask again. "What month was it?" he asked.

"One or two weeks before he died. Maybe late August."

"What else? Was it morning or night?"

"It was at night, after dinner, so six or seven."

"Can you remember anything else? What was he doing that day?"

"I don't remember," Juan said. He thought for a moment. "Wait, Mr. Hollinger was watching the Yankees after dinner. He always do that."

"Who were they playing?"

"I don't follow baseball."

"What color were the uniforms?"

"I don't know."

"Do you remember anything else? Was the game in Yankee stadium?"

Juan thought. "I think so. I remember he always wore his old-time Yankees hat when they played there."

The man at the cabana came up and put his hand on the snorkel mask that Alex was still passing from hand to hand. "Can I help you?" he asked.

Alex put the mask down, shaking his head, and the three of them walked toward the parking lot near the pier.

"How long have you worked for the Hollingers?" Camila asked.

"Six years. I started as a cook for Sonia. I also do personal training, so I work her out, too. After a year, I start traveling with them between New York City, New Jersey, and here."

Alex said, "Can you tell us what he was like? I'm trying to get a sense of why he might decide to give away a half billion dollars."

"He was a good man. Not like most rich men. He did not do evil with his money. He was—what do you call it? A believer. He believed in doing right."

Alex smiled. "And somehow Sadie Green convinced him that giving her five hundred million was right. This is going to sound totally out of left field, but—"

"Left field?" Juan asked.

"It's an expression," Camila said. "It means random. *Loco.*"

Juan smiled. "Okay, out of left field."

"Mr. Hollinger was found in the rubble of the Marriott, right?" Alex asked.

"Yes."

"Did you hear anything from him on the morning of 9/11? He was in the tower that was hit second, so maybe he called Sonia after the first plane hit."

"No, we were at home that morning, working out. Mr. Hollinger called at noon every day. He would go out to lunch at eleven and call her from the pay phone on the way back."

"Why a pay phone?" Camila asked.

"He didn't have a cell phone. Still carried change in his pocket like in the old days. Plus, I think he don't want his staff to hear him talking to his wife. He was—how should I say? Needful of her."

"Whipped?" Alex asked.

"He was an old man, happy to have a beautiful and younger wife."

When they reached the silver Mercedes, Juan sat on the trunk. The top was down and the scent of hot leather wafted up from the seats. "Speaking of phones," Alex said, "can you write down the numbers of his Hawaii house, his estate in New Jersey, and his office?"

"Why?"

"We want to see if he called John Martin in the weeks before he died."

Juan took Alex's notebook and wrote down the numbers. "I need to go. Sonia thinks I am at the store."

"Why are you helping us?" Camila asked.

Juan got in the car. "That Santiago kid. I read all the stuff they say about him and I don't think he did it from the beginning. My cousin is a boy like him. Played baseball in Cuba and now plays in college in Arizona. Something goes wrong on the team, they blame him. So, when you say you don't think he did it, I want to help."

***

At the business center Alex found an online baseball almanac. In August 2001, the Yankees had played five series at Yankee stadium. Juan had said the call happened toward the end of the month, so Alex eliminated the series with the Rangers, Angels, and A's, all of which occurred before August fifteenth.

The Yankees played three games against the Mariners from August seventeenth through nineteenth, then took a nine-day road trip before starting a three-game series with the Blue Jays on August twenty-eighth.

The only night game in the Mariners series was on August seventeenth. In the Blue Jays series, all three games were at night. He made a mental note: The call Juan was talking about took place on either August seventeenth, twenty-eighth, twenty-ninth, or thirtieth, between 6 and 10 p.m., eastern. Now he needed Hollinger's phone records.

Next, Alex called Sadie Green at the MPO office. A secretary told him she was in meetings, but promised to tell her he'd called.

Chapter Fifty-Three

Saturday, September 14, 2002

Sadie Green called the next morning as Alex pulled on the Hawaiian shorts he'd borrowed. Camila was still asleep so he grabbed his phone and walked to the balcony. The sun was coming up and the ocean sparkled, but the lawn in front of him remained shadowed. "Hello?"

"Is this Alex Vane? Your paper is an abomination—an excretion—and anyone who works there is the scum of the earth." Her voice was high and she spoke fast.

"What if this hadn't been Alex Vane?" he asked.

"Aren't you embarrassed to be working for that rag? We've issued forty press releases on critical national issues in the last year and you haven't picked up one of them. Your coverage of the buildup to this preplanned war is shameful. If we don't find any weapons of mass destruction over there, you guys will be on the hook for printing the bullshit quotes of 'unnamed official' after 'unnamed official.' Your paper is nothing more than a troupe of cheerleaders for this administration. And your absentee coverage of an unprecedented accumulation of power by a handful of media companies is criminally negligent, if not deliberately criminal." She paused. "So, how can I help you?"

"Feel good to get that off your chest?" Alex asked. "I know you've got a lot of reasons to hate journalists, but—"

"Hate journalists? How would *you* know? *You're* not a journalist, Alex. You're a typist. A stenographer for the devil. I love journalists—*real* journalists. I hate the media, and the mind-fucked, sycophantic reporters it creates. Like you, for example."

"Wow," Alex said, chuckling. "As much as I love being yelled at by you, those are complaints for another department. I'm calling to talk to you about Macintosh Hollinger."

The line was silent for a few seconds.

"What about him?" Her voice had softened.

"Well, I may as well come right out with it. Is it true that Mr. Hollinger told you he was going to donate five hundred million to MPO before he died?"

"It's about *fucking* time. I was expecting someone from the business section to call about this. Aren't you a court reporter?"

"Yes, why were you expecting—"

"I spread it around enough. You're about ten months late, but yeah, it's true."

"Ever heard the expression 'you catch more flies with honey'?" Alex asked.

"Go to hell. Are we on the record? Why are you calling me about this now?"

"Yes, we're on the record," Alex said. "I'm doing research for a piece on Mr. Hollinger and I've been in touch with his widow. She mentioned you."

"That bitch. I could barely get her on the phone. Then she ignored me."

"When did Mr. Hollinger make the pledge to you?"

"Mid-August of 2001."

"And it was a firm pledge, not just an idea he was tossing around?"

"Absolutely firm. I worked him for a year to get that donation. I earned it."

"Do you have notes on the meeting? Was anyone else there?"

"No one else was there. If I had anything solid, don't you think I would have challenged the will in court?"

"Yes, I assumed so. Did he tell anyone else about the donation?" Alex asked.

"Not that I know of. He said he was going to talk to his financial advisors and would make it official sometime in September."

"And who did you tell?"

"I told a couple members of my board of directors in strict confidence. I was gonna wait to get a letter from Mac and present it to the full board at our fall meeting."

"Did you tell anyone else before Mr. Hollinger died?"

"What does it matter?"

"It matters because … it just matters. Did you mention it to anyone else?" Alex watched a small group of birds run in and out of the shadows on the lawn below his balcony.

"No," she said at last.

"You didn't tell anyone else about the money before Mr. Hollinger died?"

"No."

"Do you know Denver Bice?"

"Of course I know him. He's the super-villain who masterminded this latest clusterfuck of a merger. He's like if Lex Luthor and Doctor Doom had a love child. You know he's aiming to take over control of the Internet, right? That's his endgame."

"When do you think he would have heard the rumors about the five hundred million?"

"I don't know. The rumors were around all fall. Once I knew Mac had died in the attacks, though, I told anyone who would listen. I talked to lawyers, but they all said the same thing. Without a change in his will, or any real proof, I had nothing. When I realized I wasn't getting the money, I drank for a few days, and then I told everyone I could think of. I figured maybe I could screw Bice and you guys at *The Standard* a little just by spreading the rumors."

"Thanks for that," Alex said. "I guess they didn't spread far. I didn't hear about them until the last few days."

"Look, I've gotta—"

"Just one more question. When exactly did you start talking to people?"

"I don't know, they found Mac in October and it took a few weeks for me to figure out we weren't getting the money. I started pestering reporters in November."

"There's no way Bice could have heard about the five hundred million sooner?"

"No. Not that I know of."

***

When he hung up, Alex went inside and found Camila sitting up in bed.

"The boxes of Martin's stuff should get here today," she said. "What do you think you're going to find?"

Alex sat on the foot of her bed, aware of her feet a few inches from his thigh. He wanted to hold them, but he didn't. He looked at her. "First, we might find out when Martin learned about Hollinger's financial plans. There ought to be a call between them sometime between August fifteenth and September eleventh. A phone record would at least give us a hint. And there may be something better. Maybe a journal entry, or a note scratched on a napkin. Something. And second, if we're lucky, there could be something about Bice. Something Martin wrote after the funeral and before he was murdered."

Camila smiled and poked him with her toes. "Or maybe something from *after* he was murdered," she said in a spooky voice.

"I'm serious," Alex said. "You know what I mean—something that hints at the interaction with Bice at the funeral. If we can figure that out, and if we can figure out who Hollinger spoke with on the phone the night Juan was talking about, we may have enough."

"Enough for what?"

"To publish."

"What good is that going to do? You can publish a story, but that doesn't mean we can go back home. Plus, who do you think is going to publish this?"

Alex stood up. "Once we publish, Rak will leave the country, if he hasn't already. The police are already after him for Downton. If Bice hired him to kill Martin, an article that even hints at that will be enough to keep them away from us. Any public scrutiny of Bice will force him to back off."

"For a while maybe, but he could still send someone else after us."

"Maybe. But what other choice do we have?" He paused and began pacing. "As far as where to publish, that's a good point. I'm not on the best terms with my boss right now."

The hotel room phone rang and Camila gave a start. "You didn't tell anyone we were at this hotel, did you?" she asked.

"No. Did you?"

"No."

They both stared at the phone for a moment.

Alex walked over to it. "Hello? Yes … yes, okay. Thank you." He hung up and looked at Camila, who was holding her breath. "The boxes are here," he said.

Chapter Fifty-Four

After a quick breakfast, they picked up two boxes from the front desk and carried them back to their room.

"Is this everything he had?" Alex asked, sitting on Camila's bed next to the boxes.

"No, the police took a couple boxes of papers and I took the stuff they didn't want. Old school papers, letters, bills—that kind of thing. I still haven't looked through a lot of this. His daughter came down and took some stuff, too."

They spent the next few hours sorting. They made a pile of phone records, one of other bills, one of student work and NYU correspondence, and one of personal papers and letters. When they finished sorting, Alex laid out the phone records and bills on his bed and left the other piles on Camila's bed.

"What should I look for?" she asked.

"Well, I'll work the phone records and you look for anything that refers to Bice and anything between August fifteenth and September eleventh that may indicate how Martin heard about Hollinger's plans. And anything relating to the interaction with Bice at the funeral."

***

By late afternoon, the sky was dark and they heard thunder in the distance. Alex had organized all the bills into reverse chronological order. Martin's last phone bill was from January 2002 and listed no calls. He read through the December, November, October, and September bills looking for incoming calls from one of Hollinger's homes. He found none.

Next, he looked for calls from Hollinger's office line. "Hollinger called Martin on July first and August twenty-eighth," Alex said.

Camila looked up from a stack of papers. "That's it?"

"That's enough. It must be the August twenty-eighth call. If he called on the twenty-eighth, they probably got together sometime between then and the eleventh. That must have been when Hollinger told him about his plans."

Next, Alex went through the rest of the calls and crossed out everything he knew would not be relevant—calls to information, Martin's daughter, NYU extensions, and all calls to or from Camila. In the end, he circled seventy-one calls he was interested in between August twenty-eighth and December thirty-first.

"What do you think they might show?" Camila asked.

"I can have James track down who owns all these numbers. Mostly, they're probably dry cleaning and food orders—that kind of thing. But maybe we'll find something interesting."

"Speaking of food orders," Camila said, "he ordered from a Chinese place on the corner every few days."

"Is it this one?" Alex pointed to a 212 number that came up twice per week.

"Yeah, that's it. I could really go for some of their Hunan shrimp right now. Somehow, they kept them crispy all the way to the door. Delivery guy must have had a deep fryer on his bike."

Alex crossed out another twenty-seven calls. "That's a lot of Chinese food. And it leaves forty-four calls to twenty-six different numbers spread over four months and twelve pages of phone bills."

"Now what?" Camila asked.

"Now we fax this to James Stacy and pray."

Chapter Fifty-Five

They ate dinner in the hotel restaurant then walked to the beach. It had rained earlier in the evening but the clouds had passed and a bright moon lit the water as they walked away from the town and its lights. After a mile, they lay on their bellies on the wet sand, chins resting on their folded arms, watching the surfers, whose outlines they could see in the moonlight far out on the water. The beach was quiet except for an occasional car passing on the road behind them.

Alex pointed to a spot where the moonlight hit the foam on the crest of a wave, turning it silver before it crashed into darkness. "Watch," he said, "it'll happen again."

Camila shot up onto her elbows. "Something's not right."

"What?"

"A car. I heard a car running. Now it's off." Camila sat all the way up and turned toward the parking lot. It was lit dimly by a few streetlights and looked deserted.

"What's going on?" Alex asked.

"Shhhh."

Alex sat up.

With her eyes still on the lot, Camila leaned over and put her mouth next to his ear. "A car parked a few minutes ago," she whispered. "I heard it come into the lot. It was idling. I barely registered it, but it just turned off."

"I didn't hear anything," Alex said.

They sat for a minute, their eyes darting back and forth, scanning the lot. A patch of the lot grew dark, then bright in a quick flash.

"What was that?" Camila asked.

"It was just one of the lights in the parking lot flickering. You're really on edge."

They sat for another minute.

"Camila, there's nothing there. Really." He threw a small handful of sand at her feet. "I'm beat, let's go back to the hotel."

She scanned the parking lot one more time and then allowed him to pull her to her feet and lead her down the beach. They walked in silence, Alex glancing at her every few steps.

Next to a pier near their hotel, a man fished from the shore. He had a five-gallon bucket and a small gas lantern sitting on a large cooler. They stopped and watched him cast far out into the water, then slowly reel his line back in.

Alex took her hand. "Can I ask you something?"

"If you skip the preliminaries."

"Do many of your students have tattoos?"

Camila laughed. "That's not what I was expecting."

"Downton had a tattoo. A few of them, but one in particular."

"I know. I was there when his mother brought it up."

The man with the fishing pole gave a hoot as his pole bent toward the water. Alex bit his cuticles as he and Camila looked on.

"What's bothering you?" she asked.

"Well, a bunch of things. But I see more and more kids with tattoos. Is this some generational thing I missed?"

The man sat on the cooler and wedged his feet into the sand, reeling steadily between jerks of his pole. An older couple that had been walking toward town paused behind the fisherman to take in the scene.

Alex watched the couple watching the man. "It's like, how can you feel solid enough? How can you know yourself enough—know *anything* enough—to get something tattooed on your body? You really have to believe, right?"

"You think all the people getting tattoos actually know what they're doing? I think a lot of them are just drunk."

"But they have something there, at least for a minute, something that feels real enough to act on. I just can't imagine that. Whenever I look, there's just nothing that … definitive in me."

The man unhooked the fish and dropped it on the beach. It flopped high at first, then lower, and finally just twitched in the lantern light, its silver-gray body covered in sand.

"I think there used to be," Alex continued. "I remember when I was little, I ran around like a wild man, full of energy, just loving everyone and everything. When my parents died, I fell apart for a couple years. Went on a bender. Got heavy. Then I regrouped, and since then it's like all that energy is pressed through a pinhole of work and exercise and women."

The couple strolled past them. The man put the fish in his bucket and walked toward the parking lot.

"That's a big fish," Camila said.

"But what should I do?"

"You need to relax."

"I'm afraid to."

"I know," she said. "You're trying to hold it all together."

Alex tried to catch her eye, but she was looking out at the water. "I've never been in love," he said. "But I think I am. With you."

"I know," she said. "Maybe you should try not to be."

"I can't help it."

"I know."

"But why should I try not to be?"

"I need to go see my father."

Camila turned away from the water. "Let's head through town. I want to get a shaved ice."

They walked to the road and left the beach at the beginning of the commercial zone. The same reggae band they'd seen their first night in Kona was playing on the sidewalk. As they approached, one of the band members called to Alex. "Hey mon, why dontcha buy a CD for the lady?"

Alex and Camila both smiled at him but they didn't stop, so he called after them, "Hey miss, make your man buy you a CD to rememba your trip!"

They passed a few stores selling t-shirts and sunglasses, then stopped to look in the window of a shaved-ice shop. A teenage girl set a giant cube of ice on a machine and stuck it into place with metal prongs. She pressed a button and a metal rod dropped onto the ice to lock it into place. She pressed another button and the rod rotated on top of the ice, shooting what looked like snow into a large paper cup. The piercing sound of metal scraping hard ice caused Camila to cover her ears.

Through the noise, Alex heard the steel drums and the man calling after passing tourists. "Hey you. Little man. You, want a CD? Hey, little man!"

Alex turned and saw Rak, a block away, walking briskly toward them. He was dressed in sunglasses and a bright blue shirt and his pasty white legs stuck out under tan capri pants. Alex recognized his mustache from *The Post's* sketch and was surprised by just how short he was.

Camila was still watching the girl catch the shaved ice.

Alex grabbed her hand. "Run!" he shouted.

She tried to look back but he was already pulling her forward.

Chapter Fifty-Six

They ran hard for a block, past shops and tourists, without once looking back. Alex slowed a few times to encourage Camila to keep up. When he finally glanced back, he saw that they were losing Rak, who was still walking.

"He's not running," Alex said, taking Camila's hand and slowing to a walk.

"What's ... going ... on?" Camila said, panting. "I knew I'd ... sensed something back on the beach."

They crossed Alii Drive onto the beach side of the street. Alex looked back every few seconds and saw Rak taking long strides with his short legs, now about two blocks away.

They passed the last of the streetlights and entered a shadowed stretch of sidewalk. Alex looked back at Rak, who was still visible under the last lights of the commercial zone. As Rak came under the light of the final streetlight, he broke into a slow trot, then a run.

"He's running," Alex said. He grabbed Camila's hand and pulled her for a long block. She was panting again as they slowed to let a few cars through an intersection. When the cars had passed, they took off again, but Camila tripped on the curb and fell into the street.

She screamed as cars swerved around them and Alex knelt by her side. Her hand was scraped and bleeding. She got up and immediately collapsed again. Alex looked down at her, then up at Rak, who was running toward them, now just a block away.

"Your ankle?" Alex asked.

"It's bad."

Alex moved into a crouch, took Camila by the waist, and lifted her up as he stood, draping her over his right shoulder as he slid between cars and crossed the intersection. On the other side of the street he stopped and looked back. Rak was only fifty yards away, arm extended, holding what Alex thought must be a gun.

Alex turned and sprinted, Camila still over his shoulder, her left arm clinging to his back. His mind was blank as he ran, lifting his knees high and straining to keep Camila level. After two blocks, he looked back again. Rak was now much farther behind and had stopped running.

"He's walking," Alex panted.

He jogged for another block then stopped. This time, when he turned to look back, he saw Rak walking in the other direction.

***

Alex dropped Camila onto the bed and slammed the door to their room. He slid the desk up against it, walked to the closet, and opened the safe. "The USB drive and the recordings are still here," he said. "At least he hasn't been in the room." He closed all the curtains and peeked through the window that looked out onto the stairway. Seeing no one, he sat on the bed next to her.

Camila gripped her ankle with both hands. She pressed it lightly for a moment, then pulled down her sock to reveal a red, swollen mass.

"What do we do?" Alex asked frantically. "I mean, we have to call the police, right? Rak knows where we are. He's here. I mean he's *fucking* here." He walked in small circles around the room, wanting to run and jump and smash things all at once. "I can't believe he's *here*."

Camila watched from the bed. "Alex, we're okay."

He took a few deep breaths, then sat on the bed and called the Kona police. "They'll be right over," he said when he hung up.

"He doesn't know we're in the hotel," Camila said, gently massaging her ankle.

"Why do you assume that?"

"If he did, he would have killed us already. This is a perfect place to kill us, right? No lobby to go through, just up a flight of stairs, kick in the door—or pretend to be room service—and bam!"

"You've thought this through."

"It's a good thing. Somehow he knew we were in Kona and—"

"Yeah, how did he know?"

"I don't know. Flight records? Maybe some other way. We're not exactly ninja spies here."

Alex went to the bathroom and emerged a minute later with a large towel soaked in cold water.

He stood beside the bed and Camila closed her eyes as he wrapped the towel around her ankle.

"Thanks," she said. "I mean, for carrying me and all."

He smiled at her, then looked up when there was a knock at the door.

"It's probably the police," Camila said.

Alex peeked through the window to see who was there, then slid the desk away from the door. Very slowly, he opened the door and, once they'd shown their ID, he invited the two officers into the room.

Pono Grady was in his early fifties, lean, and deeply tanned, with long brown hair. He sat in the desk chair as Alex sat down next to Camila on the bed. Samuel Balby, young and pudgy, stood beside the bed and took notes while Alex told them about Downton, Rak, and their chase through town.

When he told them that his apartment had been ransacked, Grady leaned back in his chair. "You didn't report it? Any man tears up my apartment, I report it."

"And I never heard of no assassin on the island," Balby added, looking up from his notes.

"Look," Alex said, "we were scared as hell, okay? We were on a plane a few hours later. This guy had just killed one of my sources and I have something he really, really doesn't want me to have."

"Look," Grady said, "it's not that I don't believe you. I do. But all you've got is a story about a man running after you, *possibly* with a gun. We're gonna do everything we can to find him, and to keep you safe. We'll check it out with the NYPD, but it's four in the morning over there, and they're pretty busy these days. We'll put Sammy here outside your door and check in on you tomorrow."

***

Once the officers left, Camila ordered room service and a bucket of ice. When it arrived, Alex wrapped her ankle in ice and towels as she made sandwiches with fresh crabmeat and dinner rolls. She ate by the sliding glass doors, looking out through a crack in the curtains and dipping her sandwiches in melted butter with lemon.

Alex sat at the desk, nibbling steamed vegetables and pushing an untouched steak around his plate with a fork. "When are you going to see your father?" he asked.

She didn't respond.

After finishing her second glass of sauvignon blanc, Camila grabbed a cup of chocolate pudding from the tray and turned to Alex. "You want some?"

"No."

"What do you think will happen if you try some?" She licked her spoon.

"I'll die," he said, smiling.

She hobbled over to him with a spoonful of pudding. "Just try one bite."

He sat up rigid in the chair, not looking at her.

"Seriously," she said. "One bite."

He rotated the chair toward her. She straddled his leg and held out the pudding.

"What are you doing?" he asked.

"I feel like a stripper."

His body stiffened as she sat on him. He looked into her eyes as she touched his cheek with the back of her hand. He felt softness and a burning lust, but both were immediately displaced by a hollow, sinking feeling. "What are you doing? I thought you said—"

"Straddling your leg and trying to get you to have some pudding." She moved the spoon toward his mouth and he took a bite.

His body tingled and his brain felt sharp. "I can feel myself retaining water already."

"What?"

"Never mind."

"Do you like it?"

"Kind of," he said. "But I kind of hate it too."

He could feel the sugar and the desire moving through him. He felt out of control and this made him angry, but he smiled at her. "Sugar is a drug," he said, trying to sound light.

She stared straight at him and adjusted her position on his leg, then squeezed his thigh by tightening both of hers. All of his awareness went to the place of contact between them and he forgot himself for a moment.

"Cam?" He stared at her. "Cam, what are you doing?"

She put the spoon in his mouth, swiveled off him awkwardly, and flopped down on the bed. "I don't know," she said.

Alex took the spoon from his mouth and put it on the desk. He looked at her on the bed, swallowed the pudding, then walked over and lay down on his own bed.

Chapter Fifty-Seven

Alex stared at the ceiling. "I'm never gonna be able to fall asleep," he said.

"Me neither."

"Let's go over this again. If we hunker down here, the police might catch him and—"

"And what if they *do* catch him?" Camila asked softly. "I say we send copies of the Santiago video to the police and the papers, you write up everything we've found about Hollinger, his money, Bice, and so on, and we disappear for a while."

Alex sat up and looked at her. Moonlight came through the curtains, lighting her face, but she was not looking at him. "We already tried disappearing," he said. "That's why we're here. Plus, the video won't be enough to get him off. They need Rak to confess—or they need some evidence on him. If they get him, maybe he'll flip on Bice. Plus, I still have the Martin calls to track down, and the phone records to get from Sonia. With another few days, I think we can get enough solid evidence to nail this thing."

She rolled over onto her side with great effort. Ice spilled onto the bed. "And then what? Even if you get evidence that Bice hired Rak to kill Martin and Downton—and us, for that matter—he will never do jail time."

"Well, I think that—"

"You can't actually be that naïve, can you?"

He rolled toward the wall.

"Bice's company has more power than most of the governments in the world," she continued. "He has the power to ruin any prosecutor, any police chief, almost any politician. You think your news story will bring him down? Plus, he *owns* your newspaper. It's bad luck. We got caught in the middle of a storm, the kind I usually like to avoid. It's just really bad luck."

He turned toward her and tried to make out her shape in the darkness. "But what about Santiago? Even if we can't get Bice, or Rak, at least we can get Santiago off. Isn't that worth doing?"

"That video isn't going to get Santiago off. Like you said, you need some evidence on Rak. Maybe the police get him on the Downton murder, but that's not necessarily going to get Santiago off."

They were both quiet. "Look," she said after a few minutes. "It's over, okay?"

"Maybe you're right, but I'm gonna try anyway."

They lay without speaking for a few more minutes. Finally, Camila said, "Do you hear the waves on the beach? They're faint."

Alex listened. "No, I don't."

"Remember what you said about being a little kid, running around, loving everyone and everything? It's still there. You just need to relax a little."

"I don't know how to relax without falling apart."

"Then maybe you need to fall apart."

***

He awoke when her chilled and swollen ankle brushed against his calf. It felt cold and hot at the same time. He felt her soft skin glide across his thighs as she lay on top of him. He realized that she was naked. He'd never wanted anyone so badly.

"What are you doing?" he asked.

"I don't know."

When she kissed him he wanted to object, but he found himself kissing her back. He wrapped his arms around her and began to roll on top of her, then stopped when he felt her cold, swollen ankle press up against his leg. They lay entwined on their sides, kissing desperately. Suddenly, she pulled away from him and leaned back. For a moment, he was devastated. Then she brought her good leg up and gripped the band of his boxers with her toes. Alex raised his hips to assist her as she pulled them down.

His body sank into the bed.

He was powerless, his mind blank.

Chapter Fifty-Eight

Sunday, September 15, 2002

Alex slept hard. When he awoke, he rolled over and reached for her but she was gone. He walked naked into the bathroom, looking for her. He opened the curtains that led to the balcony and looked out. He sat on the bed and put on his boxers, then opened the front door. Pono Grady sat on a chair, reading a newspaper.

"Where did she go?" Alex asked.

"Don't know. She left an hour or two ago. I told her I'd send an officer with her but she wouldn't wait. I can't *make* people be safe. Plus, we're spread pretty thin as it is."

"What time is it?"

"About seven."

Alex looked out at the parking lot, hoping to see her but knowing he wouldn't.

"Your story made the front page," Grady said.

Alex looked at the paper in Grady's hands.

"Couple people saw the little guy you described, but we haven't found him. We did confirm with the NYPD that a guy named Dimitri Rak is under investigation for the murder of some basketball guy last week. Matches your description. So we're gonna keep an eye on you."

"Thanks." Alex walked into the room and looked around. There was a note on the desk.

> Heading to Des Moines. I'm sorry.
> -Cam

He put on his shorts and walked past Grady. "I'm going to the fitness center."

"Okay, but I'm coming with you."

***

As Grady watched from a chair, Alex jogged for ten minutes to warm up, then set the treadmill at nine miles per hour, telling himself he would run a 5K. After five minutes, he was dripping with sweat. He wore the t-shirt he'd been wearing when Camila had climbed on top of him. He breathed in the smell of his sweat mingled with a scent he couldn't exactly identify, but knew was hers.

He looked down at the flashing numbers. A mile and a half. Almost halfway there. He thought of the crash, imagined his parents burning inside their car as a light rain fell on Bainbridge Island. His chest felt weak and all he heard was the pounding of his feet. The sun was bright on the beach, which he could see through the floor-to-ceiling windows. "I will finish this," he said to himself. He choked back a few tears and glanced at the numbers again. Almost two miles.

He listened to the thumping of his feet and tried to picture her at the airport. He turned up the speed. The thumping grew faster and he turned all his focus to his feet and his legs. Don't stop. Don't stop.

He turned up the speed again. Only a half mile to go. The sensation in his head and torso disappeared and he felt only the pounding of his feet. Don't stop.

A few seconds later, he gave up and collapsed on the edge of the treadmill, panting with his head in his hands.

When he'd cooled down, he walked up to the room and showered. When he came out of the bathroom, he called Camila but her phone went straight to voice mail. He figured she might be on the plane by now. He looked at the clock: 9:45 a.m. He lay on the bed and stared at the ceiling, then leaned on his side, picked up the phone, and dialed room service. "Hello, do you have any pudding left from last night's dinner service?"

Chapter Fifty-Nine

After finishing two plates of macadamia nut pancakes, a chocolate-chip muffin, and a vanilla latte, Alex sat on the balcony, staring at the beach and eating a bowl of chocolate pudding. Once he'd licked the bowl clean, he walked around the room for a few minutes, looked at his phone, and did five pushups before collapsing onto the floor.

By noon he was asleep.

He awoke four hours later to the digitized, Muzak version of *In Bloom*. His head ached and he fumbled around the sheets for his phone. "Hello?"

"We've been f-f-fired. Both of us."

He recognized the hurried voice of James Stacy. "What?"

"You and me, we've been fired."

Alex sat up in bed. "Let me call you back."

He walked into the bathroom and splashed cold water on his face. He looked at himself in the mirror and pushed his cheeks in with his palms. "Damn," he said softly.

He walked down to the business center, trailed by Grady, who then waited just outside the door. He opened his e-mail and clicked on one from a *New York Standard* address he didn't recognize.

From: tmeyers@standardmedia.com
To: alex_vane@standardmedia.com
Subject: Employment Termination
Date: September 15, 2002 10:02:15 AM EST

Dear Mr. Vane,

We regret to inform you that your employment with the Standard Media Corporation has been terminated. This action is being taken due to a prolonged absence from work and a failure to contact your direct supervisor, Samuel Baxton, during this absence.

A formal letter of termination has also been sent to your residence.

Sincerely,
Tracy Meyers
Human Resources Director, Standard Media

Next he opened an e-mail from James, sent only half an hour earlier. He clicked an attached PDF of the phone bills he had faxed James the day before, then dialed his phone as he scanned James's handwritten notes in the margins.

When James picked up, Alex said, "So, I get why I've been fired, but how did they justify getting rid of you?"

"The Colonel was real nice about it. Said that the c-c-company is trying to tighten up its books for the m-merger. They were happy with my work but couldn't fund a full-time researcher. I guess all their old reporters are going to have to learn how to use the Internet."

Alex got up and paced the business center. His head hurt and he rubbed his eyes. "You got fired because of the video, because of me."

"But I don't know anything."

"It doesn't matter. I'll explain later." He sat back down at the computer. "I'm looking at the PDF. Do you have Martin's phone bills in front of you?"

"Yeah."

Next to each phone number that Alex had not crossed out, James had written a name or location.

"Talk me through this," Alex said.

"I'm still stuck on why they fired me. Even if I knew something, which I don't, why would they f-fire me?"

"I promise I'll explain soon."

James inhaled deeply. "Okay … from the top of the list, the first call you didn't cross out is from August twenty-eighth."

"Yeah, that one I knew. That's from Mac Hollinger."

"Yeah, it's listed to Sonia Hollinger. Next call is August twenty-ninth. That's Shen's grocery on Fourteenth Street. Then, later that day, the 845 area code, that's his daughter's cell phone. Next c-c-call is from the thirtieth, that's a movie theater in the Village."

Alex scanned down the list, confirming that the notes James had written in the margins of the bill matched what he was saying. Most of the calls were routine, but Alex noted a couple he wanted to follow up on.

When they got to September fifth, James said, "It took me a while to track this one down because payphones are listed s-separately."

"What is it?" Alex asked. "Where's the pay phone?"

"Well, it d-doesn't exist anymore. It's a phone that used to be at the World Trade Center Plaza. Incoming call that lasted only a m-minute."

"So Martin got a call from the World Trade Center Plaza on September fifth? What day was that?"

"Wednesday."

The call happened at 11 a.m. Alex thought it could have been a call from Hollinger to arrange a lunch with Martin. He filed it in the back of his mind. "Ok," he said.

"You circled eight c-calls between the fifth and the eleventh of September. Two were r-restaurants, one was his daughter's cell again, one was a dry cleaner on Fourth Street, two were a b-b-bank. Chase Bank in the Village."

"And the other two?"

"One was to Morgan Tubbs. He's a t-teacher at Tulane."

"Makes sense. Martin was a professor, and I assume they talk to each other."

"Then it gets s-strange."

Alex looked at the next call. "September eleventh, 9:37 a.m., an incoming call for a tenth of a minute."

"Probably an answering m-machine hang-up. That's from the s-same pay phone that c-called him September fifth. The one outside the t-t-t-t—" James coughed so loudly that Alex pulled the phone a few inches away from his ear. "The one outside the towers."

Alex stood up. "What?" He remembered what Camila had told him in the park: that a caller who hadn't left a message had woken her and Martin up on the morning of 9/11.

"What I'm saying is, someone called Martin from the payphone outside the t-towers about an hour after the first p-plane hit."

Alex's mouth opened slowly. There was a black expanse where his mind had been a moment before. He saw Macintosh Hollinger emerging from the World Trade Center, alive. Then the distorted, metallic voice came to him: *There are three.*

James was still speaking. "There's no way of knowing if the call came from the same person, but it's odd, right? That someone would call Martin from that phone right after the t-towers were hit? I mean—"

"James, I need to call you back."

Chapter Sixty

Camila looked at the caller ID from the passenger seat of her mother's green station wagon. *Alex Vane.* She put the phone in her purse as her mother turned the car into the driveway of her childhood home.

"How was the flight from New York?" her mother asked.

"You already asked me that. The flight was fine. What's Papa doing tonight?"

"And tell me again what happened to your ankle, dear. I'm just so worried about you."

"I tripped on the stairs. What's Papa doing tonight?"

Her mother shut the car's engine off and turned toward her. She'd developed lines on her forehead and below her eyes, and wore thick makeup that reminded Camila of a spray tan. "Watching football. He was watching the news about Iraq, but it upsets him. I wish he wouldn't watch the news. The hospice lady came earlier today. Bathed him nicely. We gave him new meds so he's more comfortable now."

"Mama, can we go in?"

"Yes, dear, let's go in. But don't expect much from him, Cam. I know you've had your issues with how he was when you were a child, but now is *not* the time to address those concerns. You know how quiet he is these days, right, Cam?"

"Mama, it's okay. I'm okay now."

They got out of the car. Camila stopped and stared. The small house had a newness that surprised her. No flood of memories or past associations. The steps and the windows and the yard all looked familiar, but they no longer had the quality of memory.

"The leaves are about to come off the oak," her mother said, pointing at the tree on the side of the house. Camila nodded and limped up the steps.

The house smelled of bacon and lavender air freshener. Her father sat half-reclined in a tattered blue chair in the living room watching football with the sound off. She stared for a moment at the thick, rust-brown carpet and remembered playing on it as a girl.

He looked up when she walked in. "Oh, it's you. Hi. I can't get up." Camila tried to meet his dark eyes, which were set far back in his head, but he looked down at his lap. He smiled for a moment before looking back at the screen.

Camila went to him and kissed his cheek, which was prickly and cold. Then she walked into the kitchen with her mother and put her bag on the floor. The kitchen was warm, with beige cabinets and an orange electric stove from the seventies.

Her mother opened the fridge and rooted around for something. "So, why did you finally decide to come?" she asked, her head in the fridge. "I'd given up on you."

"I came to see Daddy."

"You missed your cousins."

"I know. I'm sorry."

Her mother pulled her head out of the fridge and closed the door. She held a plastic jug of milk and a small can of chocolate syrup with drips down the side. She looked at Camila. "Why didn't you come sooner?"

Camila looked at the hardening chocolate running down the sides of the can and recalled licking drips off a similar can as a girl. "I was working, then I got into something. I don't know. It's not important now."

Her mother poured a tall glass of milk and emptied the can of syrup into it. She scowled at the can, shaking it, then threw it away. After stirring the milk with a long metal spoon, she popped a straw in it and handed the glass to Camila. "Will you take it to him?"

Camila took the chocolate milk into the living room. Her father was slouched in his chair. On the TV she saw a blur of silver and black running after a blur of yellow and black. Her father's hair had thinned and his scalp looked greasy. The table next to him was piled with pill bottles and small paper cups.

She pulled up a footstool and sat next to him. "Papa, I brought your milk. Papa?"

He opened his eyes, which looked weary and kind. "You look tired, Cam," he said.

Her chest tightened. She took his hand. "Do you want some milk, Papa?"

"Chocolate milk. I drink chocolate milk now."

"That's what I mean."

She leaned over him, resting her elbow on his thigh. It was thin and hard. She held up the glass and positioned the long purple straw. He sucked slowly and she felt his thigh relax.

"Do you like the chocolate milk, Papa?"

"It needs more chocolate. Tell your mother to get more chocolate at the IGA." He sat up a little straighter and looked at the TV. "Damned Steelers."

"You want the sound on?" she asked.

He said nothing.

"Which ones are the Steelers?"

"They're in black and yellow."

She saw that they were losing by twenty. "But it says they're from Pittsburgh. Why are you rooting for them?"

"Because the Raiders are evil. They beat the Chiefs at Arrowhead and kept them out of the playoffs. Gotta root against the Raiders."

"When was that?" she asked. "I mean, when did the Raiders beat them in the playoffs?"

He sighed and squinted at the screen. "Three years ago."

She looked at the TV again, then back at her father. She was still holding the chocolate milk and her hand was wet and cold. "Papa, see how there are two clocks on the screen, both counting down? One has minutes and seconds, but the other just has seconds and resets every so often. Why are there two clocks?"

He looked into her eyes but said nothing. She could feel the irritation in him as he turned his head toward the kitchen.

"Agnes." He tried to call into the kitchen but his voice didn't carry. He turned slowly back to Camila. "One is the game clock and one is the play clock."

She took his bony hand. "What's the difference?"

"One tells you how long to go in the game and one tells you how long the team with the ball has to run their next play." He closed his eyes as he spoke. His breaths were heavy. She let go of his hand and held up the chocolate milk. He sipped weakly.

He looked toward the kitchen as Camila's mother walked out. "I need something for the pain," he said, letting go of Camila's hand and reaching toward his wife. Her mother made a small pile of pills and took the chocolate milk from her.

Tears welled in Camila's eyes as she watched her mother feed him pills. She stood. "I'm sorry I didn't come sooner," she said. "I really am."

She went to the kitchen and made a cup of tea, then peeked into the living room, where her father was sleeping and her mother was dusting a large wooden cross on the mantle over the fireplace.

Taking her tea outside, she sat on the ground under the white oak. She rubbed her ankle gently, thinking about Alex Vane and her father and her father's mother. She tilted her head back and stared up at the tree. The leaves were bright yellow, illuminated by a flood light on the garage door. She picked up a couple of leaves from the grass around her, then rubbed them together. They crackled between her fingers.

When her phone rang, she silenced it without taking it out of her pocket.

Chapter Sixty-One

Alex sat on the bed and stared at his phone. He was *not* going to call her again. After emptying a can of beer, he threw it toward the trash can in the corner. He turned on the TV and flipped channels, looking for news about the Santiago trial. Finding none, he stopped on Sunday Night Football, feeling comforted by the noise of the crowd and the warm voices of the announcers.

He assumed that the call Martin had received on the morning of 9/11 had come from Hollinger, and the thought overwhelmed him.

He ordered a burger and two more beers from room service, and they arrived as the fourth quarter started. He set the cans on the bedside table next to his notebook and sat on the bed with his food. A safety for the Raiders came across the middle and leveled a wide receiver. The crunch jolted Alex and he opened one of the beers and drank half of it in one long swig.

He reached for his notebook and wrote on a blank page.

> Hollinger called Martin from WTC Plaza 9/5 and 9/11, after the planes hit. Hollinger escaped WTC. Options: 1. Walked south two blocks, died when Marriott collapsed. 2. Called Bice, Bice killed him.

He underlined the last sentence, swigged his beer, then crumpled up the page and threw it toward the trash can.

Bice being directly involved in Hollinger's death was the only way he could make sense of his source's statement that "there are three." But was Bice the kind of person who could kill a man *himself*? And, if so, why did he do it on the morning of 9/11? Alex's thinking was slow and labored.

He looked back up at the game as the cameras scanned the crowd and the luxury boxes, showing fans holding signs and celebrities just sitting there. The shot stopped on a slight man in a gray suit sitting in a luxury box high above the field. A little graphic popped up on the screen. Alex squinted through blurred vision. He read, "Steeler's owner Clay Tunney." He was flanked by two men and the announcer said, "On his left, that's Governor Mark S. Schweiker." The camera held the shot for a few more seconds and Alex saw that the man on the right was Denver Bice. He looked crisp to Alex, clean-shaven and healthy. He wore a dark blue suit and sipped bottled water.

"Hey you!" Alex yelled at the screen. "Did you do it?"

He stood up and took a large step toward the screen, holding his head just a few inches from the warm glass, his eyes right on Bice's face. He thought of Mac Hollinger, stumbling down ninety-nine flights of stairs into the cool morning air.

He leaned back and sipped his beer, spilling some on his shirt. "You! How did you do it?" he shouted sloppily, stabbing his finger at the screen. He slammed his beer down on the bedside table then walked to the bathroom and lifted the toilet seat. It slipped from his fingers and slammed shut. He peed in the sink, walked back to the bed, and sat. When he checked the screen for Bice, the shot was back on the game.

On a clean sheet of paper, he scribbled:

> Hollinger called Martin from WTC plaza after escaping from tower. Martin didn't pick up. Then he called Bice? Bice drove down and killed him, then dumped body by Marriott. Timeline? When did Towers collapse? When did Marriott collapse? Bice's phone records? Pay phone records for 9/11? How did Bice know H's plans?

By the end, his handwriting was illegible.

After finishing his beer, he called Camila. When her voice mail beeped, he hung up, filled with longing and anger. He ordered two more beers and a slice of cheesecake, then turned back to the game.

When the girl from room service knocked on the door, Balby stuck his head in and looked at Alex. "Having quite the party in here," he said. "Don't get too drunk. In case we have to move you or something."

Once the door was shut and he was alone again, he called Greta Mori. She picked up after five rings but he hung up when he heard her voice. "What the hell am I doing?" he asked the room. She called him right back. He didn't answer.

He collapsed on the bed and propped a beer on his belly, then turned on *Survivor*. As his eyes closed and his torso relaxed, the beer spilled across his shirt and onto the bed. He didn't notice.

***

Alex awoke with a gun pressing into his forehead. The heel of a boot dug into his chest as he tried to open his eyes, which were crusted over. His head was spinning.

"Do you have the recording?" A high voice and thick accent.

After blinking a few times, Alex locked his eyes on the mustache. Rak. "How did you … why are you—"

"Where is the recording? Where is the girl?"

"What happened to Officer Balby?"

"Dead, like your black friend."

The mention of Downton brought Alex back. He blinked a few more times and stared right at Rak, terrified but pretending not to be.

"Vane," Rak continued, "you have only a moment before you die."

"I don't have it."

Rak pressed the gun harder into Alex's forehead, then shifted it quickly to the left and shot into the pillow, just missing his ear. The gun was partially silenced, but Alex's ear rang.

"The next one will be in your head. If you don't have the recording, you are of no use to me."

"If I give you the recording, will you leave me alone?"

"No, I will kill you anyway."

"Then why would I give it to you?"

"Because if you do, I'll leave the girl alone."

"You're lying."

"Possibly."

Alex moved his hands slowly above his head, as if to say he surrendered. Rak raised the gun slightly off his forehead and Alex nodded toward the closet.

Rak stepped down from the bed, head and gun still turned on Alex. He walked to the closet and turned on the light, which cast a faint glow across the room. "In the safe?" Rak asked.

"Yes."

"What's the code?"

"Three-six-two-four-three-six."

Rak reached up but could only reach the bottom row of numbers on the keypad. "Get over here."

Alex stood slowly, rubbed his forehead where he could still feel the pressure from the metal, and walked to the closet. Rak stepped out of the way, gun still trained on Alex, as Alex stood in front of the safe and typed in the code.

He reached in past the recordings of Downton and pulled out the USB drive. He turned slowly and handed it down to Rak.

"Look at me," Rak said. Alex looked down and met his eyes. "Does the girl have a copy?"

Alex's head was still spinning, his heart beating fast. "No. And she doesn't know anything. She hasn't even seen it. Leave her alone, please."

"Does anyone else have a copy?"

"Only my newspaper, but it's probably been disposed of."

"Before you die, I want to tell you something. You aren't supposed to die."

Through his spinning head and Rak's strange accent, Alex was barely registering the words. All he could manage was a weak, "What?"

"I want you to know, this is not him killing you, it's me."

Alex heard a click near the door and jerked his head around as it flew open.

"Hands up!" He recognized the voice of Pono Grady.

Rak swiveled around and fired toward the door in one motion as Alex dropped to the floor and covered his head with his arms. He heard two more shots, then the sound of the sliding balcony door opening. He looked up to see Rak disappearing over the railing.

Before Alex could stand up, Grady was past him, out onto the balcony. He leaned out over the railing, gun extended, but Rak was gone.

Alex scanned the floor for the USB drive, hoping Rak had dropped it, but found nothing.

"Officer down at the King Kamehameha Inn," Grady shouted into his radio as he ran past Alex and back out the door of the hotel room.

Alex sprawled on his back on the thin hotel carpet and stared at the ceiling. His whole body was rigid and, as he slowly relaxed into the floor, he began to cry.

Medilogue Three

Cedar View Cemetery, Iselin, New Jersey
Twelve Weeks After 9/11

Denver Bice walked across choked grass in a slick black overcoat, trailed by a blonde secretary who held an umbrella over his head. "I told you we'd be late," he said. "Fucking traffic."

The gardens around the cemetery were bare. A few evergreens dotted the landscape, but dead leaves from the oak trees covered the flower beds, making the swatches of red berries on the dogwoods the only color. An old priest in white robes stood under a large plastic canopy that covered fewer than half of the four hundred people there. A few fat drops had fallen, but it was not yet raining hard. Bice stood at the back of the crowd as the priest finished his sermon.

"We may mourn the way Macintosh Hollinger died, and desire vengeance against the terrorists who took him from us, but remember that only God gives, and only God can take away. Mac was a wealthy man, but he knew that wealth and power could not bring him into God's Kingdom. *Faith* is required. Romans tells us that 'A man is justified by faith apart from the works of Law.' *Faith alone* is required to enter into God's Kingdom. Mac had this simple faith, and in that faith, he is saved.

"And Matthew tells us, 'There is nothing covered that will not be revealed, and hidden that will not be known.' Mac knows now what we do not, and in that knowledge, he is at peace. And just as he is now unbound in the company of God in Heaven, may this also be so for us on earth. Amen."

After the casket was lowered, Bice followed the crowd to a large, white tent. He saw Sonia Hollinger next to the lavish buffet accepting outstretched hands and air kisses from a long line of people. He looked at his watch. He was missing the Steelers game. Clenching his teeth, he walked to the end of the line.

Sonia wore a neat black suit, a veiled black hat, and classic black pumps with a four-inch heel. As he approached her, he heard three different people compliment the food. "Well, given the location," she said to each of them, "we just had to do *something* interesting."

He pecked her cheek when he reached the front of the line. "Sonia, what a lovely service. I didn't know Mac was Lutheran."

She smiled. "Yes, I could not even get him to come to Latin mass with me on Christmas."

Bice took her hands. "'Faith alone.' If only it were that simple."

"Indeed."

"I'm very sorry about Mac." He pecked her cheek again and turned to leave.

Scanning the tent for his secretary, he caught the eye of John Martin. Martin wore a threadbare brown sweater over a wrinkled white shirt. He noticed a woman he didn't recognize standing with Martin and wondered how such a loser could land a woman who looked like *that.* As they began walking toward him, Bice looked down at his watch. "Damn," he said to himself. He was probably going to miss the second-half kickoff.

"Den, good to see you." Martin reached out his hand and they shook.

"It's Denver now. People don't call me Den anymore. I see you've dressed up for the occasion." He turned toward the woman beside Martin. "Who is this?"

"This is my girlfriend, Camila. She teaches at NYU with me."

Bice reached out his hand. "Lovely to meet you. NYU has a special place in my heart—any professor there is a friend."

Camila took his hand and shook it. "Nice to meet you. How do you two know each other?"

"We were Mac's students way back at Tulane," Martin said. "Can you believe that? Den came from Pittsburgh and I came from Alabama. We met in New Orleans and now we're standing at a funeral in New Jersey. It's a strange world."

Bice scanned the room for his driver. "Yes, well, I have an important—"

"What was the class?" Camila asked.

Bice smiled as he imagined her undressing in the back of his limousine. "Writing About Numbers," he said. "It was a math class for writers. I was a reporter for a while, until, you know, all this happened." He waved his arm in a sweeping motion toward the people in the tent.

"Until all what happened?" Camila asked, looking around.

Bice imagined getting a blowjob from her while watching the game in his limo as they crossed the George Washington Bridge.

"Until he took over New York City and the world," Martin said. "In case you haven't noticed, dear, we're surrounded by rich people, many of whom work for or rely on Mr. Denver Bice."

Bice heard a clinking sound and looked down at Martin's pants. Martin was fingering the loose change in his pocket. *Fucking loser.* Camila put her hand on Martin's shoulder and the clinking stopped.

"No, I just meant when I moved out of the newsroom and into the corporate side of things," Bice said, imagining dropping Camila off on the side of the road once they got across the bridge.

The clinking began again and Camila glanced at Martin. "Hey," she said. "Calm down."

Bice caught his secretary's eye across the room. "Well, I do need to be off now."

"Den, one last thing," Martin said. "You're not funding Al Qaeda in secret, are you?"

"What?" Bice asked.

"I mean, you caught a helluva break with Mac dying when he did."

Bice felt the air leave his chest all at once.

"I hope you'll at least send flowers to Bin Laden's cave in Afghanistan," Martin continued. He laughed and the clinking started again.

Bice flushed with anger. "What did you say to me?"

Camila took Martin's hand. "What kind of a joke is that?" she asked.

"All I'm saying is that at least there was a small upside from 9/11 for you and your Standard Media folks," Martin said, not taking his eyes off of Bice.

Bice stammered, "I ... what? I mean, that's the most offensive, ridiculous ... What are you talking about?"

"Just joking," Martin said. "I know you hate Arabs more than you hate losing money. I'm just saying, lucky break for you."

"John, stop it!" Camila said. "You don't know what you're saying."

Hot and red, Bice stared at Martin with cold eyes. They stood in silence as the chatter around them grew louder and then quieted. An occasional laugh echoed through the tent. Finally, Bice took three deep breaths, glanced at Camila, then looked back at Martin. "I really must be going," he said. "I have an important meeting in the city."

***

Bice watched from the back of his limousine as his assistant, Simon Macilroy, stood under the Manhattan Bridge. Rain trickled through the slatted iron above him onto his red umbrella. Small puddles formed around his feet.

Macilroy tried to kick gravel into a puddle as he scanned the deserted park. Bice saw Dimitri Rak approaching from across the small field to the north and saw that Macilroy had spotted him as well. Rak paused at the edge of the field, looked around, then walked up to Macilroy. His thin, shoulder-length hair dripped beneath a black hat.

Macilroy pulled a yellow envelope from his jacket and held it out. Rak brushed it aside and walked to the back window of the limousine. He tapped on the glass with one finger.

Inside the car, Bice cursed Macilroy under his breath. "Stupid bumbling fuck."

Rak tapped again.

Bice took a deep breath, rolled down the window and, before Rak could speak, said, "I've asked my assistant to speak with you."

Rak held out his hand and smiled. "Dimitri Rak."

Bice looked at the pale, wet hand and did not want to shake it. "I know who you are. Smedveb has told me about you."

"I do not deal with assistants. I am here as a favor to Smedveb. He says you do business with him and has asked me to assist you." He cocked his shoulder toward Macilroy. "Him, I do not know."

"Now that you see me," Bice said, "can we get on with it?" He nodded at Macilroy, who again took out the envelope and held it out to Rak.

Ignoring it, Rak said, "No. You must give it to me."

Rain was pooling in the brim of Rak's hat and pouring over its side, causing fat drops of water to fall in front of his face every few seconds. Bice stared at him. He imagined himself opening the door swiftly, knocking the little fucker down, and smashing his face into the ground until he choked on mud and gravel.

Again, Bice nodded at Macilroy, who came over and passed the envelope in front of Rak and through the open window. A drop of water splashed on it, leaving a ragged water stain.

"Damn it!" Bice yelled.

Rak and Macilroy stepped back. Bice's heart was beating fast. He looked at Rak. "Why must I hand it to you?"

"I said, I deal with you. I don't know him. You give it to me."

"What the hell difference does it make who puts it in your hand? We all know what's inside."

"What's inside?"

"The man. The name of the man."

Rak stared straight at him. "There is good reason for Smedveb to trust me. I am the best at what I do."

"That's what I've heard," Bice said. He held out the envelope. "And Smedveb told you about the money?"

"Yes, it's handled. This man must have done something very bad to you. Smedveb was quite generous."

"He knows something he's not supposed to know."

"Mr. Bice, you must relax."

Rak took the envelope, placed it in the inside pocket of his jacket, then turned and walked away.

When Rak was halfway across the field, Macilroy said, "Mr. Bice, what if Martin told others, like the girl at the funeral?"

"He probably didn't. He could barely balance a checkbook and certainly couldn't speak intelligently about high finance." Bice watched Rak disappear at the edge of the field. "And, even if he did, it won't matter. Once he's dead it would be thirdhand."

"I still don't understand why you kept the Green girl alive," Macilroy said as he got into the driver's seat.

"If she'd had any proof, *anything*, I wouldn't have. But she has nothing. She already tried to do something about it, but couldn't. Once Martin is handled, this is over."

Part Four

Chapter Sixty-Two

Monday, September 16, 2002

Alex stumbled into the bathroom at 3 a.m. and drank three glasses of water. He went back and sat on the edge of the bed, rubbed the spot on his forehead where Rak had held the gun, then collapsed.

At 5 a.m. he awoke again. He felt both thin from dehydration and bloated from sugar and alcohol. After checking around the room one last time for the USB drive, he changed into his running shorts. For a minute, he stared at the notes he had written the night before, remembering only that they had seemed important at the time. But his eyes wouldn't focus and trying to read his scrawl made his head pound. He remembered handing the USB to Rak the night before and felt sick to his stomach. Without the recording, he might still be able to put a story together, but it wouldn't have anywhere near the same impact.

He put on a pair of sunglasses and walked out into the soft morning light. "Morning, Grady," he said weakly. "I'm so sorry about Officer Balby."

"He was a good young officer. Only three years on the job. Alex, this is Officer Lucas." A tall, lean officer who'd been sitting next to Grady stood up and shook Alex's hand. "We doubt Rak will make another run at you in public," Grady continued, "but just the same, we're gonna have Lucas follow you everywhere you go."

"Any leads yet?" Alex asked.

"No. They're watching the airports. We've been talking with the NYPD."

"Nothing?"

"Well, we ..."

"That's what I thought," Alex said. "I'm gonna run anyway. The way I feel, I would be better off if he'd shot me."

"Okay," Grady said. "But I'm sending Lucas with you."

Alex trotted down the stairs and across the courtyard to the beach, trailed by Officer Lucas. The sky was light pink, turning orange. As he jogged past the pier, Alex felt his lungs fill with cool, sweet air. He talked to himself as he ran. "Three miles, then a good breakfast—eggs and coffee. Steamed vegetables. Then I will look through all my notes and make a plan. Then I will lift some weights. Then I will *act on* the plan that I make."

After twenty minutes, he turned around to walk back toward the hotel. Lucas let Alex pass him and walked fifteen feet behind him.

Alex's sweat stank of alcohol, but his legs felt strong and he was happy that his body could so quickly rebound from a binge. As he walked down the beach, he saw the interaction with Rak over and over in his mind. His recollection was hazy, but one thing Rak had said hung clearly in Alex's mind. *This is not him killing you, it's me.* He assumed that "he" was Denver Bice, but what could Rak have meant? Alex had no idea.

When he got back to the hotel, he stopped by the buffet for eggs, but took a basket of blueberry muffins instead.

***

After eating four muffins and showering, Alex called Sonia's house. "I need her phone records," he told Juan, picking muffin crumbs up off a plate by pressing into them with the tip of his finger until they stuck, then licking them off. "I may have figured out the date of the call you told me about. If I can tell who it came from, I might be able to get whoever it is to talk to me about Mr. Hollinger's plans. I need someone to go on the record about the five hundred million."

"Okay," Juan said, "come by tomorrow around lunch. We will be by the pool."

"Okay, and there's one other thing. You said that Mr. Hollinger always called his wife from a pay phone outside the towers after lunch. Is that right?"

"Yes. Why?"

"Did he always carry change in his pocket? I mean, he was an older guy. Don't people his age carry change in their pockets instead of just throwing it into a jar?"

"Why are you asking this?"

Alex decided not to tell Juan about the call Martin received on the morning of 9/11. "It's just a hunch. Probably nothing. Did he tend to carry change?"

"Yes, he did."

"Okay. Thanks. I'll see you around noon tomorrow."

After he hung up, Alex pressed into the last of the muffin crumbs with his finger, then stared out the window at the beach as he licked them off.

Chapter Sixty-Three

Camila walked into the kitchen, rubbing her eyes.

Her mother was flipping strips of bacon in a thin, non-stick skillet. She looked at Camila. "He won't eat anything anymore, but I fry it anyway. We don't know it's morning unless it smells like bacon."

Camila looked at the bacon. "When did he stop eating?"

"About a week ago. Liquids are the only calories he'll take in."

"Did he sleep in his chair?" Camila asked.

"Yes."

Camila had not slept well. Her eyes felt puffy and hot. "Should I go see him?"

"Of course you should."

Camila walked to the living room and sat on the footstool next to his chair. His eyes were closed. He seemed to her to have receded—as if overnight he had lost the energy for this world. She took his hand and he opened his eyes. "Tell her I don't eat bacon," he said.

"She knows."

"Then why does she keep making it?" he asked in a half-whisper.

"To show that she loves you."

He closed his eyes.

Camila squeezed his hand and closed her eyes too. Her fingers felt fat and warm between his. She opened her eyes and stared at him as the smell of bacon intensified. She thought he might be sleeping. She looked at the fireplace, then at the candlesticks on the mantle. She saw the wooden cross on the wall over the fireplace, bordered in gold. It had been her grandmother's cross and her father insisted it be hung in the house, even though he had stopped attending church when he was a teenager. "We keep it there out of respect," was all he'd ever said about it. She did not know if the respect was for his mother, the Church, or something else.

The small dents in the gold looked like imprints left by fingers and she wondered about all the people who had held the cross, and what it had meant to them. She felt a slight movement in her father's hand and saw that he had opened his eyes. "Take that cross when I go. It was my mama's."

She looked at him and thought she could sense a hardness all through his body. "Where did she get it?" she asked.

He grunted in a way that made her think he didn't know. "You will take the cross?" he asked.

She looked at it again. "Yes, I will take it."

He smiled at her. "Cam, get your mama, okay?" She imagined a dark cloud, lifting from his body. His voice was soft and his face had brightened a little.

She walked to the kitchen and saw twelve strips of bacon lying parallel on a paper towel. "He wants to see you," she said. "He's going today."

Her mother set down the pan she was washing and turned. "Oh no, not today. The hospice nurse will be here later."

"What does that have to do with when he will die?"

"Don't say that word."

Her mother walked into the living room and Camila followed. They sat on either side of him, Camila on the footstool and her mother on the floor, each holding a hand. After a few minutes, Camila turned to her mother. "Can you feel the hardness in him? It's like a cage. It's moving."

With flashing eyes, her mother glared at her and said, "Don't speak that way about him." Then she turned toward the wall, crying softly.

Chapter Sixty-Four

That afternoon, Alex sat on his bed and made calls to two other numbers from Martin's records. The first number rang and rang without going to voice mail. A dead end. The second was a 504 area code that James had listed as belonging to Morgan Tubbs, a psychiatrist in New Orleans. After Alex introduced himself, Tubbs said he had called Martin on a whim when looking through their yearbook from Tulane.

After a couple of questions, Alex realized that he knew more about Martin's recent life than Tubbs did. Just when he was about to hang up, Alex thought to ask, "Did you happen to have any classes with a man named Denver Bice at Tulane?"

"Hell yeah," Tubbs said in a slow and smooth New Orleans drawl.

"Do you know if he and Martin were close?"

"Don't know, but I wasn't."

"Wasn't what? Close with Denver Bice?"

"We called him Den. Guy was a crazy prick. Never understood why John hung out with him. Maybe it was some kind of inferiority thing. Anyway, he was a prick. Sorry to be blunt about it if he's a friend of yours."

"He isn't, but in what way was he crazy?" Alex asked.

"Well, he's a sociopath, by the technical definition. At least he was back then. Smart as anyone, decent looking, always got what he wanted. But couldn't empathize, didn't have any feeling, humility, or perspective. And he used to hit himself."

"What?"

"I didn't understand it at the time. He seemed to have the world by the balls. But every time he did anything wrong—like forget something or get a bad mark on a test—he'd whack himself on the head. Hard. A second later, he'd go back to being cocky old Den."

"You're a shrink now, right? Why do you think he did that?"

"I'm not sure I should say more. What does old Den have to do with Martin anyway?"

"There's a chance he's involved in Martin's death. I just need to know what he's really like. Mr. Tubbs, please."

"Most people, when they do something bad, they feel remorse, or sadness. My guess is that Den couldn't feel anything. Not joy, not love, and not disappointment or guilt either. Closest he could come was to hit himself. Like some part of him knew he'd done something wrong but he couldn't become completely conscious of it. After he'd hit himself, he'd snap back into confident sociopath mode. Go back to normal, or what was normal for him. Probably some sort of trauma in his past, but I can't be sure."

"Interesting, can you say more about what you mean about him being a sociopath?"

"Well, let me give you an example. There was a girl, Martha Morelli, who went to Tulane with us way back when. Every man south of Baton Rouge was after her. She had that New York look that was rare down here in those days. Long black hair, attitude—you know what I mean? Anyway, Den got her. They dated for a few months but then she dumped him."

"Why'd she dump him?"

"Don't know. Everyone knew she dumped him but we never knew why. We made fun of Den, though. You know how college kids are. Always talking about our conquests, making fun of each other, all that male bonding stuff. I think he was in love with her because he went around moping for a day or two."

"That sounds pretty normal."

"But he was only sad for a day or two. After that, he cracked or something. When a man gets his heart broken, he usually drinks for a couple days, then just finds another woman to fill the hole. With Den, it was as though the breakup had hit a deep wound. He stopped showing emotion, stopped looking people in the eye. He still carried himself with the same confidence. He just became, I don't know, flatter. Here's the point. A few months after the breakup, Martha started going around with some other guy. I don't remember who, but he was older, maybe a grad student. And then her apartment burned down."

Alex stood and walked to the window. "What do you mean?"

"It just burned down. Once she started going around with this guy, Den burned her apartment down, along with the rest of her building. Remember it like it was yesterday. Place was right down from campus on St. Charles Street."

Alex laughed uncomfortably. "Come on, how can you know that?"

"We all knew it. All the guys in our dorm. Of course, no one could prove it, and he was so standoffish with all of us that we could never find out for sure. But he did it. When men feel wronged in this sort of situation, most displace their aggression onto the other man. It's a competition thing. They don't want to hurt the object of their desire, no matter how distorted their desire is. But Den never showed any jealousy. Just burned down her apartment. You track her down and she'll tell you he did it."

Alex asked, but Tubbs had no idea where to find Martha Morelli. "She transferred out of Tulane after the one year. I heard she moved up north. New York, maybe."

As they spoke, blurry images of Denver Bice in the luxury box passed through Alex's head. "Mr. Tubbs, one last question. Do you think Bice is capable of murder? I mean actual murder, one on one."

"Under the right circumstances, without a doubt," Tubbs said. "To him, murder would not even need justification if he felt he was protecting himself. He's not the kind of guy who would murder for sadistic pleasure or anything like that. But if he felt threatened? Yes."

***

Trailed by Officer Lucas, Alex headed down to the business center. He looked up a 9/11 timeline and used a clean sheet of paper to write out the major events, adding the call he assumed Hollinger had made.

8:46—North Tower Hit
8:48—First TV Broadcast
9:03—South Tower Hit
9:37—Hollinger calls Martin from pay phone at WTC Plaza
9:59—South Tower Collapses
10:28—North Tower and Marriott Collapse

He figured that if Hollinger had called Martin at 9:37 a.m., he could have called Bice shortly thereafter. The soonest Bice could have picked him up was about 9:55 a.m., assuming Bice was coming from his office. So he must have killed him and dumped the body between 9:59 and 10:28.

He pulled out his list of questions from the night before and crossed off all but the last three: *Bice's phone records? Pay phone records for 9/11? How did Bice know H's plans?* Next, he opened his e-mail and wrote to James at his personal address, asking him if he knew a way to get records of calls to and from pay phones.

Finally, he returned to his room and called Bearon. "I've gotta level with you about something," Alex said. He had decided not to mention his run-in with Rak, but wanted to get Bearon's thoughts about Bice killing Hollinger.

"You finally ready to tell me what's going on?" Bearon asked.

"You know how I told you that Rak killed Martin?"

"Yeah, I started your rumor for you, you jerk. Most people just looked at me like I was a rez kid on crack. Everyone is sold on Santiago being the guy. A couple cops said they'd look into Rak, but it didn't sound like they actually would. We just don't care about Eastern Europe anymore. If his name was Mohammed they might have jumped on it."

"Yeah, but I didn't tell you why he killed him. You ever heard of Denver Bice?"

"Who hasn't?"

Alex told him about the five hundred million, Hollinger escaping from the tower, and his theory about Denver Bice and the morning of 9/11.

"Wait," Bearon said when he had finished. "Bice had Martin killed by Rak to cover up the fact that *he* killed this Hollinger guy?"

Alex opened the balcony curtains and stared out at the water. "Well, I think so, though I'm nowhere close to proving it. My guess is he got a call from Hollinger after he escaped the tower."

"And left the body in the rubble? What a sicko."

"Yeah," Alex said. "So you'd better stop spreading that rumor around. It's too dangerous now."

"Wait," Bearon said. "That's it."

"That's what?"

"You know how a couple days ago you were asking me about Sharp? Wondering if maybe he was the guy making the weird calls?"

"Yeah."

"He and Bice *hate* each other."

"What do you mean?" Alex asked, closing the curtains and starting to pace the room.

"I mean, besides being two of the most pompous assholes on earth, they have a history. *The Standard* ran a bunch of editorials ripping Sharp back when he was prosecuting corporate cases. Don't you read your own paper?"

"Usually not."

"Sharp totally had it in for Bice. Everyone knew it. And your paper went out of its way to embarrass him, probably at Bice's request."

Alex stopped pacing, opened the curtains again, and watched an elderly couple walk slowly down the beach. "That makes sense," he said, "but how could Sharp know about the video, about Downton, about Bice's involvement?"

"Who knows? But I'll bet he's your guy. Think about it. Maybe Sharp figures out Santiago is innocent. He *is* prosecuting the case, so that's not exactly a stretch. He starts digging around. Finds out about the video and somehow that leads him to Rak, and to Bice. Then he figures, kill two birds with one stone. He gets to screw with Bice, and if Santiago gets off, he gets even more exposure. An innocent kid goes free and an evil CEO gets taken down. Sharp's base would love it."

"But if Sharp somehow knew about Downton, the video, and Bice and Hollinger, why do it this way?" Alex asked. "Why make a bunch of weird calls? Why not just get the whole story out at once?"

"Too suspicious. You gotta think that if Sharp knew about Santiago being innocent, someone else might know, too. Letting it out all at once would call too much attention to him. If it got out that he was leaking information, ruining *his own case*, it would end his career."

"But how could he have known about Bice killing Hollinger?" Alex asked.

"Who knows with these guys? Maybe he was tailing him or something."

Alex thought about the calls he had received from his source and pictured Sharp, his bald head gleaming under the courtroom lights. "Wow."

"I'm telling you," Bearon said, "Sharp is a big enough asshole to do it, too. The other day I read a survey someone did about the most-hated professions in America. You know, they asked seventeen hundred people who they hated most. Lawyers and journalists came up numbers one and two. Politicians came in third."

"So what?" Alex asked.

"Sharp is a lawyer, using a journalist to become a politician."

Chapter Sixty-Five

Alex watched American Idol and began turning his timeline and notes into a story. Grady had told him that the NYPD was sending an investigator to work with the Kona police, but there had been no developments in the search for Rak. He didn't know what he would do with his story, but he wanted to have it straight when the investigator arrived. Every few minutes, he glanced at the room service menu, but didn't place an order. After an hour, he had eight pages, around two thousand words, handwritten.

He looked at the menu again and muted the TV. He'd just get a little something. He had decided on a steak with extra vegetables instead of potatoes, but when room service picked up he found himself ordering a cheeseburger and fries, a Mai Tai, and two beers. He unmuted the TV right away to drown out the voice in his head asking him what he was doing.

When the food arrived, he ate it while watching the end of American Idol. A few days off wasn't so bad. He could start back on his eating and exercise regimen tomorrow. He looked at the clock: 9 p.m. Technically, tomorrow wasn't for three hours, so he ordered two more beers.

When they arrived, Grady poked his head into the room. "Boy, what's wrong with you?"

Alex stumbled and waved Grady in. "Who knows?" Alex said, flopping onto the bed. "You wanna beer?"

"No," Grady said, taking a seat next to the desk. "Been meaning to ask you, were you there on 9/11?"

Alex stared at the ceiling. "I was there."

"Were you near the towers, I mean, Ground Zero?"

"Nah. Uptown, five miles north, in my apartment."

"You're a reporter, right? Weren't you covering it?"

Alex said nothing. Grady stood and moved to the door.

"Wait," Alex said, sitting up. "I pretended I was sick." His words were a bit sloppy and he was sweating. "I was supposed to be covering a drug case at the courthouse that day but I was running late. I saw on TV that the planes had hit and my cellphone rang a couple minutes later. I knew it was my boss and I knew he wanted me to go in. I mean, it's the biggest story of my lifetime, the most important thing in a generation. What did I do? I looked at the caller ID and put the phone down. E-mailed him later in the day and said I'd come down with the flu. Made up a whole bullshit story."

"So what'd you do?" Grady asked.

"Watched the news in my apartment. Smelled dust and melted metal and burning bodies. I just sat there. All day." Alex finished the last beer and dropped the empty can onto the bed.

"Why'd you do it?" Grady asked.

Alex picked the can up again and peered into it with one eye.

After a minute, Grady got up and walked to the door. As he opened it, Alex stood up. "Because I'm a fucking coward. Why else?"

"That why you're in here drinking alone?" Grady looked at the room service tray. "You know, for a fella in such good shape, you sure don't eat like it."

"I don't usually eat like this," Alex said. "I used to. I guess it's still in me."

***

By 11 p.m., Alex was half-asleep, watching images of Santiago float through his mind. His cell phone rang and he thought of Camila. He rubbed his eyes, rolled over, and looked at the caller ID. He jumped up from the bed when he saw the number: *000-0000*. For a few seconds, he paced the room, holding the phone tight and trying to clear his mind.

"Hello," he said, trying not to slur his words.

"Mr. Vane, you seem to have escaped a run in. You're very lucky."

"How did you know?" Alex asked, walking into the bathroom.

"You should trust the officer from New York City. He's going there to help you."

Alex ran cold water over a washcloth and rubbed it across the back of his neck. The voice sounded even stranger than he remembered. "What else would he be here to do?"

"Mr. Vane, have you connected the dots yet?"

"Almost," Alex said, rubbing the washcloth across his face. "I know who killed Martin, I know why, and I think I know how. I know that the same guy killed Demarcus Downton and that he was in my room, trying to kill me. And I have a theory about the third murder you mentioned."

"So, you know about Denver Bice?"

Alex was startled. This was the first time the source had mentioned Bice by name. He set the washcloth down and walked to the bedroom. "Well, I have a theory. Did Bice kill Hollinger?"

Slow, steady breathing.

Alex raised his voice. "Did he?"

"Yes."

"On the morning of 9/11?"

"Yes."

He sat on the bed. "Jesus. How long have you known this? I mean, how could you sit on this information and not—"

"I'm not sitting on it now, am I? Why haven't you approached Denver Bice?"

"I'm still trying to prove it. I don't know how you know what you know, but I need someone to go on record. And I need phone records."

"Whose?"

"I need the record of a possible pay phone call from the World Trade Center Plaza to Denver Bice on the morning of 9/11. I think it happened, but I need to prove it."

A long silence. "Okay. I can get it."

"Pay phone records require a subpoena."

"I'll get it for you."

"Thanks," Alex said. "Look, I know who you are. Don't worry, I'm not going to tell anyone. But let me ask you a question. Are you doing this because you want to blow up the Santiago case and get the publicity? Or because you actually want to do the right thing?" He paused. "Or do you just want to hurt Denver Bice?"

Silence.

"It's okay if you don't want to tell me. I just wanted to—"

"I want to hurt Denver Bice."

Just as Alex was going to ask whether he knew of any reason that Bice would want to keep him alive, the line went dead. Alex scribbled what he could remember of the conversation onto a yellow pad. When he was finished, he piled all the empty beer cans on the room service tray and slid it out the door.

Before falling asleep, he called Camila and left a message when her phone went straight to voice mail. "Camila, Rak found me again. He took the recordings, but I'm okay. I'm calling to … I just want to warn you. I doubt he'll come looking for you, but he might. Be careful."

Chapter Sixty-Six

Tuesday, September 17, 2002

After a long run and a six-egg omelet, Alex got a ride to Sonia's house from Officer Lucas. There had been no sign of Rak since the night he'd come to Alex's hotel room, but Officer Lucas hadn't left Alex's side since, and told him now that he'd wait for him in the driveway.

Alex walked around the side of the house to the pool. Seeing no one, he knocked on the side door by the kitchen. Sonia emerged wearing a hooded pink robe, which fell open and revealed a black bikini as she leaned in to peck Alex on the cheek. She held a frosty glass full of red liquid.

"Bloody Mary?" she asked.

"Um I—"

"Come in, honey."

She led Alex into a round room with a glass dome for a ceiling. As they entered, she retracted a wall of curtains with a button on a remote control in her robe pocket. She also muted a TV that took up an entire wall, one of the only walls not made of glass.

Alex glanced at the TV and saw the banner headline along the bottom: "President Bush unveils new preemptive war doctrine."

Sonia saw him looking at it. "It's about time. I mean, *really*."

She waved at a white couch and Alex sat down. "Where's Juan?" he asked.

She sat next to him. "Shopping. I read about what happened at the hotel," she said, sounding concerned.

Alex realized that he did not trust her completely, so her concern surprised him. "Yeah. It was a bit unnerving. Honestly, I'm hoping to get out of Hawaii as soon as I get a couple more pieces for my story."

"And where's Camila?"

"She went to see her father. He's dying."

"I'm so sorry." She no longer sounded concerned. "Have they had any luck finding the short man?"

"No, but I'm hoping you can help me track down some information that may help."

"We will have time for that." She shook her glass. "Are you sure I can't get you one of these? It's clear liquor and vegetables. I squeeze my own juice. It's practically health food."

"Okay," he said. "Just one, though."

Sonia stood slowly and led him into the kitchen. He knew she was already a bit tipsy. He thought of Camila and hoped Juan would be back soon.

She juiced three tomatoes and a stalk of celery into a tall glass, then added ice and three shots of vodka before garnishing it with a lemon wedge and another stalk of celery. "I don't do the Worcestershire because of the sugar," she said, shaking some hot sauce on top and handing the drink to Alex.

He leaned on the counter, trying to figure out how he would say what he needed to say. He took a long sip of the drink. "Sonia, I believe your husband was murdered. He made it out of the tower." He paused but she said nothing. "He called Professor Martin from the pay phone at World Trade Center Plaza. Martin didn't pick up. Then he made another call—I've had a source confirm it—and I may soon have the evidence to prove it. The man who killed him sent Rak to Hawaii because I have evidence against them." He tipped his head back and poured the rest of the drink into his mouth, then looked back at her and held her gaze.

She took a sip of her drink and closed her eyes. "Denver Bice?" she asked.

Alex almost spat out his drink. "What? How did you ..." He couldn't think of what to ask.

"Juan and I were making love and I could tell that something was off. He and I do *not* keep secrets. He told me he'd spoken to you. I truly had no idea about the money, dear, but I believe Juan. When he told me about the call he overheard, I imagined the worst."

Sonia took his hand and led him back to the living room. She sprawled out on the sofa, pulled him down next to her, and placed her feet in his lap.

"Sonia, I, uh ... Aren't you surprised? I was pretty worried about telling you that."

"I suspected that he got out of the tower for weeks after the attacks. Several people thought they had seen him. And the fact that he was in the rubble of the Marriott. It doesn't come as a shock."

Alex looked at her feet, which were caressing his chest.

Sonia laughed. "Oh, don't tell me you and Camila are monogamous?"

"What? Can we focus for a minute? It might not be a shock that he got out, but you don't seem upset to learn that your husband was murdered."

"We all deal with grief in our own way."

"And were you and Juan dealing with grief like this when Mr. Hollinger was still alive?"

"Of course we were. He was nearly eighty-four years old. He *approved.* Not everyone is an uptight white kid."

Alex heard the front door swing open. He gently shifted her feet off his lap and stood just as Juan walked in.

"Hola," Juan said.

Alex looked down at Sonia, whose eyes were now closed. "Sonia? I need Mr. Hollinger's phone records from the months before he died. Is there any chance you have those?"

She opened her eyes just long enough to say, "Juan can get you whatever you need."

Juan gestured toward the kitchen and Alex followed him. He took a stack of bills from the top of the refrigerator and handed them to Alex. "I got them faxed from the phone company after we spoke."

"Thanks," Alex said, thumbing through the bills.

"She likes you. She likes you and is used to getting what she wants."

Alex sighed. "Is there somewhere I can work on this?"

Juan laughed at him. "The bedroom where you showered the other day. Sonia will sleep for an hour or two now."

***

Alex sat on the edge of the bed and thumbed through the phone records.

He found the pages for August seventeenth, twenty-eighth, twenty-ninth, and thirtieth, and circled four different numbers. The first two turned out to be relatives, but the third number was a man named Louis Harrison. When Alex explained why he was calling and asked what the man's relationship with Hollinger was, Harrison spoke in a deep voice. "I was his financial advisor, and you know that I won't speak about his dealings."

"You're not his banker though, Mr. Harrison. Confidentiality does not extend to informal financial advising."

"I was his banker at one time."

"I'm not asking about anything formal you did for him. I'm at Mrs. Hollinger's house in Hawaii. She shared Mr. Hollinger's phone records with me. I'm trying to show that he was murdered."

"Murdered? He died in 9/11," Harrison said.

"He didn't, Mr. Harrison. I know it must be a shock, and I can't tell you anything else, but he didn't."

"I don't want to be in the paper."

"We can discuss that later. For now, can you confirm that you spoke with him on the night of August twenty-eighth, 2001?"

"This is not the first time I've spoken with a reporter. I will say a couple of things but I won't be in the paper, even anonymously. Agreed?"

Alex pressed his pen hard into his notebook, causing the tip to tear through a few pages. He needed to get someone to go on the record if his story was going to carry any weight. "Agreed," he said quietly.

Harrison continued. "Whatever you get from me is informational only and you'll have to get someone else to confirm it."

"Okay. Did you speak to him the night of the twenty-eighth about his holdings in Standard Media Group?"

"Yes."

"And can you confirm that he called you to discuss an idea he was pursuing concerning moving some of his assets?"

"Yes."

"And can you confirm that he intended to sell five hundred million of his Standard Media holdings and donate it to the Media Protection Organization?"

"Yes."

Alex thanked him and told him he would be in touch again soon. After hanging up, he sat on the bed and stared at the blank TV screen. He knew he had enough to publish now, though not enough to prove anything damning about Bice. And without the recording, probably not enough to get Santiago off, either. And without a job, he had nowhere to publish.

Chapter Sixty-Seven

Camila sat with her father all day as he drifted in and out of consciousness. He did not speak to her, but from time to time he opened his eyes and she cried and squeezed his hand. Her mother shuffled in and out of the room, straightened magazines she had already straightened, and brought in food they didn't eat.

At dinnertime, Camila left her father and walked into the kitchen. Her mother sat at the table, which was covered in steaming casserole dishes. Camila sat beside her and took a plate, staring at the bacon salad, mashed potatoes, biscuits, and corn. "We used to eat differently, Mama."

"Your father stopped eating Argentinian food a few years ago. I guess he became an American, and now we eat like it."

"I see that," Camila said.

"Oh, don't be such a know-it-all. Just because we don't eat sushi and sprouted whatever doesn't mean we're any less than."

"I wasn't saying that." Camila took a small spoonful of mashed potatoes. Her mother had placed a thick pat of butter on top and the yellow liquid pooled on her plate. She sopped up the butter with a biscuit and took a small bite. "Mama, why do you think Papa loves football?" Her mother said nothing. "Last night he was cheering for the Steelers and I asked him why. He said that three years ago the Raiders beat the Chiefs in the playoffs. He grew up playing soccer. And now because a group of millionaires from Oakland beat another group of millionaires from Kansas City in a game three years ago, he's yelling at the TV in support of a third group of millionaires from Pittsburgh—a city he's never been to and will never go to. All to get back at the first group of millionaires."

Her mother shook her head. "Oh, don't be so cynical. That game broke his heart. On Sundays he loved the Chiefs with everything he had."

"Did he ever love you like that?"

Her mother's eyes widened. Camila thought it was because she knew that, if she blinked, a tear would fall.

"Why did you finally decide to come back?" her mother asked.

"You know he hit me, right?" Her mother turned away, but Camila continued. "He hit me like his mother hit him. Maybe he used football as a way to temper his aggression, but it didn't always work. He was cruel to me, like he was to you. And we both still love him. And that's fine. It's okay to love him *and* to know that what he did wasn't okay. It's okay to know that it wasn't my fault, it wasn't your fault. All of it can pass through, like a storm, and it's okay to let it pass." Camila leaned in to try to catch her mother's eye. "It's okay to know that there's a lightness in us that can't be touched. And it's okay to love him."

Her mother turned back to her, blinking away tears. "Have some corn," she said.

Chapter Sixty-Eight

Alex was sitting on a red leather chair across from Sonia when she opened her eyes at 3 p.m.

"Sonia, I'm going to write the story. I don't know what I'm going to do with it yet, but I'm going to get it out somehow. Is there any way you can get Harrison to go on the record about the money?"

Sonia sat up on the couch and looked at him, smiling. "Why do you want to break this story, honey? What do you think will come of it?"

Alex shifted in the chair. "I don't know. At the very least, it will get Santiago out of jail."

"You're so earnest," she said, rubbing her eyes. "You're the perfect mix of selfish and selfless." She put one leg up on the couch. Her robe drifted, exposing a thigh.

Juan walked in and Alex glanced at him, then looked back at Sonia. "Sonia, please. I have enough to write the story, but it will be much better if someone will go on the record. If Harrison won't, how about you? You could tell the story of Mac, his relationship with Bice, his friendship with Martin, Sadie Green, all of it. If you'll go on the record, I can lock down the story and nail Bice."

Sonia glanced at Juan, who went to the kitchen. "I don't care to *nail Bice*."

She patted the couch and Alex got up and walked over. "But he killed your husband," he said, sitting next to her.

"Don't get me wrong. He should be punished. But he won't be. Nothing I say will do anything more than embarrass him. Men like you do not *nail* men like Denver Bice. I'm sorry

"Look, you don't need to say what you're working on. You may actually be trying to do real journalism for once in your life and I don't want to get in the way of that. But I need to tell you something."

Alex sat on the edge of a cedar planter filled with bright yellow flowers. "What do you need to tell me?"

"I told Denver Bice about Mac's money. I called him, drunk, in early September. He knew Mac's plans because I told him. And you can quote me on that."

"Why? I mean, why would you do that?"

"I was drunk. I was gloating. A gorgeous girl at the bar was flirting with me. I thought I was Captain Kirk for a minute."

"So why'd you lie when I asked you before?" Alex asked.

"Lying to members of the corporate media just comes naturally to me. I mean, *you* spend all your time lying to the public. At this point, I lie to guys like you just on principle."

"So why are you telling me now?"

"I heard you got fired. And if you got fired by *The Standard*, you must be doing something right."

"Thanks," Alex said.

When they hung up Alex sat in the courtyard and stared at the orchids. After a few minutes, he called Camila and left a message. "Hey, it's Alex. I'm still here in Hawaii. I hope your dad is okay, or, well, as okay as can be expected. Anyway, I need your help. I need advice. I need … something. Call me when you get a chance, okay?"

Chapter Seventy

Over the last few minutes, Camila thought she'd felt her father dissipate and move into the room. The expression on his face had changed, his cheeks growing softer and his eyes opening wider. He mumbled things about his mother.

"Papa, what was Grandma like?" Camila asked.

Her mother, sitting on the floor next to Camila's chair, shot her a glance. "He can't talk now, Cam. Can't you see that?"

They each took one of his hands and he smiled, sinking deeper into his chair. He looked at the cross on the mantle and Camila knew he was thinking about his mother. He closed his eyes. She imagined him as a thin wisp of smoke, thinning and disappearing as he filled the room.

He opened his eyes and looked at the cross again. "She hit me a lot," he said weakly.

Camila's mother burst into tears and looked away.

He smiled again. "She thought it would make us Christian."

He closed his eyes and was silent for a minute. He spoke once more with his eyes closed. "Will you take the cross, Camila?"

"I will," she said.

***

Camila sat once again under the oak tree. The dirt was marked with paw prints and scattered with leaves. She moved the leaves and smoothed the dirt with a stick, then looked down at her phone, which she had turned off the day before.

There were new voice mails, but she put her phone down in the dirt instead of listening to them. She stared up at the deep green leaves and billowing white clouds, feeling a deep quiet in her body.

She picked up her phone and listened to the messages from Alex. Then she dialed his number.

Chapter Seventy-One

Alex recognized Camila's number, sat up in bed, and flipped open the phone.

"Hello?"

"Hey, I got your messages."

"Hey."

Neither spoke for a moment. Finally, Alex said, "How's your father?"

"He died a few hours ago. I'm sitting under the tree I used to sit in as a little girl."

"I wish I had been there when my parents died. I miss them." Camila said nothing. "I understand why you left," Alex continued. "I mean, it hurt like hell but it makes sense."

"Tell me what's going on out there. I guess you haven't been murdered yet."

Alex laughed. "Almost, but not yet."

"What happened?"

Alex told her about Rak breaking into the room, murdering Officer Balby, and taking the video. "But it was what he said at the end that got to me. He said, 'This isn't him killing you, it's me.' And before that, he said, 'You weren't supposed to die.' What the hell could that mean?"

"I don't know. Sounds like he's watched too many dumb movies where the bad guy has to say something sinister before killing the good guy. What about the case?"

Alex told her about Bice killing Hollinger and his theory that Sharp was the source who had been calling him. She listened without speaking. "So, I have enough to publish," he concluded, "but nowhere near enough to do much real damage to Bice. And Rak is still out there somewhere."

"I guess I should be surprised, but I'm not. Maybe I'm still in shock about my father. You sound different."

"How?"

"I don't know ... softer, but also firmer."

Alex stood up and looked out at the beach. "I had a strange night. I'll tell you about it sometime. I don't feel different. I mean, I don't know how I feel." He wished she were in the room with him. "I miss you."

"I kind of miss you, too."

He sat back down on the bed. "I need to ask you something."

"Ask."

"You know how you're into trusting our intuition, feeling into people? All that stuff?"

Camila laughed. "Yeah."

"Well, I want to tell you what happened before my parents died. It's never felt right and I want to tell you."

"Okay. Why now?"

"Will you just listen?"

"Yeah."

Alex lay down on the bed, closed his eyes, and pressed the phone to his ear. "I graduated the first week of June, 1997. My parents came the week before. They hadn't visited once in my four years at NYU, so it was a big deal. I took them around to all my favorite spots, introduced them to friends. Like parents do, they reminisced about what the Village was like back in the early seventies. Is it just me or do you always imagine the Village in the seventies in those sort of off-color, pastel film colors?"

"You're changing the subject, Alex."

"So they were there for a week. We go to the graduation—six thousand of us in a big auditorium. Afterwards, they take me out to dinner, an Italian place in the Village. My mom was really into food, kind of like you. She knew in advance what restaurant we would go to. Anyway, we have a real fancy dinner and, at dinner, they seemed all weird."

"Weird how?"

Alex stood and walked to the glass door that led to the balcony. He stared out at the water. "It's hard to say. You know how after years of marriage a couple has a thing? An equilibrium? Like the relationship has become a third person? Around me they had always felt soft, like they had each melted a bit around the edges and the third person had formed in the space between them."

"Sounds kinda hippyish for you."

"You know what I mean, though."

"I do."

"At dinner that night it was like the third person, the one in the middle, had disappeared. Like they were separate people again and there was nothing between them."

"Did you ask them about it? Did you ask them what was going on?"

"No. I only noticed in retrospect. I didn't become fully conscious of it until the next day, when I found out they were dead. And I didn't really trust it anyway. I forgot about it until the last week."

"What made you remember?"

"I think it was that day we walked in the park, and you said something about Bice and Martin at the funeral. That you had a feeling something was off. Turns out you were right. I guess I've had that feeling for a long time, like something was off. Never told anyone about it, though."

They were silent for a minute.

"There's something else," Alex said. "When Rak was about to kill me, and he said what he said, I got that same feeling. Something is off and I don't know what."

"I don't know what's going on, but you're probably right."

"What are you going to do now?" he asked.

"Stay with my mom a couple days. There will be a small funeral. Then I'll head back to the City."

"Okay, I'll call soon. I'm gonna meet the New York cop later today."

Chapter Seventy-Two

Alex heard a knock and then Grady's voice outside. He sat on the bed for a moment, gathering himself. When another knock came, he walked to the door and opened it.

Grady stood beside a pale, red-haired man with freckles who held out his hand to Alex. "This is Officer Doyle," Grady said.

"Hello, Officer Doyle."

"Hi there," Doyle said. He spoke quickly, in an Irish-American accent Alex thought was from the Bay Ridge section of Brooklyn. "Let's see if we can't catch us a killer."

***

Alex and Doyle sat in the hotel restaurant, picking meat from crab legs. Doyle had ordered a local beer, even though it was only 11 a.m.

"Aren't you on duty?" Alex asked.

"Special assignment, so I can make my own hours."

Doyle got up and helped himself to coffee from the buffet. He added four sugars and enough milk to turn it off-white. He drank half his coffee in one sip and said, "So, there are rumors going around that your man is somehow connected to the Santiago case. What do you know about that?"

Alex studied the officer's pale, freckled cheeks, which were already reddening from the beer. He decided to try to find out as much as possible before telling him what he knew. "Not much," he said. "I thought I had some good leads, but what do I know? I'm just a reporter, right?"

"Well, the rumors are going around. Nothing to base it on that I'm aware of. But why would *you* become a target?"

"I was approached by a source about ten days ago who said he had a video of the night Professor Martin was murdered. Are you familiar with the details of the case?"

"Who isn't?"

Alex squeezed lemon juice onto a plate of steamed asparagus, then spoke between bites. "Well, I was approached by a man named Demarcus Downton who said he had a video and, long story short, I got it and Downton was murdered. Then someone broke into my apartment. I assume it was Dimitri Rak, the guy you're looking for in the Downton murder. Next, I came here and Rak showed up."

"But why did you come here, why not go to the police in New York City?"

"We were afraid."

"We?"

"I came with a friend. She was helping me with the story and Rak broke into her apartment, too."

"Where is she now?"

Alex looked at his plate of asparagus. "Not sure."

"And where's the video now? I should see it for the investigation."

"Don't have it. I got it while on the job so my paper took it."

"Any copies?"

"No."

"And why didn't your paper run a story on it?"

Alex folded an asparagus spear and popped it into his mouth. "You'd have to ask my boss."

"So why Kona?"

"We were trying to track down a lead we thought might be connected to the case. Turned out to be a dead end, though. When Rak showed up, Camila took off and I decided to sit tight. I had heard someone from the NYPD was coming."

Alex finished his asparagus and got up to refill his coffee at the buffet.

When he returned, Doyle was picking his teeth with a toothpick. He looked at Alex carefully. "So you're telling me you haven't found anything else? I mean, nothing that explains why Rak would be after you?"

"Well, I assume it's because of what's on that video. You've heard the rumors. Somehow he's connected to the Martin murder and he doesn't want me to talk. I'm one of only a few people who has seen the video."

"I understand that, but haven't you found anything that links him to anyone else or any reason for killing Martin, assuming he did?"

"Isn't that your job?"

Doyle smiled wide. "That's why I'm here."

***

They made a plan to meet in the restaurant the next morning and Doyle excused himself, saying he wanted to spend the afternoon reviewing the case files.

Alex went back to his room. He felt uneasy but didn't know why and, before he knew what he was doing, he had retrieved the recordings of Downton he had made at the café. For the next few hours he paced the room listening to them and jotting down key quotes that might make their way into his story. After finishing the tapes, he sat on his bed and stared at the wall. As he sat, the uneasiness intensified. There was something about Doyle, he thought. But what?

Chapter Seventy-Three

Thursday, September 19, 2002

"So, we have an idea about how to track down your man," Doyle said.

They were eating breakfast at the same table they had eaten at the day before.

"How?" Alex asked.

"Well, we figure that he knows you're here."

Alex stared at him in disbelief and pushed his empty plate to the middle of the table. "I know he knows I'm here. He tried to kill me? Twice. Remember?"

Doyle sipped a beer. "Right. So he knows you're here and where you're staying, but you haven't heard anything from him in … how long?"

"Couple days."

"We figure he hasn't wanted to come at you the same way twice. Having me here will make him even more afraid. You can bet he's watching. So we're gonna put you out on the beach, where we can see him coming."

"You want to use me as bait? That's the best you can come up with? You can't track him to his hotel, anything like that?"

"We tried that. I mean, the locals did. They visited every hotel in town. He ain't at a hotel. Best they got was a porter at a hotel who said he carried bags for a guy who fit the description, but the guy wasn't there anymore and now there's no trace of him. They checked every flight for the last ten days. And I wouldn't say we're using you as bait. I wouldn't call it that."

"What would you call it?" Alex asked.

"Look at it this way, either he's gone home, so there's no risk, or he hasn't, and we'll have a dozen guys surrounding you."

"So, how is that not using me as bait?"

Doyle finished his beer and waved his empty bottle at the waitress. "I'd call it … well, yeah, I guess we're using you as bait." Doyle laughed.

"That's hilarious," Alex said. "Really funny."

"You seen *Goodfellas*?" Doyle asked. "You know, Scorsese, De Niro, Joe Pesci?"

Alex nodded and Doyle turned and smiled at the waitress, who had come up behind him and was putting down another beer.

"You seen it?" Doyle asked. "*Goodfellas*?" She nodded. He sat up and cleared his throat, then glared at Alex and glanced at the waitress every few seconds to make sure she was still paying attention.

"I'm *funny*? I'm *funny*?" His voice had changed into a cheesy Italian accent. A bad Joe Pesci impression. "You mean … let me understand this … cuz I … maybe it's me. Maybe I'm a little fucked up maybe. I'm funny how? I mean funny, like a clown? I amuse you? I make you laugh? I'm here to fuckin' amuse you? Whattya mean funny? Funny how?"

Alex stared at him blank faced, a sinking feeling in his stomach. Hadn't Downton talked about a freckled Irish cop who did Joe Pesci impressions? The waitress was laughing and smiling, and when Alex ignored him, Doyle shifted his performance to her.

"You really are a funny guy," she said in a bad Italian accent.

Doyle pulled out his gun and waved it around the room wildly for a second before putting it on the table and high-fiving the waitress.

Pointing at Alex and still speaking with the accent, he said, "I think you may fold under questioning."

***

Back in his room, Alex called the KPD and asked for Detective Grady.

"Mr. Grady," he said, "I know how they are going to come after me. Doyle."

Chapter Seventy-Four

Alex sat on the stretch of beach he and Camila had sat on four days earlier. The sky was dark blue, turning to brown, and the moon hung over the water. He dug in the sand with a sharp rock, then looked at the parking lot, where he knew that Doyle, Grady, and six members of the KPD were sitting in darkened cars, watching him through night-vision goggles.

During his breakfast with Doyle, Alex had figured out what he had been listening for on the Downton tapes. That afternoon, he had called Bearon at the courthouse and found out that Doyle had just returned from an eight-month suspension that had started in mid-December. This had been the final piece of evidence Alex had needed to confirm that Doyle was the cop who had placed the wire on Downton. He had no idea how Bice had managed to have him sent to Kona, but he had no doubt that it had been Bice. And he had no doubt that Doyle was there to kill him.

He assumed that, at some point, Doyle would find a way to give Rak the opening he needed to get to him. It would all look like a terrible accident. A good plan gone awry. Alex figured that Doyle might even jump in at the last second and kill Rak—after letting Rak kill Alex—both to look like a hero and to destroy the evidence as a favor to Bice.

As the moon rose, the light changed from the soft darkness of twilight to a silver darkness of shadows and contrast. Alex stared out at the water, but glanced left and right down the beach every few seconds. He was terrified. He trusted Grady and his men, but still felt unsure of their plan.

"Grady, are you there?" He spoke into the tiny microphone concealed in his collar. "Tap something if you can hear me. I'm freaking out here."

He heard a tap in his earpiece.

To his right, a shadow moved. Alex sat up, rigid, then relaxed when he saw that it had been caused by a bird passing overhead. He looked to his left and saw a couple far off in the distance, walking close to the water. "There's something," he said into the microphone. His gut told him that Rak worked alone, and as the couple approached, he could tell they were both taller than Rak. After a few minutes they angled away from the water and toward the street. "It's nothing," he said.

He saw something moving far out in the water, bathed in the moonlight. He thought it was a night surfer but then noticed that, instead of moving toward the beach and side-to-side, it was coming straight toward him.

He whispered into the microphone. "Out on the water." He felt his feet begin to move in the sand, as though they wanted to stand up and run without his permission, but he made himself sit still.

"There's more movement. It's a small boat, way out on the water." Alex pushed the bulletproof vest higher on his neck, thinking that Rak could have a rifle pointed at his head at that very moment. "It's been coming for a minute or two, right at me." He had the feeling he'd had back in his darkened room the morning of 9/11. He wanted to get away, to be alone. Everything in him wanted to get up and run, but he sat perfectly still, staring at the boat. Images of Demarcus Downton appeared in his mind. Then little Tyree, sweeping his arm through stacks of blocks, laughing.

Doyle's thick accent broke the silence. "Officer Grady, I saw movement. On the water."

Then Alex heard Grady's voice. "What?"

"Way out there. A small boat."

"I see it," Grady said. "Maybe that's where Rak has been hiding the last few days."

Alex heard the beep of a radio and Grady's voice. "Stevens, Mitchell, and Sanchez. We have a possible sighting on the water. Be alert. I'm calling in the chopper." Another beep, then Grady continued. "Possible sighting out on the water. Request aerial support."

Alex watched the boat move slowly toward him and spoke into the microphone. "Grady. I'm about to bail. Where are your guys?" He knew Grady couldn't respond without giving their plan away to Doyle. He clenched his fist around the sharp rock.

Then he heard Doyle's voice. "Wait a second, I'm seeing something. Officer Grady, take your two men down to the left. I saw movement in the lot down there."

"Yes, sir," Grady said. "Kekua, Sanchez, follow me."

Through his earpiece, Alex heard a car door open and close. "Grady, what are you doing?" he asked.

A rumbling sound came up from behind him, toward the center of town. He looked back to see a helicopter appear over the hills. Grady's voice came through the earpiece, "Alex, that's the chopper. I'm going to the left side of the parking lot and will circle back. Just stay there. The chopper will take care of Rak. If Doyle makes a move toward you, I'll kill him."

Alex glanced at the boat, which was still coming straight at him, then up at the parking lot. He saw the car door open. Doyle got out and started jogging toward the beach. Out of the corner of his eye, Alex saw Grady breaking into a run toward Doyle. Alex dropped and splayed out in the sand when he heard the first shot come from the direction of the water. He glanced up just as Grady tripped and fell face first onto the beach.

The sand jumped again. Another bullet from the direction of the water. Doyle was about thirty feet away, gun drawn and in a full sprint straight toward Alex.

He covered his head with his hands.

He knew he was about to die.

The sand jumped again and Alex thought he could hear Grady shouting through the earpiece, but he couldn't tell what was being said over the sound of the helicopter, which was now passing low overhead. He peeked out from under his arms just as Doyle ran past him and stopped at the edge of the water.

Alex stared in disbelief as Doyle pulled out a second gun and began firing wildly at the boat, a gun in each hand.

Alex jumped up and ran toward the parking lot, glancing back as the helicopter shone a sharp light on the boat. Doyle was firing shot after shot at the boat. Alex's head spun with fear and confusion. What the hell was happening?

He dropped back to the sand as another bullet came from the direction of the water and struck a rock next to him. After a few seconds, he looked back again, just in time to see Doyle's brain splatter the sand at the edge of the water. The dead officer's knees buckled and he fell face first into the surf.

For the next minute, Alex lay with his head buried in his arms, gunshots all around him, the helicopter loud overhead.

Finally, he felt a hand on his shoulder and looked up to find Grady peering down at him. "Our guys rappelled onto the boat and Rak was taken alive," he said. "Rak killed Doyle. Why the hell did Doyle run up and fire like that? Didn't you say you thought he was sent here by that Bice guy? To kill *you*?"

Alex looked up. "I don't know," he said, but a single sentence hung in his mind.

You aren't supposed to die.

Chapter Seventy-Five

Friday, September 20, 2002

Alex opened the door and peeked out of his hotel room. Grady was no longer there, but two men with notebooks and one holding a microphone sat on the steps between his room and the courtyard. When they saw him, they raced up the steps.

"Mr. Vane, can we get a comment?" one yelled.

A bright light from a camera flashed in his eyes as he slammed the door. "Damn reporters," he said under his breath.

He sat on the bed and took out his recorder, then dictated the story of the night before. When he had finished, he got dressed, walked to the window, and looked out through the curtains. He could see the three reporters sitting on the stairs again. He closed the curtains, then looked at the room service menu on the bedside table.

He dialed the number. "Hi there. Can I get three orders of pancakes, three western omelets, and a pitcher of coffee? Yeah, deliver it to the three men sitting on the steps outside room 203. I'm finishing something up and keeping them waiting for an interview. Bill it to my room. Yeah. Thanks."

Twenty minutes later, Alex watched out the window as the food order arrived and the reporters tried to figure out what was going on. While they spoke with the man from room service, Alex opened the door and crept down the walkway.

In the business center, he tried logging onto his work e-mail, but it had been shut down. He checked his personal e-mail and saw a message from James Stacy.

From: james@news-scoop.com
To: alex_vane@hotmail.com
Subject: I watched the video!
Date: September 18, 2002 5:12:15 PM EST

Alex-

Called you a couple times yesterday. Maybe I shouldn't have, but I e-mailed myself a copy of that video the night you were in the newsroom with Camila. I just watched it. You NEED to get in touch with me.

I've started my own Web site. www.news-scoop.com. A whole site devoted to investigative reporting into the inner workings of the press. "All the news about the news." Do you need a job?

My first act was getting someone to leak the records of the pay phone you asked about. I'm running the site from my apartment for now. My second act might be to run the copy of that video if you don't get in touch with me soon.

James Stacy
CEO, news-scoop.com

Alex read the e-mail twice. "That little bastard," he said under his breath, smiling.

***

At 9 a.m., Grady poked his head into the business center, trailed by another officer. "I think those reporters think you're still in your room," he said, patting Alex on the back and laughing.

"That's the idea," Alex said.

"Alex, this is Detective Aliouh. He's here to take a report on what happened last night. Can we get your official statement?"

Alex led them past the reporters and back to the room, where he told Detective Aliouh everything he knew about Santiago, Rak, Martin, Downton, and Doyle. He connected Rak to the murders of Martin and Downton, and, finally, told them his theory about Macintosh Hollinger and Denver Bice.

It took three hours, and when he was finished, Aliouh said, "We'll compile our report and send it along to the NYPD, but I should say that nothing beyond what happened on the island is in our purview."

"What's gonna happen to Rak?" Alex asked.

"We're sending him to New York. We have him on attempted murder here but they have a better case in New York, so we're extraditing him. From what I could gather on the phone, the city is pretty embarrassed about this Doyle guy. I still don't get why he would just start firing like that."

"Seems like he was here to kill Rak. To protect me. But why he did what he did, I don't know."

"My guess is you'll never know what really happened," Grady said.

"Don't be so sure. I'm a pretty good reporter."

"Anyway, as far as we're concerned, the case is closed. That whole mess with the Santiago kid, all that 9/11 stuff, we wouldn't touch that with a ten-foot pole. I'm sure the folks in New York will want to speak with you though."

"I'm sure they will," Alex said, shaking the detective's hand and showing him out.

"When will that be?" Grady asked, standing in the doorway. "I mean, when are you leaving?"

"I've got a redeye tonight. Leave at ten."

"I'll pick you up at eight," Grady said.

***

On the flight from Kona to San Francisco, as most of the other passengers slept, Alex stood in the airplane bathroom with his head ducked down and his lips an inch from his recorder, dictating parts of his story. Several times, he took out the tape he was working on and inserted the recording of his conversation with Downton, memorized a quote, then swapped tapes and dropped the quote into the story. After he filled a tape, he started another.

On the connecting flight from San Francisco to New York, he wrote out a series of notes on a yellow legal pad. He planned to give a copy of the notes to the NYPD, though he knew that he would have to repeat much of what he was writing in interviews. He started with his work on the Santiago trial and his meetings with Downton. Then he covered the precise details of how he had obtained the video, the day his apartment had been ransacked, and his flight to Hawaii. He described his encounters with Rak, his four days under the protection of the KPD, and his eventual role in apprehending Rak. He also included a detailed description of Doyle and some quotes from Downton about how he had recorded the video in the first place.

Finally, he included a few pages of notes with everything he had learned about Macintosh Hollinger and Denver Bice. He knew that it would not be enough to connect Rak or Doyle to Bice, but he thought maybe the NYPD would have information that could fill in the gaps.

By the time the plane landed at JFK, he had filled twenty pages, which he stuffed into his bag as he walked off the plane.

Chapter Seventy-Six

Saturday, September 21, 2002

Alex awoke at 7 a.m. and surveyed his apartment. He stepped into the kitchen over books, clothes, and papers, and put on a pot of coffee. As it brewed, he pushed everything into the corner of the room.

He saw a red envelope wedged under the door. He picked it up and turned it over in his hands. It had no markings. He opened the envelope and pulled out a piece of paper. It was one page of Denver Bice's phone bill. A single call was highlighted in yellow. Alex recognized the number. At 9:39 a.m. on 9/11, Bice had received a two-minute call from the pay phone at World Trade Center Plaza.

This was it. It wasn't enough to convict Bice of anything, but it would certainly make things uncomfortable for him.

He poured himself a cup of coffee and smiled. As he turned to look out the window, his mind flashed and he jerked his head to look at the paper in his hand. He had expected the phone record to be an official copy from the phone company, the kind police get when doing an investigation. This was a regular phone bill—the kind customers get in the mail.

He put down the paper and paced the room, sipping his coffee. How in the hell could Sharp have gotten this? He put the coffee down and took out James's list. He called Sharp's home number and left a message.

"Mr. Sharp, Alex Vane. I need to speak with you. Look, I'm going to publish in the next couple days—at least I think so. I know you don't want me calling you, but I need a little more. And I need to know this phone record isn't stolen. Please, I can guarantee your anonymity. Call me."

After two cups of coffee, he sat down at his computer with his notes and the recordings next to him. He opened a new document, pressed play, and began to type. When the first tape ended thirty minutes later, he had transcribed five thousand words.

He took a break to check his e-mail and opened one from an address he did not recognize.

> From: l_harrison@harrisoninvestments.com
> To: alex_vane@hotmail.com
> Subject: Concerning the Matter of Macintosh Hollinger
> Date: September 20, 2002 9:29:14 PM EST
>
> Dear Mr. Vane,
>
> After consultation with Sonia—who speaks highly of you—I have determined that it is in everyone's interest that I allow myself to be quoted in your article about the death of Macintosh Hollinger. Since it is likely that the media will link me to Mr. Hollinger eventually, I would rather my statement be included from the outset.
>
> My legal advisors have copies of this statement to ensure I am accurately quoted.
>
> Here is my statement: On the evening of August 28, 2001, I received a call from Macintosh Hollinger, formerly a client of my financial advisory firm, Harrison Investments. Our professional relationship ended in 1995, but our friendship developed and I often offered him informal advice on a wide range of financial matters.
>
> On the night in question, Mr. Hollinger called me and asked what the tax consequences would be of selling $500 million of his holdings in the Standard Media Group.

At the time, he also made clear that he intended to donate all the proceeds of the sale to a not-for-profit, the Media Protection Organization.

"Why?" was the first question I asked. That evening, both Mac and I had the Yankees game muted on TV as we spoke. He loved the Yankees and was eager to get back to the game. He told me that he would explain when we met in person. But I insisted he tell me right away.

The game went to commercial and the television showed a row of Yankees leaning on the dugout. To their right, there was a row of reporters and cameramen.

"Louis, do you have the game on?" Mac asked me. "You see them? The players, the journalists?"

"Yes," I told him. "I see them."

"They lied to us," was all he would say.

Mr. Hollinger was a lovable, eccentric man, and though I never had the opportunity to try to dissuade him of this particular financial move, I doubt I would have been successful.

Sincerely,
Louis Harrison

When he finished reading the e-mail, Alex leaned back in his chair. His phone rang. "Hello?"

"Alex, it's J-James. Where have you been?"

"I'm just finishing a story that should explain it pretty well. Can you be here in an hour?"

"Yes."

"Bring the video."

Chapter Seventy-Seven

James stood in front of him, red-faced and panting. "That's a lot of s-stairs," he said, collapsing on the bed. Alex watched as a bead of sweat dripped onto his bed. "S-sorry," James said between breaths.

"Don't worry about it. You're about to help save my ass. I hope."

"That's why I'm here. I want your story to be the first on my new site. And we better get it out f-fast. Things look bad for Santiago."

"Will anyone read it on your site?"

"Leave that part to me. And what about Rak? Have you heard anything on him?"

"Nothing," Alex said. "I have an appointment with the NYPD Sunday. They want to interview me about the whole thing. But I know someone who might have heard something."

James sat at the desk as Alex dialed Bearon at the courthouse. "Hey it's me … Yeah, I know … This is important. Have you heard anything about Rak? You know he got caught and was extradited back here and—Yeah … Yeah." Alex listened. "For everything? And where are you getting this?" Alex nodded his head, smiling. "Okay, thanks."

He hung up and turned to James. "Rak is taking the rap for the Downton murder, saying he acted alone. Eyewitness from *The Post* story has him leaving Downton's apartment that night. Now the Ukraine wants him back. Says he blew up a church there ten years ago."

"What about M-Martin?"

"My guy said no," Alex said. "They don't have enough to connect him to Martin. Just that bartender, but that's pretty circumstantial."

"We'll have to change that. Santiago is gonna be convicted in the next week or two."

"Then you better read this fast," Alex said, leaning over the desk and opening the story on his laptop. As Alex lay on the bed, his buzzer rang again. His shoulders clenched.

"Don't worry," James said. "It's our mystery g-guest."

Alex sprang up and pressed the button to unlock the door at street level. A few minutes later, Lance Brickman walked into Alex's apartment wearing a neat brown suit and fingering a cigar. He looked around the apartment. "Damn son, no wonder you want to work in TV. My humidor is bigger than this shithole."

***

Alex recounted his entire story to Lance as they sat on the bed and James read his story.

"Don't you want to listen?" Alex asked James as he reached the part about Doyle and the capture of Rak.

"I can read and listen at the same t-time," James said.

"James, just how smart are you?" Alex asked.

"He's smart enough to hire me," Lance said.

"What?"

"I quit," Lance said. "After twenty-nine years and ten months, I am no longer employed by *The New York Standard*."

Alex smiled at him.

"I'm gonna work for the Internet. Don't really know what that means." He shrugged. "But James tells me you're coming on board. Says I can write whatever I want about all the bastards in the sports media. Says he'll get people to read it. Gonna rip everyone in sports a new one."

"What about your vesting?" Alex asked. "Your stock?"

"Hell with the stock. Once we run your story, it's not gonna be worth anything anyway."

Alex laughed and nodded toward James. "He said I was coming along, too?"

Not looking away from the computer, James said "I figured you would decide on the plane. I guess that makes us p-partners." He swiveled his chair around. "Finished."

"Well, how is it?" Lance said. "Was it worth you both getting fired?"

"Well, it's too long, and five things are missing," James said.

"Having you as my editor feels weird," Alex said. "Didn't you work *for me* like two weeks ago?"

"Get used to it," James said. "It's good, but c-c-can we stick to what it needs? Lance, can you call around and g-get some people to go on record about Downton? Sports people, people who knew him, the more famous the b-better. You know, heartwarming stuff."

Lance nodded. "That I can do."

"But what are the five things?" Alex asked.

James held up his index finger. "First, we need to add the evidence showing that Hollinger called B-B-Bice from the pay phone on the morning of 9/11. Like I said, I have those records now."

"I almost forgot," Alex said. He handed him the phone bill he had received that morning.

"Wow," James said. "This is better than what I got. At some point I'll want to know if you got this legally, but that can wait. Second," he held up another finger, "we need to get the finance guy who spoke to Hollinger to go on record. What was his n-name?"

"Harrison. He e-mailed this morning. I can insert that," Alex said.

"Good," James said as he put up a third finger. "Third, we need Bice's denial. Or a denial from Bice's c-camp. Fourth," he continued, holding up another finger, "we need an explanation of that black fuzz found in Hollinger's mouth."

"I'll handle the Bice denial today," Alex said. "But I'm not gonna be able to find out anything about that fuzz. Could be a million things. And, as you know, we're not getting the coroner's report."

"At least call his office so we can insert a 'no comment.'"

"And what about the video?" Alex asked.

"That's the centerpiece of the story," James said. "If we do it right, every news station in the country will be running it by tomorrow n-night."

"Okay, what's the fifth thing?" Alex asked.

James held his hand up like he was asking for a high five. "Finally, we need that source. Even if he stays anonymous, we need him to go on record and say something—anything—that connects Rak to Bice, or Bice to Hollinger on the m-morning of 9/11. We have the Santiago p-piece down cold. But without any solid evidence, the story doesn't implicate Bice. It's just a bunch of d-dots. Even though *we* know they connect, the reader won't. It could be dismissed as a crazy Internet thing."

"And you think a quote from an anonymous source will solve that?" Alex asked.

"Most p-people skim articles. They skip the attributions, they skip the B-Matter, and they scan down for the quotes. People are more willing to believe something between quotation marks. That's why j-journalists spend half their time trying to get people to say things they already know to be true."

"I called Sharp this morning," Alex said. "Haven't heard back. And, to be honest, I'm no longer a hundred percent sure he's the source. How could he have gotten Bice's *personal* phone bill?"

Lance was already on his cell phone making calls and James turned to the computer.

Alex looked down at his phone. He had a text from Camila: *I found your pole in my apartment. Dinner tomorrow? Sweet Marie's at 6:00?*

Chapter Seventy-Eight

Sunday, September 22, 2002

James Stacy lived in a large loft in Washington Heights, with two windows facing onto 160th Street. Alex stepped in, then stopped and surveyed the room. "Damn, this is not what I expected," he said.

The ceilings were high, the floors bright and shiny hardwood, the furniture modern leather.

"Doesn't exactly go with my outward ap-p-pearance," James said.

"Or your desk at work."

"My desk is messy here, too," James said. "Only place I keep messy."

James walked over to a large desk in the corner covered in trash and three computer screens set up in a U shape. "Make your c-calls," he said. "I'm gonna drive traffic."

"What?" Alex asked.

"I'll explain later."

James went to work on his computer as Alex called around for denials and inserted them in the story on his laptop. When Alex said that he was going to publish a story that exonerated Santiago, the NYPD spokesman begged him to wait until Tuesday to run the story so his bosses could have time to respond. Alex politely declined. He left a message for the coroner in charge of the bodies from 9/11, informing him that he was going to publish a story that implied that 9/11 had one less victim than reported. He did not expect a call back.

He reached a spokesman for Standard Media who said that Denver Bice had no comment. Before hanging up, the spokesman added, "If this article comes across as a disgruntled ex-employee trying to smear his former employer, we will not only sue for libel, we will use our considerable resources to—how shall I put this—correct the record in the public forum."

Alex knew he would be attacked and discredited once the story came out, and he braced himself inwardly for what was to come.

Next, he called Sonia Hollinger to go over her version of events and double-check her quotes. After a few minutes of small talk, during which she admonished him for not coming by before leaving Hawaii, she confirmed her piece of the story. When Alex tried to say "good-bye," she said, "If you ever come back to Kona, please come and see me, honey. I imagine this story will ruffle quite a few feathers. If you need to get away, you can always stay with Juan and me for a spell. We're both quite fond of you."

Alex thanked her, hung up, and turned to James, who was swiveling between screens and drinking soda. "What are you doing?" he asked.

"Driving traffic," James said.

***

That afternoon Alex met with Damian Bale, who confirmed everything he had said previously, then tried to make Alex promise to mention his new venture in the story.

When he returned to James's apartment, Alex read through the story one final time, then handed it to Lance when he walked in the door. "Take an ax to it," Alex said. "It's still too long."

"Well, you do like to hear yourself talk, don't you?" Lance looked around the apartment, then at James. "Damn, this place is nicer than mine." He waved the stack of papers in the air and took a red pen and a cigar out of his shirt pocket. He smiled. "I'm gonna sit on a park bench and smoke while I do this."

***

An hour later, Lance returned and handed the pages to Alex. They were covered in red ink and the top page was smeared with ashes held on by an unidentifiable wetness.

"You didn't sleep with it, did you?" Alex asked.

Lance laughed. "Kind of looks like it, huh? Never had a project of my own to work on. Really poured everything into it. It's a good piece. When you enter my edits, it'll be a great piece. It's gonna cause a splash if anyone actually reads it."

Alex entered Lance's changes, then e-mailed the final copy to James, who read it and corrected typos on one of his screens while running Internet search applications on the other two.

Alex pointed at the screens. "What are you doing on those computers?" he asked.

"Making sure that anytime someone types Eric Santiago, John Martin, Denver Bice, Standard Media, 9/11, Macintosh Hollinger, media conglomeration, the merger, or pretty much anything else you can think of into a search engine, our story c-comes up."

"When will it go live?" Alex asked.

"Late tonight or early in the m-morning."

"I guess we'll run it without anything from my source," Alex said. "Called him two more times and nothing."

Chapter Seventy-Nine

Alex rode the subway sixty-five blocks south and walked into Sweet Marie's. Camila sat at the counter, sipping what looked like a bowl of whipped cream. He approached her from behind and touched her shoulder as she took a sip.

Her hand gave a start and a bit of whipped cream dotted her nose. "Hey," she said, wiping away the cream.

"On a diet?" he asked.

"It's hot chocolate. And, yes, I'm limiting myself to six servings of whipped cream a day." She reached down and handed him his pole from the floor. "It was still in my apartment."

Alex took it and smiled. "Thanks."

The waitress came out of the kitchen and handed them menus. They read in silence, then put their menus down at the same time.

"Did you get the story?" Camila asked.

"Yeah, I got it. It's gonna run tomorrow on a new Web site that James Stacy started. Thinks he can sell ads and 'drive traffic' and all that."

"He's probably right. And you are now officially a *digital journalist.* Did you find out if it was Sharp who's been calling you?"

"I thought it was, but now I'm not sure. The story is good, though, and the video will be too much to ignore. It should get Santiago off. But we didn't really get Bice. We implied a lot but no real proof."

The waitress came back and Alex ordered a vegetable omelet. Camila ordered a steak sandwich and another hot chocolate.

"Are you afraid of Bice?" she asked. "He did try to have us both killed."

"A little, but I think he will want to lay low now that the police have Rak. And when this article comes out, even if most people don't believe the part about him, it will still be a major inconvenience. My guess is that he will never be caught. He'll find a way to wriggle out of this, but he's not gonna come after me again. There will be too many eyes on him. Plus, I still can't shake the feeling that he never wanted me dead in the first place."

"You think they'll come after you in the press?"

"They'll hammer me. Hammer James and Lance. Maybe even you. The story won't just mess with Bice, it will cast Standard Media in a bad light. Even if people don't believe it, it's not the kind of thing investors and board members want to see."

"Especially just a few weeks away from their merger closing."

The food came and Alex took a moment to watch Camila as she ate. Then he took a bite of his omelet and swallowed hard. "I meant to say before, I'm sorry about your dad."

"Don't be." She smiled and looked up at him. "I mean, thanks. It's okay, though. I feel okay to miss him now."

"What's it like?"

"What's what like?"

"Something's happened to you. It was happening the whole time, but now you seem different. It's why I fell in love with you. I know I am only seeing the surface, but I do see the surface."

She smiled at him. "You're right," she said. She sipped her water and was quiet for a moment. "Remember that bad feeling I told you about on the plane?"

Alex nodded. "Yeah, but I didn't really understand it."

"Have you ever done that thing where you get to work and think you left the coffee pot on at home?"

"Yeah."

"You imagine that the coffee will slowly burn away. The pot will start smoking, then the fire alarm will go off and the neighbors will have to call the police. You keep thinking about it all day, but you think you probably turned it off so you don't go home to check it. And you're too embarrassed to call your neighbor to ask him to check it. So you just worry. And it nags at you, this low-level anxiety, all day. It's mostly in the background but occasionally it smashes into the foreground and you feel terror or dread. Then you dismiss it and work for a while, but it comes back. You might even stay extra busy just so you don't have to think about it." She paused and sipped her hot chocolate. "It's the feeling that something is fundamentally wrong with our lives, with us."

"Yeah, I know the feeling. I have that even if I don't think I've left the coffee pot on."

"So what happens when you get home and you realize the coffee pot was off the whole time?"

He took a big bite and she laughed at him.

"That must have been a whole egg," she said.

He chewed vigorously and sipped his coffee.

"What happens?" she asked again.

"Relief, I guess."

"Relief that this big problem turns out not to have existed in the first place. And you can see the silliness of the whole thing—the anxiety, the dread, the scrunched up forehead."

"Yeah, but then I just find another problem, another thing to be concerned about."

"The problem is never the coffee pot. If it were, you'd just deal with it, head home and check it. But, like you said, then you find another thing to worry about. Well, imagine that relief, that 'ahhhhhh' you feel when you realize that the coffee pot was never on. Your body relaxes, your mind is clear and, somehow, you realize that the guy who was anxious all day was just a tightened up version of you."

"Okay."

"So imagine if that feeling swept over everything, your whole life. Every mean thing you have done. Every cruel thing that has been done to you. Every moment, every interaction, every bit of worry and alienation. It's like an iceberg melting inside you that you didn't know was there. You only become aware of its existence by the feeling of space and freedom that's left when it's gone." She took another sip of hot chocolate as he finished his omelet.

He studied her face but said nothing.

"What happened to me is kinda like that," she said.

"So, what are you gonna do next?"

"Finish my dinner. Go home. I have a class to teach tomorrow."

Chapter Eighty

Monday, September 23, 2002

James sat on his swivel chair with Alex on his left and Lance on his right. At 5 a.m., he clicked "upload" to make the story live on news-scoop.com. The final draft was accompanied by the video of Santiago, photos of Demarcus Downton, Denver Bice, Sadie Green, Mac and Sonia Hollinger, and Professor John Martin. It also included a photo of Rak that James had found online.

Next, James sent out a press release to over a hundred news outlets, both traditional and digital.

At 8 a.m., Lance pulled out his single sheet of sources and started making calls to his most famous contacts.

"If the right person sees the site, and mentions it, it could really help us," James said.

Every few minutes, Alex looked at his phone. He wasn't sure who he was expecting to call, but he knew that it would start ringing soon if James had done what he'd said he was going to do.

At 9 a.m., he walked up behind James, who was refreshing a web page over and over. "So, wait a minute," Alex said. "You can tell exactly how many people are reading the story, in real time."

"Yes, and how many are watching the video and how long each user stays on the s-site."

"How many so far?" Alex asked.

"Eleven."

"Hundred? Thousand?"

"No, eleven people total."

"What? I thought the Internet was supposed to be fast."

"Don't w-worry. A link is about to hit the inbox of every reporter in the five boroughs. Plus, everyone is just getting to work. Better make your calls."

Alex called Bearon and asked him to gossip about the story with anyone who came into the courthouse that morning. "Take a victory lap," Alex said. "You started leaking this thing a week ago. You're gonna be an oracle in the courthouse from now on." Next, he called a few reporters he knew from national papers. Finally, he called two former classmates with low-level TV jobs and asked them to show the story to their producers, promising them the video would make great TV.

***

By noon, Alex and Lance were watching over James's shoulder as he hit refresh again and again. The number of unique visitors to the site had hit one thousand and was climbing steadily.

"Your dreams have come true," Lance said, laughing. "You get to see in real-time how much everyone loves you."

Alex laughed. "I know, but it's not quite the same as print."

"You'll get used to it," James said.

Alex sat next to James, who looked at him uncomfortably.

"Alex, I've been meaning to ask, do you think there's any chance that C-C-. I mean that C-. That C-C-C-. That Camila would—"

"Nah," Alex said.

"I mean I felt like back at the office a few weeks ago she—"

"Don't think so."

"Well, then, once we're all rich and f-famous from this, I'm hoping that you guys can help me in that d-department." James looked back at the screen and refreshed the site traffic. "Do you two know what an exponential increase is? It's when you go from five readers an hour, to twenty-five an hour, to one hundred twenty-five an hour, and so on."

"Yeah, we know what it is," Alex said.

"Well, we're there. Turn on the TV. I'm expecting it soon. We got a thousand views in the last twenty m-m-minutes. If the rate keeps climbing throughout the day, we'll be at a hundred thousand views by dinnertime. And that's if TV *doesn't* pick it up."

Lance and Alex looked at each other. "But how do we get paid?" Lance asked.

"See the ads at the top and bottom of the page? One cent per page view, thirty cents per ad click," James said.

"What does that mean?" Lance asked.

Alex looked at Lance. "It means that if millions of people watch the video and read the story, and if some of them click on the ads, we don't have to go out and beg for jobs tomorrow."

***

That afternoon Alex clicked back and forth between CNN, Court TV, and the local news, waiting for the coverage. He imagined the frantic calls that must be taking place between Sharp and the NYPD and between TV producers and their sources. He smiled as he thought of the voice mail of the Standard Media spokesman filling up with requests for comments.

At 2 p.m., he got a call from a *Post* reporter, asking if he would be interviewed for a story about his story. He declined to comment and reminded him of the press release James had sent out earlier. After that, he got a text message from Sadie Green: *Saw the story. Wow! I take back all the nasty stuff I said to you and about you behind your back. Looks like Bice was more like Two-Face than Lex Luthor or Doctor Doom.*

By 3 p.m., Alex was receiving a call every fifteen minutes—first from local reporters, then national reporters, then TV producers asking if he would appear on a segment. He declined all of them.

***

At 4:45 p.m., WNYW did a teaser for the five o'clock news and mentioned the story for the first time on TV.

"A startup Web site has published startling accusations that could complicate the sensational murder trial of Eric Santiago and disrupt the proposed merger between Standard Media and Nation Corp. Details at five."

"Well," Lance said, patting Alex on the back, "you're gonna be on TV after all."

James plugged wires into the back of his computer, then walked to the TV and connected them.

"What's that for?" Alex asked.

"Capturing our coverage so we can use it to promote the site," James said. "Never too early to start thinking about our n-n-next story."

The news led with a summary of Alex's article and showed a still shot of the video next to the photo Alex had submitted when he applied for a job. The segment ran for five minutes and included a denial of the entire story from a Standard Media spokesman and a "no comment" from Daniel Sharp. By the time it ended, all three had muted their ringing phones.

"I guess the Internet *is* fast," Lance said.

James muted the TV. "Alex, I say you do *The Times*, and maybe in a day or two, *Larry King*. Just the classy old media stuff." James took a long drink of soda. "We want a sense of scarcity. Get the word out as wide as possible but push people toward the s-site. We've got to think long term." He leaned back in his chair. "And *Oprah*. If *Oprah* calls, we'll go."

Chapter Eighty-One

Monday, September 30, 2002

A week later, Alex walked out of his apartment building and was glad there were only three reporters and one TV crew waiting for him. He squinted in the morning light and put on a pair of black sunglasses as he walked past them. They followed him down Broadway, shouting questions.

"No comment," he said, his head down. "I've said all I'm going to say."

"Mr. Vane," one reporter yelled. "Is it true you're an alcoholic?"

"No comment."

"Then is it true that you used to drink on the job at *The Standard*?"

Alex bit his lower lip. "No comment."

"Mr. Vane, where are you headed?"

"For a walk!"

His phone beeped. As he walked, he read a text from Sadie Green: *Half of London turns out to protest a made-up war over the weekend, and what do the NY papers lead with Monday morning? Your sorry ass! But seriously, nice job on the story.*

A small man edged up next to Alex, jogging to keep up with his brisk pace. "Sources inside Standard Media say you have a personal grudge against the company, and that you fabricated the story to become famous. Do you have a comment?"

Alex ignored him. As he crossed 95th Street, the reporters turned back.

Oprah had not called, but in the last few days Alex had appeared in a feature in *The New York Times* and had done an hour on *Larry King Live*. He had turned down job offers from every local TV station, as well as CNN. The story had received over four million hits and generated eighty thousand click-throughs. Downton's video had been watched a million times and message boards had sprung up to debate the video, Santiago's reaction, and what it said about humanity. Altogether, news-scoop.com had made $145,000 from the story.

As he crossed 85th Street, Alex's phone rang and he flipped it open. "Bearon, what's up?"

"It's over," Bearon said. He was talking fast and breathing hard.

"What's over?"

"The trial. Santiago. He's gonna be released today. Can you get down here?"

"What happened?"

"Sharp is gonna drop the case. He's gonna make a huge show of it, too. Courthouse steps. *Justice being served.* All that shit. I'm hearing that they're working a case against Rak for killing Martin. You gotta get down here."

Alex stopped walking and stared at the cars going by. "I'll head down there now, but can you get a note to Santiago for me?"

***

That night, Alex and Camila stood outside Santiago's dorm on Carmine Street along with a handful of reporters and a local TV crew. "I guess the national press goes home after dinner," Alex said. Camila shivered in the cold night air.

Santiago emerged a few minutes later wearing jeans and a black pea coat, his face partially covered by a black scarf. Alex noticed the deep pockmarks on his forehead as he held out his hand. A photographer clicked away.

They shook hands and Alex said, "Thanks for meeting us. I thought we'd walk a bit to get away from all these reporters."

He turned to the group. "Head home guys. We're not making any news tonight."

Camila held out her hand to Santiago. "Camila Gray. You're back to looking like a regular NYU student."

"I saw you in court," Santiago said. "I thought you were pretty."

They walked in silence to Sixth Avenue, trailed by a photographer and a reporter who dropped away when they turned onto West Fourth toward Washington Square Park.

"What are you going to do now?" Alex asked.

"I don't know," Santiago said. He spoke in a flat monotone and didn't look at Alex as he answered.

"Are you going to enroll in classes this semester?" Camila asked.

"I don't know."

Alex looked at Camila, then back at Santiago. "I was wondering if you'd like to do an interview about the whole ordeal," he said. "You know, what happened that night, what jail was like, how it feels to be free. You probably know this was a pretty big story."

"I know," Santiago said. "I was more entertaining than the terrorists. That's what I read, anyway. I don't really know what it means."

"So, what do you think about being interviewed?" Alex asked.

"No, I'm not going to do that."

"But this is your chance to tell your side of the story, to get your version of—"

Camila broke in, "Oh, please, Alex, don't give him that line."

Santiago stopped in front of a pizza shop and inhaled. "The only bad thing about jail was the food. It was no good."

Alex led them in and bought Santiago a slice of pepperoni. They walked slowly toward the park as Santiago ate.

At the edge of the park, Santiago finished his slice and stopped to look at Alex. "Why'd you release that video?" he asked. His face was blank but his eyes flashed. "Why did you have to release it?"

Alex caught Santiago's eye. "What? What do you mean? We released it to get you out of jail, to show that you didn't kill him."

Santiago looked across the park, lit only by a few streetlights. "Maybe I was better off in there. They gave me food and a bed and some company at least. Like I said, though, the food was no good."

Alex put a hand on his shoulder. "But now you can go back to school, have a life. You know, *not* be in jail. I don't understand how you can—"

"Calm down," Camila said, taking Alex's hand. He quieted and the three of them headed toward the center of the park.

Santiago gestured toward the statue of Garibaldi, illuminated by a spotlight from below. "The finance students throw pennies at the base of the statue at the beginning of each semester," he said. "For luck." They stopped under the statue and Santiago picked up a penny. "Who is he anyway?"

"An Italian general and politician," Alex said. "He's credited with helping to unify Italy." He looked at Santiago, who didn't seem to be listening. "Eric, I've been wondering, why did you come to NYU anyway? I mean, it's not much of a baseball school and you had offers to some good California programs."

Santiago looked down at the penny. "You really want to know?"

"Yeah."

"I didn't care about baseball. I came here 'cause I didn't want my mom to see what I was going to do. You know, the drugs and peep shows and all that."

Camila said, "If you don't mind me asking, Eric, from the video it looks like you saw that something was wrong with him, with Professor Martin, I mean. Then, after he collapsed, it looked like you smiled. What was going on with you?"

Santiago sat on a slatted wooden bench near the base of the statue. Alex and Camila sat on either side of him.

"Did you know he was dying?" she asked.

Santiago looked at her. "Remember in the trial, when Sharp said that I used to kill bugs? He wasn't right about that. I never killed any of them." He looked at Camila. "In LA we had one of those little patches of grass in our front yard—a little square of grass like everyone else. You know those?"

Camila nodded. "We had one of those in Des Moines."

Santiago smiled. "We get a lot of sunshine out there, and when it does rain it usually doesn't last long. But sometimes it'll rain buckets for an hour or two. The worms will crawl outta the dirt and make their way into the middle of the sidewalk. Then, all of a sudden it'll stop raining and be, like, eighty degrees. The sun burns down hot, right on them. The worms get trapped on the sidewalk, ya know?"

Camila nodded and Santiago turned to stare into her eyes. "My mom used to shoot at flies with rubber bands while sitting on the couch. But I could never do that, ya know? I could never even wash an ant down the drain of my bathtub. I just wouldn't take a tub that day if there was an ant crawling around in there. But when the worms would get stuck out on the sidewalk, I would just watch them. The sidewalk would dry off quick in the bright sun and then all of a sudden the worms would be stuck, trying to crawl back to the wet dirt. Sometimes they made it, but sometimes they didn't. The ones that didn't just dried out in the sun and died." He paused. "I don't know who told Sharp that I like to kill bugs. That wasn't true. But I do like watching them die."

Camila was staring at him. Alex had looked away.

Santiago stood up and put his hand on Alex's shoulder. "If you want to know why I'm not going to be in your story, that's why. I know I'm broken. There's something inside me that God bent crooked when he made me and it's never gonna be fixed. That's why I should be in jail. But you and all the guys who wrote about me, you're all broken, too. You just don't know it."

"I'm not sure what you mean," Alex said.

Santiago put his hands in his pockets. "I watch the worm die and I smile about it," he said. "You see the worm on the ground, watch him die, then write a story about his tragic death."

Chapter Eighty-Two

Wednesday, October 2, 2002

Alex was sipping black coffee and reading *The Post* at a Starbucks on West 72nd when Greta Mori walked in and sat next to him. He put down the newspaper and she stared at the front page—a picture of Alex from college, standing shirtless and covered with mud in a boxing ring with two women hanging off him. The headline read "Muckraker?"

"Nice," she said, pulling her long black hair into a ponytail. "You must be so proud."

"I have to admit, that *was* a fun night. It won't be the last article either."

"Doesn't it hurt?" she asked.

"You should see the quotes inside. They are anonymous, from people I used to work with, saying I'm undisciplined, lazy. An ambitious pretty boy who would make up anything for fame."

She eyed him. "That sounds about right."

"Doesn't mean my story isn't true, though."

A group of tourists walked to the window and stared at Alex. One man held a copy of *The Post* up to the window and pointed at Alex as another man photographed him.

"Didn't expect you to call," she said at last.

"I didn't either."

"What's that supposed to mean?"

"Just that I'm surprising myself these days."

"So, how's your fifteen minutes going?"

"I'm hoping it's almost over."

"Why did you want to see me?"

Alex sipped his coffee and smiled. "I wanted to apologize. I'm sorry I didn't call when I said I would. I'm sorry I didn't return your call."

"Well, you had a pretty good reason not to, with all that happened."

A photographer came up to the window of the Starbucks, paused for a moment, then took their picture together.

"Is that normal now?" Greta asked.

"Yes, it will die down soon." He looked out at the photographer and waved. "But by tomorrow morning, you might be in the paper as the high-priced Asian call girl I'm spending all my ill-gotten riches on."

"Well, as long as they recognize me as high-priced."

They smiled at each other.

"I didn't not call you because of what happened," Alex said. "I ... just didn't call you. That's what I do, at least historically."

"Is this one of the twelve steps to recovery from being an asshole?"

"I don't know what it is," he said.

"Well, apology accepted. And I still wanna get you on the bodywork table sometime. Even if only as friends."

Chapter Eighty-Three

Wednesday, October 30, 2002

Alex was dreaming about the crash. He saw the blue Camry swerving off the road again and again, smashing the cedar tree and exploding in flames. When his phone rang, the Muzak version of *In Bloom* hovered over the scene, eventually drowning out the sound of his parents' screams and waking him up. He groped for the phone and looked at the caller ID. *Sadie Green.*

He flipped it open. "Hey, what's up?" he said, the music still echoing in his mind.

"Have you heard? I mean, have you *heard*?" Loud music and voices almost drowned out her slurred words.

"Heard what?" Alex asked, sitting up in bed.

"*The Times* piece. Did anyone leak it to you yet? The merger is off. Sonia Hollinger is pulling her money. Bice might be out. You did it."

Alex rubbed his eyes and turned on a bedside light. "Did what?"

"Brought down the evil empire!"

Alex could hear Sadie shouting and laughing. "Are you in a bar?" he asked.

"Hell yes."

"Are you drunk?"

"Hell yes. Why aren't you?"

"I was sleeping, Sadie. What are you talking about?"

"A *Times* reporter leaked me the story. It'll be in tomorrow's paper. Wait, it's *today's* paper. Anyway, Nation Corp. is pulling out of the merger and Sonia Hollinger is taking half her money out of Standard Media. And there's a rumor that Bice might be out as CEO."

"Wow. It looked like he might weather this thing."

"Anyway, I'm celebrating. I've been getting calls for weeks from Internet startups, mom and pop newspapers, and other non-profits, wondering whether the deal might fall through. The Internet is gonna stay free for at least a little while longer. A lot of people have been holding their breath over this."

"It's just one merger," Alex said. "There'll be more."

"Yeah, but this is a good start."

"I guess, but I don't really feel like celebrating. I don't know … I wasn't in this to stop the merger."

"C'mon, Alex. This is the scene in *Return of the Jedi* where they blow up the Death Star. But it's not just some dance party for the Ewoks." Her words were almost incomprehensible. "It's the remake where they show the whole galaxy celebrating. You blew up the fucking Death Star! This is a big deal."

"Bice isn't even in jail, and he's not going to be." Alex thought he heard another woman's voice, muffled by loud music.

"I gotta go," Sadie said. "Anyway, I just wanted to say you're awesome. Not that you need to get any more full of yourself. But … thanks."

She hung up without saying good-bye, and Alex went back to sleep.

***

At 5 a.m., Alex drank coffee on a bench outside the corner deli as he read the story.

> Nation Corp. Pulls Out of Merger
> Cites Bad Publicity and Declining Stock Price
> Hollinger Widow Said to Contemplate Divestment as CEO Bice on Hot Seat
> Wednesday, October 30, 2002
>
> In a stunning about face, Nation Corp., the world's largest cable and Internet service provider, is backing

> out of a planned merger with Standard Media. Though a final vote of the board will not take place until next week, multiple sources have confirmed that the merger is off.
>
> The Standard Media stock price has dropped 10% over the last month after a story on news-scoop.com, an Internet start-up, implicated its CEO, Denver Bice, in an elaborate plot involving conspiracy and murder. Though no substantial evidence against Bice has emerged, and no charges have been filed, the rumors were enough to damage the merger.
>
> Sources inside Nation Corp. say that a key element was a planned divestment by Sonia Hollinger, the widow of Macintosh Hollinger.
>
> To make matters worse for the CEO, who has defended himself vigorously in the weeks since the story broke, an executive inside Standard Media says that Bice himself may be at risk. According to the executive, who declined to be identified, a rift exists on the board of directors between those who want Bice out, and those who want to continue to back him.

Alex stopped reading when he got to the B-Matter. He sighed with satisfaction and watched the cars go by, then finished his coffee and walked back to his apartment.

Chapter Eighty-Four

Denver Bice leaned back in his black leather chair. He took five breaths with his eyes closed, then opened them and took five more. He looked down at the copy of *The Times* on his desk, pounded his fist on it, then picked up the phone and dialed.

After five rings he left a message. "Laurence, it's Denver. Are you avoiding my calls? We can still fight this. There's more we can try. Call me back. I'll be in the office all day."

He pulled the small key from his pocket and opened the bottom drawer of his desk. He took out the gun and the flattened NYU hat and placed them on the desk. From the back of the drawer he pulled out a tattered Polaroid photograph and placed it face down on the hat. He was staring at it when his phone rang.

"Hello?"

"Denver, it's Gathert."

"Yes, hello Chairman Gathert. Before you say anything, just let me say that we can fight this, it's—"

"Denver. It's over. The deal is off. You're out."

Bice looked down at the gun. "Chairman, this is just a bargaining tactic. Nation Corp. wants us to lower the price. It's not over."

"Denver, you're out."

He picked up the gun.

"Look," Gathert continued. "You've done a helluva job for us, and no one believes the crap they're saying about you, but we can't go forward with you at this point. I think you understand."

Bice closed his eyes. "I understand," he said. He saw his father's body on the edge of the stream behind their house. Blood pooling in frozen shoeprints.

"Good," Gathert was saying, "it'll be easiest for everyone if you just clear out quietly today. We've got to put a new face on this as soon as we can."

Bice opened his eyes and hung up the phone. He still had the gun in one hand and he picked up the photograph with the other. He heard the thud of Hollinger's head hitting the sidewalk. *When you hurt someone, you deserve to be punished.* He breathed deeply and turned the photograph over in his hand. Bice as a young man stood smiling on a vast green lawn, his arm around the shoulders of a beautiful young woman with a striking smile and long dark hair. "Martha Morelli," he whispered. He smelled cedar trees and mist and saw the blue Camry sliding off the road. He passed the gun from hand to hand, then slowly lifted it up to his head. *When you hurt someone, you deserve to be punished.*

He pressed it hard into his temple, his index finger on the trigger. He heard the roar of the river again, the thud of Hollinger's head, and the screams of Alex's mother, trapped in the car as it burned. "Martha Morelli." He smelled cheap Scotch and felt belt lashes on his back. *When you hurt someone, you deserve to be punished.*

His finger pressed slightly on the trigger. *I deserve to be punished.*

He looked down at the NYU hat and his finger relaxed. He set the gun down on the desk.

He put the hat on, tucking his ears in carefully. He put the gun in the drawer and pulled out a headset and a small black box with two silver wires running from it. He connected the box to the back of his cell phone. He put on the headset and connected it to his phone.

He dialed Alex Vane.

Chapter Eighty-Five

"Even for a pre-season game, Madison Square Garden is the best," Lance said as they rode the escalator down into Penn Station. Alex and Camila stood in front of him, Malina, Tyree, and James behind him.

"Can we look around the station before we go to the game?" Malina asked. "Little Tyree has never been here."

They all walked toward the center of the station. When Tyree saw the soaring ceiling and giant schedule board, he tugged at Malina's hand. "Look, *Muppāṭṭi*. Look how high it is. Can we go under it?"

Malina turned to Lance, who was walking next to Alex. "Is it okay?" she asked.

Both men nodded and they all followed the little boy as he ran toward the center of the station. A dog led by two officers sniffed at his heels as he ran by.

Lance turned to Malina. "Is this his first game?"

"Yes," Malina said. "Mine, too. And thank you. I do appreciate the invitation."

"Thank Alex." Lance said. "It was his idea."

"But Lance's tickets," Alex said. He turned to Malina. "It's the least I could do. I promised Demarcus I would get him onto the floor."

They walked in silence for a moment, then Lance turned to Camila. "What about you? This your first game?"

Camila nodded. "I used to watch football with my dad a little," she said, "but I'm not much of a sports lady."

Lance laughed. "A sports lady? Is that what they call them these days?"

Camila wrapped her arm around Lance's. "Oh, be quiet," she said.

They stopped in the center of the station. "I'll buy you a hat when we get in there," Alex said, "then you will be a *real* sports lady."

Camila crinkled her nose at Alex, then wrapped her other arm under his.

"Look what he's d-doing," James said, pointing at Tyree. He was jumping toward the schedule board thirty feet above him and swiping his hand as though it was just inches away.

***

They took their seats courtside—James on the end, Lance next to him, Alex in the center, Camila next to him, and Malina at the end with Tyree on her lap.

A hot dog vendor came by. "Who wants one?" Alex asked. "I'm buying."

They all nodded and Lance said, "I don't know. Are the hot dogs carb-neutral, dolphin-safe, and all that crap?"

"No," Alex said, handing the vendor the cash, "but I'm making an exception today."

Alex gave everyone a hot dog, sat down, and took a big bite. He turned to Lance. "You don't think the Knicks have *any* shot at making the playoffs?"

"You can scratch that dream. Only upside is maybe they'll be bad enough to get that Lebron kid in the lottery next year."

James said, "Maybe you oughta write a p-piece on it. You know, 'Ownership Guts Franchise to Save a Buck.' Four years ago we're in the finals, and now this?" He waved his hand at the players who were warming up on the floor. "I think the sports press needs a wake-up call."

Tyree got off Malina's lap and stood right at the edge of the court, jumping up and trying to reach the scoreboard fifty feet above him.

The stands were filling and James pointed across the court to the front row on the opposite side. "L-look who it is."

Alex turned and saw Daniel Sharp laughing next to a tall blonde woman. He wore jeans and a black blazer with a Knicks hat.

"Must be phase two of his mayoral marketing campaign," Lance said. "Start pretending to care about the Knicks and Yankees."

Alex laughed. "Maybe I should go see if he wants to go on the record about Bice."

One of the players came over and slapped Lance on the shoulder. He was a light-skinned black man in his late thirties, with specks of gray in his short hair. "You gonna write some nice stuff about us this year, fatty?" he asked.

"Don't work for *The Standard* no more," Lance said. "And aren't you too old to be playing basketball? I thought you'd be an assistant coach by now with your old rickety ass." He handed the player a card. "News-scoop.com."

The player looked at the card and tucked it into the pocket of his warm-up pants. "Who are these folks?"

"Alex and James—work with them at the new venture. Camila Gray, she teaches at NYU. And that's Malina and Tyree Downton. They're Demarcus's kin. Everyone, this is Ben Davis, but we call him Chicken Legs. Came up in Brooklyn six or seven years behind Demarcus."

"He used to school me in the park," Ben said to Malina. "One time—I'll never forget it, I was ten years old—he jumped over my head for a lob dunk. In a game. Never seen anything like it."

Ben walked over to Tyree, who was still jumping toward the ceiling. He grabbed him out of the air. "You wanna play here someday?" Ben asked him.

"I don't know. Can you touch the scoreboard?"

Ben held Tyree in his left arm and reached up with his right arm, leaning forward onto the tips of his toes. "Not quite," he said.

"Can anybody jump that high?" Tyree asked.

"Your granddad could. He could have jumped up and grabbed on." Ben put him back down and jogged onto the court.

Alex smiled at Tyree, then looked down at his phone and froze. He had one missed call. The caller ID read *000-0000*. His voice mail beeped and he dialed. He shot a look across the court at Daniel Sharp, who was chatting with players.

As Alex listened to the message, his mouth opened slowly.

"You have made Bice pay for *some* of what he has done." The voice was weak and slow but still tinny and distorted. "He has done more. Terrible things. And he deserves to be punished. *You* were supposed to catch him, *you* were supposed to punish him."

An announcer's voice boomed through the PA system: "Ladies and gentlemen, welcome to Madison Square Garden and a new season of New York Knicks Basketball!"

The crowd applauded as Lance sat next to Alex and patted him on the shoulder. "Get off the phone, man."

Alex pressed the phone to his ear, his head spinning. "Remember that he who hateth his life in this world shall keep it unto life eternal. And he who loveth his life shall lose it. Have you figured out what it means, Mr. Vane?"

The message ended.

Alex sat up and Camila took his hand. "Who was that?" she asked. He turned to her but said nothing. Confusion spread across his face, then fear. "What's wrong, Alex? Who *was* that?"

"The source."

"Who?"

He met her eyes. "I have no idea."

Thanks for reading.

If you'd like to hear about my upcoming books, including the sequel to *The Anonymous Source*, here's how:

Sign up to receive an occasional newsletter from me: http://acfuller.com/newsletter

Find me directly:

On Facebook: www.facebook.com/acfullerauthor
On Twitter: @acfullerauthor
At acfuller.com

Get the sequel to *The Anonymous Source*:

The Inverted Pyramid

Uneasy lies the head that wears a crown.

/

July 13, 2017

Pre-orders available May 1, 2017

Acknowledgements

Before beginning *The Anonymous Source*, I'd heard that writing a book was, to some extent, a collaborative process. And as I read through the final draft, I recalled with fondness and gratitude the support, encouragement, and advice I received from the following people and organizations over the two and a half years it took to complete this book.

For offering a wonderful place to teach for the last four years: the students, staff, and faculty of Northwest Indian College and the Port Gamble S'Klallam and Suquamish tribes.

For providing support to a wonderful community of writers, including me: the Pacific Northwest Writers Association.

For providing a quiet, clean, lovely place to work: the staff at the Kitsap Regional Library.

For their lessons and encouragement, three English teachers who were especially important to me: Sonya Brooks, Judith Stickney, and Naomi Schwartz.

For their support over the years: Willa, Jeanne, Marie, and Hameed.

For their brilliance and mentorship: the professors of the NYU School of Journalism. (The dead professor in this book is not based on any of you). And special thanks to Professor Michael Norman for teaching me how books work.

For being the book's first reader and first fan: Teri Fink.

For their feedback and encouragement early in the process: Susan Simmons, Josie Foster, Lisa Lenz, Susi Korda, Cliff McCrath, Michael Lassoff, Cherie Martin, and Cody Raccoon.

For providing necessary feedback at a critical time: my early editor, Aviva Layton.

For valuable feedback toward the end of the process: Denise Anderson Foreman, Melanie Hart Buehler, and Pam and Stan Birch.

For connecting me with my publisher, offering excellent feedback in the final hours, and being a friend through it all: Ina Zajac.

For her tireless work guiding this book across the threshold: my amazing editor, Julie Molinari.

For her quick and excellent work: my proofreader, Maggie Dallen.

For capturing the book in a way I couldn't have imagined: my cover designer, Greg Simanson.

For providing great advice about marketing and social media: Sophie Weeks and Kathy Marks.

For her talent, energy, and spirit: my early book manager, Jamie Green.

For all their support, encouragement, and babysitting: my extended family of Fullers, Allens, Cosbys, and Andersons. Special thanks to Fred and Diana Allen.

For providing mentorship, advice, and good books: Robert Dugoni.

For their support and advice down the home stretch: the members of my Launch Team.

For inspiring and teaching me something new every week: the authors, agents, journalists, and publishing professionals who have appeared on the WRITER 2.0 Podcast.

For letting me go to sleep early so I could get up and write: my daughter, Arden, and son, Charles. I couldn't have done it without you!

Finally, to the readers for whom I wrote this: My hope is that you have as much fun reading it as I did writing it.

50283801R00219

Made in the USA
San Bernardino, CA
18 June 2017